Pengarron Land

Pengarron Land

Gloria Cook

CANELO

First published in the United Kingdom in 1992 by Headline Book Publishing

This edition published in the United Kingdom in 2019 by

Canelo Digital Publishing Limited
57 Shepherds Lane
Beaconsfield, Bucks HP9 2DU
United Kingdom

A CIP catalogue record for this book is available from the British Library.

Print ISBN 978 1 78863 405 2
Ebook ISBN 978 1 78863 072 6

Look for more great books at www.canelo.co

Printed and bound in Great Britain by Clays Ltd, Elcograf S.p.A.

To my husband Roger, my daughters Cheryl and Tracy, and all the wonderful people who have helped and encouraged me in the writing of this book.

Chapter 1

Kerensa Trelynne lingered on the shingle beach of the little Cornish cove where she lived. It was the first day of a new year, 1753, and in the spring she would begin a new life. She would miss all the familiar sights and sounds around her, things she had taken almost for granted all her seventeen years. The dramatic horse-shoe-shaped cliffs of the cove, formed of black granite, and part of the mild southern coastline. The weathered lichen-covered rocks she had climbed over, exploring every nook and cranny. The ever-present winds that swept her face and lifted her hair. The constantly changing, eternal beauty of the sea.

Trelynne Cove was one of the many coves and creeks and inlets of Mount's Bay, the bay taking its name from St Michael's Mount, a large high rock, graced by a habited castle, out in the sea and known to fishermen and mariners alike as the Cornish Mount. It could not be seen from the cove, sheltered from view by the outward curve of the cliff.

Kerensa leaned against her grandfather's rowing boat, shabby now, its paint flaking and lower timbers needing replacement. The air was sharp but here she was sheltered, warmed by a mellow winter sun which heightened the pungent smells of dried seaweed and the worn-out crab pots stacked clumsily close by. Even though the boat and crab pots had not been used in years, to Kerensa they were a vital part of the cove.

It would be a wrench to leave all this; it was as much a part of her home as the solitary tumbledown cottage above the beach, and her scrap of garden which produced masses of wild flowers. Kerensa knew every rock of the cliff, every mood of the waters that invaded the lonely shore. She had watched them contentedly throughout her life, changed with them through each successive season. She loved them all with a passion, but she loved Clem Trenchard, the young tenant farmer's son whom she was going to marry, far more. It would be hard to leave all this, strange to wake up to the sounds of noisy farm animals instead of screeching gulls and the lapping or crashing waves, but she would wake in Clem's arms.

Kerensa would miss her grandfather too. After her mother had died when Kerensa was seven, he had raised her. He was the last of the Trelynnes and after his death the cove would pass to her. She and Clem planned to use it as a retreat from the busy farm life. Kerensa was pleased the cove would always belong to her.

She was reluctant to go back inside the cottage this morning, but she had her grandfather's breakfast to prepare. He had spent all of last night out somewhere, probably in an alehouse with his gambling cronies, and was sure to come home to Trelynne Cove ravenously hungry. She turned back up the shingle towards home.

–

Two miles further along the coast Sir Oliver Pengarron was standing on the rugged clifftop at Pengarron Point, the place to which he always came when troubled or in need of solitude. He was making plans for the new year.

Oliver had spent the last eight years rebuilding the fortunes of his family estate which his late father had allowed almost to founder. After much hard work and bloody-minded determination on his part, his business interests were at last successful. On the 1,500 acres of land he had been left he had knocked the two dozen tenant farms into shape, achieved a high-yielding home farm and oak timber plantation, and was breeding the finest horses in the country. Gradually he had bought back the pockets of land his father, Sir Daniel, had sold or lost at the gaming tables, winning some back by the same means as they had been lost. There was only one piece of land left to repossess. It had not been sold or lost by his father. Trelynne Cove had been gifted away, by his great-great-grandfather, Sir Henry Pengarron, to Jacob Trelynne, Kerensa's great-grandfather, for saving him from being trampled by a

2

runaway horse. The locals had quickly dubbed it Trelynne Cove and Trelynnes had lived there and continued to work on Pengarron land up to the present owner's day. Old Tom Trelynne preferred to make his living by more dubious means.

Sir Daniel had thought Trelynne Cove too small and insignificant to bother about, but to Sir Oliver it was a matter of honour not to allow it to remain in another's hands. A smile crossed his intense dark features. He was contemplating a proposition he was about to put to Old Tom Trelynne. Confident of the outcome, he drew in one last deep satisfying breath of tangy sea air and held it for a moment before turning to reach for the reins of his horse.

Allowing Conomor, his sleek black thoroughbred, to have his head, Oliver raced the half mile from the headland on to the cliff track. Keeping the grey, undulating sea in view he followed the track at the same pace until sighting the small shingle beach in isolated Trelynne Cove. Conomor picked his way deftly down the steep rocky path as it wound its way in the shape of a figure three to the front of the cottage. Smoke drifted lazily upwards from its one chimney, and as they approached the chorus of the sea reached out beguilingly as peaceful waves lapped their way up the shore.

Kerensa was singing happily at the top of her voice and was startled at the suddenness of the loud rapping on the cottage door. Very few people ventured down to Trelynne Cove, rarely anyone as early as this, unless it was one of the disreputable-looking characters her grandfather called his friends.

Leaving the breakfast preparations, she wiped her hands on her apron and cautiously opened the heavy wooden door. She was even more surprised when she recognised the tall proud-looking man standing there in the chill air. What reason could the Lord of the Manor have to be here in Trelynne Cove?

'Good morning, my lord,' she blurted out, pushing back a straying lock of rich dark auburn hair from her eyes; eyes that were grey-green like the winter sea and always bright and enquiring. Now, her brows were raised in curiosity, her small oval-shaped face mirroring her surprise.

'I want to speak to Tom Trelynne,' Sir Oliver informed her brusquely, in his firm cultured voice.

Kerensa did not reply at once, just stared up at him.

Impatiently he bent to lean one arm against the door jamb. Deliberately bringing his strong dark face close to hers, he snapped, 'Well, girl! Have you lost your tongue? Where is Trelynne?'

Oliver Pengarron's strikingly handsome face showed none of the harshness and debauchery she'd expected from his reputation as a hard-drinking womaniser who spent many hours at the gaming tables. His nose was long and straight, his cheekbones high, and like most of his forebears he possessed hair and eyes as black as the deepest night. It was the first time Kerensa had seen him at such close quarters and she found it disconcerting to look straight into those eyes. She took a step back from him, a not unbecoming flush tinging her pale cheeks.

Kerensa was determined not to be intimidated by this man so, lifting up her chin, she clasped her hands firmly together and said, 'My grandfather is abroad somewhere, my lord. I am expecting him back at any moment.'

Oliver Pengarron was studying her, moving his eyes up and down her slender body in undisguised familiarity. Not much past girlhood, Kerensa moved with a natural grace and poise that evaded most of the women he knew. Her skin glowed clear and healthy and she exuded a gentle innocence which he found appealing. Beneath this he sensed an adventurous spirit tinged with obstinacy.

Kerensa stepped well back into the room, her face growing crimson under his steady scrutiny, although more from anger than embarrassment. Pengarron moved his arm from the door jamb, took off his tricorn hat and bowed to her in mock chivalry.

'I'm obliged to you, Miss… Miss Trelynne, is it?'

'Ais, that it tes, m'lord. Miss Kerensa Trelynne. My granddattur.'

Oliver whirled round. Having the ability to scramble over the rocks and cliffs like a surefooted animal, Old Tom Trelynne had crept silently up behind him. The old man was hideous and stunted. He reminded Oliver of a throwback to the prehistoric race of dwarf-like people who were said to have crossed the sea from Europe and settled in

West Cornwall. It was they who had probably given rise to the many legends of goblins, fairies and little people; it would not have been difficult to harbour such superstitions looking at Old Tom. He had a leathery brown face, short claw-like hands, filthy grizzled hair, and one over-long tooth. Old Tom gave Kerensa a broad smile. 'Tes all right, m'dear,' he croaked, 'you shut the door an' keep yerself warm. Don't reckon tes you Sir Oliver 'as come a visitin'.'

Kerensa reached for the latch but before closing the door looked first at Old Tom, then Sir Oliver, and back to Old Tom again. What on earth did Sir Oliver Pengarron want with her grandfather? What had the old man been up to now? It must be something serious to warrant the baron's presence here. She went straight to a window and peeped out at them.

Oliver glared angrily at the closed door. He had been thinking it would be a pleasure to wait with the girl until her grandfather's return, an unexpected bonus… He quickly dismissed her from his mind. The purpose of his visit to Trelynne Cove had nothing to do with wenching but with the wretched little man now leering up at him, exposing his long yellowing tooth.

'Ye 'aven't come a visitin' my granddattur, 'ave 'ee?' asked the old man, adding with a hard edge to his croak, 'cus 'ee better not 'ave. I'll excuse 'ee fer any other reason, yer bein' of the quality 'n' that, but not with 'er. Anyone who lays as much as a finger on 'er will end up with a slit gizzard.' Old Tom drew a dirty finger across his throat to illustrate his point.

'It is you I have come to see,' Oliver said stonily. 'I have a proposition to put to you, Trelynne.'

'That so?'

Oliver pointed down to the shingle. 'We'll talk down there.' With long easy strides he led the way along the well-worn path from the cottage door until he could feel the smooth pebbles of the beach crunch under his boots.

Old Tom followed him slowly, shrugging his scrawny shoulders and scratching his grizzled hair, all the while speculating on the reason for this unexpected visit. When he reached the younger man's side, looking out across the sea, he lit a foul-smelling pipe. Oliver's face tightened at the acrid smell of the home cured tobacco and the equally distasteful odour of the old man's unwashed body. It amazed him that this dirty little man should be the grandfather of the extraordinarily pretty, neat and clean girl in the cottage.

Kerensa still watched them from the window. They had their backs to her. Sir Oliver was a muscular, straight-backed man and towered over her grandfather, who stood with his heavy ragged coat pushed back, elbows stuck out, and his thumbs rammed into his waistcoat pockets. He was puffing pipe smoke towards Sir Oliver.

Worried thoughts raced through Kerensa's head. What was going on? What were they talking about? She knew Old Tom lived just one shaky step ahead of the law. Had he gone as far as offending Sir Oliver and was therefore about to be hauled off to prison? Or, worse still, had the baronet arrived to mete out his own personal form of justice? It was rumoured he was a terrible man to cross. Her grandfather was a bit of a rogue, Kerensa had known that for years, but she loved him and was concerned for him. If only she could hear what they were saying.

Oliver avoided looking at the old man and watched the sails of the fishing boats from the nearby fishing village of Perranbarvah as he spoke. They were racing one another back from the mackerel grounds to the busy fish market at Newlyn to get the best prices for their catch. The fishermen were proud of their thirty- to forty-feet luggers which skimmed with great rapidity over the waters, and which could be seen from any position in the cove.

'I want to buy this cove, Trelynne,' Oliver said with the quiet firmness of a man used to getting his own way.

'That so?' Old Tom rubbed his dirt-streaked, stubbly chin and spat a ball of saliva on to the shingle. 'How much yer off'rin'?'

'Twenty guineas.'

'Not int'rested.'

'Nonetheless, I intend to buy this land. Name your price.'

'Les see now… Shall we say, two 'undred?'

Oliver rounded on the old man. 'Don't be ridiculous, you old fool! I'll give you thirty guineas and not a penny more.'

Old Tom looked up through narrowed eyes. 'Now look 'ee 'ere, I got no call to sell this 'ere cove, tes my 'ome, so if yer wants it, tes not goin' to be cheap, young sir. Trelynnes 'ave been livin' 'ere fer years 'n' years, ever since my grandfather Jacob worked in the Pengarron stables. Course, Pengarron Manor was a fine place in they days. Not like it is now, all run down an' any'ow,' Old Tom put in sarcastically. 'With my son Robert dead of the typhus, all this 'ere will be my granddattur's one day to do with as she pleases when I be dead 'n' buried.'

Reaching inside his caped overcoat Oliver pulled out a fat leather pouch. Old Tom watched eagerly as, from a side pocket, he produced a flint and steel and a long thin clay pipe. Oliver carefully filled the pipe with sweet-smelling tobacco, lighting it with deliberate slowness. The old man scowled when the pouch, flint and steel were returned, unoffered, to their places.

'From what I've heard, Trelynne, the day when you'll be dead and buried may not be too far ahead.' Drawing in deeply, Oliver blew smoke into the old man's face. 'You've made a lot of enemies over the years and now you're up to your scrawny neck in gambling debts. I've heard there are some as far away as Penzance who are ready to collect their rightful dues. Perhaps one dark night…'

'So 'ee knows 'bout that, do 'ee? Well, tes true enough I'm des'prit fer money right now, but I've got my granddattur to think 'bout.'

'Very well, Trelynne, I'll give you an extra ten guineas to give to her and will find employment for her on my estate.'

The old man stayed silent. Oliver's stern face showed signs of relaxing. In a thoughtful mood Old Tom took several steps away to where the shingle turned into coarse sand and turned his back to the sea. He spat heavily again before looking up, his wrinkled face sly and cunning, and held to one side.

'Y'know, I've done a lot of wicked things in my time,' he said, 'but I've always done right by that young maid in the cottage. Always kept 'er clothed an' well fed, even let that young preacher feller learn 'er 'er letters 'n' such. There's bin no workin' on a mine face or as a kitchen skivvy fer my little Kerensa. She was 'bout to get 'erself married to young Clem Trenchard, who's father do farm on yer estate.' Old Tom's face overran with mischief and malice. 'But I d'reckon she could do better fer 'erself.'

'What the hell are you getting at?' Pengarron demanded.

Old Tom licked his lips and rubbed the sleeve of his coat across his mouth in a rapid movement. 'I'll not move an inch off this 'ere land fer less than an 'undred guineas fer meself... an' yer promise to marry my granddattur.'

'What! Marry your granddaughter! Have you gone mad, Trelynne?' His face livid with anger, Pengarron strode menacingly towards the old man.

'Mad? No, not me, Sir Oliver,' returned Old Tom, putting up his arms as if to protect himself. 'I d'appen to know there's two reasons fer 'ee bein' so eager to get this 'ere cove an' bit of land. One is it would make a good place to land contraband in, an' everyone knows 'ee fer bein' a freetrader. An' the other is yer want it tacked back on to yer estate, don't 'ee? Can't bear to think of me ownin' it, can 'ee? Bin eatin' away inside of 'ee ever since I turned 'ee an' that mealy-mouthed Besweth'rick boy out of 'ere all they years ago... I'm right, ain't I?'

Oliver's face was black with fury. The insulting remark aimed at Arthur Beswetherick, his long dead friend, and the suggestion that he marry the old man's granddaughter, were almost too much to bear.

'Do you really expect *me* to marry kin of *yours* Trelynne?' he snarled between clenched teeth.

The old man's silence and smirking expression spoke for him.

'All right, you old cuss, I'll give you the two hundred guineas you asked for at first.'

Old Tom sniggered. He knew there was no shortage of money in the other man's pocket, or his bank. He could ask for double the amount, and probably receive it, but it wasn't a large sum of money he was looking for. He wanted only enough to clear his heels and set himself up again, while being comfortable in the knowledge that Kerensa would want for nothing during the rest of her life.

'Course there would be one or two other gentlemen who would be willing to pay me an 'an'some price fer this 'ere cove, an' fer the same reason as you, what with so many lookin' to get in on a bit of freetradin' these days... or to buy it just fer the pleasure of keepin' it from 'ee. Yer not that popular yerself, are 'ee, m'lord?'

It was Oliver's turn to remain silent. He moved some distance away, to be as far removed as possible from the sight and smell of the evil little man. He tapped out the contents of his pipe to meet a gentle incoming wave and watched the ash break up and bob away on the clear ebbing water. From the outset he had been confident an agreement over Trelynne Cove would have been settled, if not quickly and easily, at the least to his satisfaction. The last thing he had expected was this wily weasel of an old man to produce such a startling proposition.

He had always hated the thought of former Pengarron property being in the hands of such a scoundrel. He would not rest until he got it back. Of course to allow Old Tom to sell it to anyone else was unthinkable. But to get it back by agreeing to marry his granddaughter? Oliver's father would simply have taken her and the old man up to the top of the cliff and thrown them off. He'd have few qualms himself about taking Old Tom up there this very minute and wiping the smirk off his hideous face for ever. But the girl...

Strange, though, the old man bringing up the subject of marriage. After negotiating the return of his property, Oliver's next plan was to take a wife. He had stayed a bachelor far longer than most of his contemporaries, one reason being the habit of many ladies of genteel birth of systematically bleeding their husbands dry of their wealth, pride and prestige. He was not going to allow that to happen to him, but the time had come to put up with the inconvenience of a wife if there was to be an heir to the Pengarron estate. It was a matter of some irritation that there were no suitable ladies of his own class apparent. They were either married already, exceedingly unattractive, or not of childbearing age. Not even a half-decent widow was to be had.

Of late he had considered looking outside his own circle, but a penniless girl of the lower orders, half his age, the granddaughter of a common criminal...

Oliver watched the last red sail of the fishing luggers disappear behind the outline of Mother Clarry's Rock, a smooth-shaped spur which jutted out to form the seat of the mythical witch, reputed to have sat on it on nights bearing a full moon in order to gloat over her evil misdeeds. No one knew the exact origins of the legend, lost a long time ago in the hazy mists of antiquity.

Kerensa Trelynne's sweet face came to mind. She was comely enough; indeed from the moment she had opened that door Oliver's baser instincts had been stirred. He had seen enough of her to realise she had many pleasing attributes, and looked as though she would readily bear healthy babies. If he didn't produce an heir, the estate would one day pass to one of his disapproving distant cousins at Zennor. An amused smile touched the corners of his mouth at the thought of their outrage if he did marry and produce an heir by a girl of Kerensa Trelynne's pedigree. It would be worth marrying the girl just to see their faces, and those of the rest of the County's gentry – not that he had ever cared a damn what anybody thought of him. He wanted Trelynne Cove, and one way or another he wanted the girl in the cottage. If he agreed to Old Tom Trelynne's ludicrous proposition he wouldn't come out too badly, and anyway he could always find a way out of the marriage at a later date. But for now he was furious at not having the upper hand.

He turned coldly on Old Tom.

'Very well, Trelynne, I agree. Collect your money tonight from Painted Bessie's alehouse. But after I've fulfilled my part of this agreement you had better not take one single step on to Pengarron land ever again. If you do, I will be sorely tempted to kill you myself with my bare hands!' He threw the alarmed old man backwards on to the sand. Before Old Tom could regain his feet a wave rolled up the shingle and soaked him.

–

Kerensa gasped in alarm to see her grandfather unceremoniously hauled off his feet and dumped into the bitterly cold sea. She flew out of the cottage, passing Sir Oliver as he strode away from Old Tom without attempting further hurt. She helped her grandfather coughing and spluttering all the way back to the cottage, and ushered him inside the cosy warmth. He drank down a mug of hot tea in two noisy gulps, then wiped his stubbly chin with the back of his hand before he told her the reason behind, and the outcome of, Sir Oliver's visit to him.

'Marry him? Sir Oliver!' Kerensa screamed. 'Are you mad, Grandfather?'

'That's what 'e said,' replied Old Tom, massaging the angry red marks appearing on his throat. 'It's fer yer own good, Kerensa.'

'What do you mean, for my own good? Just what kind of nonsense are you up to this time, Grandfather? I'm not moving from this spot until you tell me everything that went on between you and… and that man out there.'

She waved her hand angrily towards the window where she could see Sir Oliver, his arms folded, waiting impatiently by his horse. 'For a start, you can tell me what he's doing just standing there.'

Old Tom knew by the set of her jaw and the flash of her eyes that Kerensa meant exactly what she said. ''Ee's waitin' to 'ave a word with 'ee, m'dear,' he said sheepishly.

'Why? To discuss the wedding arrangements?'

Old Tom hung his head at the stinging remark.

Kerensa was used to her grandfather's involvement in dubious schemes and his having to extricate himself hastily from all manner of troubles. From the time she had been old enough to cook, clean and look after the cottage for both of them, she had chided him like a naughty child on such occasions. But this latest scheme of his was beyond her comprehension. He knew how much she loved Clem and was looking forward to marrying him. How could he so cruelly upset their plans, ruin their future, break their hearts, by striking a bargain that was totally unnecessary, and one to which she would never have agreed had she been consulted at its outset?

'Pour me another cup of tay, cheeil, an' I'll tell 'ee everything.' Old Tom looked appealingly at her from the chair on which he'd sunk down.

Kerensa poured his tea and pushed it towards him, the hot liquid spilling on to the well-scrubbed table.

'Come on, me 'an'some, sit down a minute, won't 'ee? It won't sound 'alf so bad when I tell it to 'ee prop'ly.'

In between gulps of tea Old Tom told Kerensa every detail of his conversation with the black-haired baronet waiting outside. Kerensa sat with her hands clasped together on the table as she listened. When her grandfather had finished his tale, her face was drained of all colour.

'And what about Clem? Where does he fit into this arrangement of yours?'

She spoke so softly Old Tom had to strain to hear her voice. Ashamed, he looked away and shrugged his shoulders. It was a habit of his, not wanting to accept responsibility for his actions.

'Ye'll just 'ave to ferget young Trenchard. Honestly, Kerensa, I did it fer the best fer 'ee. Just think of yerself as Lady Pengarron, up there livin' in the Manor 'ouse. I know Sir Oliver 'asn't done it up like the rest of the estate and tes in a bit of a state now, I'll grant 'ee, but ye'll soon get the place all done up nice in no time. The cove'll still belong to 'ee in a way, an' twill be better 'n' bein' a farm labourer's wife, scratchin' fer a livin'. Besides, m'dear, I need that money quickly. My life went be worth a mite if a knife finds its way into my back one night...'

'Why do you need that money? More gambling debts?' Kerensa asked harshly.

'Ais, I've 'ad a run of bad luck,' Old Tom answered, without looking at her.

'I see. But you didn't have to involve me in your foolish schemes.'

Old Tom looked worriedly out of the window. 'Be a good little maid, eh, an' go out an' 'ave a word with 'im? 'Ee's waitin' fer 'ee.'

'We'll see about that!' Kerensa wrapped a warm woollen shawl around her shoulders and stood at her grandfather's side, looking down at his slouched figure. He met her eyes for only a moment before gazing sightlessly into the empty tin mug cradled in his hands. He wriggled about on his chair, made more uncomfortable by her accusing face than by his clinging wet clothes.

'You really think that what you have just done is for my good,' she said, bitterly, 'but you have sold me to that man in just the same way as you have sold the cove and our home. It will be hard to forgive you for this, Grandfather.'

As she closed the door behind her the old man slumped forward, placing his forehead in the palms of his dirty hands. Old Tom had never had any time for his long-suffering wife whom he'd often beaten, even up to her early death some twenty years ago. He'd been just as cruel to Robert, their only child; surly and indifferent to his quiet mousey daughter-in-law. With Kerensa, though, things had always been different. He had first seen her at a few months old, following a prison sentence for poaching, and for some inexplicable reason she had struck the only chord of love and kindness in the otherwise heartless man.

'I did it fer the best fer 'ee, Kerensa,' he said to her empty chair. 'Ye'll see. One day ye'll see...'

Oliver watched her intently as Kerensa walked gracefully towards him. He was holding Conomor's bridle as he stroked the horse's velvety neck. He stared at her for some time before speaking, taking in every detail of the girl he had agreed to take as his wife. Pain and anger had clouded the brightness of her large eyes.

Kerensa held her head high and met his bold stare. The harsh look on his face emphasised the few lines on his forehead and the tightness at the corners of his wide cruel mouth.

Nodding in the direction of the cottage, Sir Oliver said icily, 'Has that cunning old swine in there told you everything?'

She nodded, ignoring the insult. 'You must want the cove very much to agree to such a thing,' she said, keeping her anger in check.

An east wind suddenly whipped up about them, wrapping the plain grey skirt of her dress about her legs. She shivered violently and pulled her shawl in tighter round her slender shoulders.

Reaching for Conomor's reins Oliver slapped them a few times in the palm of his hand. 'I'll send someone over to collect you on the morrow,' he said.

'Sir Oliver, I will not go through with this marriage.'

'You have no choice!' His face clouded over, his voice was like thunder.

'Please listen to me. My grandfather is old, I'm sure he didn't mean...'

13

Oliver paid her no attention but glared at her as she spoke. If she'd thought to change his mind, it was out of the question now. He wanted to lay hold of her fragility, rob her of innocence. A few weeks under his domination and her spirit would be broken. She would never challenge him again. And was he not doing this girl an honour by consenting to marry her? How dare she baulk, argue, defy him? Abruptly he swung up into the saddle and with no more than a curt nod started back up the rocky path.

Kerensa watched him disappear into the distance with cold fury building up inside her. She ran down to the beach and thrashed at the pebbles with her feet. How could this have happened without her knowledge and consent? How would Clem react with their future together threatened like this? It was hardly believable, ridiculous. It would be almost laughable – if Sir Oliver wasn't so frightening.

She stalked up to a tall outcrop of rocks, climbed to the highest point, and thought of Clem. Old Tom had kept her mainly in the seclusion of the cove and it had been at the Methodist Bible classes, in tin miner Jeb Bray's cottage on Lancavel Downs, they had first met. They had quickly formed a shy friendship which soon changed into an easygoing companionship. Old Tom hadn't seemed to hold any objections to the boy, later the young man, who regularly walked her home after services in Perranbarvah's parish church as well as after the Bible classes.

True, the old man hardly spoke a word to Clem, being inclined only to scowl if they met face to face. But, Kerensa had been overjoyed when he didn't refuse their plea to get married.

Clem's father was a tenant farmer on the Pengarron estate and Clem was building a lean-to on to Trecath-en Farm for them to live in when they were married. The lean-to was almost completed, with only the roof to be put on, and Clem worked on it every moment of his spare time. Granite, readily attained from the fields, made up the walls, while Nathan O'Flynn, as the Pengarron Estate's head forester, had helped with a supply of timber scraps for a sturdy oak door, the window frames and furniture. Kerensa too had spent many happy hours working towards their joint future, sewing bedding and curtains (some from material Old Tom had given her, probably smuggled in or even stolen).

The sea no longer seemed so gentle but ran high to match her mood. Kerensa scrambled down from the rock and ran back to the cottage to give her grandfather a piece of her mind. He had no right to sell the cove, her inheritance, her dowry to Clem. He had no right to try to deny her of living and loving with her chosen husband.

–

Oliver usually galloped Conomor along the clifftop for several miles of a morning. Today was different. He turned off after a mile and headed inland, taking the shortest route back to Pengarron Manor. The damp air grew heavier as they progressed and when they headed landwards, misty rain driven forcefully by the east wind met horse and rider full on. They quickly left the stunted, skeletal bushes of the clifftop behind and reached the boundary dividing Ker-an-Mor, his home farm, and Trecath-en Farm, their hedgerows littered with untidy dead foliage. Rose Farm soon took over from the strip of Trecath-en Farm and when they reached the end of the narrow rutted cart track Conomor's hooves were pounding over the grounds of Pengarron Manor. As the commanding building of the Manor house came into sight the sky overhead was as darkly grey as Oliver's mood.

Entering the quiet stableyard, he hurriedly dismounted, throwing the reins over Conomor's proud head.

'Jack! Jack! Where are you?' he shouted.

A cheerful-looking skinny boy aged about twelve years came running across the wet cobbles and doffed his cap to his master. 'Yes, m'lord?'

'See to Conomor then take Meryn and ride over to the Reverend Ivey. I want to see him at once. Tell him it's urgent and I'm not to be kept waiting. I'll be in my study.'

'Right away, m'lord.'

Jack grinned to himself as his master stamped across the stableyard and entered the Manor through a kitchen door. He led the elegant black stallion away to its stall. 'Goin' to be one of they days, is it, boy?' Jack said to the horse in his sharp as yet unbroken voice.

There were not many horses kept now in the rambling stables at the back of the Manor. Apart from Conomor, there was Meryn, a small grey pony, Nessa, an old black mare, and Derowen, the chestnut mare used by Nathan O'Flynn, the estate's gamekeeper and head forester. Jack was the only stableboy, and with the groom Barney Taylor more often than not laid up with rheumatics, he was skilled enough in his job for Sir Oliver to trust him to attend to his mount.

Whistling cheerfully as he rubbed Conomor down with fistfuls of straw, Jack jumped as a heavy hand clamped down on his skinny shoulder.

'Oh, tes you, Nat,' he said, the relief on his narrow face giving way to its broadest grin. 'I thought 'twas his lordship coming back.'

'From the way you jumped then, lad, he wouldn't have been all that welcome. Something amiss, is there?'

'I don't know for sure, Nat. I got to ride and fetch the Reverend Ivey for his lordship. He says tes urgent and he's not to be kept waitin'. Anyway, he's in a proper bad mood about something. I'll be off the moment I've done with Conomor here.'

Nathan O'Flynn, a thickset Irishman in his early thirties, pulled a wry face and took off his cap to run a large flat hand through his mop of bushy dark hair. 'I've got a few minutes to spare, lad, so I'll finish Conomor for you if you want to go now.'

Jack hesitated. He didn't want Sir Oliver to think he couldn't be bothered to finish his allotted tasks, but the sooner he set off to the parsonage at Perranbarvah two miles away, the more likely he would see the Reverend Ivey before he left his home on parish business elsewhere.

'I'll be off right now then. Thanks, Nat.' And with another grin he slapped a handful of straw into Nat's hand. Ducking under Conomor's belly he made his way further along the stable to Meryn's stall. It was only a short time before the pony's hooves were heard clattering out of the stableyard.

Conomor whinnied to Nathan O'Flynn as if in complaint of Meryn's outing whilst he had not received his usual long early morning gallop. 'There, there, my beauty.' Nat's voice was mellow, soothing. 'I don't know what's up either, but if it's trouble ahead, we'll hear of it soon enough, so we will.'

—

As was his custom, at half of the hour past noon, Clem Trenchard stopped work to eat his crib. He had spent the past few hours hard at work combing the ground of a sloping three-acre field with a plough pulled by a quietly natured ageing but strong horse. Wiping sweat from his brow Clem looked critically back over his work. He nodded with satisfaction at the straight lines he had made in the shallow earth, cut despite the huge granite boulders that stubbornly protruded above the ground or wickedly lurked below it, ready to snare the plough of an unwary farmer.

Clem liked to be outside, and alone, while he worked. He was glad his father, Morley, had stayed behind on the farm to assist with the calving of their roan dairy cow. A sudden outburst of barking from his black retriever bitch, Charity, brought a smile to Clem's clearly defined, fair features. This was the companion he did not object to, and she followed him faithfully and determinedly everywhere he went.

Knowing it was crib-time, Charity came bounding across the wet earth, her coat glistening from the heavy drizzle that had persisted all morning. Man and dog, used to all weathers, plodded over to the shelter offered by a stretch of low natural hedge, leaving the horse to drink from a small trough in the corner of the field. They dropped down comfortably to eat, Clem on a boulder, Charity lying across his mud-laden boots.

Clem pulled a canvas bag out from under the shelter of the boulder. From it he took out a tin box containing an enormous pasty. Charity watched and fidgeted as he broke off a corner of the largely potato and turnip pasty with its scant addition of meat. 'Here you are, girl,' he said, ruffling the retriever's damp straggly ears. Bolting down the corner of pasty Charity sat alert, a begging paw on Clem's knee, her long pink tongue hanging loosely as she resumed her hopeful watch.

As he ate Clem rubbed his leg above the knee, the flesh tender where he'd been pitched forward on to the plough when it had jarred, with a terrific shudder, against a huge hidden outcrop of granite. When the pasty was eaten they shared cold water from a flask. Charity searched her master's coat for any overlooked pasty crumbs while Clem, deep in thought about Kerensa, with eyes closed, idly squeezed a handful of wet gravelly soil.

A good-looking youth of nineteen, with every maid in the district having an eye on him, Clem had quickly learnt from childhood how to exploit and replenish the land. His tall lean body had been made tough and agile by constant hard work. With his fine silky blond hair, clear blue eyes, and the knowledge he would have his father's tenancy one day, he was one of the most sought after bachelors in the district. But much to the disappointment of the rest of the female population Clem had a mind and eye only for Kerensa Trelynne.

He was roused from his pleasant daydream when Charity became alert, her body tense, ears pricked back. 'What is it, girl?' he said, looking around.

A short time later a rider appeared at the top of the field. Locating Clem with his dog, he rode swiftly down to them, his horse's hooves throwing up clods of earth. It was Nathan O'Flynn on Derowen.

'So there you are Clem,' the Irishman said, his face serious. 'I've been looking about for you this past hour. I've got something to tell you and you're not going to like it, that you're not.' Nat sat down beside Clem and handed the puzzled youth one of the bottles of ale he'd brought with him.

'Thanks, Nat,' said Clem. 'Father wouldn't approve but I'll be glad to take a few drops with you. So… what's this news I'm not going to like, then?'

Charity deserted Clem to make a big fuss of Nat in the hope he had brought with him something to eat. Nat waited for Clem to take a long swig from his bottle before going on with his news. Clem watched in amused curiosity as the other man's drawn features pulled his eyebrows together in one long straight line like a hairy caterpillar. Charity abandoned Nat as soon as it became apparent her hopes of getting a titbit were fruitless.

When she'd settled down again over Clem's boots, Nat said, 'It's Kerensa I've come about, Clem.'

He was instantly concerned. 'There's nothing wrong, is there? I only saw her last evening.'

Nat looked his young friend full in the face. 'The only way I can tell you is just to say it to you outright. Clem, there was talk in the marketplace today that Kerensa is going to marry Sir Oliver.'

'What? You must be mad, Nat! How can you say such a thing?' At first Clem's face paled. Now it was deeply flushed with anger.

'I wish it was mad I am, Clem, but I fear it may be true. I came out to find you myself, before you heard it from the village gossips.'

Springing to his feet Clem sent Charity rolling several feet away, knocking over his bottle to smash on the stones at his feet.

'But why!' he cried. 'I don't understand. Why should she? What on earth is going on, Nat?'

'I don't know for sure, Clem. It seems to have something to do with Old Tom's cove. I've known for some time that Sir Oliver's been looking for another place to land contraband and Trelynne Cove would be ideal, but it can't be done easily with that old rascal about. I do know that first thing this morning his lordship turned up at the stableyard with his face as black as thunder. He sent young Jack off to Perranbarvah to fetch the Reverend Ivey up to the Manor and apparently old Beatrice overheard some of their conversation. Well, later Adam Renfree comes across Beatrice roaring drunk in Marazion and he was too late to have stopped her from babbling to all and sundry about what she'd heard. It seems Old Tom would only agree to sell the cove to Sir Oliver on condition he makes Kerensa his wife.'

Clem felt unreal, numb. He could see Nat. He knew he was standing there in front of him in the field, in the rain that had now turned into a steady downpour, but he felt as though he was in a dream. A terrible, mocking dream. Back on her feet, Charity licked his hand. He didn't expect to feel the warm, rough wetness and was surprised he did.

'Clem—'

He was further surprised that when he spoke his voice actually made a sound, that it could be heard. 'I've got to see her, Nat. I won't believe Kerensa is going to marry anyone else, let alone that man, unless she tells me herself. You may have got this all wrong anyway, if as you say Beatrice was drunk.'

'I only hope you are right,' Nat said, standing up and putting a hand on the young man's shoulder, 'but Beatrice is well known for her sharp mind, even when drunk.'

Clem's blue eyes were wide and fierce. 'Even if what you say is true, I won't let Kerensa marry that arrogant devil. No one can force her to and I won't let them!'

'Be careful, Clem,' Nat reasoned with him. 'Once Sir Oliver has his mind set on something, he won't be easily shaken.'

'Thanks for taking the trouble to come and tell me, Nat.' Clem pulled his collar tight about his neck and grimaced up at the sky. 'Come on, girl,' he called to the young bitch.

When he reached the old horse Clem unhitched it from the plough and urged the animal over the cloying mud, Charity running and leaping at their side.

Nat drained his bottle and pushed it down into his coat pocket. He shook his head as he mounted Derowen then pulled his cap down over his eyes against the rain. Following the path Clem had taken up the field he could just make out the youth's fair hair as he rode in the direction of Trelynne Cove.

Chapter 2

For the first time in her life Kerensa was truly alone. Unable to face the hurt and betrayal in her face, Old Tom had packed his meagre belongings in an old sack, and a few hours after Sir Oliver's visit the grizzled old man had left Trelynne Cove. He would only tell Kerensa he was not going far away and would be watching over her until he'd witnessed her wedding. After that he intended to get a berth on a ship and sail away to a new life; once settled, he would send word so she would know he was safe and well. Kerensa did not believe him. She thought it more likely her grandfather would waste all the money he was to collect from Sir Oliver on gambling and cheap gin, thereby making the agreement that was to break her heart all for nothing.

Fearing trouble from one of his debtors, Old Tom begged Kerensa to leave the cove and ask for a night's lodgings at the home of one of her Methodist friends. She had adamantly refused to leave her home, especially if this was the last night she was to live there, and maintained her intention to stay even if it meant being alone.

Kerensa stood in the rain and watched her grandfather trudge up the winding path to the top of the cliff. Tears caught in her throat as she lifted a heavy hand to wave goodbye to him, then despondently she went back into the cottage, shivering in her wet clothes. Taking off her dress she hung it to dry over a line strung up close to the fireplace, then placed her shoes in the hearth. All her actions were automatic, from throwing a log on the fire, putting on a dry dress – the only other one she owned – to clearing away the unused breakfast dishes. The cottage seemed so empty.

Old Tom had left his pipe behind. It lay forlornly on the corner of the table, forgotten in his haste to go. Kerensa touched its grimy bowl with a fingertip. It was hard to believe her grandfather was responsible for wrecking her plans for the future. He had always been kind and caring. She couldn't remember much about her parents, only that her mother who had been quiet, gentle and always smiling, had died six months after her father; he dying of typhus in some foreign port. Of him Kerensa could only recall that he'd been loud-voiced and sullen. Since then Old Tom had taken good care of her and she had never lacked life's necessities.

He had offered no resistance to her friendship and growing romance with Clem. He'd known that although she had enjoyed her life in the cove, in the latter years she had been lonely and was looking forward with joyful anticipation to family life on Trecath-en Farm. How could he wish her to live her life without Clem, knowing she loved him so much? To spend her life with a man much older than herself and renowned for his bad character and single-mindedness in getting his own way. She would be forced into a totally different way of life, have to mix with a class who usually despised her own; moreover some of the gentry with whom Sir Oliver Pengarron associated were as unsavoury in their own way as the people her grandfather mixed with.

She sought refuge in her bedroom, sat shivering in the cold on her bed. But here there were too many poignant reminders of Clem. A lock of his fair hair, tied with ribbon and wrapped in a neckerchief of his, lay under her pillow. There was a picture on the wall made of dried pressed primroses, milkmaids and pink campions he had gathered for her.

She went back to the other room but soon could bear to be inside the little cob-walled cottage no longer. The familiar things that were so much a part of her life seemed to crowd in on her, the atmosphere becoming more and more claustrophobic. She could not think straight and needed to clear her muddled mind as to what to do about Sir Oliver and what to say to Clem. Throwing her shawl over her shoulders, she stepped back into her shoes and went outside into the rain.

She walked up and down the beach until her legs grew weary then sat on a large flat rock near the shoreline, pulling her shawl in tighter to keep out the wet and chill. Wistfully she looked out to sea, but drew no comfort from its familiar sights, smells and sounds. Even the waves seemed to move dejectedly on their passage up the shore, each one bidding her a mournful salute.

She had sat on this rock many, many times. With Old Tom who had told her fanciful tales of smugglers and pirates. To reflect and seek comfort on the awesome wonderful journey she knew nothing of as she grew from girl to woman. Here, she and Clem had shared their first shy kiss. She had never before sat here with her heart breaking as it did now.

Gulls that nested up high in the cliffs were circling overhead, screeching, and Kerensa took a fancy they were mocking her. It wouldn't have surprised her to see Mother Clarry, perched up on her seat, maliciously gloating over her fate. She was cold and wet but did not feel the wind or rain.

Clem found her standing on the shoreline, the icy water soaking her shoes and the hem of her dress, and she seeming neither to notice nor care. She looked lost, forlorn, her expression one of bewilderment as he ran towards her. He took her into his arms at once, holding her close, but her body was tense and unyielding.

She said: 'I knew you would come.'

'What's going on, Kerensa?' he asked earnestly. 'Nathan O'Flynn sought me out in the fields to tell me you're going to marry Sir Oliver. Tell me it's not true.' He took hold of her face and searched her eyes for his answer.

'It is true, Clem,' she told him miserably. 'I'm afraid I have no choice in the matter.'

He shuddered at her words and gripped her tightly by the shoulders. 'You do have a choice, my love, to marry me and not that man. I don't understand how this could have happened.'

'My grandfather made an agreement with Sir Oliver.'

'But they couldn't possibly hold you to such a thing!' he exploded, shaking her as if to make her see sense. 'It was none of your doing.'

Kerensa pulled away from him, and reluctantly Clem let her go. 'We can't talk out here in the rain,' he said. 'Let's go inside and get ourselves warm and dry.'

Taking her by the arm, Clem led Kerensa into the cottage. Once inside he threw logs on the fire to build up a comforting blaze while she half-filled a battered kettle with water, hanging it on the hook over the flames to boil for tea. Neither spoke, but stared into the cavorting orange-red flames until the kettle began to sing. It acted like a signal to Clem, as though he had suddenly become aware of his surroundings.

'You're shivering, my little sweet,' he said, and feeling he must take charge of the situation, added, 'You go and change out of that dress and I'll make the tea. Then you can tell me exactly what happened this morning.'

The dress Kerensa had taken off earlier was almost dry. 'I won't be very long,' she said, pulling it off the line and going into her bedroom.

When she returned Clem was sitting at the table with two mugs of steaming hot tea in front of him. Kerensa gave him a brave smile as he got up to help her put her wet dress up on the line next to his dripping jacket. She put her shoes in the hearth once more, beside the boots Clem had placed there. She sighed at the thought of how the clothes hanging together on the line, and the shoes and boots standing side by side in the hearth, looked for all the world like things shared in the comfortable intimacy of marriage.

'Come and drink your tea,' he said gently. 'Old Tom been doing a bit of freetrading, has he? When I looked in the cupboard to find you something to eat I noticed quite a few suspect packages in there.'

Kerensa nodded. 'The whole neighbourhood's flooded with tea, so I've heard. Everybody has tea., coffee and spices, and brandy in plenty since... since Sir Oliver's last contraband run.'

Pulling a chair closer to the fire Kerensa sat down and sipped her tea, the hot liquid spreading a welcoming warmth inside her, but otherwise her spirits could not be lifted.

'Don't worry, my love,' Clem tried to reassure her. He crouched down in front of her, lightly resting his arms on her lap, and gave her the boyish grin she liked so much in him. 'We'll think of a way out of this somehow.'

'I only hope we can,' she murmured. Kerensa relinquished her grip on her mug to push fine strands of fair hair away from Clem's eyes.

Haltingly, she told him the details of the agreement made over the cove that morning and how she had come to be involved in it.

In turn he told her how Nathan O'Flynn had heard about it from Adam Renfree, the Pengarron Estate's home farm steward. Kerensa shuddered as she pictured Sir Oliver's drunken servant broadcasting the news to all who cared to listen; she could only hope Adam Renfree had quickly removed Beatrice from Marazion's busy marketplace.

'I'm so afraid, Clem. I can see no way out of this. I've gone over and over it in my mind. What can we do? My grandfather is my legal guardian and I'm honour bound to comply with his wishes. Then there's his safety to consider. But most of all there's the fact that if Sir Oliver wants anything, he will be determined to have his own way.'

'I don't care what Sir Oliver says or does!' Clem said vehemently. 'I'm going up to the Manor house to tell him you aren't going to marry him.'

Alarm spread across Kerensa's face. 'Please don't, Clem. You know what he's like. It may only serve to make things worse than they are already. Sir Oliver is not the kind of man you can just go up and tell things to.'

'But you can't go through with it, Kerensa. They can't make you, and I won't let them!'

'It's not as simple as that, Clem. I only wish it was.'

In agony he reached for her small soft hands and kissed her chilled fingers, keeping his eyes on her lovely troubled face.

'We could go away together,' he said, appealing to her.

'But what would become of my grandfather? And your family too for that matter, Clem? They might be evicted from Trecath-en Farm.'

'Sir Oliver would never throw my family off the farm. He's always been pleased with my father's work since he took over Trecath-en.'

'We can't be sure of that. No one's ever crossed that proud man and got away with it lightly before.'

'But it's me you'll be going away with,' he argued. 'Sir Oliver will know my parents wouldn't approve. It's me he would be angry with, not them. And as for your grandfather, I know you love the old boy, Kerensa, but he's asked for any trouble that comes his way. Where is Old Tom?'

He followed Kerensa's gaze as she looked sadly across the room to the wide bench on which lay the rolled up mattress and blankets where her grandfather usually slept.

'He's gone,' she said, very quietly.

'Gone where?'

'He wouldn't say, only that it won't be far away and he'll be watching over me. He's collecting his hundred guineas from Painted Bessie's tonight.'

Clem huffed. 'I'd like to meet him outside that kiddleywink and wring his ruddy neck for doing this to us!' He immediately regretted his outburst at Kerensa's pained reaction. He said, more soothingly, 'You mean he's left the cove for good?'

'Yes,' she said miserably. 'Packed up and gone.'

Clem raised himself and wrapped her in his arms. He kissed her cheeks softly. 'You shouldn't stay here alone, my little sweet,' he said. 'Pack some things together and come back to the farm with me. You can sleep with Gran and Rosie. The family will be glad for you to stay.'

'No, Clem,' Kerensa returned, with sudden firmness. She freed herself from his arms and rose to stand and stare at the fire. 'Sir Oliver is sending someone here to collect me tomorrow, and here I must stay. He won't like it if I'm not here and we must do nothing to antagonise him.'

'I can hardly believe this is happening,' said Clem, coming to stand behind her. 'I was only thinking this morning that it won't take me much longer to finish building the lean-to for us to live in, and now...' He spread his hands helplessly, then easing Kerensa round to face him, enclosed her in his strong arms.

She snuggled her cheek against his rough working shirt. He caressed her hair, winding tendrils of it round his fingers. They stayed quiet for several minutes, trying to shut out the world and the terrible thing looming over them.

Then Kerensa said in a whisper of a voice, 'Perhaps if we don't make a fuss, Clem, then maybe Sir Oliver will not insist on going through with this marriage.'

'Dear God, Kerensa, I hope you're right, but the one thing I am sure of is that I'm not going to give you up. Not ever. No matter what happens. I love you too much.'

Unlike his usual chaste shows of affection, tonight he kissed her long and hungrily, the pain in his handsome face threatening to overwhelm them both.

They talked and argued for hours. Kerensa lit candles against the rapidly growing darkness. Despite the freezing rain and the sharp winds blowing in off the sea, the cottage was warm and cosy as Clem fed the fire at regular intervals with logs and pieces of driftwood. They sat huddled together before the blaze.

'We must be prepared to face the fact I may have to marry Sir Oliver, Clem,' she said wretchedly.

'How can you say that?' he returned, viciously prodding the fire with a poker.

'Because of all things I said earlier, and because Sir Oliver was so angry when I tried to speak to him.'

He pulled her round to look at him. 'You believe the situation is cut and dried already, don't you?'

'I… I don't know,' she answered, pressing her face against his shoulder as tears jewelled the corners of her eyes. 'I believe our only hope is not to do anything that would make Sir Oliver go on with it just to serve his pride, his arrogance, his… do you understand what I'm trying to say, Clem?'

'Yes, my love,' he said at last, breathing into her sweet-smelling hair. 'I'm afraid you're probably right.'

They kissed tenderly, clinging tightly to each other, then Kerensa told him he ought to go.

'Let me stay the night,' he pleaded.

'No, my love, it wouldn't be right. You know what might happen with us feeling the way we do at the moment. It would only make things more difficult for us, and your family must be getting worried about you by now.'

'I wish you'd change your mind… but I understand.' He kissed her in a way that tempted her to waver and tell him he could stay.

'When will I see you again?' he asked, when finally he let her go.

'I don't know where Sir Oliver intends to have me taken to tomorrow,' she said, frowning deeply.

'I'll find out easily enough. He won't be able to keep it a secret. I'll try to see you. Don't worry, my dearest love,' he added, with an optimism he was far from feeling. 'I love you, Kerensa, no one will keep us apart.'

'I love you too, Clem… always remember that.'

She clung to him a little longer before he opened the door and stepped out into the cold wet hostile night.

–

After Clem had gone Kerensa barred the door. Wrapping herself in a blanket, she sat on the old rug her grandmother had made and gazed dejectedly into the fire. She had sat in much the same way on winter evenings as a child with Old Tom. He had made hot chocolate for her from cocoa beans smuggled in from Spain which he had ground down himself, and although it was rather a fatty drink Kerensa had found it delicious with sugar added. As she sipped the chocolate he had told her many wild and colourful stories, then tucked her into bed. She did not go to bed that night, and her eyes did not close in sleep until dawn broke to chase away the darkness of the night.

Twenty-four hours had passed from the time Sir Oliver had rapped on the cottage door, when a tapping on the window roused Kerensa from a fitful sleep. Her head and limbs ached as she got unsteadily to her feet. Her arm felt painfully numb where it had been trapped under her body as she slept. As she rubbed her arm the tapping became more persistent, and wrapping the crumpled blanket around herself against the coldness, she looked apprehensively out of the window to see who was there.

She thought it might be Clem. It wasn't, it was a cock robin, come for the crumbs she scattered on the window sill each winter morning. Snatching up the remains of a loaf of bread from the table Kerensa went outside and broke off pieces for the robin. It had flown away when she unbarred the door. She stood at a short distance and watched the bird fly back to the sill, its brown and red body bobbing up and down as it pecked up the crumbs.

There was a mist out to sea giving visibility of no more than fifty feet over the shifting grey water, but on shore it was dry and the sky overhead held only a hint of a shade of greyness.

Kerensa walked down the path to the beach and scattered breadcrumbs over the cold black rocks. A flock of screeching gulls materialised as if by magic, rapidly clearing the rocks back to their former state.

When the last gull had flown off, apart from the gentle roll of the sea, all was quiet, oppressively quiet, with a feeling of remote unfriendliness in the air. At other moments when Kerensa had been alone and looked at these surroundings, she had felt herself to be the only person in the world; today she heartily wished she was.

When she returned to the cottage the robin had gone and sadness overwhelmed her again. Tomorrow, the bird would find no one to feed him crumbs of bread.

Once inside she set to work, vigorously raking out the ashes of the fire. She threw dried seaweed and kindling wood in the grate but it took her longer than usual to light them. Her fingers were stiff and clumsy, not from the cold but because she was angry. It was a feeling she was unfamiliar with and it made her feel guilty and uneasy. She was angry at everything and everyone and felt like throwing things around the cottage. 'Proper mazed' her grandfather would have called it. She was angry at a situation that was to force her into a marriage she neither sought nor desired. Angry at the two men who had included her in a bargain they had made, as though she had no right to feelings or opinions, hopes or wishes for herself.

She was even angry at Clem, this because of the guilt she felt at his distress and the worry that he might communicate with Sir Oliver and make matters worse. It was the anger she felt with herself that hurt the most. Why hadn't she faced her grandfather and Sir Oliver together yesterday and bluntly refused to have any part in their unfair, ridiculous agreement? Kerensa was hurt and confused, and anger supplied her with a wall of defence to protect her vulnerability.

What would happen, she wondered, if she refused to take one step out of Trelynne Cove with whoever it was the proud, arrogant man sent to collect her? But all the arguments she'd put to Clem the night before kept flooding her mind, and, she mused, Sir Oliver would probably be so angry, he'd ride down to the cove and haul her up on his big black horse and take her away himself. No, she decided she had no wish to be humiliated. Whatever she had to do, she would do it with dignity. But as she tidied up the cottage more angry thoughts only served to add to her misery.

She made a pot of tea but had no appetite for breakfast. While sipping from a mug at intervals, she packed a small battered trunk with the things she treasured. She would take with her a gilt-edged mirror her merchant-sailor father had brought back from the Barbary Coast for her mother; the cheap tin, fish-shaped brooch bought for her in Marazion market by Old Tom; a lace handkerchief she'd found abandoned on the roadside; a tiny green medicine bottle washed ashore amongst some driftwood; and the faded leatherbound Bible given to Jacob Trelynne by Sir Henry Pengarron. And the love tokens given to her by Clem.

Folding the few clothes she possessed she laid them carefully over and around the things that meant so much to her. She did not open the bottom drawer of a chest in the corner of her bedroom and tried not even to look at it. Among other things lying neatly arranged in the drawer was the linen she had stitched and embroidered to take to Trecath-en Farm with her as Clem's bride. She decided she would not take them now, and probably not at all.

Carrying the trunk from her bedroom she put it down by the outside door of the other room, and with this done, once again went outside into the cold morning air.

As she paced aimlessly up and down the beach Kerensa wished the crunch, crunch of the smooth pebbles under her feet could drown out her thoughts and diminish her anger and misery. Eventually, she found herself on the shoreline next to the outcrop of granite, and not having the will to climb to the top, sat desolately on a rock at the bottom.

When Nathan O'Flynn rode down into the cove a short time later he found her sitting on the rock, scratching idly at the coarse sand with a piece of rotten driftwood. She did not turn to see who it was as he took long steps to reach her.

'Kerensa,' he said softly.

During the summer before Clem had taken Kerensa to Ker-an-Mor stables to see a newly born foal. Nat had been there that day with other interested estate workers and it was then they had first met. With her sparkling grey-green eyes, the burnt copper sheen of her rich dark hair, and her captivating smile, Kerensa had turned many an appreciative head.

He was shocked now at the depth of sorrow in her pale young face as she turned and looked up at him. 'Haunted. That was how she looked, kind of haunted,' he was later to tell Jack and Barney Taylor.

'Hello, Nat. Have you come for me?' she said quietly, her voice remote.

'That's right, m'dear,' he answered, sitting down beside her. Picking up a handful of pebbles he tossed them one by one into each approaching dull grey wave, only speaking when his hand was empty. 'I'm taking you to Perranbarvah. It's been arranged for you to stay with the Reverend Ivey until... until you're married,' he said in an apologetic fashion.

They sat for a moment watching a latecomer on its way to join the fishing fleets at Newlyn. The speed of the lugger, with its entourage of scavenging gulls following in its wake, encouraged Kerensa to her feet. She threw the driftwood away with a careless movement. With her back straight, head up, and chin forward, Nat was fascinated by the look of determination that kindled her eyes.

'I'll get my things.'

Nat stood beside her and put out a hand lightly on her shoulder.

'I'm so sorry for you Kerensa, for you and Clem. If ever you need a friend...'

She gave him a faint smile. 'Thank you, Nat.'

It took but a few minutes to secure her trunk on Derowen's back. Frowning at its size, Nat said, 'What about the rest of your things, Kerensa? You must have more than this.'

'It will do for the time being,' she said firmly.

He glanced all around. 'Is your grandfather about somewhere? I could arrange to collect the rest from him, or perhaps he'd like to bring them over to the Parsonage himself later on?'

'He's gone – for good, Nat,' Kerensa informed him sharply. 'I don't know where he is.'

'When was this?'

'Yesterday.'

Nat whistled through his teeth. 'If Sir Oliver knew you'd be alone here last night, he would have sent me over for you yesterday. I'll come back and put a padlock on the door. It might keep the scavengers out for a while when word gets out the cove is deserted.'

He had brought Meryn, the grey pony, with him and helped Kerensa up to sit side-saddle on the animal's sturdy back. Unused to riding, she sat stiff and upright. As Nat turned to mount his own horse, she called his name.

Turning back, he said gently, 'Yes, m'dear?'

'Nat, do you think there is a chance Sir Oliver will change his mind?'

He looked down to the ground and kicked away a stone in front of his foot.

'No, Kerensa,' he replied grimly, 'I'm afraid I do not.'

–

As Kerensa and Nathan O'Flynn were travelling to the tiny fishing village of Perranbarvah, the Reverend Joseph Ivey moved about its bitterly cold parish church. Built of granite, small and sturdy to combat the effect of the wind and sea, the church today did not provide the Reverend with the feeling of tranquillity he usually found there.

He shivered and fidgeted all the way through his morning prayers. Feeling the need to linger he rose, and laying aside his prayer book walked back down the aisle and scooped up the handful of brittle dead leaves that had blown in as he'd entered the arched doorway. He then made an unnecessary check on the faded kneelers of the front pews, all hanging like sentinels on their hooks. Then, with a finger to his chin, he studied at length the stone floor beneath his feet, as if there he might find a solution to ease his troubled mind. After that he moved across to the tiny St Luke's chapel where he knelt to pray, but still he found no peace.

Finally, in full Sunday morning solemnity, he climbed up into the pulpit. He swept his eyes around the empty church and coughed apologetically as though he was keeping an impatient congregation waiting for a long overdue sermon. Feeling rather silly, he looked down at his hands resting on the pulpit's edge and picked off imaginary drops of candle grease from the wood with a well-manicured fingernail.

A sudden scratching at the heavy door by a straying animal looking for shelter caused the Reverend to jerk up his head, a guilty blush burning his wrinkled cheeks. On hearing the cat mew pitifully at not being able to gain admittance, the parson offered up a quick prayer of silent thanks that it wasn't Mrs Tregonning, his housekeeper. Proudly responsible for the cleanliness of the church, at a time when most church buildings had been allowed to fall into serious states of disrepair, she would have frowned reproachfully at his actions.

Throughout all of this, the problem the Reverend was turning over and over in his mind was the forthcoming marriage of the bad-tempered owner of Pengarron Estate to the goodly natured young girl from Trelynne Cove.

He had arrived at the Manor house as soon as he'd been able following the hasty summons from Sir Oliver. Although he and Sir Oliver enjoyed a close friendship, the Reverend could never forget that with most of his parishioners living in or near to poverty, it was Pengarron money that kept the small church at Perranbarvah functioning adequately and in reasonably good repair.

The Reverend had been parson of the church, dedicated to St Piran, from the time of Oliver's infancy, he being the only surviving Pengarron baby. He had baptised the child, and with a paternal eye watched Oliver grow up through an overindulged childhood and a reckless high-spirited youth. He had missed him during the years spent with his regiment as a young man.

It had been the Reverend's responsibility to teach Oliver, an intelligent, assertive boy, until he had entered public school. The Reverend liked Oliver far more than he had liked Sir Daniel, Oliver's father, who had been an amoral, unfeeling man. It was to the Reverend that Oliver, as a distraught ten year old, had turned for comfort when his mother, Lady Caroline, had died in childbirth.

In the eight years since Oliver had taken over the running of the Pengarron Estate, following his father's death, he had often discussed important matters with the Reverend, on occasion sending requests for him to call at the Manor. As he'd ridden to the Manor house the day before, the Reverend had mulled over the possible reasons for the urgency of Oliver's summons.

From the moment he entered Oliver's study it was apparent a crisis of some kind was at hand, but on hearing the reason for the younger man's ill humour, the Reverend had been deeply shocked. He'd been too ill at ease openly to point out to Oliver that he'd brought this intended marriage upon himself. He'd tried from time to time to do so, in a roundabout way, but Oliver Pengarron was not a man to listen or be reasoned with, when in one of his infamous adverse moods.

As more of the tale had unfolded the Reverend had become more and more perturbed, particularly so when he realised the agreement made over Trelynne Cove would force a girl into a marriage to which she would not have consented given her own choice.

Eventually he had agreed to call the banns. There would be no going back, and Joseph Ivey stood in his church feeling guilty and ashamed of his weakness in not standing up to the baronet.

The Reverend met Kerensa and Nat as he was leaving the church-yard. He greeted them cordially as they trotted the last few yards towards him. Kerensa gladly accepted the Reverend's offer to stroll through the churchyard with him to the Parsonage, while Nat rode on along the cart track with her trunk.

'You are most welcome, Miss Trelynne,' the Reverend said, offering her his arm. 'Mrs Tregonning, my housekeeper, has a room prepared ready for your stay.'

Thankful to be able to ease her aching limbs from the uncomfort-able journey, Kerensa took his arm and with a shy smile said, 'Thank you for your hospitality, Reverend.'

The Reverend Ivey coloured guiltily. They strolled through the churchyard. The church and Parsonage were built halfway up a steep hill and looked down over the cluster of closely built cob cottages of the fishing village below.

The Reverend sighed as he watched the fisherfolk, busy about their work in the crisp winter air.

'It won't be easy for you, my dear,' he said gently, 'all this sudden change in your life.'

'I was not born to marry a baronet, Reverend, that much is certain,' Kerensa remarked miserably. 'I want to marry Clem, and we are hoping Sir Oliver will change his mind and settle for a different agreement over the cove.'

The Reverend Ivey knew this to be highly unlikely. Sir Oliver Pengarron was a man of his word, and if he had agreed to marry Kerensa Trelynne then he would do just that. The Reverend tried to think of a way to comfort Kerensa. 'Sir Oliver is not entirely a bad man...'

'I find that hard to believe,' she retorted quickly.

'Well, there's been many a charitable deed he has done quietly for his tenants, estate workers and others in the parish, Miss Trelynne.'

'Really?' Turning her head she looked down over the cottages at the wide still strip of grey sea. 'That does surprise me.' Then looking earnestly at the parson, she went on, 'Oh, look, Reverend, I want to marry Clem, I love him and he loves me. You know that, we've talked to you about it. Can't you talk to Sir Oliver? Please,' she pleaded, 'he might listen to you.'

'I...' The Reverend was embarrassed and made temporarily witless. 'I'm afraid it... it would do no good.'

Kerensa sighed loudly and all the energy seemed to go out of her body, 'And I was afraid you would say something like that.'

She walked on, the Reverend keeping hold of her arm but staying one step behind.

The winter sun, growing in strength and height, illuminated the scarlet berries of the hawthorn bushes growing on hedgerows either side of the gate leading to the back of the ivy-clad Parsonage. Kerensa reached up and lifted a few berries on her fingertips.

'I suppose I'll find out more about Sir Oliver if I really do have to marry him,' she said stiffly, then turned her attention to the clumps of snowdrops growing against the shelter of the parsonage wall.

'Try not to become bitter, my dear. I don't approve of what has happened, but your grandfather did what many would have done in his position, to secure a good marriage.'

'A good marriage! But who for?' Kerensa asked, getting a little heated. 'I don't want this *good* marriage and I can't understand why Sir Oliver would want to marry me. I don't know anything about being a lady, and the rest of the gentry won't want anything to do with me. Surely you don't approve of people marrying out of their class, Reverend?'

She was looking him straight in the eye and he was taken by surprise at the question. 'I don't really believe it's a good idea, but… but I also believe that all people are equal… like the Good Lord does… we all have our value, worth. Your future will be difficult for you, but the only way forward now is to try to forgive and forget. When you've settled in, why not go into the church and sit awhile and pray? It will help, I'm sure.'

Unaware of how uncomfortable she was making him feel Kerensa warmed to the elderly parson with his kindly face; without his wig he had long wisps of grey hair encircling his high shiny pate, like an egg in a basket.

'Yes, I think I will,' she said, giving him a trace of a smile, 'and visit my mother's grave at the same time.'

The smile erased some of the sadness from her lovely young face, and slightly eased the burden of the Reverend Ivey's guilt.

–

Mrs Tregonning was a plump, middle-aged, bustling sort of woman. She fussed over Kerensa as she showed the girl up the dark creaking stairs to her room. It soon became apparent that Mrs Tregonning strongly disapproved of Sir Oliver, frequently referring to him as 'he up there'. Kerensa wasn't sure whether to find this shocking or amusing.

Entering a bedroom that overlooked the sea, Mrs Tregonning smoothed down the thick quilted bedcover on a bed twice the size of the one Kerensa usually slept in, then fussed with the fire burning heartily in the hearth.

'I do hope you'll be comfortable here, my handsome,' the plump woman carried on breathlessly, 'though there isn't much for you to take comfort in at the moment. I couldn't believe it when the Reverend told me why he'd been summoned up to the Manor yesterday. Summoned indeed! The trouble with he up there is he's got no patience, more's the pity. When he says jump, you jump, or watch out for it. And your grandfather… well! How could he do such a thing? Marrying off his only grandchild in a business deal, and to he up there of all people! Then there's poor Clem to think of. What's that poor soul going to do. That's what I want to know. I don't know what my late husband would have said about all this, God rest his soul. We both worked at the Manor in Sir Oliver's father's day. My, it was a grand place in they days before Sir Daniel let it get run down, and he was a worse man even than he up there is now. Now, my handsome, I don't want you to worry about nothing while you're here, I'll look after you.'

'Thank you, Mrs Tregonning,' Kerensa began. 'I…'

'I suppose he up there will send word about the wedding arrangements? Not that you'll have any say in the matter.'

Mrs Tregonning prattled on and on, and although Kerensa was sure she meant well, she had a distinct feeling the housekeeper was enjoying making a drama out of her misery. Kerensa was relieved when she eventually bustled out of the room, leaving her alone.

The room was light and airy, but so much larger than her own small bedroom in the cottage that Kerensa fought back the feeling that she was shrinking into obscurity. She took no interest in her surroundings but walked to the window to look out over the sea, hoping to gain some solace in its familiarity. It didn't work and she looked down at the garden below. The delicate movements of a greenfinch as it flitted along the high wall enclosing the spacious garden caught her eye. She watched its confident performance until a jealous robin protecting its territory chased the greenfinch away. Kerensa gripped the curtains: the rivalry of the two birds had served as a cruel reminder of Clem being ousted from his rightful place as her husband. Turning sharply back into the room she unpacked her trunk, but did not put Clem's lock of hair under her pillows. It was too precious to her to be glimpsed by Mrs Tregonning's curious eyes.

When she had freshened up from the journey Kerensa quietly slipped out of the Parsonage, grateful not to be faced on the way by the chattering housekeeper. She made her way to her mother's grave, the headstone simply bearing the words, 'MARY TRELYNNE, 1716-1743'.

Her mother had been a good woman. Everyone who'd talked of her did so from fond memories. Gazing down at the lonely grave Kerensa realised she knew little of her mother's death. She pondered on this for a few moments then bent and scratched at the lichen intruding on the granite around her mother's name.

'I wish you were still alive,' Kerensa whispered, 'then you could tell me what to do. Perhaps you could've put a stop to what Grandfather did. I'm so frightened, Mother. I can't bear to lose Clem and I'm so afraid for him. If Sir Oliver won't change his mind, what will I do? What will my future be like… living as his wife? Watch over me, please, Mother, help me if you can.'

Kerensa wiped away silent tears then, covering her head with her shawl, left her mother's resting place and entered the old Norman doorway of the ancient granite church.

Chapter 3

A week later, during the first hour after midnight, Oliver Pengarron was back in Trelynne Cove. Partly sheltered from the winds that veered around the cliffs and the light mist blowing in off the sea, he and several other men were concealed behind the largest rocks on the shingle beach close by the shoreline. There were more men stationed up on the clifftop with a long line of pack ponies, mules and carts. There was nothing to shelter them from the cold gusting winds that sliced their way across their path and pierced through their clothes. In an effort to keep warm, they rubbed chilled hands together and tugged in rough working coats against tense bodies.

They were there on that bleak moonless night to smuggle in uncustomed goods. Trelynne Cove, typical of the small coves, creeks and fishing harbours of Mount's Bay, afforded a clear run for contraband to be brought across from France and the Channel Islands. There were no caves at Trelynne Cove in which to hide the goods but access was easy, with its path leading from the cottage, so contraband could be carried up to the livestock and carts and stealthily conveyed inland along the well-worn cliff track.

In total there were over seventy men secretly hovering about the cove. Miners, fishermen, farm labourers and local craftsmen, all eager for a small share of the tea or tobacco brought in, and the few shillings that would put more food in the bellies of their all too often hungry families. All the men had made smuggling runs before, if not for Sir Oliver then for other men of forceful character who could command their respect, or even in some cases in groups of their own. Some of the fishermen among them brought in goods in their own boats, cleverly hidden in folded sails or hollow spars or under anonymous canvas.

One of the men crouching patiently behind the rocks was a young fisherman, Matthew King. Known as the 'Barvah Giant' for the extremity of his height and hefty bulk, he scanned the sea through wide excited eyes for the first sign of an approaching vessel. Brought up in a quiet, austere, religious household Matthew was grateful to be involved in the excitement and possible dangers of the smuggling ventures. He was well accustomed to pulling in heavy nets of writhing fish and it was no daunting task to him to carry the four and a half gallon tubs of gin and brandy, two at a time, across his massive chest up the steep dark cliff.

A man moved carefully up to his side. 'See anything, Matthew?' he whispered.

'Nothing yet, Hunk. Shouldn't be long now, though. I d'believe Cap'n Solomon don't like to hang about, do he?'

Hunk Hunken was the lander of the operation, second in command. While Sir Oliver Pengarron planned the run with the captain of the vessel, arranged to borrow the ponies, mules and carts for the night and for some of the goods to be carried up to London a few days later, Hunk was in charge of recruiting the men and for tipping off those who hid the goods about when to be ready.

Hunk scratched his long nose before answering Matthew. 'That's true enough. I just hope nothing goes wrong tonight, what with Sir Oliver being in such a bad mood and all. Mind he don't hear we talking, I heard un giving someone his tongue just now for doing it.'

'Mmm,' acknowledged Matthew King. His expression changed at the thought of the reason for the baronet's bad mood. Sir Oliver must know that most of the men here tonight did not approve of what he was doing to Clem Trenchard and Kerensa Trelynne, the girl who by right should be sleeping safely in the cottage above them. The men felt they had no right to be here in the cove. That feeling challenged Sir Oliver's authority and that was what he hated most.

Matthew and Hunk exchanged rueful glances when Sir Oliver crept up behind them. He had been working his way round the groups of men, checking on their readiness for the task ahead.

'Boats ready to put to sea, Hunken?' he asked, under his breath.

'Aye, m'lord, saw to it meself,' Hunk replied.

'Good. Are you ready, King?'

'That I am, m'lord,' Matthew answered. He couldn't make out Oliver's features but he knew they would be tense and severe and that he would be monitoring all their responses to him for signs of dissent.

The sky was dark and smudgy. A few feet away waves rolled then crashed on the rocks but the ones that reached the shingle seemed only half-hearted in their progress. Oliver felt that way about this run, rather than triumphant as he'd anticipated he'd be on repossessing Trelynne Cove. He was almost disinterested, totally lacking the usual controlled excitement he felt when undertaking an illicit operation. He had dampened the spirits of the other men. They were more tense than usual, too, and wanted only to finish the night's work ahead and go home to their beds.

Hunk Hunken shivered and pulled his neat beard between forefinger and thumb. He was uneasy, even though there was no firm reason for him to be feeling this way. There were only a few Revenue men stationed at Penzance and an inept elderly Riding Officer at Marazion, who had been ensconced there for many years and whom the authorities seemed to have forgotten to retire. Hunk was sure the Riding Officer was taking bribes from Sir Oliver to turn a blind eye to his well-organised runs. A more duty conscious Revenue man could be stopped in a chase by dropping a tub of spirits in his path, although not all could be counted on to be interested in self-gain. Quite recently a man from Breage had been hung just for hindering an officer. There was always good reason for secrecy and caution but it wasn't that kind of worry that was attacking Hunk tonight; dodging the Customs was part of the game. He felt he and the others wouldn't be there if something underhand hadn't occurred. It wasn't right and he was afraid it would bring them bad luck.

The men were like taut springs, ready to jump into action, their heads spinning round or jerking from side to side at the slightest noise. Even so, some risked Sir Oliver's wrath and snatches of whispered conversation were indulged in to offset some of their tension.

'Wonder what's comin' in tonight.'

'The usual, I 'spec. Wine, brandy, tea, lace. P'raps bales of silk fer gowns to dress that poor little maid in when she becomes his wife,' came a sarcastic reply, but not aimed at the other speaker.

Among the fishermen: 'At least with his lordship's frequent runs tes stoppin' some of they blamed tinners runnin' like vultures and bein' so violent over a wreck.'

'Aye, hope there'll be some French salt comin' in. Tes better fer the pilchard curin'.'

Elsewhere: 'I d'believe she's comin' in from Guernsey.'

And somewhere else: 'Now don't 'ee be tempted to 'ide somethin' fer yerself, mind. You went want Sir Oliver comin' after 'ee.'

Hunk Hunken continued to peer round the horse-shoe shape of the cove, searching intently for a reason for tonight's unease. He longed to light his pipe and let the strong tobacco take away the sourness in his throat.

Matthew King fidgeted with his belt buckle, made tight by a furtive downing of four tankards of homemade ale and several plates of thin watery broth in another smuggler's cottage on the way there. With Sir Oliver in close proximity, Hunk knocked urgently on the fishermen's arm for him to be still.

At a sudden whinnying from a pony the men looked up anxiously and held their breaths. When all was quiet again, with only the sounds of the whistling winds and the shifting sea, Matthew silently eased his belt loose by three holes before it stopped his breathing.

A miner close by with congested lungs cleared his throat. Oliver drew in a deep angry breath and Hunk inwardly sighed and was relieved that Clem Trenchard had elected to stay on the top of the cliff with the animals.

'The coast should be clear all night, sir, I d'reckon,' Hunk whispered, although not feeling that confident.

Oliver nodded his agreement. He was peering through the darkness, listening hard for a different sound through the strangely muffled waves in their eerie misty world.

A few moments later he asked, very quietly, 'Did you see that?'

'Aye, sir.'

They had seen the light overhead of miner Ted Trembath's snout lantern, signalling back to a vessel out at sea, the silhouette of which, made hazy by the mist, could be just made out by those with better eyesight.

'I'll get the men ready, sir.' Hunk moved off, hunched over and padding like a farmyard cat.

The rhythmic splash of oars brought the men on the beach expectantly to their feet. On a signal from Sir Oliver they made their way down to the water, some to unload the incoming boat, others to row their own boats out to the waiting ship, which had dropped anchor in deep waters, a safe distance from submerged rocks. Some of the men on the clifftop moved to form a chain along the length of the cliff pathway, to take the goods and pass them upwards to be loaded on to the ponies and mules and into the carts. They would work quickly. If there were any Customs men about the most dangerous time during a run was the unloading and reloading of the cargo.

It had been decided not to take the animals down the narrow rocky pathway in the dark for fear of accidents. Clem moved two ponies closer to the path's edge to await the first tub-carriers with their heavy burdens. He stood in front of the ponies, borrowed for the night from the Wheal Ember mine, their bodies well greased, their tails and manes clipped so they could not be caught in the event of trouble. He held on firmly to their bridles, every few moments tossing back his head to remove the damp strands of hair that threatened to get in his eyes.

Clem was anxious for the run to be over, then he would seek out Sir Oliver and challenge his right to take Kerensa away from him. He had worked out so many sentences and phrases in his head, a counter reason or appeal for each of Sir Oliver's expected retorts or angry threats. It would not be easy, might even as Kerensa feared make matters worse, but he had to take the risk. He could not go on any longer and just do nothing about it.

Further along the line of ponies and mules, the excited boy standing beside Ted Trembath, who was on watchman's duty, tapped his brother's arm.

'What happens now, Ted?'

He ruffled the boy's untidy hair and grinned at his growing delight. 'Well, Davey boy, we'll keep watch up here for Revenue men and their cutters out at sea while they below bring the goods ashore and carry 'em up here,' he said as quietly as his strong voice would allow. 'Then Clem 'n' the others will put 'em on the carts 'n' animals and take 'em off to the hides.'

'Where are the hides, Ted? Do we know anyone who takes the goods in?'

'Tes best 'ee don't know who takes in what, boy. The folks who're able to take in goods tonight will stick a bottle in their eaves. I can tell 'ee, though, the hides are all different places—hayricks, churchyard, hollow trees and the like.'

Davey Trembath's curiosity was not yet satisfied. 'What about the Revenue men, Ted? They have muskets, don't they? If they find us up here will they shoot us?'

Ted Trembath looked seaward before answering, for signs of a Revenue cutter bearing down on the smuggling vessel. Satisfied nothing ill-favoured to their cause was lurking about he swept his eyes over the beach and cliff path. He sensed rather than saw the activity below, of men working quickly in an attitude of stealth, their bodies poised ready for trouble as the first tubs of spirits were passed arm to arm along the human chain. Men sweating and trying to silence their grunts, concentrating in the darkness so as not to drop a tub, smash it and waste the precious liquid. Men savouring the contents of their burdens, hoping that Sir Oliver wasn't in such a bad mood tonight as to deny them a tub to be taken away later and shared out among them. Ted could hardly see the men but could hear the crunch of their boots on the shingle which no amount of care could keep silent.

'Don't 'ee be concerned about the Revenue men,' Ted said to his brother, hoping to allay any fears he might have; a nervous man could endanger a smuggling run and he began to doubt the wisdom of bringing Davey with him. 'There'd only be a few of 'em and they'm more likely to be afeared of we with we outnumbering 'em; what with Sir Oliver being behind the run and we being on his land.'

'Then why all this need for secrecy?' Davey asked, with the scorn of youth.

Ted gave his brother a slight cuff round the head that told him not to be so stupid. 'Don't 'ee ferget tes against the law, boy. And another good reason fer keeping an eye out fer the Revenue men is if they don't try to arrest 'ee on the spot, they've bin known to follow 'ee to the hides, seize the goods next day and arrest they people who took 'em in.'

As the younger Trembath enthusiastically took in all this information Clem was looking behind them to see if anyone was coming up the cliff path. There was no one to be seen but he heard a noise and his body froze. Primitive instinct told him it was not a smuggler. Creeping along the side of the ponies, Clem urgently nudged the man nearest to him.

Daniel Berryman of Orchard Hill Farm, a short stocky man of middle years, looked around. Acting as batman and armed with a staff to deter the Revenue men, or in the event, troublemakers of a different sort, he whispered hoarsely, 'What is it, Clem?'

'I think we're being watched,' he hissed back.

Daniel moved forward to peep past the ponies. His head moved from side to side as he concentrated hard while staring into the misty darkness. Straightening up he beckoned Clem to his side. 'You're right, boy. See over there? There's about five of 'em.'

Clem followed Daniel's pointing finger to where the outline of a small group of men could just be defined.

'Do you think it's the Preventive men?'

'Dunno. We'll wait till they get closer, boy. We don't want a panic for no good reason.'

Davey and Ted Trembath spotted the mysterious group of men advancing steadily towards the smuggling party at the same instant. Ted clutched his brother's arm. 'Quiet, boy. Don't move.' Ted's voice was harsh.

'They've got uniforms on…' Davey sounded frightened.

'Hush, Davey.'

'Who are they, Ted? Tes the Preventive men. It is, isn't it?' The boy squirmed against Ted's tightening grip. 'What'll we do, Ted!'

The boy's voice had risen steadily; the other men on the clifftop became quickly aware of what was going on.

'Damn it!' exclaimed Daniel Berryman to Clem. 'Keep they ponies still, boy. I'll see who tes.'

A cry went up: 'We've been betrayed! Ambush!'

It was repeated by others. Ted, the eldest of four brothers, gave Davey, the youngest, a hard push. 'Run, Davey! Run for home!'

At the outbreak of shouting there was a sudden panic among the strangers and two turned and ran away.

Davey took off across the springy grass, dodging out of the way of a smuggler running in the opposite direction towards his brother.

'Light the beacon, Ted!' the man cried, amidst the growing commotion. 'There's not enough Preventive men to do anything 'gainst we but there may be a cutter out there after the ship.'

After making sure that Davey was on his way Ted was already racing to the cliff edge. He dashed his lantern into a huge pile of damp furze and kicked at the pile until the beacon was well ablaze as a warning to the smuggling vessel of the possible danger.

The cry of ambush had been taken up below. Oliver dumped the tub of brandy he was lifting back into the rowing boat that had come ashore.

'Out of here!' he ordered, at the top of his voice. 'Move!'

With the help of the towering Matthew King, Oliver pushed the boat out into waist-high, freezing water then they turned together to join the scramble up to the clifftop. They gathered up a fallen man in one co-ordinated sweep of powerful arms and guided him as he stumbled over the shingle.

Amid the shouts and scuffles Daniel Berryman thrust himself forward, and by the light thrown out from the beacon saw he was facing three uncertain-looking Revenue men. They were taking steps forward and then backward, as if they didn't know whether to exert their authority and try to make an arrest or turn tail and run after their fleeing companions. Daniel was not going to risk having a musket ball tearing into his body, and slashed at the legs of the nearest Revenue man with his staff. The man fell like a dead fly, howling in agony, and Daniel snatched up his musket.

Clem tried for all he was worth to hold on to the ponies but they were alarmed and whinnying and edging themselves forward. Their restlessness turned to panic as more and more men rushed past them, and Clem was threatened with being dragged under their hooves. He decided it was safer for himself and the ponies to let them go. As they bolted away he found himself on the end of a musket barrel held by a Revenue man who, although nervous, looked as if he intended to take a prisoner, perhaps thereby ensuring he had something to bargain with for his own safety at the end of the night's fray.

Clem's heart missed its next beat but was whipped up with fury. He hadn't come here tonight to take part in his enemy's misdemeanour only to be robbed of the opportunity to challenge him by being taken into custody or perhaps killed by another. With a cry of rage he ducked rapidly under the firearm and thumped both his clenched fists with all his might into the softest part of the Revenue man's belly. The musket went off, its ball thundering harmless up into the air. The Revenue man doubled over. Clem pushed him to the ground, ripped the musket from his hands and smashed it useless on a granite boulder.

Now he was stirred up, Clem looked around for more Revenue men. He pushed through two miners attempting to put a tub of brandy on a skittish mule then saw the back of the last Revenue man scampering off into the darkness. He had tossed aside his musket and it quickly joined the other in a broken heap on the turf under Clem's furious hands.

Four or five others of the back ponies had panicked at the outbreak of the fracas and the sudden light from the beacon. They broke away from the line of agitated animals, heading off in all directions. Men cried to one another to get out of their way. Two fishermen reaching the top of the cliff path in front of Hunk Hunken were knocked off their feet and trampled by flailing hooves. Hunk shouted and waved his arms at the ponies, and checked by his actions from doing further injury to the fallen men, they raced away inland, rapidly becoming engulfed in the darkness.

Another pony slipped and checked itself on the greasy surface before rearing up in front of a small thin boy who had appeared across its path. Ted Trembath, running back from the beacon, recoiled in horror and shouted something to the boy. Unable to hear in the confusion, Davey Trembath, who hadn't been able to get through the mêlée of milling bodies and animals, raised his arms and attempted to grasp the pony's reins. He succeeded, but the pony, its eyes bulging in terror, kicked the boy to the ground, his arm breaking in several places as the animal resumed its crazed journey.

Ted ran after them, screaming in abject horror. The pony, with Davey being dragged along with his broken arm tangled in the reins, was heading for the cliff edge.

'Davey! Davey! For God's sake, boy, let go!' Ted's anguished words were lost among the shouts of the other men and the surge of the sea fifty feet below. He watched in frozen horror as the terrified pony and his thirteen-year-old brother hurtled out of sight.

Ted moved on trembling legs to the cliff edge. Some of the other smugglers, including Clem and Daniel Berryman and the two Revenue men they now held prisoner, slowly joined him. They all looked down in stunned silence where the boy and the pony had disappeared. Nothing could be seen but inky blackness. Murmuring broke out but the horror remained. Davey's last scream was still echoing inside their heads. Ted Trembath began to moan, then sobbed and wailed, holding his sides and shaking.

Oliver had been the last to come up from the cove, ensuring first that the other men had safely reached the top. He skirted round the men attending the trampled fishermen and roughly pushed through to the group huddled near the dying embers of the beacon. After the commotion all had gone quiet.

'What on earth is going on here!' he shouted. 'Has someone gone over?'

Ted Trembath answered, his voice thick and throaty. 'It was Davey. He was dragged over the side by one of the runaway ponies.'

Oliver glanced over the cliff. From that position it was a sheer drop on to treacherous rocks. He drew in a long deep breath through his nose; no one could survive such a fall.

'What frightened the ponies?' he asked severely.

No one answered. Throats were cleared, feet were shuffled, heads lowered. But no one spoke.

'Speak up, one of you!' he demanded, looking from face to face, resting momentarily on Clem's. 'Was it the shout of ambush? What's been going on up here? Was there a good reason for the panic or—'

When he saw the two terrified men in uniform trying to conceal themselves among the other men, he reached out and grasped the one in Daniel Berryman's clutches. 'What the hell are you doing here?' he shouted in fury.

'Nothing like this was supposed to have happened, sir,' the Revenue man blurted out, while quaking in his boots. He was terrified he and his companion were about to follow Davey Trembath over the cliff.

'Then just what *was* supposed to have happened?' Oliver hissed, pulling the man closer and shaking him violently. 'Out with it, man!'

'It... it was the old Riding Officer... at... at Marazion, sir.'

'What about him!'

'He... he... he informed us there'd be a landing here tonight. Said if we didn't... didn't come along... and... and... he'd report us for being slack in our duties. We didn't mean no harm, sir, not on one of your runs. We was hoping just to seize some of the goods and scarper.'

'Have you any idea why the Riding Officer was so keen for you to come here tonight?' Oliver snarled, gripping the Revenue man even tighter.

'I... I don't know for sure, sir. But there was a strange little man coming out of his office this evening, all wrinkled up he was, ugly and dirty, with only one long tooth in his whole head.'

'Old Tom Trelynne!' spat Ted Trembath, who had been listening intently. 'Was it him who informed the Riding Officer, man?'

The Revenue man shook with fear as Ted advanced on him. 'It could'a been, mister. I don't know for sure.'

'I believe the old man said he lived here, sir,' the other Revenue man put in hastily, hoping the smugglers would go easy on them if they seemed co-operative.

'Aye, he—'

'Sounds like Old Tom,' Oliver said grimly, interrupting now he had heard enough.

'Aye, sir,' said Ted, his voice unusually low. 'I'll get that little bastard for this, if it's the last thing I do on this earth.'

'Go back to Ashley Hinton,' Oliver told the quaking Revenue men. 'Remind him that I pay him well to turn a blind eye to my free trading ventures. If anything comes of this tonight, I swear there will be hell to pay. Now get out of here, and be very sure to keep your mouths shut!' He pushed the Revenue man he was clutching towards his colleague. Daniel Berryman and Clem let him go too. In an instant they had both turned on their heels and scurried off, one limping badly, the other holding his stomach.

Hunk Hunken looked after them. 'D'reckon they'll find their way back to Marazion in the dark, sir?'

'I don't give a damn about them! Get this place tidied up, Hunken, and make sure the fishermen sail back to Perranbarvah. I don't want a single trace left to show we were here. We'll take the goods we've managed to bring ashore to one of the hides. You can tell the men I'll pay them as usual.'

Oliver turned to speak to Ted Trembath but found Clem standing in his way. The younger man stood his ground.

'Get out of my way, Trenchard!' Oliver snapped.

'I want to talk to you, Sir Oliver,' he said coldly.

'This is not the time for discussions, pleasant or pretty, and if it's about what I think it is, I certainly have nothing to say to you on the matter. Now help get these animals out of here.'

Clem realised he would be foolish to carry on with what he wanted to say, but saw no reason not to rub salt in the baronet's recent wound.

'It's your fault the boy's dead,' he said, as if triumphant over something.

'Get out of my way,' Oliver repeated, 'if you don't want to follow him over the cliff.'

Clem's face was strangely aglow in the firelight as he stepped aside and wandered off into the darkness.

Oliver kicked at the embers of the beacon, sending a shower of red sparks up into the night sky.

Unaware of the tragedy that had happened on shore, Hezekiah Solomon, owner and captain of the vessel *Free Spirit*, shouted orders to weigh anchor and put to sea. A careful watch was kept for any patrolling Revenue cutters but none were sighted, and *Free Spirit*, her captain and crew, sailed to safety further along the coast, to the lee side of Pengarron Point.

Long after the last of the men had left, and there was no sign of the *Free Spirit*, Ted Trembath remained on the clifftop looking out over Trelynne Cove. He pulled off the red handkerchief he always wore around his neck and wept bitter tears into it for his beloved lost brother.

–

Mrs Tregonning was up early bustling her large, sombrely dressed frame around the parsonage kitchen.

Clem tapped on the door, opened it slightly, and softly called out, 'Mrs Tregonning, are you there?'

'Come on in Clem,' she called back. 'I saw you pass the window. Sit yourself down and we'll have a nice cup of tea.'

As he entered the big cosy room Clem noticed the woman's puffy red-rimmed eyes.

'I take it you've heard about Davey Trembath, then?'

'Yes,' she said, sniffing back fresh tears, 'Jack rode over and told the Reverend about it a short while ago. It's dreadful, dreadful. Fancy taking that poor little boy out like that last night. And his poor mother, how's she going to bear it, that's what I want to know. Isn't it bad enough that he up there involves half the neighbourhood in his wrong doings, without children getting involved in them too.'

The tears of the distraught woman could be held back no longer and ran freely down her chubby face. Clem rounded the table and with an effort he enclosed Mrs Tregonning in his arms. After a moment or two she pushed him aside, her face a picture of embarrassment as she noisily blew her nose.

'Better now?' Clem asked kindly.

'Yes, my handsome. Sorry about that,' she answered briskly, dabbing her cheeks with a handkerchief. 'Come on now, sit yourself down. I'll pour us a nice cup of tea.'

Clem sat down at the table laden with things in readiness for the breakfast of the Reverend and his guest. He sipped his tea, keeping silent until Mrs Tregonning was quite composed.

Carefully he said, 'Does Kerensa know what's happened?'

'Yes, poor little maid. Been crying her eyes out she has, what with Old Tom being more than likely responsible for the boy's death. Now everyone knows I don't hold with smuggling, although it's no wonder that men do it with times being so hard, and the government not giving a darn about what happens to we down here, but like everyone else, I believe there's none worse than a man who informs on his own kind. As if that poor little maid hasn't got enough to put up with already...' She threw up her podgy hands in a helpless gesture and sighed deeply.

'Can I see Kerensa?' Clem pleaded, 'Just for a little while.'

Mrs Tregonning very slowly placed her cup in its saucer.

'I don't think that would be a good idea, Clem, she—'

'I promise I won't upset her,' he interrupted urgently.

'I'm sorry, Clem. It's up to the Reverend, not me, who sees his guests in his house, but I'm quite sure he wouldn't allow it. Besides, it will do no good to either of you at the moment. Why not leave things as they are for the time being?'

'There might not be much time left for us, Mrs Tregonning. I need to know if Kerensa's had the chance to speak to Sir Oliver. She's hoping to talk to him out of this marriage he's got planned.'

'If you were in church on Sunday, Clem, you would have heard the first banns being called.'

'I know about that,' he said, grimacing at the reminder. 'I managed to talk to Kerensa out in the garden, the day before yesterday. She told me up till then he hadn't sent word to her about anything, or been over to see her. I have to know what is happening, you do see that, don't you?'

'Of course I do, Clem. I only wish there was something I could do to help you, but I do know he hasn't been in touch with the dear maid. I don't want to turn you out, but you really ought to go now, Clem. With this dreadful business over young Davey Trembath, he might well ride over to see the Reverend. It will only make matters worse if he catches you here.'

'You're right,' Clem said reluctantly. 'I'll leave it this time, but I'll look for another chance to see Kerensa. Thanks for the tea… tell Kerensa I called and I… just tell her I called will you, please?'

Mrs Tregonning nodded understandingly.

Charity was waiting for Clem outside the kitchen door. She jumped about excitedly at her master's feet, then sensing his doleful mood as he strode off, she fell in soberly at his heels.

'What are you doing here, Trenchard?'

The stinging question hurled at his back came from Sir Oliver Pengarron. Clem turned sharply round to face his father's landlord. Clem was six feet two inches tall but Oliver looked down on him by a good three inches more. Five yards of hard frosted ground lay between them and Clem stared back into the dark eyes that pierced keenly into his.

'I called at the Parsonage to find out how Kerensa is,' Clem muttered, his voice as cold as his feelings were for this man he had always disliked and now hated.

'The girl is to be my wife, Trenchard, it's of no concern to you how she is,' Oliver snapped. 'In future keep away from her, or your father will be the only Trenchard to farm on my land.'

Clem said nothing. Their eyes parried for supremacy in a silent battle of unspoken challenges; Oliver tapped his riding crop against his leg, Clem clenched his fists. It was Clem who looked down first. Charity nuzzled his hand but he pushed her away.

With a jerk of his head he said coldly, 'I've got work to do.' Turning again he followed Charity, as she bounded on before him, to begin his day's work.

Oliver smiled superciliously after the fair-haired youth, then with long strides he reached the Reverend Ivey's front door. Mrs Tregonning showed him into the parson's neat study and with her disapproving nose up in the air retreated to inform the Reverend of his visitor and to fetch Kerensa from her room.

He entered his study dressed in preparation for riding, his kid gloves held loosely in his hand.

'I'm on my way to the miners' cottages on Lancavel Downs to call on the Trembath family,' he explained, after bidding Oliver a solemn good morning. 'They are not regular worshippers in my flock now their interest lies in the Methodist prayer and Bible classes, but they may allow me to offer them some comfort.'

'They might,' Oliver agreed. 'Matthias Renfree has been with them all the morning. They regard him as something of a preacher now, although like John Wesley himself, young Renfree encourages the likes of the Trembaths to attend church to make their communion.'

The Reverend glanced at the other man with a shrewd look in his watery brown eyes. He was always amazed by the way Oliver knew everything that concerned, or occurred in, the local district.

A little tap on the study door was followed by the arrival of Kerensa, with Mrs Tregonning fussing around her.

'Good morning,' she said quietly to both men, her hands toying with a damp handkerchief. She was dressed in the better of her two dresses, the one she wore to church. It was simply styled in pale blue dimity with subtle lace trimming. Because she felt cold her shawl was draped over her shoulders and crossed over, the ends tied at her waist at the back.

Oliver studied her face. Although her eyes were red from weeping it did nothing to detract from her loveliness. Her eyes seemed larger than he remembered and she looked lost and so very young.

When he moved his gaze to Mrs Tregonning's plump face his features noticeably hardened. The housekeeper made no attempt to leave the room so he switched his attention to the Reverend Ivey.

'I don't want the girl to see or speak to Clem Trenchard,' he ordered. 'If he calls here again you are to make it quite clear she cannot see him.'

Before the Reverend could return an answer, Kerensa rounded angrily on Oliver. 'I will see or talk to anyone I like, *when* I like.'

'You most certainly will not!' he snarled at her. 'As my future wife, you will act accordingly. From now on you are not to associate with people such as Trenchard.'

'But I come from people such as him!' Kerensa snapped back. How dare this man aim an insult at Clem after the hurt he had caused him?

She would not tolerate it. Her cheeks were highly flushed and she began to shake. Mrs Tregonning put a hand of caution on her arm.

'Yes, I'm afraid I know that only too well,' Oliver returned sarcastically, determined to have the last word, as he was wont to do.

'You don't have to marry me.' At first Kerensa thought she had said the right thing. Now he could say, 'No, you're right, I don't have to, do I? I've made a mistake, you may go home.' But she had spoken angrily, returned his sarcasm, and he was furious. His presence dominated the room, she had felt it as she entered. Now he puffed up his chest and tilted his head even higher.

'I will do whatever I want,' he said, icily and evenly.

Fearful of another angry interchange the Reverend Ivey coughed loudly. 'I suggest you both calm yourselves before things get out of hand.'

Kerensa was unnerved but glared at Oliver. For the second time within a few short minutes his dark eyes beheld another's in mutual animosity, and as Clem had gone, Kerensa looked away first. She moved across the room and sat down near the window, folding her hands on her lap. Mrs Tregonning followed and stood protectively at her side.

The Reverend breathed an audible sigh of relief. Oliver began to converse with him as though the two women were not in the room.

'The two fishermen who were hurt last night will receive a few shillings a week from the estate until they are fit to return to work. I don't want to be accused of allowing people to starve. It is a great pity they were among such a panicky lot of men last night.'

'Yes, indeed,' the Reverend said, non-committally.

Mrs Tregonning snorted and received a withering look from Oliver.

'The injured fishermen were John Roskilley and Ebenezer Laity, weren't they?' the Reverend said. 'I understand the Trembath boy was the youngest child of the family and his mother's favourite.'

'That's all correct,' Oliver replied. 'Will and Curly Trembath were on their core down the mine last night, but they've joined their brother, Ted, in the search for Old Tom Trelynne.'

He looked pointedly at Kerensa as he mentioned her grandfather. She looked up sharply at him, a guilty flush on her face at Old Tom's supposed involvement in the tragedy.

'It's a great pity that all the Trembaths were not on their shift last night,' the Reverend said, drawing their attention, his face full of concern. 'I do hope there will be no violence.'

No similar hope could be detected on Pengarron's stern face.

'I will, of course, cover the funeral expenses if the boy's body is ever recovered.'

'That is very good of you, Sir Oliver, and no less than I've come to expect from you. There's many a gentleman who cares nothing for the ordinary folk.' The Reverend Ivey seemed anxious for his remarks to reach Kerensa's ears.

But if the parson was hoping that Kerensa would see Sir Oliver in a better light, it didn't work. She looked at the baronet with cynicism on her face. As far as she was concerned he saw the working class as nothing more than dirt beneath his feet which he felt free to treat in any way he chose, and any sympathetic gesture he made towards those who had suffered on the smuggling party was performed merely to please folk like the Reverend.

'Yes... well.' Oliver cleared his throat and shifted his stance. 'I came here today to arrange for her,' he indicated Kerensa briefly with a movement of his head, 'to ride over to the Manor house and see what is to become her new home. I daresay you will escort her over, Reverend?'

'I'll be glad to,' the parson answered.

'With your lordship's pardon, there's something I would like to say,' put in Mrs Tregonning, much to Oliver's annoyance. 'The Manor house is not fit and proper to be lived in, what with the way it's been allowed to become run down these past years. If Miss Trelynne, here, is to live as a lady up there, it will need a thorough cleaning right through for a start, and she will need staff to help her run it as well.'

Oliver knew of the woman's strong disapproval of him and his manner of living. He disliked her, too, particularly for her outspoken tongue. Her tone reminded him of a verse from the Reverend's sermon, taken from St James' Epistle on the previous Sunday morning service: 'But the tongue can no man tame; it is an unruly evil, full of deadly poison...'

He said, abruptly, 'I am not interested in any opinion of yours, woman.'

Then he turned to Kerensa, 'Come up to the Manor at three o'clock tomorrow afternoon. You will find me in my study.' He looked hard at her for a moment. She had been staring at him curiously since the Reverend Ivey's rejoinder to his remark about paying for Davey Trembath's funeral. Despite himself, Oliver found her appealingly innocent and fragile.

He gave Mrs Tregonning, who was hanging over Kerensa's shoulder, an icy stare before continuing, 'There will be no need for a chaperon. Beatrice will be there.'

'I'll see Miss Trelynne arrives safely at the appointed time,' the Reverend said, smiling lightly.

'Good. A good morning to you, Reverend.' And with nothing more than a quick nod in the direction of the two females, Oliver took his leave.

–

Later in the day Oliver found Ashley Hinton in his dreary lodgings over candlemaker Edward Hill's workshop in Marazion. He reluctantly shook the moist podgy hand offered to him by the elderly Customs Riding Officer, who looked as though he was part of the cluttered furnishings in his makeshift office. The two men sat down to a discussion over a glass of strong clear gin, drawn from a tub of one of Hinton's pay-offs.

'Good to see you, Sir Oliver, good to see you. Yes indeed, good to see you,' Hinton said, in his irritating hissing voice, while smiling much wider than was necessary.

It was always difficult to hold an intelligent conversation with the grossly overweight, cross-eyed man, of whom the locals would remark, ''ee be one stick short of a bundle.'

Oliver fixed him with a cold stare. 'Do you know why I'm here, Hinton?'

'Um, yes. Last night. Shame about the boy, yes indeed.' Ashley Hinton gulped a large mouthful of gin, taking no care to prevent a further stain adding to those already soiling his unkempt shirt and jacket.

'Yes, it is a shame, Hinton,' Oliver agreed, tapping his riding crop on the leg of the table that lay between them, 'and a great pity also that you inclined your ear to Old Tom Trelynne. I take it it was he who informed you of last night's landing in the cove?'

Hinton moved about uncomfortably on his squeaky chair. 'Yes, I believe it was. Well, the thing is… was, you see… I thought a couple of men having a quick look round would show those higher up that we do try to detain smugglers and seize uncustomed goods. Smuggling is… um… rife all along Mount's Bay, from Land's End to the Lizard.'

'And so what if it is?' Oliver said, in challenging tones.

'I was threatened… if I didn't… there weren't meant to be no trouble. The men weren't meant to be taken along the cliff so far.'

'What!' Oliver banged his fist down hard on the table, making Ashley Hinton jump in fright and spill more of his drink. 'Are you telling me that the old man took your men all the way to Trelynne Cove, Hinton?'

'Um, yes, Sir Oliver. I believe he did.'

Pulling a handkerchief from his pocket, Oliver very carefully wiped the inside and outside of his glass before drinking from it.

'But it puzzles me,' he said a moment later. 'With me about to marry his granddaughter, why would Old Tom want to make trouble for me? I can hardly marry the girl if I'm sent to prison for smuggling.'

Ashley Hinton squirmed about and scratched his bulbous stomach. He looked about his office with blinking eyes, and with puffing and hissing noises coming from his throat like an enormous kettle about to boil.

'Um… with the greatest respect, Sir Oliver, in your position you would be most unlikely to be apprehended, let alone brought before the court. And certainly not convicted.'

'Yes, Hinton.' Oliver nodded thoughtfully. 'I'll grant you that is true. So what is the reasoning behind Trelynne's betrayal? He had no need of money, so it could not have been for any reward.'

'Well, the thing is, the old man… um… I wasn't really sure who he was at the time, you understand… well, I got the feeling the old man didn't want anyone hanging about the little cove.'

Oliver's face relaxed and a glimmer of understanding shone through his eyes. 'Now I'm beginning to see what last night was all about,' he said slowly.

'Oh, do you, Sir Oliver?' Hinton laughed in an embarrassed fashion. 'Oh, that is good, excellent in fact. That is good. I'm so glad to have been of some help.'

Hinton reddened from his neck upwards, watching in nervous fascination as, with the tip of his riding crop, Oliver lifted papers and documents on the table.

The Riding Officer was told, 'You did not have to act upon Trelynne's information, Hinton, or allow him to guide your men to the cove.'

Hinton licked his fat lips, his eyelids blinking rapidly as papers and other articles amid the clutter were tipped on to the dusty floor.

'Why didn't you just ignore him?'

Gulping like a fish out of water, Hinton looked helplessly around the room.

'Well! Speak up, man!' Oliver snapped.

It helped the Riding Officer to find his tongue.

'I… well, the old man threatened to inform my superiors of our little arrangement… if I didn't.'

Oliver stood up abruptly and drained his glass. 'Be very sure that nothing like this ever happens again, Hinton. Instead, have the good sense to come and see me at once. Good day to you.'

Ashley Hinton had got clumsily to his feet. He bowed over and over again. 'Good day to you, Sir Oliver. Yes, indeed, good day. It was a pleasure to have your company…' But he was talking to thin air.

Chapter 4

Pengarron Manor had stood in its sheltered valley for over two centuries. Planned and built by Sir Arthur Pengarron, it had replaced the more modest dwelling of his ancestor, William Garres, the illegitimate son of Sir Ralph Garres, a French aristocrat who had crossed the English Channel with William I.

Built three storeys high, of local granite, the building made Kerensa feel small and insignificant as she stood before its massive oak door. The Reverend Ivey had escorted her along the two miles of narrow winding lanes and cart tracks from Perranbarvah and up the long gravelled carriageway that led to the front of the imposing Manor house. Now she regretted her insistence that the Reverend leave before announcing her arrival, he being urgently required back in the village to assist in the journey of the soul of one of his flock into the next world.

Kerensa had ridden over on Meryn, the pony Nathan O'Flynn had brought with him to the cove, now to be kept temporarily in the Reverend's stable. She was a little more used to riding, having gone out to Trelynne Cove in Nathan's charge to secure the remainder of her possessions bottom drawer and all. Even so, she was relieved now to be on firm ground. When a skinny boy in tattered clothes had appeared, and with a cheery smile had taken Meryn away, Kerensa had smiled back, wishing she could think of something to say to detain the boy a little longer.

Left alone in the circular courtyard, with a statue of a cherub in a fountain at its centre, she'd twisted the bow at the neck of her cloak and wondered if anyone was watching her from behind the heavy drapes of the innumerable windows. At the door she stopped short and peered at its curiously shaped brass knocker. It held the likeness of a wolf's head, giving her an even greater feeling of apprehension. She was not looking forward to seeing Sir Oliver again and had been steeling herself to appeal to him, even challenge him, to agree to an alternative arrangement for securing Trelynne Cove back into Pengarron ownership. As she left the Parsonage, Mrs Tregonning had urged her to be careful in what she said to him, saying ominously that she did not have to make a journey into Hell to meet the Devil. Kerensa prayed her courage would not fail her at the vital moment.

She had no idea what to expect once inside the building and very much wanted to turn and run away. Gingerly she reached out to use the door knocker, only to realise the door was slightly ajar. She was uncertain what to do and this added to her discomfiture. Should she knock and wait to be admitted within or had the door purposely been left open for her to enter unannounced? She decided on the latter and pushed the door just wide enough for her to slip through.

She stepped into the great hall, which like the rest of the house was panelled in dark oak from the plantation that sheltered the building, the valley and parklands in an almost perfect arc.

Portraits of Pengarron forebears looked down on her from their lofty positions ascending the wide stairway. Some looked benevolent, while others held that same air of disdain in their dark eyes as the present-day baronet and Lord of the Manor. Some had fought for their monarchs, like Arthur Pengarron who received the first baronetcy from King Henry VII, and Sir Edward who helped repel the parliamentarians on St Michael's Mount. Others had built up the family fortune by farming the land.

Kerensa knew nothing of this as she looked about her. Everything was layered in dust, from solid-looking oak chests, perhaps holding bygone secrets, and tall cabinets with smeared glass, to semi-circular tables and the swords and shields that hung from the walls. Hangings and draperies, once richly embroidered, were faded where the sun had leached their colours. The over abundance of spider's webs was so pronounced, it seemed to Kerensa they might bring down the splendidly decorated ceiling at any moment. The floor beneath her feet had seen no polish for many months, if not years, and she'd have felt no surprise if an army of mice had materialised to march across it.

As Mrs Tregonning had said, it would take a lot of work to make the huge house habitable, if the remainder of it was in the same condition. Kerensa frowned and wondered what sort and how many staff Sir Oliver retained. She glanced at the portraits of past Pengarrons and thought by the look of them they would not approve of the condition their home had been allowed to lapse into. Apparently the decline had begun in Sir Daniel's day, but why hadn't his arrogant son stopped and reversed it? He was meticulous about everything else it seemed. Kerensa had observed that he kept himself and his clothes clean. Had it something to do with his Devil-may-care attitude? Unfortunately, she surmised, she would only know the answers to these questions when she got to know him better – and the time had come to face him on his own ground.

There were many roads leading off to the left and right of the hall. Kerensa bit her lip as she tried to decide which one led into Sir Oliver's study.

A woman padded into sight, breathing like a bronchitic and grunting to herself like an old sow. An old woman, appallingly dirty, with many chins over which there was a constant dribble of something unpleasant and discoloured. Added to this was a fat, bright red nose, squinting eyes, and a huge rounded bosom that hung down over her waist. Many years before a person such as this might have been burned at the stake as a witch on the grounds of her appearance alone, and Kerensa watched her approach with a growing sense of horror.

When the woman saw the girl standing so still just inside the door she stopped and peered at her through short-sighted eyes.

'What do 'ee want, cheeil?' she rasped, breaking off to cough in each and every direction.

Kerensa swallowed hard, her throat dry. 'Sir Oliver is expecting me.'

The crone screwed up her hideous face. 'Yourn never the new missus? Yourn so young! Why, tedn't seemly, tedn't seemly atall. 'Ee'll be in 'is study, I d'believe. That door there, cheeil.'

Kerensa mouthed the woman a silent 'Thank you', forced a grim smile and hurried off to the appointed door. Even Sir Oliver was preferable to the old crone. She took a deep breath and knocked twice.

After a pause came the command: 'Come in.'

Oliver was sitting at his desk, clicking a quill pen between white even teeth. An old black retriever lay sleeping at his feet.

'Ah. Three of the clock already, is it?'

He looked tired and Kerensa could just make out the tiny lines beginning to form at the corners of his eyes. Devil's eyes, Mrs Tregonning had called them. Kerensa didn't know his exact age but thought him to be nearing thirty, although she supposed if he ever smiled he would look younger and make the difference in their ages seem less dramatic.

'I... I think I am a bit early,' she replied quietly, looking around the room rather than directly at him.

'Come in and sit down,' he said.

From the corner of her eye Kerensa could see him pointing to a padded leather chair on the other side of his desk. Leaving the door open she self-consciously crossed the wooden floor, stepped on to the colourfully patterned carpet on which the chair rested and sat down.

The study was a complete contrast to the hall; its floor and furniture, windows, glassware and ornaments, highly polished, the air fragrant instead of musty. Well, at least you like to sit and work in clean and comfortable surroundings, Kerensa thought, and couldn't help wanting to look over and compare the rest of the Manor to the hall and his study.

The old dog woke up and noisily spluttered as it limped its way round to see its master's visitor and without invitation placed its head on her lap. Glad to be given this distraction Kerensa patted and stroked the dog's rough neck. It seemed a friendly old thing – in stark contrast to its master. Oliver leaned back in his chair. 'That is strange,' he said, 'Dunstan doesn't usually care for strangers but he certainly seems to like you.'

With Charity in mind, able to think of nothing else to say for the moment, Kerensa remarked, 'There are a lot of these dogs about in the parish, aren't there?'

'Indeed there are. They have been bred on Ker-an-Mor, my home farm, for many years. Many are now mixed with the local mongrels.'

'He's very old… Dunstan.'

'About the same age as you are. Well, Kerensa, what do you think of my house?'

It was strange to hear this man use her Christian name in such a natural intimate way. So very different to Clem. His very presence dominated the room. Unable to relax or concentrate, she looked up at him and said the first thing that came into her mind.

'The Manor house is different to what I expected.'

He kept silent, waiting for her to go on.

'Well, I thought there would be servants rushing all over the place, yet despite the state of the huge hall out there it doesn't look cold or draughty or as if… as if…' She searched her mind for the right expression. 'As if the place is haunted.'

'I have never seen a lost spirit or heard ghostly footsteps in the night,' he said, a hint of amusement lighting up his eyes and chasing away their tiredness. 'I've heard it said more than once that Lady Agnes Mortreath, my maternal great-great-grandmother, would not allow manifestations and other such silly things in the house. You will find no ghosts in Pengarron Manor, my dear.'

Kerensa felt young and exceedingly stupid. She was greatly relieved when the old crone appeared again, saving her from having to reply. The old woman made noises like an enormous flatfish struggling out of water as she only just managed to hold upright a tray of tea things. Dropping the tray with a clatter on a table near to the roaring fire, she gave Oliver a hideous lopsided grin.

''Ere 'ee are, me 'an'some, 'ad un already in the makin' fer 'ee. Ye'll need warmin' up on a cold day like this. So, this is yer little maid, is it? Gis on with 'ee, boy,' she said, giving Oliver a flick of her hand across his shoulder, ''er's nought but a little small cheeil, bless 'er 'eart. Pretty little thing too.'

'Thank you, Beatrice,' Oliver said, bluntly.

Ignoring the dismissal she turned to Kerensa. 'Let me take yer cloak for 'ee, maid, or 'ee went feel the benefit of un when 'ee goes outside again.'

Instinctively Kerensa wanted to pull her cloak tighter, feeling that by relinquishing it she would be made even more vulnerable. But Beatrice was leaning forward to take it from her so reluctantly Kerensa eased Dunstan's head off her lap and stood up, untied the bow with trembling fingers and passed the wrap to the old woman. She quickly sat down again, to be out of range of the old woman's wide variety of nauseating smells.

"Ee's a good boy really, me 'an'some,' Beatrice told her, 'fer all 'is temper 'n' tantrums. Born yellin' as lusty as the best of 'em, 'e wus, an' 'twas me who delivered 'im an' all 'is dead brothers 'n sisters. Ais, underneath it all, 'e's a good boy. Don't 'ee ferget now.' She prodded Kerensa painfully on the collar bone and Dunstan growled a warning at her.

'Thank you, Beatrice!' Oliver had raised his voice but his expression was tolerant.

With a cough and a loud grunt she turned heavily around and waddled out of the room with Kerensa's cloak over her arm, puffing and blowing at every step.

Oliver looked as if his amusement had grown while he watched Kerensa's expression throughout Beatrice's glowing appraisal of him. She had stared at Beatrice as if seeing her worst nightmare appear before her eyes, and when she had handed over her cloak she had made awkward movements as if to wrap her arms about herself, as though she were improperly dressed. Her chair was close to a window and the sun broke through the grey sky to bathe her for a moment in a beam of bright light. She was wearing the deep green silk dress which he had had sent over to her. It complemented the colour of her eyes and she needed only a wreath of flowers in her auburn hair to give her the appearance of a woodnymph.

'Did you find Beatrice rather overwhelming, my dear?' he asked, with a short laugh.

Kerensa was taken aback by the way the laugh gave his stern features a tranquil benevolence she had not thought possible before.

'I've never met anyone quite like her before,' she answered, but the memory of Beatrice's eccentricity was fading as she forced herself to concentrate on the one thing she had been wanting to say since her arrival. The knots in her stomach that had formed early in the morning in anticipation of this moment tightened painfully. 'Sir Oliver, I want to ask you something.'

'Oh, do you? And what is that?'

His face rapidly returned to its former expression, his body instantly alert and his bearing more upright. Kerensa could almost feel the attitude he had adopted; that of a predator ready to strike at its helpless prey.

Clenching her hands so tightly together her nails dug into her flesh, she blurted out, 'Please will you reconsider this marriage? I could never be a suitable wife for you... and I want to marry someone else. I'm sure that you can find—'

'You can pour out the tea now,' he cut her off in cold tones.

'What?'

'I said, you can pour out the tea.'

'But, but, I was saying—'

Oliver leaned forward. He said very slowly, 'Mark well my words, Kerensa: the matter is not open to discussion.'

She had cherished one faint hope for Clem and herself, that she might succeed in a direct appeal to the man, but deep down inside she had believed he would scatter it away into nothing. Kerensa now determined she would not plead with him or even show any anger. The old dog grumbled as for the second time she gently removed his head from her lap to stand up. With a dignity beyond her years she moved to the table where Beatrice had put the tea tray, but her hands shook as she poured from a silver teapot. The extravagant heat of the fire did nothing to dispel the numbing chill spreading throughout her slight body. She had failed and her feeble attempt had been over so very quickly.

Thinking it a small wonder it was tea and not spirits he was drinking what with his reputation, Kerensa placed a cup and saucer very carefully on the desk in front of Oliver, who accepted it with a brisk thank you.

She held her own cup and saucer with extreme care; never before had she drunk tea from wafer thin, bone china. She was dubious about drinking anything prepared by the dirty-looking old woman, but the hot strong tea helped to soothe her. Not wanting to prolong the uncomfortable silence, or to give Sir Oliver the satisfaction of knowing how much hurt he had caused her, Kerensa decided it would be she who spoke first.

As naturally as she could, she asked, 'Is Beatrice your only servant?'

'She's my old nurse actually, and no, she is not my only servant, although she is the only one I have in the house now. She is supposed to clean the few rooms still in use, but as you noted in the hall, she's something of a lazy slut. This room looks like this today only in honour of your intended presence. I spend little of my time here and have been happy to leave things as they are over the last few years. I do have three excellent gardeners, and staff in the stables at the back of the house.'

'What happened to the other house servants?'

'They left over the years, for various reasons, but mainly because they couldn't get along with Beatrice.'

Or more'n likely you, Kerensa thought, in a moment of spite.

'There's no need for you to be afraid of Beatrice, she obviously took to you. And like Dunstan, Beatrice doesn't take to many.'

Kerensa was pleased Dunstan liked her but of Beatrice she wasn't so sure.

'Since agreeing with your grandfather to take you as my wife, I've given a lot of thought to the Manor house,' Oliver continued. 'I want to see it returned to a degree of its former glory – although I have no interest in entertaining on a grand scale, balls, dinner parties and the like.'

Kerensa was relieved to hear this. It would be difficult enough adjusting to a new way of life as this man's wife. To have to take on the duties of running a huge house where even the ceilings were three or four times higher than those she was used to was awe inspiring. The mere thought of socialising with the members of the gentry whom Oliver Pengarron associated with filled her with trepidation.

'Therefore,' he was saying, 'I shall be employing more staff. Three will be sufficient to begin with, I should think. A good cook, a kitchen skivvy, and a maid for you.'

'A maid?' Kerensa leaned forward in surprise and carefully placed her cup and saucer on the desk. She wondered what Clem would think of her having a maid. It would hurt him all the more, this new way of life she was being cast into, him realising that he could never have provided these things for her.

'Do I have to remind you,' he said impatiently, 'that as my wife you will become Lady Pengarron? Of course you'll have a maid. Beatrice can potter about as she likes, she will always have a place here. I will ask the Reverend Ivey to make the necessary inquiries for the servants, unless you know of three suitable women yourself. It is you who will have to deal with them.'

Kerensa brightened at his last remark. From the time Mrs Tregonning had broached the subject of taking on staff at the Manor, she had had many daunting thoughts as to what these servants would be like. She had not expected for a moment to be offered the chance of choosing them herself.

'I know of some very nice women who might do,' she said, then frowning deeply she added doubtfully, 'they go to the prayer and Bible classes on Lancavel Downs.'

'I have no objections to people of a Methodist mind. All I require is that they are honest, reliable and hard-working. The Reverend Ivey and Nathan O'Flynn will be too busy to escort you everywhere you may wish to go in order to recruit the staff, so I'll send Jack my stable boy over to the Parsonage. He's young but totally trustworthy. As soon as you've engaged someone you can start them off by cleaning through the house. I'm sure the Reverend's inquisitive housekeeper will be pleased to offer you advice if you need it. All other arrangements I will give to the Reverend himself. I shall be away a lot of the time so it will afford you a good opportunity to get things into some sort of order. Now, is there anything else you would like to know?'

Kerensa looked up at Oliver from under long curling lashes.

'Yes. Do you know, or have any idea, where my grandfather is?'

'No, I do not. For all I care Old Tom Trelynne is in Hell!'

Kerensa flinched at this sudden outburst, but kept her composure. Surely it was a reasonable question to ask. Oliver Pengarron had seen her grandfather at Painted Bessie's the night he had left the cove; Old Tom might have said something. And from what she had gathered yesterday, Oliver Pengarron was making enquiries into her grandfather's whereabouts; he might have learned something. Why did he hate Old Tom so much? Could there be something more than straightforward anger at not getting his own way entirely in the business agreement over Trelynne Cove, and Old Tom's supposed betrayal of the smuggling party that irritated him so?

You ought to be feeling guilty over Davey Trembath's death, Kerensa thought resentfully, staring at Oliver, while stroking his dog. If you hadn't made that bargain with Grandfather you wouldn't have been smuggling in the cove, and nor would poor Davey.

She was deeply perplexed at the conflicting faces of the man across the desk from her. Some folk inferred he was a depraved monster, yet the Reverend Ivey liked something about him and seemed anxious for her to see it too. Sir Oliver's filthy servant, Beatrice, doted on him, and while he apparently did not suffer fools gladly, he tolerated her slovenliness and even showed affection for her.

As the Lord of the Manor, a titled gentleman, Sir Oliver Pengarron held his superiority over her own class with an impatient, scathing manner, showing no care for Clem's hurt feelings. But then he had made that generous gesture to see to Davey Trembath's funeral if the body was found.

This was only the third time she had spoken to the man at close quarters, and she had seen more moods in him than she had in her grandfather during all the years he had brought her up.

What would living with him be like? For certain, nothing like it would have been with Clem. She had felt a little nervous at the new responsibilities she would have taken on as Clem's wife, and she knew him through and through. He was always kind and gentle, never given to 'tempers 'n' tantrums'; he would have treated her like a delicate rose petal.

Kerensa sighed, her heart sinking lower than she could ever imagine. It was going to be overwhelming living with Oliver Pengarron. But as she sat opposite him, staring into his unreadable dark eyes, she made a pact with herself to never show him her fears.

She said, very quietly, 'May I go now?'

'You may do as you please,' he answered, pulling across a sheet of vellum to write on and dipping his quill into a silver-trimmed inkwell.

He had made this final remark sound more as if he was ordering rather than giving her any choice in the matter. She was dismissed.

Kerensa left the huge house to wait outside for the Reverend Ivey's return. She sat on the top step outside the gigantic main doors, under a window from which she could not be seen. She remonstrated with herself for playing into Oliver Pengarron's hands by showing an interest in the future servants of his house. That had been tantamount to admitting defeat. She would not readily co-operate with him again... even if it seemed that God's help was needed for anyone who dared not to.

–

Clem trudged his way past the poorly built mining cottages on the edge of Lancavel Downs, a vast stretch of bleak but starkly beautiful moorland. Despite a howling wind, toddling children clothed in tattered hand-me-downs were playing fretfully outside their damp homes.

A group of hardy miners, soon to go on their core at the Wheal Ember mine, were languidly hanging about smoking pipes, their rough calloused hands stuffed into coat pockets. Their voices dropped to whispers when they saw Clem approach. Not one of them could think of anything worthwhile to say to the bereft young man, and after brief nods in his direction, they all adopted a deeply thoughtful expression as he passed them by.

The gloom that had descended on the mining community since Davey Trembath's death was still painfully apparent. Death was no stranger on the Downs, whether in a mining accident or through illness caused by the poor living conditions. The death of Davey Trembath was a different matter altogether. His was a death caused by betrayal, an unforgivable occurrence even to those whose consciences forbade them to take part in the illicit smuggling, and, before two nights past, unheard of in the area.

No one spoke openly about what had happened though there were those who knew the truth. According to the tale being circulated, Davey had slipped and fallen over the cliff edge while not taking due care as he waited for his two brothers to come off their core at the mine. No one had denied or questioned it, not even from an official source; which was of course the reason for the story.

The sky was dark and cheerless as Clem headed for Jeb Bray's cottage, set a little apart on the edge of the mining community. He had to leap out of the way of the snarling teeth of Beelzebub, a vicious one-eared mongrel belonging to the equally malignant miner, Colly Pearce, who bawled out a foul oath at the barking dog from inside his cottage as Clem passed.

He looked about for Charity but she'd had more sense than him. Having skirted around the back of the cottage she was waiting for him up ahead. Reaching the dog's side, Clem patted her head as she sat outside the home of the Trembath family. He bowed his head in respect, quickly passing by the bleak cottage where strips of frayed sacking were strung up at the window.

He was glad at last to reach Jeb Bray's cottage, which like Hunk Hunken's was somewhat superior in style and construction: Hunk's on the strength of his Captaincy at the mine, while Jeb's, a devoutly religious man, was according to him thanks to his faith in the Lord Jesus Christ. Clem was greeted at the door by Faith Bray, Jeb's wife, a kindly woman with an ever ready maternal instinct.

'Good morning, Mrs Bray,' he said, fidgeting about as though eager to be on his way. 'I'm told I can find Matthias Renfree here.'

'You can indeed, Clem. Come on in a minute, m'dear. He's just having a word or two with Mr Bray.'

'It's all right, Mrs Bray, I have my dog with me. I'll be content to wait for Matthias out here.'

'Oh, well, if you're sure, Clem. He'll be but five minutes, I believe. I'll tell him you're here.' Faith Bray was far too tactful to remark to Clem on his change of circumstances. She put a motherly hand on his shoulder and gave him the kind of smile that said without words how sorry she was before she closed the door.

In a few minutes Matthias Renfree left the Brays' cottage, greeting Clem with a warm handshake. The two fell in step, Charity following behind, to walk back down to the farms on which they worked.

'I'm surprised to see you up here, Clem,' Matthias said, watching him closely in between each careful step over the marshy ground.

'I went over to Ker-an-Mor first of all. Your father told me I would find you here.'

'I started work early so I could have a few words with Jeb before he goes on core.'

'I thought perhaps you were visiting the Trembaths. How are they now?' Clem sounded evasive and Matthias raised his eyebrows.

'The Trembaths are still distraught, but it isn't them you want to talk about… What is it, Clem? Has Kerensa spoken to Sir Oliver?'

Clem stopped walking and looked back over the stark moor, the bracken and heather, like his hopes, colourless and swept by relentless winds. He blinked moisture from his eyes and Matthias wasn't convinced this was entirely due to the cold wind.

When Clem felt the need to confide in someone he always chose Matthias Renfree. Only four years older than himself, they had been firm friends since the time Morley Trenchard had worked on Ker-an-Mor Farm before he'd gained the tenancy of Trecath-en.

Having shown a keen intelligence from his early years, Matthias had been schooled by the Reverend Ivey under the sponsorship of Sir Daniel, and later Sir Oliver. This had been done on the understanding he would one day take over his father's stewardship of Ker-an-Mor Farm and the adjoining stud stable. Adam Renfree had managed Ker-an-Mor for over thirty years, continuing an unbroken tradition of Renfrees working in loyal service of the Pengarrons going back two hundred years. A hard drinking, hard swearing man, he had nurtured a wish for his son to follow in that tradition. Unbeknown to anyone but the Reverend Ivey, Matthias would have preferred to enter the priesthood, but he felt honour bound to fulfil his father's hopes and the Pengarrons' expectations. A lapsed Anglican of many years' standing, Adam strongly disapproved of his son's involvement with the newly formed Methodist society. For Matthias, organising prayer and Bible meetings, teaching children some basic lessons, and the ability to give spiritual comfort when it was needed, fulfilled the greater part of his own spiritual needs. Some folk now called him Preacher Renfree and he was a sensitive, respected father figure to many. It was this aspect of his friend that Clem needed now.

'I saw Kerensa earlier this morning,' he said miserably, running a hand through his hair. 'She was in the churchyard, just standing there, so still and so small, staring down at her mother's grave. Oh, yes, Matthias, she's spoken to him, but he wouldn't even listen to her.'

Matthias was shorter than Clem, but as he was standing on higher ground their eyes met on the same level. He knew better than anyone how much Clem loved Kerensa Trelynne, and it hurt him to witness his friend's distress. Matthias liked to walk alone on the moors, and on a clear summer day would feel at his closest to God. Now, it seemed, a hundred malevolent spirits were abroad in the howling wind all about them.

Repressing a shudder, he said, 'I can't think of anything to say to ease your pain at this moment, Clem. As for Kerensa, she is going along with a decision she will have to live with for the rest of her life. All we can do is, pray for her, and for the strength you will need to face the future.'

'Without Kerensa I have no future. It tears my heart in two to think of her belonging to anyone else but me, especially to that man. What sort of a life will she have, Matthias? I've heard the Manor is not fit for pigs to live in. Then there is his drinking, his gambling, his women…' A fierce look entered Clem's sad eyes. 'If Kerensa ever needs me, at least I won't be far away.'

Matthias had not missed that hard look. Very seriously he said, 'Be careful, Clem. I know Sir Oliver better than you do. I've seen him drinking with my father on occasions as if there were no tomorrow. He's not an easy man to cross. It takes a brave man, or a fool, to try.'

'I don't care about that, I don't care what happens to me any more. I swear if he ever hurts Kerensa, I'll… I'll…' Breaking off, Clem turned hurriedly to wipe away tears with the sleeve of his jacket before walking briskly on.

Matthias caught up with him, wisely keeping his counsel until they had left Lancavel Downs where they petered out on to Ker-an-Mor farmland.

As they closed in on the sturdy buildings of the farmyard, he said, 'What are you going to do now, Clem?'

Shrugging his shoulders, he answered miserably, 'I don't know. Go back to work, I suppose.'

'If it's any comfort to you, the picture painted of Sir Oliver is far blacker than it is true. The Manor house is an awful state, I grant you, but while its cleaning is badly neglected, the building itself is not in ill repair. And while Sir Oliver does drink and gamble, and has been involved with too many women of doubtful reputation, he's far too intelligent to have let it get out of hand.'

'What are you trying to tell me, Matthias?' Clem blazed. 'That Kerensa is going to marry a paragon of virtue!'

'No, no, of course, not,' said Matthias hastily, while visibly reeling from Clem's unexpected outburst. 'I was only trying to say—'

'I'm going to lose the girl I love and who loves me and we can do nothing about it because of the power and position that bastard holds over us. Make up your mind! One minute you tell me to be careful, the next that I should not mind too much. Is that it? You all want me calmly to step aside and just let her go, don't you? If you ever fall in love with a woman in the same way that I love Kerensa, Matthias Renfree,' Clem spat out the words, 'you'll know what it feels like if some high and mighty bastard snatches her out from under your nose, and laughs at you into the bargain.'

'Clem, look—'

Turning abruptly on his heel, Clem stormed off.

'Clem, wait, Clem!' Matthias began to run after him but stopped after a few steps. If he judged correctly by the rage on Clem's face, should he attempt to stop him, he might well be beaten to the ground, friend or not. Matthias was badly shaken. He had seen a lot of people made momentarily bitter while in distress, but never before had he encountered such a look of pure hatred.

Chapter 5

On her return from the Manor, Kerensa told the Reverend Ivey in a dull matter-of-fact voice what had been said between Sir Oliver and herself. Not wanting her to brood, the Reverend allowed Kerensa just one day of solitude to come to terms with the changes in her life. Feeling she would be better kept busily occupied, the next morning over breakfast he brought up the subject of the three female servants.

Kerensa, pale and listless, showed no enthusiasm for the subject as she picked at the plate of food in front of her. A feeling of guilt still persistently gnawing its way through him, the Reverend pressed her for the names of the women she thought to be suitable. Two she had in mind were sisters of Matthew King and lived down in the fishing village with the rest of the over abundantly blessed King family. At the Reverend's suggestion Kerensa agreed that their father be asked to call at the parsonage at his earliest convenience.

Solomon King arrived later in the morning with his father, a sometimes genial, sometimes prickly old man, who was the official head of the family. They came dressed in their Sunday best suits and sat awkwardly on the edge of their chairs, turning their caps round and round in rough brown hands.

Heading the formal discussion, the Reverend explained to the two fishermen that their granddaughters and daughters respectively were being offered the positions of cook and housemaid, to start immediately, at Pengarron Manor. Kerensa listened quietly throughout, having very little to say. When the Reverend had finished, the Kings, father and son, respectfully entered into a brief discussion between themselves. They then agreed to the offer, grateful to have two of the superfluous unmarried females of the family off their hands. Privately they thought it a shame their womenfolk would come into contact with Sir Oliver but at least they could keep an eye of Christian concern on young Kerensa Trelynne.

As Solomon and Grandfather King took their leave they shook hands with the Reverend and Kerensa, promising her, 'We'll pray mightily for thee, maid.'

With the afternoon not yet far advanced Kerensa set off for the Manor with Ruth and Esther King. Bestowed with the advantageous height characteristic of their family, and seven and eight years respectively her senior, the sisters were considered to be suitable escorts for Kerensa. She preferred leading Meryn to riding him, walking along with the sisters who had to adjust their own long ungainly strides so she could keep up with them.

Ruth and Esther King, with their heavy bone structure and mousey brown hair pushed in under tightly knotted scarves, were not at all attractive but, like all women who constantly handled fish, they had flawlessly clear skin. They had been toughened by a life of near poverty and arduous labour in the salting cellars. Kindly natured, they walked protectively along on either side of the girl they looked on as a 'dear little maid'. Despite their strange situation the three fell into friendly conversation as they travelled.

When they reached the Manor house, Jack once more appeared out of nowhere to lead Meryn away. Kerensa led the sisters round to the back of the building to enter by the kitchen door. Jack had shyly told her the Manor house was empty; Sir Oliver was away on Ker-an-Mor Farm and Beatrice sleeping off a bottle of cheap gin in one of the outhouses. Kerensa was relieved by this news. She had not relished the thought of another meeting with either of them so soon. She was pleased though to see Dunstan again as he limped his way from his basket by the kitchen fireside to greet her, but the old dog made it quite plain he wanted nothing to do with her companions.

They found the kitchen and its ancillary rooms in an unsanitary state which brought about many exclamations of disgust from all three. Ruth vigorously banked up the fire that was threatening to breathe its last while Esther fetched water from the pump in the yard in the biggest receptacle with a handle she could find, a cross between a bucket and a jam-pan, putting it on the hook to boil for cleaning up some of the filthy mess.

While they waited for the water to boil, Kerensa gingerly led the way through the other rooms of the huge house. Warily, they looked all around. The sound of their footsteps echoed behind them as if they were being followed by some of the long dead Pengarrons, curious as to who these strangers were and what they were doing there. Many of the rooms were locked, and apart from the study Kerensa had already visited and a small bedroom obviously used by Sir Oliver, those they could gain access to were layered in shrouds of dust and cobwebs, and deposited with mouse droppings.

'Bless my soul!' Esther kept exclaiming. 'It will take months to clean up all this mess and have the house fit to live in. It's a good job I won't be needed to cook for a while yet.'

'Do you think Sir Oliver ever comes into these rooms, Kerensa?' asked Ruth.

'I've really no idea,' she replied. 'For some reason he doesn't seem to mind Beatrice's laziness, and appears to be fond of her too.' Kerensa ran a finger along the stair rail as they looked down over it to the great hall below, frowning as she held the finger up to study the dirt collected on it. 'Beatrice herself is just as dirty as this,' she said, 'but it will be as well for us to be careful what we say to her. Sir Oliver told me she will always have a place here.'

'Oh, I'm not bothered about her,' laughed Ruth. 'Likes her drink too much does that one. I don't think we'll be seeing much of her.'

'That water must be good and hot by now,' Esther put in. 'Shall we go downstairs and make a start?'

'You go ahead. I'll be down in a moment. We could do with a dish of tea first, if you'd like to find the things to make one,' Kerensa said, trying to sound natural.

Esther and Ruth exchanged curious glances at this but did as they were asked and without question.

Not really knowing why, Kerensa slowly walked back into Oliver's room. Even though he was nowhere in the house she felt his dominating presence everywhere, especially in his study, and here where he slept. There was the subtle scent of expensive cologne, mingled with those of brandy and tobacco. She moved about the room, lightly touching some of his personal belongings with the feeling of being an intruder, nervously looking back at the doorway at regular intervals, fearful he would suddenly appear.

His clothes were strewn about and Kerensa picked up the discarded garments one by one, smoothing out the creases and carefully placing them over the back of a chair. Untidiness fitted in well with his unpredictable character, as did the bottle of brandy and glass she discovered on the bedside table. The bed had been carelessly made and after straightening the covers, she traced a finger along the embroidered initial P that curled its way on the wide hem of the lace-edged sheet.

She found nothing on his dressing table to give her even the smallest hint into the depths of this enigmatic man; there was only a hair brush, a clothes brush, and a pipe filled with unlit tobacco. Cautiously, Kerensa opened the door to a clothes closet, and with her fingertips touched the sleeve of a lavishly embroidered, sea blue dresscoat. She tried to picture what Sir Oliver would look like in such a garment. Most handsome, she decided reluctantly, and had a vision of him at a social function, never-empty glass in hand, talking wittily with the gentry, the ladies throwing themselves at his feet. Such an eligible unmarried man would be hotly sought after... what on earth would they think of his decision to shun their company and marry below him? A lady would surely not be content simply to have the Manor house cleaned through, to share Sir Oliver's basic manner of living. Kerensa was thankful it would suit her.

Deep in thought, she was startled when Ruth called up the stairs that the tea was brewed and ready to pour. With rapid guilty movements she removed her fingers from the dresscoat and shut the closet door.

The room overlooked the stableyard and as she passed by the window Kerensa glimpsed Jack down below, grooming Meryn, his lips pursed as he whistled a favourite tune. The sight brought Kerensa back to reality. She left the bedroom and ran down the wide stairway, a faint smile on her face at last.

The following day Kerensa found Jack the most pleasant of company as they rode to Lancavel Downs. Jack himself was captivated by Kerensa's gentle loveliness, and from a shy beginning, took delight in giving her simple instructions on how to ride Meryn more comfortably. She was pleased to take his kindly meant advice, and as they trotted along she listened with interest as he told her some of his past.

He knew little of his own background; his first memories of his life were as an orphan among travellers who lived by criminal practices. Jack was taught to steal and this he had skilfully done. At the age of about eight, on a busy market day in Marazion, he had had the misfortune to try to steal the pocket watch of none other than Sir Oliver himself. Jack had received the severest thrashing of his life, but his fortunes had changed when Sir Oliver had offered him the job of stableboy, and with it the chance of a new start. It was obvious to Kerensa that Jack had left his previous way of life well behind him; it was also obvious that as well as being his benefactor, Sir Oliver was something of a hero to the boy.

Again Kerensa found herself confused as she considered the contradictory things she'd heard about Oliver Pengarron's fickle nature.

'You like Sir Oliver, don't you, Jack?' she asked, wanting to learn more.

'Aye, miss, I do that. Oh, he d'like for things to be done proper in the stables, and heaven help 'ee if they'm not, but he's fair enough most of the time.'

'You don't find him a hard master, then?'

Young though he was, Jack had the perception to realise something of what was going on inside her head. He looked at her evenly. 'Folk d'tell tales about his lordship.'

'Do they?' Kerensa said, but she thought that even if Jack didn't believe them, some of them must be true, there were so many.

She talked of other things. Jack was greatly impressed when Kerensa mentioned she could read and write and his admiration was not lessened when she stressed that her skill stretched to no more than her own name and the most simple of words. By the time they reached Lancavel Downs, across potholed ground and muddy ditches, she had promised Jack she would show him what his name looked like when written down on paper.

Leaving Meryn with Jack and Nessa, the old mare, Kerensa braced herself against the bitterly cold wind and enquired from Faith Bray as to the whereabouts of the cottage of Colly Pearce and his sister, Rosina. In place of the motherliness of old, Faith Bray's manner was subservient to the point of bobbing a curtsey. Kerensa felt lonely and disappointed by Faith's attitude as she left the Brays' doorstep and hurried away to the Pearces' cottage.

Rosina Pearce was a lame girl of the same age as Kerensa. Frail and nymph-like, she was blessed with a pleasant disposition. She answered the door immediately to Kerensa's knock, then grabbed Beelzebub by the scruff of his neck as he lunged viciously at her visitor. With surprising strength for one so small, Rosina pushed the snarling mongrel back into the cottage, slamming the door shut behind her. She stood outside with Kerensa, the dog yapping and scratching at the door to get out.

'Hello, Kerensa,' Rosina smiled sweetly. 'I'm sorry about that, and I'll have to ask your forgiveness for not inviting you inside.'

'I understand, Rosina,' Kerensa said, smiling back, relieved that Rosina was treating her in the same way as she'd always done. The two girls had become acquainted at the Bible classes on the occasions Rosina had been able to attend because her brother, Colly, was on his core down the mine. Everyone knew Colly Pearce for a cruel man who constantly ill-treated his younger sister, getting himself into fights and drinking away all their wages. Kerensa had suggested Rosina to the Reverend Ivey as her maid and he had been pleased at the prospect of getting her away from the wretched life she led.

Kerensa knew Rosina was fiercely loyal to her brother, she defended him every time someone sympathised with her or criticised Colly, but Kerensa was nursing the hope that nevertheless Rosina would agree to leave him and become her maid at the Manor house. Kerensa knew Rosina better than the King sisters and felt she would make a familiar ally in her new life, but knew it might take some persuasion to get her away from this bleak unfriendly place.

Rosina was shivering and Kerensa felt guilty for taking her out of the cottage.

'I won't keep you long, I can see that you're cold.'

'It's quite sheltered by the Hunkens' chicken coop,' Rosina said, pointing to a large hen house not far away.

When they were huddled close together beside Hunk Hunken's chickens Kerensa threw the edges of the voluminous cloak that Mrs Tregonning had loaned her about Rosina's small frame. They giggled while agreeing there was room for at least half a dozen girls of their size within its confines.

Then Kerensa said, 'I suppose you know about my new... the changes in my life, Rosina?'

'Yes,' she replied simply. 'I was sorry to hear about your trouble.'

'Thank you. Well, rather than sit about feeling sorry for myself I've been given an unexpected chance to make things a little more bearable for myself in the future. A new staff is being taken on at the Manor, and Sir Oliver has given me permission to make the arrangements, so I'm trying to surround myself with people I know and trust. Ruth and Esther King have agreed to be the new cook and housemaid and have already started work. He says, Sir Oliver, that I'm to have a maid. I've come up here Rosina because I'm hoping you will consider taking the position.'

Her deep blue eyes widened in surprise. 'I can't. It's very good of you to ask me, Kerensa, but Colly couldn't manage without me to look after him, and I have my work at the mine. Thank you for taking the trouble to come and see me, though, for thinking of me.'

'Oh, please don't say no straight away, Rosina,' Kerensa implored. 'Think about it. The work will be so much easier than dressing ore at a cold mine surface.'

'There's nothing to think about, I will never leave Colly. My duty lies here with him,' Rosina returned firmly, but sadly.

Kerensa was very disappointed but felt she had no right to add to the strain Rosina already lived under. She marvelled at the other girl's serenity, despite all she had to cope with, and hoped she would have the strength to face her own future in much the same way.

'I'm sorry you can't accept, Rosina,' she said. 'I wanted you to be the first person I asked. Please go back inside and warm yourself again.'

'I'm sorry too, Kerensa, I hope you find someone else to suit you.'

Kerensa sadly watched the slight form of Rosina Pearce as she limped back to her cottage, her long corn-coloured hair swaying below her tiny waist. It was said Colly Pearce was responsible for that limp and Rosina had had it ever since Kerensa had known her. Kerensa would have been pleased, despite not being able to marry the man she loved, if she could at least have managed to get Rosina Pearce away from her bullying brother. It would have been some small comfort.

With this hope dashed, she sought out the home of another Wheal Ember bal-maiden, Alice Ford, the only girl of her own age she had had the opportunity of becoming friendly with after spending so much of her life in the cove.

Alice, an infectiously happy but outspoken girl, readily accepted the job. 'I can hardly believe it!' she said, jumping about excitedly and shaking her hazel curls. She grabbed Kerensa's hand and dragged her along to her family's cottage.

'Just wait until I tell Mother, and Father when he comes off his core. They'll be some proud of having a daughter as a lady's maid instead of one fit only for cobbing. No more having my ears deafened, eh?'

The few people who were about looked on curiously as Alice, chattering all the way, finally pulled Kerensa through the door of her home. 'Sit down,' she said, still excited. 'I'll fetch Mother and we can have a good natter.'

Kerensa sat down on what amounted to no more than a couple of old sacks stuffed with straw, but it was comfortable. She grinned at the thought of Alice with her runaway tongue telling her mother the news, and resolved to stay as long as she could in the company of the Ford women before she had to go back to the Parsonage. She would send word to Jack to find himself a sheltered spot.

The Fords lived in one of the numerous hovels thrown up a half mile from the workings of the Wheal Ember mine. They had moved there eight months ago having always moved about the county, living on the fortunes of the lodes underground, moving on when the tin or copper ran out and the mine closed down. Now Alice would have a more permanent job, less arduous than hammering rocks into suitable size for the stamping machine, working in grand surroundings, much cleaner, dry and warm in the winter. Her two pennies a day, invaluable to her family's poor income, would be impressively increased and her father would not have to rely so much on smuggling to supplement their harsh existence. Alice would no longer have to suffer the regular sight of mangled bodies being brought up from accidents below, be there at first hand worrying about her father and younger brothers. Best of all she wouldn't be living among some of the hardest, coarsest men in Cornwall, made so by their hopeless way of life. Truly, the offer was the answer to her prayers.

She kept telling Kerensa that over and over again with her mother present as they drank mugs of smuggled tea and chewed on coarse barley bread. Despite the rigours of her life Alice maintained a refreshing sense of humour, and despite Kerensa's breaking heart made her laugh. Kerensa left the Fords' cottage feeling that Alice would offset some of the gloom and despair she felt about her future.

'Some funny goings on in this parish, if you d'ask me,' said Mrs Ford, as she and Alice stood at their doorway and watched Kerensa riding away with Jack.

'Who cares about that?' said Alice dreamily. 'It's brought me and the rest of us good fortune. Who knows what else'll come out of it.'

Mrs Ford shook her head. 'I don't know, tedn't right, tedn't natural for an ordinary young maid to marry into the gentry. Kerensa'll be plunged into a life she don't know nothing about. Don't you feel sorry for her, Alice?'

'What for! Oh, because she can't marry Clem you mean? I suppose that's a bit sad for her – but, Mother, what more could a maid want than to be married to a handsome, powerful, wealthy man? Talk about dreams coming true!'

'But tes said Sir Oliver Pengarron's a wicked man. You might not like working at the Manor, my girl, when he's around. You'll have to watch that mouth of yours. Wouldn't do to get on the wrong side of him.'

'I know, I know.' But Alice was too elated to be worried about her new master for long. 'And whatever happens at the Manor, it means Clem Trenchard is up for grabs now!'

It was arranged for Alice to begin work at the end of the week, her first job cleaning through the entirety of Pengarron Manor with Ruth and Esther King. Like the King sisters, part of her wages would be sent home to her needy family. All three were to live in at the Manor proper from the day of the marriage.

–

Mrs Tregonning joined Kerensa and the King sisters occasionally at the Manor. Having worked there in Sir Daniel's heyday she was invaluable at helping in the arduous task of making the huge house fit to be lived in again. She remembered how things had been and knew how they should be. She taught the others the correct way to clean the porcelain, china, crystal and cut glass, the things made of precious metals, and the dark oak furniture and panelling.

'Couldn't keep nothing clean and tidy when Sir Oliver was a boy,' she said one afternoon as they all sat, with Kerensa, round the huge wooden kitchen table tackling the collection of large pewter plates and tankards taken down from shelves in the hallway. Jack was there too, having slipped in for a mug of tea, and Mrs Tregonning was in her element having such an eager audience. They all longed to learn more about the powerful baronet; Kerensa, something of what her bridegroom was like, the others, more about their new master. Kerensa listened and worked moodily, feeling that nothing she touched in the huge house would ever mean anything to her. It was all a thankless task, not like the things she had made so lovingly for her marriage to Clem.

'How's that then?' Jack asked Mrs Tregonning, grinning impishly, while munching on one of her oat and apple biscuits. He was content; he adored Kerensa already, felt that not only was he getting a beautiful new mistress but that he had never eaten so well, and this was only the beginning.

'Yes, go on, Mrs Tregonning,' Alice urged chirpily. 'I've only been in the parish a few months and I don't know much about Sir Oliver.' She shot a guilty look at Kerensa, knowing that she did not share the same feelings at having her life so suddenly changed, but the girl had her head bent over a pewter tankard.

'Well, he'd run in and out of the house all day long,' Mrs Tregonning explained authoritatively, handing out cleaning cloths. 'His boots full of mud, clothes ripped, covered in scratches and bruises. He used to give poor Lady Caroline, God rest her soul, nightmares – getting into fights, climbing trees, riding his pony at breakneck speed. And his nursery, heavens above! You'd be lucky to see an inch of floor under the heaps of clothes and all his toys and his paintings. How he liked to paint in them days.'

'Really?' said Esther. 'Wonder if he does it now.'

'I don't know – give that plate plenty of elbow grease, Alice – gave it up for dallying with wanton women, I shouldn't wonder. And there was plenty—'

'I don't think we want to hear about that,' Ruth interrupted quickly, sensitive to Kerensa's feelings; there was no need to make matters worse for the girl by referring to *that* side of life and the probability that the baronet wouldn't be keeping strictly to the marriage bed.

It hit Alice hard at that point just how distressed Kerensa must be feeling deep down inside, and how much it must be costing to hide it from the others. She passed her another clean cloth and smiled sympathetically.

Kerensa smiled back faintly and pushed the plate of biscuits towards Jack. 'Have as many as you like.' Then she turned the tankard upside down and rubbed vigorously at its bottom. She listened carefully to Mrs Tregonning's prattling but never asked a question, just storing up the knowledge in case it was useful in the future. She was not going to allow the others to try and read her muddled mind.

At the end of their first day there she had left a note on Oliver's desk asking if all the doors could be unlocked. Four days later she'd gone into his study to find a huge bunch of keys lying on top of her note. Picking up the keys, she was outraged to see he had dashed heavy lines through all her misspelt words and placed the correct spellings over the top of them in his bold handwriting.

Alice had come running at her cry of indignation. 'What's up, are you hurt?'

'It's this!' Kerensa waved the note in the air and told Alice about Oliver Pengarron's gall. 'Does he suppose I've had the same education as him?'

'Ruddy cheek,' Alice agreed. 'He should be impressed you can read and write at all.'

'Oh, I don't want this life, Alice,' Kerensa sobbed, crumpling on to a nearby chair. 'I just want Clem.'

Alice wrapped her arms around her and Kerensa held on to her source of comfort and let the floodgates open to release some of her wretchedness.

Alice smoothed her hair and patted her arm and stayed quiet until the tears stopped. 'Better now, m'dear?' she said, using the tone her mother employed for comforting her and her brothers.

'Yes,' Kerensa whispered, raising her head and pushing away wet strands of hair from her face, then nestling her head against Alice's shoulder. Alice was a much bigger girl; her life of hardship out in the world that Kerensa had not known had given her a maturity that Kerensa found comfort in. 'Isn't it bad enough that I have to marry the beastly man, am expected to supervise the cleaning up of his filthy house, and then he has to be spiteful about my efforts to do it! Oh, I'm so glad I've got you, Alice.'

'Well I'll always be here, won't I? Don't let him get you down, Kerensa. But if he does, you just come and tell me. We'll soon think of a way to get our own back on him.'

Kerensa was alarmed at this. Alice had already shown in some of the outrageous things she said to Mrs Tregonning and Beatrice that she spoke first and thought afterwards. 'We'd better not do anything like that, Alice. We could end up in all sorts of trouble.'

'Pah! We can have a ruddy good time making plots against his Bigheadship even if we don't do anything. He won't know what's going on against him in our heads!'

'Oh, Alice,' Kerensa couldn't help smiling. 'The things you say.'

'And I'll always be here saying them, won't I, m'dear?' Alice planted a kiss on the top of Kerensa's head.

She took Alice's hand in her own. 'One thing's for sure, Alice, if he ever reduces me to tears again I won't let him see them,' she said, rallying defiantly.

As the days went on the Manor house began to show a dramatic change. The furniture was highly polished and the silver, bronze and brass painstakingly returned to their original condition. Glassware and window panes sparkled, all the household linen was washed, pressed and aired, the carpets and heavy drapes beaten free of layers of dust. The floors were swept, polished and scrubbed clean, while the ornaments were carefully cleaned and dusted. It was necessary for craftsmen to be sent for from Marazion and further afield to do the delicate tasks like cleaning the portraits and miniatures, to make certain repairs, and reach ordinarily inaccessible places.

As the Manor house was transformed, Kerensa took to wondering why Sir Oliver had allowed it to become so rundown. She could see he was unconventional in some of his attitudes but she was sure he took pride in his position and family name. She dismissed the thought that he might care more for people than possessions; she had heard of his apparent kindness but had yet to see it for herself. She surmised that the previous condition of the house spoke clearly of an earlier desire to deprive it of a mistress—but why did he have to change his mind now and agree to take her!

Despite her resistance to the place, and all it stood for, Kerensa was captivated by some aspects of the Manor. She took to wandering through its many rooms and was fascinated by some of the things she found. There were interesting caskets, carved or painted or inlaid with parchment, mother of pearl or tortoiseshell. Some contained aged documents, others, personal effects of Oliver's forebears, like writing materials and toilet requisites. While some were graced with their own stand, all were ingeniously fitted inside with drawers and compartments. Still more were locked, sending Kerensa on flights of fancy as she tried to imagine the secrets they held. What were their owners like? Had they lived a happy life here? Had any of them, like her, had their hearts torn apart by a scheme that stopped them from being with the one they loved more than anything in the world. Perhaps one or two had met a gruesome death… Kerensa smiled grimly. She could almost wish ill-fortune on the house's present owner.

In a corridor on the second floor she found an arming chest. This too was divided into compartments of varying sizes and contained breastplate, chainmail, swords, and a complete suit of armour. She conjured up an amusing picture of Sir Oliver in the armour and for the first time in weeks laughed out loud. The armour had been made for a much shorter ancestor and he would be squashed up in it. Perhaps if Sir Oliver had been there he would have looked down at her disdainfully from his great height and proudly told her the armour was of Greenwich vintage, fashioned in the royal workshop of King Henry VIII no less.

Kerensa often slipped into the large rectangular ballroom to gaze for lengthy periods at the creatures from myth and legend carved on an old oak cabinet there. Rubbing a finger gingerly over the raised figures as if she expected them to come to life, she wondered with the burning curiosity of a child how the stories ran. She was intrigued to discover in the library a clothbound book containing colourful pictures of the very same creatures. Drawn and painted in a child's hand, each picture was signed 'O.P.'

So Mrs Tregonning was right about Oliver Pengarron's penchant for painting. He had filled the book prolifically and, even to Kerensa's inexpert eye, well. She had been in every room of the house now and had detected no evidence that he still painted, but then thankfully he spent so little time there. Kerensa had a picture in her mind of Sir Oliver as a child sitting in front of the cabinet in the ballroom, studiously painting a likeness of the mythological creatures and leaving the inevitable mess behind him. She closed her eyes tightly to shut out the vision. She did not want to think overmuch of that hateful man who was ruining her life. She blamed him entirely now for her predicament. She had still not seen or had word from her grandfather, and missed him terribly. She thought of him only with affection now, believing that Sir Oliver with his superior birth and intelligence had no right to have allowed an ignorant old man to outsmart him.

The desk in Oliver's study had been made in the reign of a Tudor monarch and was carved with the initials of each successive owner. Standing as a piece of furniture in itself was the box containing the family Bible. When Kerensa lifted the outer cover of the huge heavy book she could just decipher the scrawled writing in which was inscribed Oliver's full name: Oliver Richard Edward Ruan Charles. So many names for just one man. She also discovered the date of his birth, the twenty-fourth day of December, in the year 1719. It came as yet another shock to realise he was twice her age.

She allowed none of these extraordinary items to interest her for long. Kerensa insisted on working as hard as the other women, stretching herself to her full physical and mental capacities to ensure she slept through some part of each night, and to give herself little time to dwell on her fears for the future.

Oliver appeared once or twice a week to work in his study. He eyed Ruth and Esther, and Alice in particular, when Kerensa introduced them, but after that showed no interest at all. If he was pleased with the improvements they had made to his home he made no mention of it, and Kerensa had swayed to Mrs Tregonning's insistence that she wear the green silk dress while he was there and not be seen doing any of the heavy work.

–

Whereas Oliver's frequent absences made it easier for Kerensa and the others to work, Beatrice was deliberately obstructive to them. She was rude to Ruth, Esther and Alice, and more so to Mrs Tregonning, whose presence back in the Manor she bitterly resented. Things came to a head one afternoon after Mrs Tregonning left to return to the Parsonage to prepare the Reverend Ivey's evening meal.

'I dunno what 'is lordship's thinkin' of, lettin' she back in 'ere,' she grumbled from her chair by the fireplace. 'Wus nothin' but a stuck up ole mare back in the ole days.'

Coming through the kitchen with a huge pile of fresh linen, Alice stopped and glared angrily at the old woman. Never one to be slow to speak her mind, she said in a raised voice, 'Here, you got no call to take on like that about Mrs Tregonning. She's been a great help to us, not like you – always sitting on your fat backside and sneaking off to get drunk. You should learn to keep your mouth shut!'

'An' 'ere yerself, Miss 'igh 'n' Mighty. You got no call to chitter on me neither. I've been 'ere workin' fer the Pengarrons all me life, 'is lordship'd soon put 'ee in yer place if 'e wus 'ere to 'ear what 'ee jus' said. Now, jus' mind yer own shut-up, or I'll lam one on 'ee!' Beatrice screeched back, snorting and grunting between sentences.

Putting the linen on the table Alice placed her hands on her hips, shaking her head of curly, light brown hair.

'Come on then, you slobbering fat witch. You just dare!'

Beatrice did dare. She treated Alice to a vicious slap across the face that sent the girl hurtling across the kitchen first to thud into the table, then on to the floor.

'Beatrice! Why on earth did you do that?' Kerensa had run to the kitchen to find out the cause of the shouting and had witnessed the slap from the doorway. 'Tell Alice you're sorry!'

Beatrice waddled across the scrubbed floor until she was face to face with Kerensa.

'The only thing I'm sorry fer, m'dear, is I didn't scat 'er blamed 'ead off. I'm takin' meself off 'til 'is lordship's back fer good, and 'ad 'ee wedded 'n' bedded.'

Turning her head away from Beatrice's foul breath, Kerensa's face was scarlet with embarrassment.

'Where are you going?' she asked as the old crone made her way to the door.

'Don't 'ee mind 'bout me, maid,' came the reply. 'Ais, we'll soon see who's who 'n' what's what round 'ere later on.'

Ruth and Esther had watched everything in bemused silence, looking from one face to the other. To lessen Kerensa's embarrassment they turned back to their work as she helped Alice on to her feet. As Beatrice slammed the door behind her Alice rubbed her painful, red cheek and, glancing at Kerensa, turned her head away, to smile a little wickedly.

Kerensa worried about what Oliver's reaction would be to Beatrice leaving so abruptly. It was the old woman who usually took him in a tray of tea on the afternoons he was in his study. Kerensa did this herself the next time he appeared. He was standing beside the fireplace, an elbow resting on the mantelpiece, reading from what looked like an official document. He didn't look up or offer a greeting as she entered and placed the tray on a nearby table.

Smoothing down her dress with nervous hands, she waited silently to be given attention. When at last Oliver did glance at her his face was serious.

'Yes. What is it?' he said, returning his eyes at once to the document.

'It's... it's about Beatrice. A few days ago, she left the Manor.'

'Why?'

'There was a bit of an argument and she stormed out,' Kerensa explained rapidly, 'but she said she would come back.'

Much to her surprise, Oliver threw back his head and laughed.

'I thought this would happen. Who was it she took exception to? Mrs Tregonning?'

'Yes, it was, but... it was Alice she argued with.'

'Beatrice and that woman didn't like each other in my father's time. Beatrice will be back when she is good and ready.'

Kerensa swallowed hard, relieved he wasn't angry with her over Beatrice, but still worried about the old woman's welfare.

'Beatrice had somewhere to go, didn't she?' she asked, then bit her bottom lip as she waited for him to answer.

'Oh, yes, Painted Bessie's alehouse more than likely. She spends nearly as much time as she does here.'

He reached across the desk to lift her chin with a finger and gave her a disarming smile. 'You don't have to worry about Beatrice, my dear. She can take care of herself.'

It was the first time he had touched her and the remark Beatrice had made about the intimacy she would soon have to share with him lingered in Kerensa's mind. She moved quickly out of his reach and all traces of joviality left his face.

'Pour the tea before you go,' he said stiffly.

He didn't thank her for doing so and made her feel more uncomfortable by watching her intently until she left the room. Kerensa leaned heavily against the outside of the study door and breathed a tremendous sigh, wondering if from now on, this was how her life would be.

—

As the wedding day drew near Oliver arranged for a dressmaker from Marazion to call at the Parsonage. Mistress Hilary Gluyas was an elegant middle-aged woman; she arrived on a wet afternoon with a carriage full of sample gowns, accessories and materials.

At Kerensa's insistence Ruth, Esther and Alice were present at the fitting, while Mrs Tregonning presided over the proceedings with the air of a wealthy matron purchasing the trousseau for her own daughter. The Reverend Ivey had left much earlier, prudently making a hasty decision to retreat to the farthest end of his parish.

Kerensa felt none of the excitement of the other women as they wondered at and touched the fine fabric of the gowns and other garments Mistress Gluyas draped over every available chair in the parlour. With thirty years' experience behind her of dressing the ladies of the gentry, she had quickly worked out an entire wardrobe for Kerensa in her head.

The dressmaker had no interest in the humble background of her newest customer, it was of no concern to her, what with the bridegroom prepared to pay an exceedingly generous amount to have his young bride suitably attired. She prudently ignored the endless prattling of Mrs Tregonning as she advised Kerensa on what materials and style of gowns to select.

'You will look best in gowns of a simple cut and discreet decoration, Miss Trelynne, complementing your youth, beautiful hair and superb clear skin. The colours… ivory, peach, various blues, and green, which suits you so well. Delicately embroidered petticoats, trimmed with the minimum of lace, bows, ruchings and ruffles. On the gowns, what would you say to small flowers, palm fronds and curling motifs, Miss Trelynne?' Mistress Gluyas smiled graciously.

Mrs Tregonning got an answer in first. 'Yes, I think that would all be most suitable, Mistress Gluyas. Miss Trelynne is only a little small bit of a thing, we don't want her to be overdressed like some of the ladies I've seen. Now, I remember Lady Caroline, Sir Oliver's late mother, she had such style…'

A loud, 'Ahem,' from the dressmaker silenced the housekeeper.

Kerensa said, disinterestedly, 'That sounds all right, thank you.'

'You'll look so lovely, Kerensa, I can see you now,' Alice said, her face shining with delight. She was disappointed she had a much rounder, bigger boned body than Kerensa. Now the two of them were firm friends, with Kerensa relying on her, she would have asked if she could have tried on some of her gowns. Just to see how they looked, how they felt, only that. Alice gingerly stroked a pair of cream-coloured kid gloves richly decorated in silks and sequins. 'Just look at these… will you choose them?'

'All right,' Kerensa smiled wanly, 'just to please you, Alice.'

From the other accessories, she chose an emerald green silk fan and a plainer one of cream parchment – Mistress Gluyas said, 'They'll do for now, I'll have one made to match each gown later' – several pairs of coloured stockings, two lace-edged caps and two more pairs of gloves. She felt a blush coming on when she agreed to satin nightgowns and hoped they would not be made of flimsy material, then insisted on plain white shifts and discreet stays. Mistress Gluyas maintained that fichus were not strictly necessary but Kerensa again insisted, intent on having no exposed bosom for anyone's eyes to look upon, gentry or otherwise.

Then came the question of the circumference of the hoops to wear under the gowns. Kerensa said moodily, 'They must be kept small. The doors of Pengarron Manor may be very wide but I still want to feel free to move about.'

Mrs Tregonning looked apologetically at Mistress Gluyas but the dressmaker said understandingly, although knowing it was not the truth, 'It's only the pre-nuptial nerves. Now, Miss Trelynne,' turning to Kerensa, 'I will take your measurements. I sent over this green silk dress you are wearing on Sir Oliver's orders but it is not a good fit. I did not realise you were quite so dainty.'

As Kerensa was pulled and turned under the measuring tape, Alice tugged at her own brown curls and wished she could be measured for a dress as a maid of honour.

Esther asked Kerensa shyly, 'Have you any idea what style you'd like the wedding dress to be?'

'Something simple,' Ruth said quickly, suddenly afraid that Kerensa would be made to look ridiculous on that dreaded day.

'As long as it is simple, I'll be happy to leave the colour and design to Mistress Gluyas,' Kerensa said, with a distinct sigh.

'As you please,' Mistress Gluyas said, putting her tape measure away now all the fitting and choosing was accomplished. 'There is only the question of footwear left. I have brought nothing small enough with me for you to try on so I'll arrange for a shoemaker to call on you tomorrow.'

Before leaving she took a glass of port wine and gave a firm promise that most of the wardrobe would be made up and delivered before the wedding day.

The rain had stopped, the sky stained a sulky grey, when Kerensa saw the dressmaker away in her carriage. As the wheels spattered over the muddy ground she did not go back inside but walked on to her mother's grave. She did this every day, sometimes looking around in the hope of seeing Clem, yet at the same time fearful she would. She had not seen or heard from him since the day she had stood on the same spot and told him of Sir Oliver's clear intention to marry her. She had kept on hoping the baronet would still change his mind, but with the servants chosen, the Manor house cleaned through, and the wedding dress ordered, there seemed no hope for her and Clem. Looking wistfully in the direction of Trecath-en Farm, she wondered what he was thinking and doing, if he was thinking of her.

Free Spirit was moored up to the pier at St Michael's Mount, having returned the night before following two weeks' stay at Roscoff. But for the one man on watch, Hezekiah Solomon, its gentleman owner, was alone on board in the process of making a thorough inspection of his vessel. As their duties were fulfilled the rest of the crew had made their way to the alehouse, gin shops or the more outlying kiddleywinks where smuggled spirits were more easily taken and drunk on the premises.

'Good morning, Hezekiah. I trust everything is in order.'

Hezekiah Solomon turned around and smiled a warm welcome to his friend who had just climbed on board from a rowing boat.

'Good morning to you, Oliver. I can assure you everything is very much in order.'

Oliver grinned; he knew this to be true of all things that concerned Hezekiah Solomon. A fastidiously tidy man, he was elegant and flamboyant in his style of dress and manners. His neat, finely boned body was scented always with expensive French perfumes, his long white hair tied back with colourful silk bows, a lace handkerchief always at his wrist.

No one seeing Hezekiah Solomon for the first time would take him for a seafaring man, much less one often involved in bringing in contraband from France or the Channel Islands. Or taking it off a colluding East Indiaman out in the English Channel, and landing it in secluded coves and creeks of the Cornish coast.

Oliver himself knew little of Hezekiah, even his age, but reckoned him to be about ten years his own senior. Oliver wasn't particularly curious about Hezekiah's background – whether he had a wife or not – he would have found such domestic talk boring. Oliver liked him for his intelligence, superb wit and skill at the gaming tables. It is said that opposites attract, and Oliver and Hezekiah were a complete contrast to each other in appearance. Hezekiah's hair, which he had specially dressed, was as white as Oliver's was black, he was as effeminate-looking as Oliver was masculine, his clothes as colourful and fashionable as Oliver's were discreet and functional.

It was four years since Hezekiah had suddenly walked into Painted Bessie's clifftop kiddleywink. Conspicuous by his colourful appearance, he had caused a stir amid the bluff miners, fishermen and few farm labourers crammed into the ramshackle alehouse. It was as well that night that Painted Bessie, a degenerate, heavily rouged woman in her fifties, was as hard as she looked. With her highly pitched, common voice she had swiftly stilled the hubbub caused by Hezekiah's arrival. Miners and fishermen had no time for each other's way of living and needed only the flimsiest excuse to break into a fight. Painted Bessie kept a wary eye on the two factions in case there was trouble brewing.

Oliver had been in the kiddleywink with Hunk Hunken, making arrangements, and recruiting men, for a contraband run. People were used to seeing him there from time to time and his presence went without comment. He and Hunk had been deep in discussion, and after Hezekiah's arrival they'd paid no attention to the small, effeminate-looking man sitting but five feet away. That was, until an agonising scream coming from the stranger's direction had made them look up sharply. Colly Pearce, a big brute of a miner, was on his knees beside the stranger's table, a silver-handled stiletto impaling his right hand to the table top.

Oliver had watched in fascination as the stranger cruelly twisted the blade in Pearce's hand, before very slowly drawing it out and holding the bloodied pointed length of steel before the miner's anguished gaze. His steely blue eyes narrowed to slits, Hezekiah had then shown the blade to the hushed occupants of the dark shabby room.

'The next man who is foolish enough to offer me an insult will have his throat cut. Is there anyone here among you who would care to try?' His voice was clear and silvery and strangely musical, and all the more terrifying for it.

Some men had shook their heads, others had murmured negative monosyllables. All had returned to their drinking.

Clutching at Oliver's arm with trembling fingers, Painted Bessie had whispered fearfully, 'What shall we do, m'lord?'

Oliver had impatiently pushed her away. Standing up, he'd moved to the stranger's table and held out his hand.

'Sir Oliver Pengarron, sir,' he had said. 'Pleased to make your acquaintance. I believe I speak for everyone here when I say that the writhing scum on his knees here has received what he deserves. He's nothing more than a liar, a cheat and a bully.'

Murmurs of agreement came from every direction as Hezekiah shook Oliver's hand.

'I'm pleased to make your acquaintance also, Sir Oliver,' he returned. 'Hezekiah Solomon at your service, sir, owner and captain of the ship *Free Spirit*, currently anchored at St Michael's Mount.'

Hezekiah Solomon smiled the smile of an angel before wiping his blade on Colly Pearce's dirty shirt and replacing it inside his elegant leather boot. Then he bent his perfumed head and whispered something in Pearce's ear. The miner wailed and his eyes bulged bright in terror.

A short time later Oliver and Hezekiah left the kiddleywink together.

'If it's not an impertinence,' Oliver said, 'may I ask what Pearce said to you that earned him a well-deserved hole through the hand?'

'It's no impertinence, Sir Oliver. The man suggested I would have no interest in the fairer sex, but I can assure you, I most certainly have.'

Oliver laughed. 'In that case, Captain Solomon, if you would care to accompany me, I know the very place of entertainment where we might pass what remains of the night.'

It was the same place that Oliver had in mind for them now, once Hezekiah finished his inspection. Sitting down on the gunwale Oliver filled his pipe and lit the tobacco with sharp impatient movements.

'You look as though you cannot wait to reach our intended destination, Oliver,' Hezekiah remarked.

'To tell you the truth, I'm fast losing my desire to go at all.'

'Oh, and why is that?' Hezekiah asked, raising his thin arched eyebrows.

'I've got something on my mind,' Oliver replied grumpily, staring down at his outstretched feet.

Hezekiah sat down beside him. 'Do you want to talk about it?'

'You wouldn't believe it, Hezekiah.'

'Tell me anyway.'

Drawing on his pipe with a sigh, Oliver blew smoke into the cold air.

'In a week's time, I am to be married.'

'You're what! Have you got some luckless female with child?'

'No. Not that.' Oliver sprang up and thumped his fist on a water barrel. 'Trelynne Cove, the place where we tried that unsuccessful landing, was once Pengarron land. Recently I purchased it back. At an exorbitant price, I might add.'

'Go on.'

'As part of the bargain, I agreed with that wretch Old Tom Trelynne that I would marry his granddaughter.'

'You agreed… good Lord! I have heard tell of this Old Tom character, but I didn't know he had any kin, let alone a granddaughter.'

'Well, he has, and I've got to marry her,' said Oliver moodily.

'I don't know what to say,' Hezekiah said, bringing a hand up to his chin, his eyes wide in amazement. 'What's she like, this girl?'

'Nothing like her grandfather, thank the Lord. She's quite beautiful, actually, but very young.'

'Ah, a virgin?'

'I'd stake my life on that.'

'Every man hopes to marry a virgin, of course, but even that does not qualify a village girl as a suitable bride for a gentleman. Surely you can get out of this marriage, Oliver?'

'I intended to take a wife this year, Hezekiah,' he said, picking at the wood of the water barrel and receiving a frown from the captain who couldn't bear to see anything less than smooth and perfect. 'I want a son, an heir to my estate. I've worked damned hard rebuilding it and I want to see it passed on to the next generation, the fruit of my loins, not one of those damned awful distant cousins I have residing at Zennor. I've looked around carefully at all the available ladies and none of them are suitable – a pretty grim lot actually. I wanted Trelynne Cove back and got myself a bride into the bargain, it's as simple as that.'

'As simple, Oliver?'

He paced the deck like a caged animal for several moments. 'Enough of this talk!' he exclaimed. 'I have Trelynne Cove, and Old Tom can rot in Hell!'

'But surely, Oliver,' persisted Hezekiah, 'the cove wasn't so important that you had to agree to marry the girl who lived in it.'

'I've ridden up to the Point many times to think about it, Hezekiah,' he said with a long deep sigh. 'I set out one morning with the intention of regaining my family's land. I became carried away by my own pride and utter determination to achieve that desire… It will be the first and only time I will be outwitted like that.'

He moved to the other side of the lightly swaying vessel and gazed down into the moving water. Hezekiah joined him, and neither spoke for a long time.

Finally Hezekiah said, 'Do you want to marry this girl?'

Oliver shrugged his broad shoulders. 'I know I want her,' he told his friend, and the lazy waves below.

Chapter 6

Four weeks later to the day that the bargain had been struck over Trelynne Cove, Oliver and Kerensa were married. The parish church of Perranbarvah was packed to capacity for the occasion. Sitting importantly in the front pews were members of the local gentry; the Harrts, the Ransoms, the Courtises and the Coles; and Oliver's sour-faced cousins from Zennor.

The middle pews were taken by the traders of a higher social standing from Marazion, along with Mistress Hilary Gluyas, Mrs Tregonning, Adam Renfree and Nathan O'Flynn. Crowded together on rough benches, or standing at the back, were many of the estate workers and all the tenant farmers, except for the Trenchards, and their families. Much to the consternation of the occupants of one of the back benches, Beatrice waddled into the church, reeking of gin and perspiration, and pushed her way in beside them.

There was much talk when Oliver entered, walking briskly up to the front of the church with Hezekiah Solomon as groomsman on one side. On the other was the fat elderly Sir Martin Beswetherick, owner of neighbouring land to the Pengarron Estate and the main speculator of the Wheal Ember mine. The younger females in the congregation, some stealthily, others openly, eyed the handsome figure of the tall baronet. They had never before been treated to the sight of Sir Oliver in his court dress. Elegant in garments of deep sea blue, he also wore his ceremonial sword, the hilt of which was encrusted with semi-precious stones, the sword knot made up of bunches of blue ribbons.

Mrs Tregonning, who was repeatedly dabbing a handkerchief to her eyes even though the ceremony had not yet begun, was outraged at the sight of Hezekiah Solomon.

'Just look at him,' she whispered behind her hand to Adam Renfree sitting next to her. 'He looks quite ridiculous, like one of they court dandies.'

Hezekiah was dressed even more flamboyantly than usual. His dresscoat and breeches were scarlet. Layers of Brussels lace overflowed at his wrists, while his gloves were lavishly embroidered, each buttoned with three tiny rubies. The ruby and emerald pin on his tasselled necktie matched the buckles glittering on his kneebands and low-heeled pumps. He had no need to wear a wig. His abundance of long white hair fell easily into extravagant curls, and was at that moment tied at the nape of his neck by a wide scarlet ribbon.

A subdued crowd had gathered outside the church and they moved apart to make way for Kerensa and Jeb Bray as they walked through the churchyard from the Parsonage. With still no sign of Old Tom, Jeb had agreed to be substitute in her grandfather's place. With her skirts unceremoniously hitched out of the mud, Kerensa held up her chin and nodded to those in the crowd she knew. She had no care for her dress, a beautiful but discreet creation in ivory silk and satin (Mistress Gluyas believing her colouring did not suit the traditional white and silver), and the self-control she was determined to keep showed on her face. But inside her heart ached for Clem. She hoped he wasn't there, stationed behind a wall or one of the gravestones. She could not have borne to see him at that moment. If he spoke her name, if he pleaded with her with his eyes to come to him... it was all a torment to her and Jeb Bray knew it. He motioned for the people gathered around the church doorway to move aside. He stopped with Kerensa just outside the entrance.

'Now, m'dear,' he said gently, 'are 'ee going to be all right?'

'I'll have to be, Mr Bray, won't I?' she said in a small voice.

'Do 'ee want to stay out here for a little while? Make him wait?'

'Not with everyone watching.' She took a deep breath and tried to smile at Jeb, but couldn't. 'This is not going to be the wedding I dreamed of and I might as well get it over with.' She mentally determined to shut herself off from what she was about to do.

Inevitably, Kerensa captured the most attention from those inside the church. On a signal from the Reverend Ivey, the small band of hired musikers announced her arrival. She walked slowly up the aisle, holding on tightly to Jeb's arm. He carried out his duty reverently, refusing to be intimidated by the increasingly exalted company as they progressed to the bridegroom's side.

Oliver did not turn round to see Kerensa walk towards him. The music stopped when she reached his side. Neither looked at each other. Both stared ahead. When the Reverend turned to face the couple he too looked through them and not at them, as though he wished to inform the congregation he did not approve of this marriage. He had officiated at a great many weddings, but on this day, in the church he had favoured the most in his long ministry, he could not bring himself to look upon this as a holy sacrament.

Clearing his throat and taking a deep breath, he began to speak the words of the ceremony in the hushed church.

'Dearly beloved, we are gathered in the sight of God, and in the face of this congregation, to join together this man and this woman in Holy Matrimony.'

Is this all really happening? Kerensa thought. She felt she was not really there, but in a mysterious other world, like the strange creatures carved on the cabinet in the ballroom of Pengarron Manor.

'...signifying unto us the mystical union that is betwixt Christ and his Church... and is commended of Saint Paul to be honourable among men...'

Honourable... The word ran through Oliver's mind. Some here would think me not to be honourable... but it was her grandfather's wish that I marry her.

'...and therefore is not by any to be enterprised, nor taken in hand, unadvisedly, lightly, or wantonly... but reverently, discreetly... and in the fear of God...'

A moment of panic seized Kerensa. Wasn't she entering this marriage unadvisedly and wantonly? Certainly not reverently, not when she had promised herself to Clem.

'...Therefore if any man can show just cause, why they may not lawfully be joined together...'

Oliver breathed in deeply, tightening the corners of his mouth. Might that young fool Trenchard be somewhere in the church, and about to cause a scene and turn the ceremony into a farce? The moment passed. Oliver expelled the breath and relaxed.

'Who giveth this woman to be married to this man?'

The hand given by Jeb Bray to Oliver was small, soft and cold. He held it lightly as he repeated his vows in a clear voice. Kerensa's were barely audible. When Hezekiah Solomon placed the tiny gold ring with which he had been charged on the Reverend's prayer book, he did so with a dramatic flourish. As the Reverend blessed the ring he gave Kerensa a brief smile of encouragement. Her face quite frozen, she was unable to return it.

Removing his other hand from its resting place on the hilt of his sword to take Kerensa's left hand for the giving of the ring, Oliver turned, finally, to look at his bride. He was completely taken aback by the depth of the composure and the delicate, almost supernatural beauty he saw in the expressionless young face that turned to look up at his. Firmly, but gently, he pushed the ring down her finger, his dark eyes laying siege to hers, as time itself seemed to hold its breath in the ancient Cornish church.

The bells pealed out in celebration through heavy rain as the couple left the church. By this time a much larger crowd had gathered outside to see Kerensa Trelynne emerge as the new Lady Oliver Pengarron. Most of them stared at the baronet in stony silence to show their disapproval at what he had just made her do, but the few who wanted to keep in with the Lord of the Manor for their own ends clapped and cheered. Oliver was unconcerned as he led Kerensa to the waiting coach. She forced a brave smile this time for her sympathetic onlookers, but took no care to hold up her dress as it dragged behind her in the muddy path.

Barney Taylor, standing smartly to attention, opened the carriage door. He was about to offer his hand to help his new mistress inside but Oliver swept her up in his arms, lifting her in himself as if she were no more than a small child. He shook hands with the Reverend Ivey and accepted the best wishes of the guests who were not to attend the reception at the Manor. He was then accosted by his angry cousins, furious at the possibility of their inheritance slipping away if he sired an heir by this girl, with recriminations over his marriage, vowing their intention of never accepting her as part of the family. Oliver looked jubilant as he sent them away, red-faced and outraged by his stinging retorts.

Before climbing into the carriage beside Kerensa he threw a handful of silver coins into the cheering crowd. It caused a rush of ragged children, and some older greedy individuals among them, and angered members of the gentry who were endeavouring to get into their carriages out of the rain.

Kerensa had been peering out of the windows on each side of the carriage before Oliver joined her. She was anxious to know if her grandfather had appeared to witness the final part of the agreement he'd made with the man who was now her husband. But Old Tom Trelynne was nowhere to be seen.

Nor was Clem Trenchard.

When the carriage moved off, Kerensa was visibly shivering. Without a word, Oliver pulled a blanket from the seat opposite and placed it round her shoulders. Kerensa quietly thanked him, but for the rest of the journey over the rough muddy roads, neither spoke. She looked out of the window at the bedraggled seagulls scavenging the thawed ground of the ploughed fields. Red-stemmed coltsfoot was appearing in the hedges and dripping lambstails nodded from the awakening hazel bushes.

Oliver glanced occasionally at his bride, her face half-hidden by the short pearl-encrusted veil flowing from her headdress. At one point he reached out to touch the cold, white hand that now wore his ring, but changed his mind. Instead he settled comfortably back against the upholstered seat to muse over the celebration he had planned at the Manor.

It would be the first time for many years there had been any kind of entertainment there and he had ordered a wealth of food, ale and spirits to be prepared for the thirty or so invited guests. Without the sobering company of his cousins the proceedings promised to be even more enjoyable.

Keeping up a Pengarron tradition, Oliver had arranged for generous quantities of food, ale and rum to be laid on at the separate celebrations to be held in honour of his marriage in the fishing village, on Lancavel Downs, and at Ker-an-Mor Farm. It had earned him further disapproval of the local Methodists, and the grateful anticipation of the heavy drinkers of the local populace who were not going to boycott the parties. Oliver didn't care much what anyone thought of him today. He intended to enjoy himself to the full, and if it provided a break in the tedious, wretched lives of others less fortunate than himself, so much the better.

Ruth, Esther and Alice, attired in new servants' uniforms purchased by their master, were nervously waiting in the great hall when the carriage pulled up outside on the wet gravel. They bobbed awkward curtseys to Oliver and Kerensa before hurrying off to get trays of champagne, port and wine to offer the guests following in the carriage's wake. They had been disappointed not to have been able to be present at the wedding ceremony itself.

Leading the way into the ballroom, where the reception was to be held to the accompaniment of a full string orchestra, Oliver coolly informed Kerensa she was to stand beside him as they received their guests. When this was done he abruptly left her to stand alone while he engaged Sir Martin Beswetherick in conversation over the latest profits to be obtained in tin and copper ore. Kerensa felt slighted at his extreme bad manners in leaving her so, when he must know only too well how difficult the situation was for her. She was also smarting at the way the gentlemen among the guests, with the exception of only one, had eyed her up and down crudely when they'd been received.

Only the dandy Hezekiah Solomon had shown Kerensa any real semblance of courtesy or friendliness. She was relieved when he came to stand beside her.

Hezekiah had been looking forward to meeting this working-class girl whom Oliver had reluctantly agreed to make his bride. He had secretly taken in every detail of her appearance and agreed with Oliver's assertion that she was beautiful. Hezekiah liked her soft accent, her bearing, and in particular her air of innocence. He envied Oliver his wedding night.

'May I say, ma'am, you look absolutely enchanting in your wedding gown,' he said, beaming his angel smile at her.

Kerensa trusted that smile and returned a charming one of her own. 'Thank you, Captain Solomon. Are you a friend of Sir Oliver's?' she hoped he was. It would be good to like at least one of her new husband's friends.

'Indeed I am, ma'am. We also do… business together.'

Kerensa decided she liked this butterfly of a man. Although his clothes could not be said to be easy on the eye, he helped her feel at ease in an otherwise painfully awkward situation.

'I hope we may also become friends one day, Lady Pengarron,' he went on.

'I'm sure we will, Captain Solomon,' she readily agreed, feeling flattered for no accountable reason.

'So you're acquainting yourself with my wife, are you, Hezekiah?' Oliver interrupted them.

'I am indeed. A most pleasant task, too, I assure you. I congratulate you on your choice.' Hezekiah said this with a small bow to Kerensa, his eyes not leaving her face.

'In that case, my friend, you can drink to our health and future sons.'

Oliver had taken a tray of champagne from Alice. He thrust a glass at Kerensa. She took it from him, but with no intention of drinking it. Hezekiah took a glass for himself, inclining his head to Oliver and Kerensa with another angelic smile.

'To your health and to your future, Oliver. Yours too, ma'am.'

'Thank you, Hezekiah.' Oliver downed his champagne with a toss of his dark head. 'Now for a decent drink, my friend. I have a fine cognac I want you to try.'

Hezekiah bowed again, and withdrew.

Oliver turned to Kerensa and treated her obvious discomfiture with an irritable gesture.

'Why not get yourself something to eat?' he muttered.

The two men joined their circle of friends, leaving her to glare angrily out of the window.

As darkness began to fall some of the guests took their leave, but were quickly replaced by others. They now numbered seven in all, three of whom were women. Though fashionably dressed they looked cheap and gaudy, their faces heavily made up to disguise their age; one also wore several patches to hide the pockmarks on her hard face. After scathingly greeting Kerensa they ignored her, except for the odd knowing look interspersed with raucous laughter as they joined in obviously vulgar innuendoes at her expense.

As the evening drew on the party changed to a more frolicsome mood, of a nature Kerensa found both embarrassing and distasteful. The three women fawned over Oliver and the other men, and like Sir Martin, tucked in hungrily to the remains of the food. Kerensa remained in the ballroom for a further hour, not eating, not drinking, not moving. If anyone noticed when the quiet young bride slipped away from her own wedding celebrations, they didn't seem to care.

Kerensa was relieved to find the kitchen deserted. When Esther, Ruth and Alice had been told they were no longer required they had left to join their families in the village celebrations, Esther and Ruth to a quiet supper in the fishing village, Alice taking Jack to the noisier bonfire party on Lancavel Downs. Dunstan, who had sought her company so often in the four preceding weeks, raised his head, greeting her with a friendly grumble. Kerensa ran over to him and threw her arms around the old dog's neck, not caring at all that he was dribbling down her gorgeous dress. She hated its finery of ruching, tiny bows, silk flowers and gleaming pearls, knowing it was nothing like the dress Old Tom had once proudly talked of having made for her wedding to Clem.

'Hello, boy, I'm so glad you're here,' she told Dunstan miserably.

Discarding her headdress and veil Kerensa wrapped herself in a shawl Alice had left over the back of a chair. She put more logs on the fire and a kettle of water on the hanger to boil for tea. Dunstan ate the large meal of chicken, tongue and bread she put down for him. She could eat nothing herself.

From time to time raucous laughter could be heard coming from the ballroom. Icy rain pattered against the window panes. Kerensa had never felt so lonely in all of her life. She wished that even the loathsome Beatrice might shuffle into the kitchen to keep her company. She settled herself into the lumpy low chair the old woman used, close to the warmth of the fire.

She had stared into space, becoming oblivious to all noise and her surroundings for so long that when Beatrice suddenly appeared in front of her, she cried out in fright.

'Tes all right, me 'an'some, tes only me,' Beatrice rasped. She smelled heavily of gin and was almost breathless. 'I come to see 'ow yer doin'.'

'I'm doing – I'm all right,' Kerensa said quietly. She stood up and offered the old woman her usual seat, hoping it would encourage her to stay and talk.

'I don't think yer all right at all,' Beatrice said, flopping down heavily in her chair. 'Ah, that's better. Sorry to turn 'ee out but tes the only chair that's comfy fer me old backside.'

Kerensa chuckled, intent on showing Beatrice that she really was all right. She pulled up another chair and sat close to her, trying to look as if she wanted only to have a good gossip.

Beatrice wasn't fooled. 'Yer not right, young Kerensa, an' I'll call 'ee that fer now. You'm mis'rable and frightened. Got yer weddin' night a'ead of 'ee an' prob'bly wond'rin' what's goin' to 'appen to 'ee. That's why I'm 'ere, to reassure an' tell 'ee all about what 'ee prob'bly know nothin' of.'

'I'm really glad to have your company at the moment, Beatrice,' Kerensa said, feigning heartiness. 'I could do with someone to talk to, but I don't want to talk about him… Sir Oliver… and as for… I don't even want to think about it.'

'Well, you ought to talk about it, might be a bit of a bleddy fright if 'ee don't knows what 'appens, if 'ee don't know a bit about men. You 'aven't got a mother to turn to an' that's what a maid needs at a moment like this.'

Kerensa made an impatient face. 'Mrs Tregonning was married, she's told me over and over all about it.'

'Huh! All in gory detail, I 'spec, knowin' that old mare. Damned woman, should keep 'er mouth shut! Tedn't necessarily like whatever

108

she said to 'ee. Let me tell 'ee right now, Kerensa, it can be good, with an understanding man. And Oliver – and that's what 'e is to 'ee now, no more Sirs – 'e's a man like that.'

Kerensa turned her head away. 'I know you mean well, Beatrice, but I…'

'Don't want to talk about it.' Beatrice bent forward. 'You'll be all right with 'im. I know 'ee don't want to 'ear nothin' good about un, but b'lieve me, m'dear, 'e's a good man, and if I'm not mistaken you'll be good fer 'im.'

'If you say so, Beatrice,' Kerensa said wearily, knowing that if she protested the old woman would only go on along the same track. She had come to say her piece and it was better to let her get it over with.

Kerensa got up in a panic as Beatrice wrestled with her weight getting out of her chair. She held out her arms and Kerensa ran into them.

'I'm going now, me 'an'some,' the old woman said gently, stroking the girl's hair in motherly fashion. 'Like I said, ye'll be all right with 'im, don't 'ee ferget now.'

And Kerensa was alone again with only the old dog for company.

She sat back in Beatrice's chair and waited.

–

A hand shaking her shoulder woke her with a start. It was dark. The room was cold, the fire having almost burnt itself out. Oliver placed a single candlestick on the table. Kerensa blinked and rubbed her eyes.

'What… what time is it?'

'Late,' he answered simply.

The only noise was the persistent rain on the window panes as Kerensa became aware of the silence of the Manor house.

'Where are all your friends?' she asked.

'They're gone. I turned them all out fifteen minutes ago.'

The silence in the house was heavy, ominous.

'The girls? Are… are they back yet?'

He stood tall and straight, his arms crossed.

'The two tall ones I've sent to bed,' he informed her, 'the other one is waiting in your dressing room for you.'

'Oh.' A snuffling noise across the room offered her an excuse to stay longer in the kitchen. 'Dunstan,' she said wildly. 'I think he wants to go outside.'

She wanted to delay the inevitable climb up the stairs to the master bedroom with its huge four-poster bed. If this had been her wedding night with Clem, though she would have been a little shy and he as inexperienced as she was, she was confident their love would have been wonderfully and successfully consummated in the lean-to of Trecath-en Farm. But spending the night with this other man, now her legal husband having full rights to her body, was a different prospect altogether.

Even from the other side of the kitchen he was overwhelming her with his vibrant sexuality, sending palpable signals to her sharpened senses. She could feel them all about her, was engulfed by something she did not know how to cope with, nor had any understanding of.

She had thought only Clem would ever totally possess her, and yet here she was, about to become a sort of sacrificial lamb to this other man. A man old enough to be her father. She beat back her panic, harshly scolding herself into a state of reasonable self-control. At least he looked nothing like fat Sir Martin. His broad muscular body and fine dark looks helped a little to dampen her fears of what he might do to her. But now, despite Beatrice's kindly reassurances, her mind was a frightening turmoil of questions she could not ask and would only know the answers to after the events of the night ahead. Oliver Pengarron had made love to so many women. What was he used to? What would he ask of her? Would he be patient with her as he exploited her maidenly innocence? Having kept her eyes rooted on Dunstan for several moments she looked back at Oliver. How would he find her? And would she be able to respond to him in any way... would she want to?

Oliver seemed to be reading her wild thoughts. 'I'll see to Dunstan,' he disappointed her. 'You go on up. Come on, boy.'

Kerensa was relieved that Alice was sensitive enough not to employ the indelicate talk usually indulged in on a friend's wedding night as she helped her out of her wedding dress and into one of her new silky smooth nightgowns. She was grateful that Alice made no mention of the wedding or the reception or the bonfire party she had attended, but spoke only of how exciting it had been to ride behind Jack to and from Lancavel Downs on the little grey pony.

'I should have stayed here with you, though,' she said, as they spoke in whispers for fear their voices would travel from Kerensa's dressing room into the master bedroom. 'If I'd have known you were going to spend so much time alone in the kitchen…'

'Don't feel guilty, Alice. But I will be glad to have you close by in the future.' She stopped Alice's hands as they moved towards her head. 'No, I'll see to my hair, in the… other room, it'll give me something to do.'

Alice was very nervous for Kerensa now. 'Are you frightened?'

'Yes, I… I just wish it was the morning.' And she pulled the ribbons at her neck tighter together.

'I'll say a prayer for you,' Alice said, hugging Kerensa firmly and giving her a peck on the cheek.

'Thanks, Alice,' Kerensa replied, grateful for the encouragement. Squaring her shoulders and resolutely holding up her head, she said, 'I'll go in now before I feel even worse.'

'Good night… good luck,' Alice said, crossing her fingers. She clutched her hands to her heart and her eyes filled with tears as she slipped away to her own bedroom.

Oliver was already in the master bedroom, standing by the hearth in much the same way as he had done in his study on the day she had told him Beatrice had left. This time he held a brandy glass in his hand. His dresscoat and waistcoat were strewn carelessly on the floor, his necktie pulled loose. Light from the fire flickered across his face, one moment enhancing his handsome features, the next lending dark shadows to them to suggest overpowering wickedness lurking within.

'Can I pour you a drink, my dear?' he said amiably. 'A little wine or champagne perhaps?'

'No, thank you. I don't drink alcohol,' she said, trying to keep her voice normal and looking disapprovingly at his glass.

'It will warm you,' he persisted, his eyes moving over her in a distinctly appreciative caress.

'I don't want anything, thank you. Anyway, I'm not cold.'

Kerensa felt helpless to counteract his intimate observance of her. The large master bedroom was stuffily warm, the smell of his brandy heady and strong; this powerful combination threatened to dull her wits and she wanted to keep herself sharp and aware of what was going on. Or did she? Perhaps it would be more welcome to have all her senses limited and dimmed.

She moved to pull aside a heavy damask drape, slightly opened the window, and watched as raindrops slid down the glass and formed miniature rivulets. Then she walked quickly to her dressing-table and picked up a hairbrush. That morning Mrs Tregonning had swept her hair up into a halo around her head. She pulled out the pins and began brushing it down with unnecessary force, acutely aware that Oliver was watching her every movement. When satisfied with her hair she blew out some of the candles, feeling strangely more secure as the room grew darker.

In a quiet husky voice, Oliver said, 'Come here, Kerensa.'

His words inexplicably beckoned her to him and she came and stood facing him, facing the inevitable. She held her breath as he put down the brandy glass and stretched his hand towards her. The dancing flames on the logs of the fire brought her deep auburn hair alive and turned her skin to a silky golden glow. With the lightest touch he ran a fingertip down the glossy length of her hair and round the ends where it curled under on her shoulders. She shivered inwardly as the same fingertip then ran a gentle coaxing path down the smooth creamy column of her throat. Kerensa tried in vain to see past the darkness of his magnetic, shameless eyes. Oliver smiled with a gentle charm as he pondered her expression.

It was the same expression he had seen on her perfect face the day he first rode to Trelynne Cove: apprehension, curiosity and wonder.

He gazed into her eyes. He was again stunned by the depth and complexity of them, their bright colour now fully exposed by the firelight.

He looked so different to the man who had been unfeeling towards her earlier in the day that Kerensa found herself smiling back at him. Oliver lowered his hand to his side and Kerensa turned her head away. Her eyes alighted on the four-poster bed. Ignoring the prick of niggling panic in her stomach she moved away and climbed up on to it. The quilted damask counterpane was folded back to the foot of the bed and she dug her toes into the thick warm soft blankets. She sat with her chin resting on her raised knees and her hands clasped tightly in front of her.

Oliver sat beside her, so close their bodies touched. He took her left hand in his and turned her wedding ring round and round with his finger and thumb, waiting patiently for her to look up at him.

'I won't hurt you, Kerensa,' he said softly. 'Do you believe me?'

'Yes,' she whispered truthfully, and without knowing why, she did feel she could trust him.

He put his other arm around her tiny waist, pulling her even closer to him, bunching the stuff of her nightgown in his fist. They sat and watched the curtain billow, in delicate little dances, where she had opened the window. Oliver moved so her head rested first against his shoulder and then his chest. Kerensa could hear the steady rhythm of his heart beating, the steady rhythm of a man who was very much in charge of his life. But was he as sure of his feelings? She had seen him in moods that could change with startling rapidity. She had not expected this moment of quiet gentleness from him and gradually she relaxed against his body.

Oliver closed his eyes to concentrate on the fresh tender smell of innocent youth that was so much a part of Kerensa. It was a fragrance he had soon become aware of, pervading the huge old house like an early spring come to refresh the winter of the dingy long neglected rooms. He felt her eyelashes flutter against the bare skin of his chest and when she moved slightly her warm breath caressed the hollow at the base of his neck. It was a place where he was acutely sensitive and he shivered. Kerensa looked up at him as if she was surprised. He could wait no longer. It had been four long weeks now since he had first ached to kiss her soft inviting lips. He lowered his face to hers. Kerensa tightly closed her eyes. The moment had come and there was no going back. His kiss was so very soft and she could taste the sweetness of the brandy on his lips. His next kiss followed at once and there seemed to be no end to the way he gathered her into himself.

—

By habit Sir Martin Beswetherick was no early riser. The morning after the Pengarron wedding was no exception. It was eleven o'clock when his aged servant, Judith Teague, threw back the heavy drapes to allow the entry of a cheerful sun. Sir Martin lay back on his pillows snoring aloud, his mouth wide open. Judith Teague shook the elderly grey-haired gentleman.

'Wake up, Sir Martin, wake up!' she shouted down his ear. 'You've got a visitor downstairs.'

'Eh! What? What's going on, for damme's sake?' he blustered. 'Oh, it's you, Judith. What's that you say?'

'You have a visitor, sir. Sir Oliver Pengarron.'

'Am I expecting him? S'pose I am or he wouldn't be here, eh? Show him up, Judith, and send up my breakfast too. I'm starving, I could eat a horse this morning.'

Sir Martin struggled and snorted, levering his overweight body to a sitting position, affectionately watched by Judith. She had been with the Beswetherick family since Sir Martin himself had been a babe-in-arms, and he now sixty two years old. She was well past the age of useful work, but Sir Martin was happy to let her feel needed by doing light tasks about the house. One of these tasks, dressed neatly in a black dress covered with a white apron, was to awaken him from his slumbers when he was resident in his smart new townhouse in Marazion. Sir Martin had lived there nearly all year round since his beloved wife, Lady Ameline, had died. Judith plumped up Sir Martin's pillows then left the room to attend to his breakfast, and send up his visitor.

A tap on the bedroom door was followed immediately by Oliver, who rarely troubled himself to wait to be admitted anywhere, striding straight into the room.

'Ah, Oliver, dear boy, pull up a chair and we'll have breakfast together.' Sir Martin pointed to a chair and Oliver, who was broadly grinning at the older man, carried it across to the bed and sat down, putting his feet up on the covers.

'No breakfast for me, Martin, thank you. I shared an excellent one earlier this morning with my wife.'

'Wife? Wife?' A moment of perplexity on Sir Martin's persistently red face gave way to a lecherous smile. 'Of course, the pretty little red-haired thing, I remember now. Quite a bash we had after the ceremony. Things last night go satisfactorily, did they, eh?' he added wickedly.

Oliver leaned back comfortably in his chair.

'Mmmm, well enough, I suppose.'

'New to it all, was she, eh? You think yourself lucky, m'boy. I've missed my regular comforts since my Amy died. It's a good thing some of the village maids are willing to oblige, for a few pence, from time to time.' Sir Martin's fat sides shook as he laughed heartily then entered upon a fit of hoarse coughing.

A footman brought in a tray well laden with poached eggs, fried gammon and sausages, thick slices of white bread and butter. A large pot of Congo tea was complemented with glasses of spring water. When the footman was dismissed Oliver poured tea for them both. He sipped from his cup thoughtfully while Sir Martin tucked in noisily to his late breakfast.

'Hezekiah sails for France tonight on the evening tide. He's due back in two weeks,' Oliver said.

'He enjoyed the celebration last night,' Sir Martin said, putting a whole sausage on his fork and stuffing it in his mouth. When he could talk again, he asked, still chewing on the meat, 'What are you doing here, anyway, Oliver? Was I expecting you?'

'I have business in Marazion this morning. I thought I'd call on you and tell you about the next contraband run. Hezekiah will bring in the goods. Now the fuss has died away over young Davey Trembath's death I think we can use Trelynne Cove again, as well as our other spots.'

'Dreadful business that,' slurped Sir Martin. 'The boy's body been found yet?'

'Not yet.'

'What about Old Tom?' Sir Martin munched.

'No. Him neither. I had men on lookout all day yesterday, at the church and the Manor, but there was no sign of him. I have an idea he's not too far away though. He'll meet with a bad end one day and if Ted Trembath doesn't find him first, I hope he'll cross my path...'

'Quite so, my boy.' The slurping continued. 'Why d'you marry that little girl anyway?' asked Sir Martin, suddenly looking up from his food.

'She's Old Tom's granddaughter, remember? She was part of the bargain for the cove.'

'Was she indeed! You've got the better part of the bargain there, Oliver, I should say,' bellowed the fat old baronet, spitting food in all directions.

He smiled sardonically. 'Mmmm... One of my more astute moves, I admit, particularly if she's a good childbearer.'

'Ah, so that's it, is it? It's sons that you want, eh? A man needs a son to carry on his name. S'pose it is high time you settled down. You're the same age my Arthur would have been, aren't you?' Sir Martin's flabby face contorted in his effort to think. 'Yes, that's right. Arthur would have been thirty-five next Michaelmas and you're a small bit younger. Arthur would have liked her, your little wife. As I remember, the two of you were always fighting over women... or sharing them. With the wedding night over he might well have been planning how to seduce your little wife, were he here to!' Sir Martin bellowed again.

'Yes, and I his, no doubt. I often wish Arthur was still alive, Martin. These past ten years have been lonely without his companionship.' They were serious for a moment, each lost in their own thoughts of the past.

'Anyway, my boy, you have someone to keep you company now. I don't see much of my brood these days, sons or daughters. They seem to want to spend all their time in London, with the exception of William. He and Rachael have taken up permanent residence at Tolwithrick and are happy and comfortable there. It will be his one day soon, when I'm dead and laid to rest in the family chapel.'

'Huh, you fat old coot, you'll live to be one hundred and ten. I'd bet my wine cellar on it.'

Sir Martin roared with laughter and choked on a huge mouthful of best gammon. Hastily he reached for a glass of water to wash it down as Oliver sprang up to pound on his back. The elderly gentleman's nightcap slipped off, while more water soaked the bedcovers than ended up down his throat.

'You young swine, Pengarron,' he gasped, 'nearly responsible for my early demise there. You! Risk the contents of your overflowing cellar on a losing bet? Huh! That'll be the day young Preacher Renfree takes up drinking and turns atheist. Now, be so kind as to pour me another cup of tea.'

'Matthias Renfree would certainly like to see me drink less,' returned Oliver as he refilled the other man's cup.

Sir Martin resumed his breakfast.

'Your little wife, Oliver. She involved in this Methodist business?'

'Yes, but she'll be attending St Piran's with me now.'

'Quite right too. Been confirmed?'

'Yes, apparently, but for the life of me I can't remember her taking Communion.'

'Overlooked that one, eh? Mind you, she is a discreet little thing. Probably sat at the back of the church hiding away from the wicked Lord of the Manor, along with all the other local virgins.' Sir Martin tore off a chunk of bread and stuffed it into his mouth with a teasing glint in his eyes. Oliver met it with a wry smile.

'S'pose you'll be hurrying home to the nest again tonight, eh, my boy?'

Oliver drained his teacup and wiped his mouth, tossing the napkin on the bed.

'Perhaps,' he said, studying his fingernails.

Sir Martin eyed him for a moment, then they both laughed loudly.

Getting rapidly to his feet, Oliver retrieved the riding crop he'd tossed on the bed as he entered the room.

'Oliver?'

'Yes, Martin?'

'What's your little wife called?'

'Kerensa.'

'A pretty name. Bring her over to my next supper party. She'll be fine with Rachael to look after her. Now, my boy, before you go, kindly fill my cup again.'

—

Alice was uncertain what she ought to do at first that morning. With the King sisters she had risen early, envying them as they'd started work in the kitchen. She went reluctantly upstairs and hovered outside the master bedroom, wondering if she should go in to help Kerensa dress for breakfast. She was about to knock tentatively on the door when it was suddenly opened and Sir Oliver appeared before her. Jumping back in fright, Alice clapped a hand to her thumping heart. Recovering quickly, she dropped a curtsey.

'Good morning, m'lord.'

He raised an enquiring eyebrow.

'Good morning to you…?'

'It's Alice, Sir. Alice Ford.'

'Alice.' He inclined his head to her. 'You may go in to her ladyship now.'

Alice returned his direct look without a trace of servility.

'Thank you, sir.'

Sir Oliver held the door open for her, forcing her to lower her head as she passed under his outstretched arm. Running energetically down the stairs, he left Alice to close the door herself. She found Kerensa facing her, her face half smiling, half frowning, as she struggled to close the hooks on the back of one of her new dresses.

'I didn't expect him to hold on to that door like that,' Alice complained loudly. 'It made me feel proper silly.' She dashed a hand to her mouth, 'Oh, I'm that sorry, I'm forgetting myself. Good morning, m'lady.'

'Don't call me that please, Alice… not when we're alone. You're my friend, after all,' Kerensa said, breathless from her efforts to reach the hooks.

'Well, if you think it proper. Better not let his lordship hear me calling you Kerensa, though. I doubt he would approve.' Alice moved behind her, nimbly fastening the stiff hooks. 'Don't know why you're trying to do this yourself, you have me to do it for you, remember?'

'Don't nag me, Alice Ford,' Kerensa chided her friend good-humouredly, 'I'm not ready to change my whole way of life in one day. I'll brush my own hair too.'

As Kerensa moved to her dressing-table, Alice went in the opposite direction and stood at the head of the bed. She stared down at the indentation left in one of the plump pillows. Picking up a solitary strand of long black hair, she wound it tightly around a finger.

'He'll take some satisfying,' she murmured to herself.

'What was that you said?' Kerensa asked, looking at Alice's reflection in the mirror.

Coming straight to the point but feeling embarrassed so turning her back, she said, 'What was it like last night? Did he hurt you? Was he cruel? I couldn't sleep a wink all night worrying about it.'

Kerensa couldn't bring herself to look at Alice and instead gazed down at the brush in her hand. Her body was still feeling the effects of Oliver's lovemaking. There was a constant tingle on her lips, and where he had so delicately touched her. He had been patient and thoughtful of her youth and inexperience, and after he had withdrawn from her had immediately taken her back into his arms and held her close against him all through the night. There she had lain, feeling warmed through and somehow comforted, breathing in his masculine smell and feeling small and young and yet having taken on a new maturity. In the early hours of the morning he had teased her out of her nightgown and she had felt a fresh vulnerability as he had made love to her again, and it had been like a continuation of what had happened between them earlier in the night.

How her responses to him had been and how she had made him feel, she did not know, and did not want to think because it only accentuated her feeling of betraying Clem's love. It was his lovemaking she should have received last night; he loved her and she loved him, and it should only have been with Clem that she shared this most intimate of all things.

'No, Alice,' she said, after a long silence. 'He wasn't cruel to me, but I'd rather not talk about it… or think about it. You see, when I think of Clem, it hurts so much that it wasn't him.'

'Yes, of course, I suppose I shouldn't have mentioned it. But I wanted to be sure you were all right.'

Kerensa went to Alice and took her hands. They faced each other with their faces burning. 'It's so good having you around, Alice.'

'Whatever happens, Kerensa, I'll help you through,' Alice promised.

Kerensa went back to brushing her hair and Alice pointed reprovingly at the clothing strewn about on the floor.

'He's an untidy beggar, isn't he?'

'Never mind that now. Sir Oliver wants to hold family prayers in the great hall in ten minutes. Will you tell Ruth and Esther now, please?'

'Prayers!' Alice's face showed utter disbelief. 'Who'd have thought it?'

–

The prayers were performed with enough reverence to grace even the most renowned of clergymen, and Sir Oliver left the Manor house soon after breakfast. Alice was smoothing out the muddied, silk skirts of the wedding dress when Kerensa sought her out in her dressing room, flopped down on a chair and crossly folded her arms.

'What's the matter? Has something upset you?' Alice had been ready to rush to the defence of the other girl if need be.

'Ruth and Esther won't let me do any work. Not even lift a plate off the breakfast table. They're insisting I'm not to do anything they're supposed to… it wouldn't be in keeping now I'm mistress of a grand house.' Kerensa waved her hands in irritation. 'When I tried to explain that I'm used to hard work, that I like to be busy, to be useful, they suggested I go to my sitting room, make myself comfortable, and sew!'

Alice looked sympathetically at the girl who at that moment looked like a petulant child.

'I see… they're right in a way, Ruth and Esther, you'll have to get used to a lot of changes.'

Kerensa looked even more cross. 'But I can't spend the rest of my life embroidering 'O's' on silk shirts, Alice!'

'Now, let me think,' she said soothingly, 'what sort of things do ladies do?'

She chewed on her lip as she concentrated. Kerensa leaned forward hopefully.

'I know, they spend a lot of time in their gardens, don't they?'

'Talking like this makes it sound like a game,' Kerensa said dolefully. 'But it isn't, Alice! My whole life has been turned upside down and I still can't get Clem out of my mind. I feel like a traitor. I let all this happen, and if I'm unhappy it's no more than I deserve. I'll just have to make the best of it.'

She got up and looked gloomily out of the window to where Jake Angove, the Manor's head gardener, was attending to a square of earth where straight rows of rose trees grew. She pictured herself asking him for advice on what to grow and where to grow it, and wearing dainty gloves, cutting blooms and laying them in a long wicker garden basket. Alice stood at her side and put an arm around her shoulders.

'It wasn't your fault, Kerensa. You had no choice. If my father says I'm to marry someone for the good of the family, I'll go ahead and do it. Us women don't have much say in the matter.'

'Maybe not, but that doesn't make me feel any better.' Kerensa lifted the skirt of her powder blue, floral-patterned gown and shot a reproachful look at her satin slippers. 'But I'm not going to turn into a lady overnight,' she murmured.

'Eh?'

'You haven't thrown my old things away, have you, Alice?'

'No, of course not. I thought if you don't want them no more, as they wouldn't fit me, I was going to ask you if I could pass them on to Rosina Pearce. Here, what are you up to?'

'I'm going to wear one of my old dresses and shoes to go out in the garden and Rosina can have the rest, and I'll have something made up for her. At least now maybe I can do something useful for someone else. Perhaps I could ask her to come over here to the Manor and we could all have tea together. I want to keep in touch with her.'

'Oh, don't ask her to come over here, Kerensa,' Alice advised. 'That brute of a brother of hers wouldn't like it and he'd only make her suffer for it. Benefit Cap'n Solomon put a ruddy hole in his head instead of his hand backalong!'

'Yes, it was, and it's a pity I can't invite Rosina. But at least you can keep an eye on her when you visit your family and we'll do whatever we can for her.'

Feeling much more comfortable in her own familiar things, but thinking it strange to be wearing what once had been her Sunday best for gardening in, Kerensa hurried outside. On the way she was waylaid by Esther who informed her that there was hardly any food left in the larders. Suddenly feeling like giving orders, Kerensa said loftily, 'Sir Oliver's told me the Manor has an account at Araminta Bray's grocery shop. Ask Alice if she would take Meryn and the small trap into Marazion and order enough food to restock the larders. They can bring back what we require immediately and the rest can be sent over... oh, and while she's there she can call at Mistress Gluyas' to see if any more of my things are ready.'

–

Alice had listened open-mouthed as Esther had recounted this to her later. It seemed Kerensa was not by any means going to be a meek mistress to them. She smiled to herself as she visualised Kerensa delivering her orders, her small chin forward, her grey-green eyes sparkling with determination. Perhaps Sir Oliver too would have a surprise or two ahead of him, she thought, as she struggled with a wide cumbersome package tied up with red ribbon, on her way back to the trap having completed her morning's errands in Marazion.

'Hey, Alice!' came a shout behind her. 'Wait there, I'll give you a hand.'

Alice turned, and waited with interest for Clem Trenchard to catch up with her. Gratefully she handed over the heavy package into his outstretched hands.

'You're a welcome sight, Clem,' she told him. 'I've got a trap outside Araminta Bray's being loaded up with provisions for the Manor's kitchens. In town shopping yourself, are you?' She was dying to find out what he was doing and how he was feeling.

'No, just hanging about, don't feel much like working,' he replied in a dry flat voice.

They waited at the trap as Araminta Bray's errand boy put the last basket of foodstuffs in, then Clem put the package down beside them.

'What's all this for?' he asked moodily, inclining his head at the overflowing baskets.

'There's hardly any food left in the Manor. You wouldn't believe how much the wedding guests ate yesterday,' she answered him, watching his face closely for any reaction. 'Nothing but greedy pigs, the lot of them. When I think of how long it took us to prepare it all.'

'Huh,' he murmured, moving aside foodstuffs in one of the baskets to see what it contained, 'there's enough in here to feed my family for a month.'

'And there's more to be sent over later on. I came over with an order Ruth and Esther had made up but this lot was already being prepared.'

Clem fingered the sumptuous ribbon and bows on the package.

'It's a dress,' Alice explained.

'For Kerensa?' He looked sharply at her.

'Yes. I just collected it from Mistress Gluyas' establishment.'

'Mistress Gluyas? He's not mean with his money then. Are you going back to the Manor now?'

Alice hesitated before she admitted she was; Clem's voice seemed normal enough but his face was gaunt, his eyes unnaturally cold.

'I've nothing to do for an hour or so, can I keep you company part of the way?' He was already holding out his hand to help her up on the trap.

'Well… I… all right, Clem,' she ended brightly, hoping to lift his solemn mood.

He took the reins and held Meryn at a steady trot as they left the town behind them. After a while Alice leaned forward and looked up under Clem's bowed head. His eyes were fixed on the road ahead. He looked in need of friendly conversation.

'Fancy me driving a pony and trap,' Alice said chirpily, 'Jack reckoned I'd have no trouble. Meryn there is a quiet pony. Jack said Meryn's been to Marazion and back so many times he'd find his way in the dark.'

'Aye, this pony won't give you any trouble.'

'Haven't seen you at the meetings lately,' she said.

'Haven't been anywhere much lately.'

Alice let her shawl slip back from her shoulders. After the persistent rain of the day before the sun was pleasingly hot, the air fresh, the atmosphere clean, as though spring had decided to declare an early appearance.

Still watching the road, Clem said, in a voice that did not match the fine weather, 'Do you like your new job, Alice?'

'Oh, yes,' she replied enthusiastically. 'It's much better than dressing tin ore for a living.'

'I used to watch Kerensa walking to and from the Manor with those two tall King women. I prayed that for just one day she'd be alone. I wanted to talk to her so much. I even thought of kidnapping her to get her away from—'

'Oh, Clem,' Alice put a comforting hand on his arm.

Clem had had a lot of comforting hands reaching out to him, but none of them helped to ease his heartbreak.

He pulled Meryn to a halt and faced the girl beside him. He had lost weight, and the eyes in his pale face seemed to have lost their deep colour. Where men were concerned Alice had never been forward in her life, but she reached out and clasped his hand tightly in both of hers.

'I'm sorry for you, Clem,' she said softly, 'I wish there was something I could do to help.'

'How is she, Alice?' he returned earnestly. 'You can tell me how she really is.'

'Kerensa is well, Clem. Honestly. At this moment she'll be out in the gardens with Jake Angove.'

'I didn't believe she'd go through with it,' he said, shaking his head slowly. 'My family convinced me to keep out of the way and do nothing, but I should have spoken to her again! Made her see reason!' His voice had steadily risen with emotion, then he seemed to choke. 'She might even believe I don't really care… that I don't love her after all.'

'Kerensa doesn't believe that, Clem, I'm sure she doesn't.'

He grasped her by the shoulders. 'Alice, will you promise me something?'

'It depends what you want me to do, Clem,' she answered, disturbed by his intensity.

'If ever he does anything to hurt her, if he ill-treats her in any way at all, will you tell me? Promise that you'll tell me.'

Chapter 7

As the days of February passed slowly into March, each one became progressively warmer, bringing clear blue skies and tranquil seas. Trees, shrubs and bushes displayed the first glimpses of their summer splendour. Spring daffodils and celandines appeared alongside the paler hues of the primroses which were splashed in clumps on common land, roadside verges, ditches, and ranged across the cliffsides. The budding gorse bushes were not to be outdone and burst forth with their own deep yellow to add to the glorious wild golden beauty.

Farm workers pulled off their shirts to feel the sun's caressing warmth on their back as they tilled the fields and planted their crops with high hopes and a heavensent prayer for a bountiful harvest to offset another poverty-stricken winter. The Wheal Ember tin mine was considered to be doing well with only two fatalities and one lost limb since the start of the new year. The mine Captains and the speculators, who had money invested in it, were confident that with the splendid amount of good quality ore being brought to daylight from its awesome depths out under the sea, ample cash would be made at the next tin stamping. At Perranbarvah the fishermen were grateful for the whiting, pollack, skate, and mackerel in particular, which filled their nets out at sea, and the pilchard catches that could still be coaxed into the seine-nets on shore.

As she had promised, Beatrice had duly returned to the Manor the day after the wedding. For the most part she caused no trouble, limiting the work she did to insisting she carry in the three o'clock tea tray Kerensa shared with Oliver in his study, on the infrequent occasions he was actually there. The old woman doted on her new mistress despite the changes she'd brought, and much to Kerensa's dismay she was clutched to the other's ample, smelly bosom at every opportunity. Despite that, Kerensa soon became fond of Beatrice too. Ruth and Esther tolerated her provided she kept out from under their feet. Alice ignored her.

While the people who lived and worked around them got on with their lives Kerensa was learning what it was like to be the baronet's wife. From the beginning Oliver made it clear that he was to be master in his own house and he expected her to obey his every wish without question and to keep the servants in line. Although daunted by his expectations, Kerensa found if things ran smoothly in the house he took little interest in it. His habit of staying away from home for several days at a time gave her some welcome breathing space to adapt to living in the huge Manor house with its history that seemed to press in on her from all sides and live with her in the present.

If time stood still for Oliver in his ancestral home and in his memories, he raced on regardless with his life and into the future. Kerensa could not forgive him for forcing her into the marriage but knew it would be foolish to live at loggerheads with him and risk bringing his wrath on herself, and perhaps the servants. She must at least make life as bearable as possible. She decided to study Oliver when he was at home, and find out what she could about him while he was away, and use what she learned to try to ward off his more negative moods, which imposed themselves on the whole household.

She had little success at first. He watched her as much as she tried to watch him, and she was nervous that he would consider any such scrutiny an invitation to the marriage bed. She was prepared to submit to her duty in that respect, and while she could not complain to herself because he was always considerate and not too demanding of her, she was certainly not going to give him any idea that she was encouraging him. He was in many respects a complex, unreadable man but she was beginning to feel that he was occasionally won over by her determination to be calming and unobtrusive, and her attempts never to be too sulky or quarrelsome. It was not a hard task to steal glances at his handsome face.

Kerensa's greatest pleasure came from the time she spent in the gardens under the fatherly supervision of the crusty-tempered, heavily white-bearded, Jake Angove. The head of the Manor's three gardeners Jake was twin brother to Nick Angove, Marazion's blacksmith. Although to others he could be surly and indifferent, Jake had willingly taken Kerensa under his wing, silently wishing just one of his many granddaughters possessed the girl's grace and dignity.

The spacious, beautifully landscaped gardens to front and back of, and at each side of the Manor, had been designed by Oliver's grandmother. Kerensa had been all round them many times with Jake, discussing their various points and making plans for their further development. She was fascinated to learn from him that the lady responsible for them, Lady Mary-Anne Pengarron, had also been a Pengarron bride from a working-class background. Oliver's outrageous grandfather, Sir Charles, had been an elderly bachelor when he had inherited the title and estate.

'He was proper wild,' Jake told Kerensa as they ruthlessly pulled up weeds together. 'Didn't give a darn for what people said about him, did old Sir Charles. He married the woman he fell in love with. My, that woman! She was nothing like you, m'dear. She had a temper like a devil, swore worse 'n' any man I've ever heard, and screamed like a banshee with it.'

'And she designed all of this?' Kerensa said incredulously, waving both arms in all directions.

'Ais, that's right. You wouldn't think a woman like her would have had it in her. Sir Charles adored her, and she adored Young Oliver when he came along.'

Kerensa sat back on her heels and looked at Jake in amazement, her mouth wide open. 'You call him Young Oliver, Jake?'

'Ais, have done all his life. From the time the little beggar run over my tilled ground trampling my seedlings as a tacker.' The gardener tugged his long wiry beard and winked at her. 'Reckon that's where he do get some of his ways from, eh? His grandparents? I never did give him no mind, myself. Here, m'dear, next time he starts one of his rantings and ravings, just you think about what I just told 'ee.'

Kerensa felt a smug satisfaction to have this secret told to her about her proud husband. She laughed and wondered if she should tell Alice.

'Young Oliver,' she repeated to herself before renewing her attack on the weeds.

One afternoon, with Dunstan contentedly plodding beside her, Kerensa stopped to listen to some rather mysterious noises she heard coming from a small wooden hut at the back of the stableyard. Full of curiosity she peeped around the open door. The inside of the hut was fitted with benches and shelves, each one bearing varying sizes of cages and boxes, blankets and foodstuffs. She stepped inside. Dunstan did the same then flopped down lazily in the doorway.

Kerensa peered into some of the boxes. They were empty. Looking up at the sound of a fluttering noise directly above her head she found herself looking straight into the beady wide eyes of a fully grown tawny owl.

'Oh, what are you doing up there?' she gasped in surprise.

The owl blinked a welcome to her from its high vantage point.

'Good afternoon, m'lady,' said Nathan O'Flynn, cautiously stepping over Dunstan to stand beside Kerensa.

'Good afternoon, Nat,' she whispered back, not taking her eyes off the owl. 'He's beautiful, isn't he? Does he live here all the time?'

'Only until he gets better. He's got a twisted leg.'

'And you're looking after him?'

'His lordship is actually. He came across him a couple of nights ago. He's looked after injured animals and birds in here since he was a small boy. I just take over when he's away.'

Kerensa was both surprised and impressed by this piece of information. She peered over the tops of the other boxes, stopping at the sight of a curled up bundle of grey fur. 'What's in here? It looks like a squirrel.'

'It's a squirrel, sure enough. I found it myself only this morning. It had its foot chewed up in a gin trap.'

'Poor little thing, it's only a baby. Will it recover, Nat?'

'Can't say for sure. I'll ask his lordship to have a look at it this evening. He's got more of a way with 'em than I have. He has Beatrice make up ointments and potions from herbs and things.' Nathan ran his large hand through his bushy hair and angrily frowned. 'The little thing was caught in a trap – set, I suspect, by that rogue Colly Pearce. His lordship won't be too pleased about it, that he'll not.'

Kerensa delicately stroked the sleeping grey form with her finger.

'Are there any more little creatures in here, Nat?'

'Only old Esau, the field mouse. He's been here for ages and ages.'

Kerensa looked up at the tawny owl's hooked beak. The owl moved its head on its short neck and blinked at her.

'Don't you worry about Esau, m'lady. He's safely tucked away inside his lordship's pocket at the moment. Goes round with his lordship quite often, even in the Manor house, but his lordship says nothing for fear of provoking screaming females all over the place.'

'I'm not afraid of mice,' she said proudly.

The large bird with its mottled buff plumage seemed to nod its agreement.

–

Oliver spent much of his time away from the Manor working with Adam Renfree, the steward of the Estate's home farm and horse stud. Ker-an-Mor Farm, at three hundred acres, was a bare mile from the Manor, and barley was planted and harvested right down to the cliff edge. From one angle it overlooked the east side of St Michael's Mount. The two men often rode there to share meal breaks together, drinking wine and eating pies and pasties ably made for them by Esther King and Jenna Tregurtha, Adam's woman friend.

They enjoyed this time together, Oliver relaxed in the genial company of his own gender, the rough and ready Adam having no care for differences of class. He took a man as he found him. Watching the sun gild the magical castle on the Mount, they sat on their coats to discuss the conditions of the other farms rented out on the Estate.

'Trecath-en's doing well, but I'd expect no different from Morley Trenchard,' Adam said, 'though I b'lieve he's having a small bit of trouble with his son, Clem.'

'Why? Taken to drink, has he?'

'Huh! Not with Matthias looking out for him. No, he's moody and uncooperative. But I s'pose he'll snap out of it.'

Oliver looked deeply into the glow of the bottle of wine he was holding up to the rays of the sun.

'He had better,' he remarked slowly.

Oliver felt no guilt over Clem Trenchard's heartbreak. In Oliver's class marriages were made mainly for financial or political reasons, or to fuse two eminent families together to make them more powerful. The gentry were brought up to do their duty to their families in all aspects of their lives; there was no room for sentiment and one was expected always to behave with decorum. Clem Trenchard's sulky behaviour had earned only Oliver's antipathy. If Kerensa was similarly heartbroken she hid the effects well and there was nothing sulky about her attitude.

In fact, you're rather spirited, Oliver mused, his mind drifting off to the times he'd overheard Kerensa laughing with Alice, sharing what was obviously a private joke. When he made his presence known to them they resolutely straightened their faces, but when they thought he wasn't looking the audacity of the expressions they passed between one another made him wonder if some of these jokes were at his expense.

'Polcudden and Barvah Farms are doing well, Orchard Hill not too bad. It's just the Richards on Rose Farm who're lagging behind with their tilling and planting,' Adam said.

'We'll keep an eye on them,' Oliver replied, coming back to the matter in hand, 'but that young man Richards will never make much of a farmer, I fear. How are the Berrymans managing with the loss of so many calves through their defective bull?'

'Well, 'twas pretty bad and Daniel is hoping to make up for it this year with the bull we've loaned him, but you know Daniel, sir. He don't let much get him down for long. I've never lost sleep over Orchard Hill Farm.'

'You still friendly with that attractive widowed sister of his?'

Adam Renfree's jaw fell.

'How on earth did you know about that? I haven't broadcast it about.'

Oliver leaned back on his elbow to allow the sun to warm his face. With a smile relaxing his dark features he said, matter-of-factly, 'There's very little that escapes my attention, Adam.'

'Dear life, I'll be damned,' said Adam, looking at the other man with a mixture of disbelief and respect, 'I haven't even told Matthias about my friendship with Jenna Tregurtha.'

'Would he object?'

'No, not Matthias, he seems to like everybody. Besides, it's not as if I'm about to give him a stepmother.' Adam waved his pasty crust in an arc, obscuring his view of the ant-sized figures of people crossing the causeway between Marazion and the Mount. 'Did you know they Wesley brothers will be preaching hereabouts in the summer, sir? Matthias is getting all fired up about it already.'

'Yes, I know that too,' Oliver said with a boyish grin. 'The Manor is full of Wesleyan followers. I've overheard them talking.'

'You don't mind that, sir, – or the Reverend Ivey?' Adam asked seriously.

'I have no cause to hold anything against the Wesleys or their ilk. Nor has the Reverend Ivey. He gets on very well indeed with your son, Adam. I've joined in many an interesting discussion with them, debating the whole subject.'

'Well, you always did have a proper thirst for knowledge, and you're more tolerant than most people think,' Adam said drily. 'I must admit, though, I assumed the Reverend shared the views of the majority of Anglican ministers and despised this Methodism business. Got no interest in none of it myself.'

Oliver said no more on the matter. He greatly respected Adam Renfree, who had taught him and his boyhood friend Arthur Beswetherick to ride the sturdy Pengarron stud ponies from the time they could walk. As they grew, he and Arthur had followed Adam about the farmland, the three of them entering into an easy compan-ionship. Together they had spent many carefree hours labouring at harvest time, tilling and planting the land, tending livestock, learning the intricacies of the stud animals and riding hard across the cliffs. Adam Renfree was a burly man possessing an uneven temper and a finely controlled drinking habit. Oliver knew how much his farm steward held the church in contempt, and disapproved of his son's interest in matters spiritual.

'We're getting far better results from the crops now we're using Tull's drills and plough,' he remarked, looking back across the fields, 'we have crops growing in places not dreamt of in my father's time.'

'Aye, people will always need feeding,' Adam nodded. 'I just hope this hot sun so early on doesn't mean we're in for a dry summer.'

'Mmmm, Beatrice is already giving out warnings of scorching ground and the springs and rivers drying up,' Oliver said soberly.

Adam Renfree let out a long sigh. 'Is she?'

A ladybird alighted on the back of Oliver's hand. He was not as superstitious as most Cornish men and women, but regarded it as sacrilege to kill a ladybird, even if unintentionally. He put a finger out in front of the little creature, counting the seven black spots on its red back.

'Careful,' said Adam, rising to his knees, his eyes kept fast on the ladybird, 'you got seven years of good luck there.'

Both men watched with bated breath as the ladybird crawled obligingly on to Oliver's finger, explored the lightly tanned skin for a short while, before spreading its wings and flying away inland, leaving its pungent smell behind.

The mesmeric moment over Adam sat back again and reached for the wine bottle.

'When we're finished here, sir, think I'll head back to the farmyard to have a look at old Bethy. She's an old girl to pup, and may need a bit of help.'

'Will they be pedigree or is it an unknown sire?'

'They'll be as black as pitch, sir. More grandchildren of old Dunstan.'

–

On the surface of the Wheal Ember mine, scattered about the towering engine house, were many ramshackle wood and corrugated shacks and sheds, and enormous heaps of mine waste and building materials which blighted the once beautiful landscape. It was a sight that continually offended the eyes and senses of Oliver Pengarron. He felt no differently as he rode up to the mine early one afternoon with the intention of seeing Hunk Hunken, its underground Captain. Leaving Conomor to wander at will, he walked briskly to the shafts.

Giggling bal-maidens nudged one another as he passed by them, leaning over to whisper in the nearest ear and encouraging the small ragged grinning boys working with them to imitate the tall man's strides. Oliver ignored them until he saw Rosina Pearce working quietly among them. She caught his eye because she was in the simple grey dress that Kerensa had been wearing on the day she'd opened the cottage door to him in Trelynne Cove. Even from a distance Oliver could make out dark marks on her arms as she hammered at the rocks. He sighed heavily. It was obvious the girl's brother had been beating her again. Oliver wished heartily that Colly Pearce wasn't so adept at poaching without being apprehended, then he could be sent to prison at the maximum sentence and the girl could be given some much needed relief. He couldn't abide unnecessary cruelty.

He moved away and turned his back on the workers to gaze out across the sea where the swell of the water rose and fell like the gentle breathing of a sleeping child, and overhead gulls floated lazily on warm thermals.

Oliver was in a contented mood. He had repossessed all of his family's land, and the one part of the last transaction he had so furiously baulked at was not turning out to be the demeaning experience a gentleman might have supposed. Kerensa was not coarse-mouthed and common, or subject to uncleanliness, with no concept of how to better herself, as were most of the women who were presently gawping at his back. She showed an interest in the running of his house, and spent time working in his gardens; she showed an interest of sorts in him because he had noticed she often stole glances at him.

It was just after two o'clock and men and boys were gathering around the top of the wooden ladders, waiting their turn to go down into the black depths when the last of those on the morning core had surfaced. All wore the large round hard hats with dripping tallow candles attached to the front to light their way underground. Pasties wrapped in brightly coloured kerchiefs were stuffed inside their shirts or peeping over the tops of pockets.

Some of them looked across at the man clad in white linen shirt, riding breeches and black leather boots. They assumed correctly that Sir Oliver was waiting for Hunk Hunken to come to grass with the men finishing their core.

They moved back to give room to the first exhausted miner to clamber out on to the surface and lie on his back to regain his breath. His breathing came in loud rasps. Although the man was about thirty-six years of age, old for an underground miner, he could easily be mistaken for twenty years more. Such was the lot of a man working and breathing in damp cramped conditions where no fresh air could be found.

Gradually, more blackened, sweat-streaked men and boys, some as young as eight or nine, appeared on the stony, sparsely grassed clifftop. They blinked hard as their eyes painfully adjusted to the bright sunlight, thankful to have survived the core without explosion or other incident, and not to have plunged from fatigue off the thousands of wooden rungs of the ladders to certain death.

Hunk Hunken, a tough but likeable ginger-haired man in his late twenties, staggered over to Oliver as soon as he noticed the baronet close by. Oliver had turned to watch the ascending men, giving each one a curt nod as they acknowledged his presence. He waited several minutes for Hunk, who was bending forward with giant hands on his thighs, to recover his breath. When the mine Captain was at last able to straighten up, he furiously rubbed his pale blue eyes against the light. Finally he was able to speak.

'Good afternoon, m'lord! Phew! It's like the bowels of Hell down there.'

Having taken a water flask off Conomor's saddle, Oliver passed it to Hunk.

'I believe you enjoy it underground, Hunk Hunken, bowels of Hell or not,' he said pleasantly.

This was another ordinary man in whose company he felt at ease. Hunk took the flask with a nod of thanks, gulped several mouthfuls of water, swilling out huge spits of dust and swallowing the rest. Rubbing his hand across his face, he left channels in the dust on his cheeks and beard.

'Reckon I do have an affinity with the depths of the earth, sir,' he answered Oliver at last, 'same as the farmer does with the surface. We're both trying to get a living out of it. I take it Cap'n Solomon is due in soon, then?'

'Three nights from today. Can I leave you to make the usual arrangements?'

'Aye, sir. Trelynne Cove, or the little place beyond Pengarron Point this time?'

'Trelynne Cove, and we'll keep a look-out as before.'

Straightening to his full height Hunk flexed his arms and moved his head from side to side, the strain in his muscles from the arduous climb to the surface beginning to subside.

'You still reckon Old Tom's about somewheres, then?'

'I'm sure of it,' Oliver informed the mine Captain, 'he'll show up sooner or later.'

'Trembath brothers won't go to Trelynne Cove to run goods, sir.'

Oliver sighed. 'I'd offer them the usual payment but Ted would not accept it. He's been up on the cliff where Davey went over, staring out to sea, many times since that night. I am wondering if he shares my suspicions concerning old Tom.'

Hunk met the other man's dark eyes and they both looked in the direction of Trelynne Cove.

A small girl hurrying on bare feet towards the miners waiting to descend the ladders captured their attention. Her long straggly hair streaming out behind her as she ran, the girl stopped in front of the man who had been the first to grass.

'What's up me 'an'some?' Carn Bawden asked his daughter.

'Mam sent me to tell 'ee to tell Ted Trembath, 'fore he goes down the shaft, his brother's body been found, washed up in Perranbarvah,' the girl gasped out between deep intakes of breath.

Carn Bawden looked across to Ted Trembath who had been with his two brothers, they having not long come to grass. There was no need for Carn Bawden to repeat his daughter's tidings, Ted Trembath was staring at him with a face like granite.

'I heard the little maid, Carn,' Ted murmured. 'Perranbarvah beach she said?'

'Aye, Ted. I'm sorry,' Carn Bawden replied, hugging his daughter to him. Without looking down he said to her, 'You're a good girl, Heather, you run along home now, off you go.'

Heather glanced up at the serious faces of the miners who had now fallen silent. Without a word she bolted through their legs and away from the scruffy buildings.

Oliver and Hunk Hunken moved in and joined the group of men. Hunk stretched out his hands to Ted Trembath, and in slow movements, Ted placed his tools in them.

'I'll take them back to your cottage, Ted,' Hunk said grimly. 'Yours too, Will... Curly.'

The two younger Trembaths repeated their brother's actions.

'Is there anything else I can do for you, Ted?'

Blinking back tears he answered, 'Just... just make sure Mother's all right, will you, Hunk?'

The mine Captain nodded.

Putting a hand firmly on Ted's shoulder, Oliver spoke.

'I'll ride on ahead, Ted, to see what can be done.'

'Thank you, sir,' the Trembaths whispered in unison.

When Oliver reached Conomor he found the girl Heather Bawden looking up at his horse from a distance, her eyes glowing with admiration. She jumped back guiltily when Oliver passed her and gathered up the reins. He mounted and surprised the girl, as she edged nervously away, by smiling down at her. Very shyly, she smiled back and attempted a makeshift curtsey. A few moments later Heather was happily skipping home to show her mother the shiny sixpence she was clutching tightly, a sixpence Sir Oliver Pengarron himself had given to her.

Some two hours before Oliver had spoken to Hunk Hunken, the Laity, Drannock, and King children had been playing near to a shallow salt water pool on Perranbarvah's beach when a scream from one of the tiny girls brought the others running to her.

'What's up with you, Becky Laity?' Paul King, who reached her first had asked. At seven years old he followed the family trait and was head and shoulders taller than his counterparts.

Tiny Becky Laity had not answered. Her eyes stood out large and glazed as she pointed among the rocks. Paul King peered past her upraised arm and stifled a scream of his own. Taking the toddler's hand and shielding her eyes from a further look at the distressing sight, he led her away to meet the other running children.

'What's going on, Paul? What's she scream for?' It was Bartholomew Drannock who wanted to know, the wilful eldest son of the King family's seine-boat partner.

'She saw something awful, that's what. There's a body over there among the rocks, and a stinking horse's body beside it.'

'See it, did 'ee?' asked another child.

'Ais, I did,' Paul said, a shiver of horror passing through his grubby body, 'and it was proper awful. Better get back quick and tell Tas and Grandtas... they'll know what to do.'

'You lot can go back,' Bartholomew Drannock said scornfully, 'I'm going to have a look at they bodies first.'

Paul left Becky in the care of an older girl then ran on before them, leaping expertly over the rocks and shingle on his gangly legs. He ran past the cottages and down the narrow quayside. Brightly coloured sails hung up to dry on spars surrounded the men busily making or repairing nets, tarring ropes or working on the upkeep of their boats.

Grandfather King, always the first to sense a change in the weather or direction of the wind, or to see the silvery flash of fish at sea, looked up from the net spread over his knees. He moved his pipe to the other side of his mouth as his grandson ran towards him with the smaller children endeavouring to keep up in his wake.

'Solomon,' he said to his son, hard at work behind him.

'Tas?'

'It's trouble comin'.'

Solomon King collected his sons, Matthew, Mark and John, his nephews Jeremy, Josh and Christopher, and his brother Jonathan, to gather around the head of the family. If Grandfather King said there was trouble coming, no one doubted his word.

Bartholomew Drannock had joined the other children by the time Paul had told his grandfather, father, and the rest of his family of Becky Laity's gruesome discovery. The children, with the exception of Paul and Bartholomew, were ordered away to join their mothers in the fish salting cellars. Grandfather King sent a man to inform the Reverend Ivey, another to Matthias Renfree, yet another to Pengarron Manor, and one more still to Mrs Trembath and the mining community. With the two small boys to point out the exact spot, he sombrely set off with his sons and grandsons to reclaim Davey Trembath's body back from the sea.

Since her marriage Kerensa had been allowed to travel the short distance to Perranbarvah unescorted, presumably because Oliver now felt that Clem Trenchard would not be so troublesome in trying to see her. While the children from the village below were rushing to Grandfather King, Kerensa had been standing beside her mother's grave with the Reverend Ivey. She had been about to discuss the details of her mother's untimely death with him. She felt it was a matter left unsatisfactorily explained from her old life and it had become a matter of some importance to her to learn all the facts behind it. Her interest, however, had been caught by the steady trickle of people who were gathering below in a fair-sized crowd on the little quayside.

The Reverend had slipped aside to gain a better view, concern crossing his face as he watched the scene with her.

'I had better go down and enquire what is wrong,' he said gravely.

'All the boats are in,' said Kerensa, frowning. 'What else could it be?'

A fisherman ran through the lychgate at that moment and answered their anxious questions. Kerensa gripped the Reverend's arm, a feeling of unreality sweeping over her as the fishermen told them what was happening.

'I'll come down presently,' the Reverend said in solemn tones. When the man had gone he turned to Kerensa. 'I'll take you in to the Parsonage, my dear.'

'No!' she exclaimed. 'No… I mean, I'll be all right. I'd much rather stay here in the fresh air. Please, Reverend, you go down to the village, you'll be needed down there.'

'I'm not sure…' he began, but at the pleading in her eyes he said, 'Very well Kerensa, perhaps it would be best if you were to stay here.'

Shame and fearfulness dominated her as the elderly parson left Kerensa alone. He threw one last worried look back at her before he disappeared round the side of the lychgate. Kerensa sat down dejectedly on the dry grass beside her mother's grave, sadly touching the petals of the speedwell flowers that spread their blueness like a gently undulating summer sea over the graveyard. The sound of voices brought her back on her feet again. A pregnant woman with a struggling infant in her arms, and dragging another protesting child by his hand, waddled around from the side of the church building. Managing to free his hand the child ran away from his mother, leaving her to call ineffectually after him to stop. He only halted when he saw Kerensa standing in his path.

'Hello,' she said very softly, holding out a hand to him.

The child, swaying from side to side, locked his fingers together and pouted at the pretty girl standing before him. When his mother caught up with them she dropped a perfect curtsey to Kerensa despite her burdens and tried to retrieve the boy's hand, but he only stuffed them firmly under his armpits.

'Good afternoon, my lady,' the woman said, 'I apologise for my son's behaviour, but he's not being at all co-operative this afternoon.' The woman's voice was clear and cultured, and out of keeping with her clothing.

Kerensa was surprised and it took her a moment to speak.

'He's got a nice smile, your little boy,' she volunteered.

'All of my boys are rather strong-willed,' the woman explained, smiling pleasantly. She held out her hand to Kerensa. 'I'm Jenifer

Drannock. My husband Samuel is a fisherman from the village.' The woman inclined her head towards the village, rapidly becoming alarmed as she saw the gathering crowd below.

'It's not a fishing accident,' Kerensa hastily reassured her, 'some of the village children have found Davey Trembath's body by a salt pool on the beach.' She took Jenifer Drannock's hand. 'I wish we could have met in different circumstances to this. Mrs Drannock. I see you know who I am.'

Jenifer made another futile attempt to take her son's hand as she said, 'I am relieved it's not another tragedy. Will you excuse me if I go down to pay my respects with the others?' The infant in her arms began to wail and beat at her with tiny clenched fists.

'I'll take the little one if you like, Mrs Drannock,' Kerensa offered without hesitation, 'you'll manage much better without him.'

Jenifer studied Kerensa, who was as pale as a white primrose. She recalled the supposed connection between Old Tom Trelynne and Davey Trembath's death and she felt sorry for the girl.

'Are you sure, my lady? He may ruin your lovely riding habit. I brought flowers to put on my mother-in-law's grave and he tore most of the heads off. And he's always being sick.'

'That doesn't matter,' said Kerensa, anxious to have the infant's company to vanquish some of her own wretchedness. 'I'd really like to take him for a while. What's his name?'

'Jack,' replied Jenifer, handing over her son. 'He's not long been fed and should stay dry for a while. I'll try not to be very long.'

The other little boy tugged at Kerensa's skirt.

'I'm called Charles,' he said politely.

Kerensa smiled warmly at him. 'Hello, Charles. Be a good boy for your mother,' she told him kindly.

The baby was aged about eight months and a miniature copy of his brother Charles. He didn't seem to care at all that his mother and brother were leaving the churchyard without him. Kerensa hugged his little body close, hoping he would not sense her uneasiness as she paced up and down with him.

'Well, Jack. You're a lovely baby aren't you?' she told him.

Jack didn't know. He pursed his fat lips together and his eyes seemed to cross as he stared into her face, then clutching at the satin ribbons on her bodice, he tried to cram them into his mouth. Kerensa gently rubbed her nose against his and Jack rewarded her with a chuckle, and a long wet dribble down her neck. She kissed the top of his downy head and held him closer.

After ten long minutes she saw no change in the stillness of the villagers below.

'Let's go and see if Mrs Tregonning has something nice for you to eat, shall we, Jack? I ought to tell her what's happening anyway.'

He chuckled again, then returned to the now sodden ribbons clutched in his equally wet fist as he was carried towards the parsonage.

—

If a man farmed the sea for a living he soon became used to tragedy upon its awesome vastness, and of the putrid conditions of a waterlogged body. Altogether the King family had seen several, but confronting them didn't get any easier. As soon as they arrived at the grisly scene Paul and Bartholomew Drannock were ordered home and Grandfather King quickly set his sons and grandsons to work by the salt pool.

With their neckerchieves pulled up to cover their mouths and noses, Jeremy, Josh and Christopher cut the seaweed-strewn reins that had joined boy and pony together in their death plunge and the weeks spent in the devouring sea. They deftly tied ropes around the pony's legs and kicking away crabs, flies and other shore scavengers, the brothers dragged the rotting carcase of the animal a long, long way along the shore. Rounding a large outcrop of rocks, accessible only in a deeply receding tide, they piled the remains with driftwood and dry seaweed. Setting the putrefying mass alight they stood well back, away from the stench-bearing smoke. When the fire had consumed all the pony's flesh they were to bury what was left deep enough to avoid any health hazard and to conceal the location from curious children. As the brothers stood and silently watched the blaze they rubbed their stinging eyes.

Beside the pitiful scraps left of the once handsome boy, Solomon, Matthew and Mark carefully laid out a tarpaulin. Their faces grim under their neckerchieves, they were helped by Jonathan and Grandfather King to lay a small net over Davey's body. On a count of three they skilfully twisted the net round to contain the body, and reverently placed it down on the tarpaulin. Solomon and his brother wrapped Davey Trembath up into a neat parcel, finishing it off with firmly tied rope.

With the gruesome task completed the King men stood respectfully in a circle around the body, their kerchieves pulled down, as Grandfather King said a few words of prayer. Hoisting the small bundle on to their shoulders, Solomon and Matthew, following Grandfather King and Jonathan, formed a sombre procession for the short journey back to the fishing village.

Down on the shoreline Mark King was comforting his younger brother. John, one of the youngest members of the King brood, was violently retching into the water. It was the first time he had witnessed the vile consequences of what the unrelenting sea does to those lost in the depths of its deceptive majesty.

–

Jack was almost full of tiny broken off pieces of Mrs Tregonning's saffron cake. He sat happily on Kerensa's lap, his tiny face smeared with dribble and bright yellow crumbs.

'Here, give the little mite to me,' Mrs Tregonning cooed, 'and I'll wipe his face clean before he gets you all mucky too.'

But Jack had taken an instant dislike to the Reverend's plump housekeeper and rubbed his sticky face into Kerensa's shoulder and stubbornly clung to her.

Mrs Tregonning was affronted. 'They Drannocks will breed like they Kings,' she sniffed, passing Kerensa a damp cloth to wipe the crumbs off her dress.

When Jack's interest in the cake waned Kerensa put him down on the spotlessly clean floor to see if he could crawl. Jack made no attempt to move but stretched out his arms towards her and loudly protested.

Kerensa rushed to pick him up again and spoke softly soothing words until his puckered red face was smoothed out and cheekily smiling. She paced the floor with him for several minutes, bobbing him up and down as she moved.

'Shouldn't think they'll be much longer now,' Mrs Tregonning said. 'Mind you, I don't know what people want to stand and gawp for anyway. 'Tis all a bit ghoulish if you ask me. It's a thing I've never done myself… just being nosey, most of them.'

Kerensa sighed. 'I think I'll take Jack out in the fresh air.'

She showed Jack the Reverend's daffodils and polyanthus. He was not impressed by them and was sick down the front of her dress. Knowing very little about babies Kerensa playfully bounced him up and down and Jack was sick again. Finally her restlessness got the better of her and very slowly she followed the path the Reverend and Jenifer Drannock had taken until she arrived at the back of the waiting crowd down in the village.

People were standing with arms folded and talking in respectful whispers, the work for the day forgotten. Kerensa felt conspicuous in her riding habit against the drab clothes of the fishwives as they turned to look at her in surprise. Matthias Renfree had arrived and was talking with the Reverend a good distance away from the quayside. She squeezed apologetically through the groups of fisherfolk until she was on the quayside out of the Reverend's sight.

If he saw her he would insist she return to the Parsonage or even go home to the Manor, but Kerensa knew of the fishermen's strong superstitious fear of clergymen being on a quayside and knew the Reverend would not set foot upon it himself.

Jenifer Drannock was standing in a doorway with a group of other women. Spotting Kerensa with her son, she came forward to take him back, watched with great interest by the women she'd stepped away from. Jack turned his head abruptly away from his mother.

'He's all right with me, Mrs Drannock,' Kerensa said. 'I'd like to hold him for a bit longer, if you'll allow me to.'

'Well, if you're sure, my lady. I'll come for him if he starts to cry.' Jenifer placed her hand on Jack's bottom and lightly smiled. 'He's still dry at the moment,' she added, then returned to her neighbours.

Kerensa nodded nervously at the faces staring at her. She received courteous nods in return before the eyes turned expectantly to the place where the Kings were expected to appear with the boy's body.

A few more tense minutes passed by before the Kings' appearance with their burden caused a spontaneous movement forward and an outbreak of sympathetic raised voices. At the same moment a heavy hand grasping Kerensa roughly by the shoulder and whirling her round made her wince.

'There's no need for you to be here,' Oliver told her harshly.

'I want to be here,' she returned feebly, jerking Jack up to a more comfortable position.

Oliver glared at the child his young wife was holding. Jack only gave the tall man who had loomed up suddenly in front of him a disinterested look, and carried on chewing the wet ribbon he was tightly clutching.

'Get rid of that brat and go home without delay,' Oliver hissed.

'But I—'

'Do as I say. Ted Trembath and his brothers will be here soon and there's no knowing the mood these people may take. I don't have to remind you of your grandfather's supposed part in all this, do I?'

Kerensa saw her husband narrow his eyes as he spoke and by now knew well enough, from his stance: the subtle change in the darkness of his eyes, the tiny vein that appeared from nowhere in his neck; that in this mood he would not be argued with. She knew also he was probably right in what he said. She found Jenifer Drannock at her side, silent pity on the woman's face as she reached out for her son. The baby's fist had to be forcibly removed from Kerensa's dress, and he screamed and fought against his mother.

Kerensa pushed her way through the fisherfolk, her mind telling her that the concerned looks on the brown weather-ravaged faces she rushed past were hostile to her. She ran back up the hill to the Parsonage stable, tears searing her eyes as she left it up to Meryn to find their way home to the Manor.

Chapter 8

The following day the coroner from Marazion rode over to the church where the boy's body had lain overnight and gave permission for it to be buried. Thomas Cole, a gambling acquaintance of Oliver's, took very little time in deciding the only evidence he required was a positive identification of the deceased. This was given by Ted Trembath by means of the remnants of his brother's clothes, and the beaten tin medallion Davey had always worn around his neck. Ted had made the medallion himself for Davey's fifth birthday, and hanging it on a thin strip of leather, the boy had worn it with pride.

Except for a few maintenance men in the engine house on the mine surface, Wheal Ember closed for the afternoon of the funeral. Davey Trembath's body was taken home after the coroner's examination, his pathetically small coffin borne along on a bier pulled by two black ponies from the Ker-an-Mor stables, and three hundred men, women and children walked reverently in line behind the cortege.

Mrs Trembath insisted on walking the long twisting miles, supported by her remaining sons, to take Davey back to the church. Led by Faith Bray, the mourners filled the air with the harmonious sounds of Celtic voices. They sang hymn after hymn without pause or break, collecting other mourners along the way until the slowly moving procession reached the small church in Perranbarvah.

In deference to the ailing, grief-stricken mother the Reverend Ivey conducted a brief service. He tactfully made no comment on the manner of the boy's death, only recalling to the small portion of mourners who could gain admittance inside the church, the boy's devout Christian way of life, and comforting them with the knowledge that young Davey had exchanged his cross of suffering for a crown of joy.

Mrs Trembath sat stiff and upright, her face set like cold stone throughout the service. Davey had been her favourite son. His father had died in an explosion down the mine during the same hour Davey had struggled his way prematurely into the world. He had fought for his life over the first weeks and thereafter had been a sickly child. With three other sons well able to provide for the family, his mother had seen no reason for him to work underground and Davey had joined the bal-maidens on the surface until he was twelve.

But he had felt ashamed to be left 'at grass' while such younger boys worked and earned more underground, and by all accounts led more exciting lives. He had begged his mother to allow him to work underground too and finally she had relented while remaining fearful for his safety. Mrs Trembath had had no knowledge that Davey was joining Ted on the night of his death and she was never to forgive her eldest son for robbing her of her youngest.

Ted Trembath would never forgive himself either for allowing Davey to go with him on that fateful night. He searched without success in his pockets for his kerchief as tears streamed down his face as the mourners sang another Wesleyan hymn around the graveside.

'Jesu, lover of my soul.
Let me to thy bosom fly,
While the gathering waters roll,
While the tempest still is high,
Till the storm of life is past,
Safe into the haven guide,
O receive my soul at last.'

It had been Davey's favourite hymn. Ted reached for his mother but she would not part the hands she held tightly gripped together. Oliver had joined the family at the church door and Mrs Trembath had not replied to his offer of sympathy. Ted gave him a look near to hopelessness across the graveside and Oliver returned it with one of compassion while at the same time attempting to convey to the distraught miner that he shared in his guilt and shame.

The bell in the church tower knelled its mournful note as the coffin was lowered into the ground. People were suddenly jostled aside as Sir Martin Beswetherick unceremoniously shoved his way through to stand next to Oliver. Sir Martin took little notice of the remainder of the burial, mainly confining himself to casting lecherous glances at Rosina Pearce. A man of strictly Anglican concerns, he snorted at every few words that Matthias Renfree said as the young man gave a short address at the Reverend Ivey's invitation.

It was a hot day and the mourners were uncomfortable in their black clothes. The sun gained in strength to burn through coats and shawls on the backs and shoulders of the people below. Mrs Trembath, her face still set in the same expressionless mask, threw a handful of dry earth on her son's coffin, then stepping back tilted her head to look up at the golden-white rays. The new expression on her face suggested she thought the sun had insulted her by shining so.

Kerensa sat in a secluded corner of the gardens at the back of the Manor house, twisting her skirt between taut fingers. Dunstan lay at her feet, looking up at her every now and again with concern in his old brown eyes. He struggled clumsily to his feet when alerted by sounds from behind him. Kerensa thought it was Oliver returning from the funeral. It wasn't. It was Clem Trenchard.

Rushing to her feet, she looked fearfully all around.

'Clem! What are you doing here? Oliver... he may come back at any moment.'

Clem raised his hands to still her fears.

'Don't worry. I won't stay long. I just had to see you, Kerensa.'

She looked thinner and paler than he had ever seen her before. A little girl lost in the storm of life, like the words of the hymn, and Clem loved her. He loved her more than ever and wanted to hold her, to tell her everything would be all right. He fought back a mounting desire to take her in his arms and do just that.

'Have you been crying?' he asked instead, looking at her closely.

Kerensa ran a trembling finger under each damp eye. 'Just a little. Did you go to the funeral, Clem?'

'Yes. I joined the procession on the road to Perranbarvah. I overheard the Reverend Ivey offering Sir Oliver and Sir Martin Beswetherick a glass of port so I hurried over to see you.' He moved closer to her and took Kerensa's hand. 'How are you, Kerensa? I mean, really?'

Dunstan growled jealously and sidled forward between them.

'I have everything I need, Clem,' Kerensa answered him quietly. 'You must not think of me now, but make a new life for yourself.'

'I doubt if I can ever do that,' he said softly.

'I'm so sorry.' She gripped the hand holding hers. 'I feel so terrible about what I've done to you. I can never ask you to forgive me. You look different, so unhappy, and I blame myself for putting you through this misery.'

'That doesn't matter, my love. I don't blame you, tis his fault! That, that…' Clem could not say the bitter words emblazoned on his heart. 'What I want to know, my love, is if he ill-treats you?'

Kerensa wanted to look away but could not. She knew Clem wanted to hear that Oliver was cruel to her, that then he would almost certainly plead with her to run away with him. But even a lie told to be kind would bring terrible consequences for Clem if he challenged Oliver in any way.

'Oliver demands his own way in most things, but he doesn't ill-treat me,' she said wearily, torn inside by the disappointment on Clem's face as she destroyed this forlorn straw he had clutched at. 'Not at all. Please, Clem, you must go. If he comes back and finds you here…'

He sighed deeply and jerked up his head to hide the hopeless tears that had sprung to his eyes.

'If that's what you want, Kerensa, I'll go now,' he said, persuaded only by the fearfulness she harboured for him and the entreating look in her eyes. 'But if ever you need me, send Alice for me and I'll come straight away.' He kissed her hand and Kerensa's heart missed a beat, but when he reached out to hold her she pulled away.

'Please don't, Clem. I'm another man's wife now. You must forget me.'

'I'll never do that,' he told her vehemently, kissing her hand again, 'as long as you love me I'll have a reason to carry on.'

Fresh tears sprang to her eyes and this time she did not stop Clem taking her into his arms. She held on to him closely and he buried his face in to her neck, gently caressing her hair.

'Kerensa!' Alice Ford came running towards them. 'Sir Oliver… he's riding up the carriageway now.'

Clem reluctantly let Kerensa go. It was not easy to relinquish the warm soft body he had not held for so many weeks. He had no care for Alice's presence as he took the liberty of brushing his lips against those of the girl he loved so much.

'Hurry, Clem,' Alice implored him, 'you must leave, and pray to God no one saw you come here. Don't worry about Kerensa, I'll look after her.'

'I'll hold you to that, Alice Ford,' he said grimly. He turned quickly and left the two girls alone.

–

Oliver slammed every door he passed through until he reached Kerensa in the pleasant surroundings of the sitting room that once had been his mother's and was now claimed by his wife for her own. Kerensa looked at him from her armchair in surprise. He had never before entered the room while she was there and his presence was unexpected. She was momentarily fearful that he knew Clem had visited her in the garden but he only glared irritably back at her.

'What a bloody awful afternoon!' he declared, tossing his tricorn hat to land expertly on the table next to the tray from which Alice was serving tea. Dropping down heavily in the armchair opposite Kerensa, he added moodily, 'Is there any chance of getting something to eat?'

'I'll see to it right away, m'lady,' Alice said at once. Like Ruth and Esther King, whenever possible she addressed her mistress rather than her master.

Once she left the room Oliver's eyes darted back to Kerensa.

With a dismissive wave of his hand at the tea tray he said stiffly, 'Get me a large brandy, will you?'

It was an order, not a request, and it angered Kerensa.

She snapped back, 'Have you never heard of the word "please"?'

Carefully, and deliberately slowly, Oliver placed the tips of his fingers together and studied them as though he'd never seen them before.

'Please… my dear.'

Kerensa knew the courtesy was not meant. She inwardly fumed and took her time to fetch a bottle of brandy and a glass from his study. She kept her back to him as she poured out a small measure, and did not look at him as she held out the glass.

Oliver swirled the fiery liquid around in the glass as he waited for her to sit down, then draining it in one toss of his head, held it out to her again.

'Another, if you please.' He scrutinised the second measure of brandy at his leisure, sipped it and sighed deeply. 'That's better,' he said maliciously. 'At last.'

Where Oliver was of a mind to upset her, Kerensa was equally determined in not allowing him the privilege of showing him he'd succeeded. She sat down again, sipping slowly from her cup until her anger abated.

'How were Mrs Trembath, Ted and the others?' she asked in a quiet voice.

The question brought a slightly wondering look to his face before he answered it; he marvelled at the way she had spoken, as if she had many years' experience of entertaining nobility itself to tea.

'They were distraught,' he told her. 'I don't think that she will ever come to terms with the boy's death. Nor Ted. He's taken to haunting the cliff overlooking the Cove these days.'

'I wish things were different, then people wouldn't have to resort to smuggling. Then this… the tragedy would never have happened.'

'Men indulge in freetrading for more reasons than that they happen to be poor, Kerensa. There's greed, excitement, comradeship to be found. Not to mention the pleasure of cheating a greedy government of its exorbitant taxes.'

'Why do you do it, Oliver?' Kerensa looked down into her teacup as she spoke. She knew full well of his involvement in much of the smuggling around the Mount's Bay coastline but had not talked of it to him before. She wondered, as he hesitated, had she spoken unwisely?

Oliver sank himself deeper into the armchair, his long legs stretched out across the room, and said simply, 'Because I want to. My ventures are well supervised, quicker and safer if there's no treachery afoot, and I allow violence of no kind. It's not unknown for a whole village to be slaughtered to keep secret the identity of smugglers who are little more than murderous thugs.'

Kerensa shuddered at this. She'd had no idea such a thing had ever occurred and realised how sheltered and secure her life had been in Trelynne Cove. She thought of her grandfather and wondered if he had ever used violence in such a way.

Alice entered with a tray of dainty cakes, wedges of pork and ale pie, thinly cut bread and butter, and fruit. She had to walk around Oliver's long legs to put the tray down on the table, but on the way out she left the room by skirting round the back of Kerensa's chair.

'That girl,' Oliver said, waving his brandy glass towards the door, 'she's got plenty of spirit. I like her. I hear Clem Trenchard has taken to hanging about her now. Did you know?'

Kerensa coloured and looked out of the window. 'No, I did not,' she said drily.

Oliver enjoyed these games of cat and mouse he frequently played with her. He enjoyed the way he could change her youthful expression from curiosity to delight, from hurt to relief or vice versa, by just one carefully chosen remark. If Kerensa chose to laugh at him with her maid, it didn't hurt to keep her in her place.

He studied her profile. She was as beautiful from this angle as she was face on and he resolved to have portraits painted of her one day from all angles. Oliver became serious as he thought about the reason why she had turned her face away from him – the mention of Clem Trenchard. Did she still yearn for him? What went on inside that lovely young head of hers? Would he be able to probe that deeply? Perhaps not, but then it didn't really matter... did it?

As the sun continued its journey upwards through the sky, the shadows in the room deepened. Kerensa watched the last chink of sunlight disappear from the corner of the window.

'Nathan says the tawny owl can be released tonight,' she said conversationally. 'Apparently it wasn't too badly hurt after all.'

He wasn't listening to her. And he had forgotten all about the harrowing funeral as he remembered how soft her body was against his, how tightly she closed her eyes and clung to his neck when they came together. He watched her mouth moving as she spoke and with a fierce urgency wanted to kiss it, to smother her words, to feel the soft sensation of her warm lips. He quenched his immediate desire, deciding to wait until later and increase the pleasure to be taken at his leisure.

'Oliver?'

'Mmm?'

A puzzled frown had appeared above her eyes at his silence.

'I… I was saying, it's a good thing the tawny owl is well again.'

'Yes, it is,' he agreed with her.

Kerensa was confused. She thought she recognised the look in his dark eyes, but in her naivety she wasn't sure.

He changed the subject suddenly. 'So what were you doing holding one of Samuel Drannock's brats the other day?'

'Oh, you mean little Jack. He was fretting so I offered to take him from his mother for a while. She had Charles to see to.'

'I noticed she will be in childbed again quite soon. The Drannocks will be as good at breeding as the Kings.'

Kerensa recalled Mrs Tregonning's similar remark. 'How many children have they got, I wonder?'

'Five or six at least,' Oliver said, picking up a wedge of the pork and ale pie and breaking it slowly in two. 'Like children… babies, do you, Kerensa?'

'Oh, yes, very much so.'

'Good.' Without taking his eyes from her face, Oliver bit into one half of the wedge of pie and chewed it slowly, leaving Kerensa in no doubt what he had in mind.

Morley and Florrie Trenchard were more than relieved when Clem took to walking Alice Ford back to the Manor from the regular Bible classes held at Jeb Bray's cottage. They had been deeply worried about the effect on their elder son when Kerensa Trelynne married Sir Oliver. They knew how shaken Clem had been when the girl whom they had come to love themselves had actually gone through with the marriage.

Morley had remonstrated many times with Clem over his moroseness and lackadaisical attitude to his work on the farm. Spending time with the cheery Alice meant he no longer hung restlessly about the farmyard or vanished with Charity his dog for long secretive hours. Perhaps now his parents' prayers were answered and Clem would be bringing a bride home to Trecath-en Farm after all.

Alice was excited that it was her Clem sought to sit next to in the miner's cottage, and unlike Matthias Renfree, was unaware he paid attention to nothing or no one while there. She delighted in his company at other times and didn't seem to notice when he was quiet and sullen.

Clem spoke little unless it was to ask questions about Kerensa. Other matters held small interest for him.

'Does Kerensa mind not going to the Bible meetings any more?' Clem asked. He and Alice were strolling side by side in the evening sunshine, following the path running in twists and turns beside a narrow tinkling river on Trecath-en pasture land.

'No, I don't think so,' Alice replied, pulling off the heads of long grasses as they moved along, 'she gets on so well with the Reverend Ivey anyway. He's such a sweet old soul, isn't he? Besides, whichever way you look at it, we worship the same God, don't we.'

'Does she see much of the Reverend, then?'

'Usually once a week.'

'At the Parsonage or the Manor?'

'Depends.' Alice went on gaily answering his questions. She was always more pleased when Clem was talking instead of having to draw him out of one of his prolonged silences. 'It's been at the Manor since young Davey Trembath's funeral, she's been rather upset by that.'

'Is she all right?' he asked quickly.

'Oh, yes. I think she's just waiting for things to settle down a bit, then she'll be out and about again.'

'She looked so pale when I saw her last.'

'Well, it may be she's pregnant, Clem.'

'What!' he exclaimed at the thoughtless remark, his arms held in mid-air in the act of throwing a stick for Charity. 'Is she?' he demanded, with an anguished look at Alice.

'No, I don't think so. Forget I mentioned it, it was silly to say such a thing,' Alice said meekly. Then wisely changing the subject she asked, 'How's your family keeping, Clem?'

'They're well enough,' he said moodily, finally throwing the stick for the impatient dog.

'And Kenver? I've never met your brother, he sounds very nice.'

'He is, but what makes you say that?' Clem said, ignoring her hint to be invited to his home.

'Kerensa told me about him,' she replied, 'she sounds very fond of him by the way she spoke of him.'

Clem sighed heavily as he searched about for another stick to throw.

'That's another tragedy that happened when Kerensa married that man,' he said angrily. 'Kenver adored her. She'd spend hours sitting on his bed talking to him. I believe he misses her as much as I do.' He hurled a stick away with great force. 'Kerensa shouldn't have had to change anything if she didn't want to!'

'A good wife follows her husband, though, Clem,' Alice said pointedly to his face, then turned away to watch Charity come bounding back. She added in a small voice, 'I know I would.'

For the first time Clem looked critically at Alice Ford. She had none of Kerensa's grace and beauty, nor the ethereal quality to be found in Rosina Pearce, nor even the clear skin of the King sisters. But her hair was full of shining bouncing curls and if a man troubled himself to give her a second look he could find other becoming things about her. Her eyes were hazel brown, a shade lighter than her hair, her mouth pink and inviting, and her young body moulded into generous curves. Alice was sweet and honest, and with a start Clem realised he actually did enjoy being with her.

Alice was the closest person to Kerensa now and she readily chatted about her and the new life they shared in the Manor, and although it usually annoyed him to have to sift through all she said to get the information he wanted in the first place, there had been the odd moment when her cheerfulness had made him smile. Meeting her gave him a reason to carry on, it gave him something positive to cling to in his miserable existence. He knew he should be grateful to her for this small measure of comfort; he received none from anybody else. His mother and grandmother said it was 'time he pulled himself together', his father was at the end of his patience with him. Matthias Renfree didn't know what to say to him any more. The rest of the parish had lost interest in him and speculated only on how the Pengarron marriage was working out and how soon an heir would be born. Only Alice Ford tried to understand how he felt, how he suffered, and was willing to befriend him in the way he desired at the moment.

Clem threw Charity's stick again and on impulse held out his hand to Alice. Shyly she held out hers in return and Clem took a step towards her to claim it. Her hand was warm and alive and its touch brought back feeling to his body, sensations he'd not felt for many weeks.

They walked on, hand in hand, to the shade of a clump of elm trees.

'It'll be getting dark soon,' Alice said, 'we should be making our way back.'

But Clem didn't want to go back yet, back to the cosy farmhouse where the rest of his family were contentedly getting on with their own lives. It was in too stark a contrast to his belief that life was not worth living. This was one of the few times he didn't want to be alone, and Alice was the best company he had had for many weeks.

'Not yet, let's sit down here for a while,' he said persuasively.

'The ground'll be getting damp,' she said doubtfully.

Clem took off his jacket and laid it out on the ground.

'Just for a little while… please, Alice,' he appealed.

With a bright smile, she said, 'All right, Clem.'

She made herself comfortable and he sat down beside her.

'I don't want to go back yet,' he said quietly, looking up at the bunches of leaf-like fruits on the branches overhead. 'Not for ages.'

He put his arm around her shoulders and Alice gingerly leaned against him. Neither felt the need to speak. Alice watched the sky quickly darken, with a warm feeling in the pit of her stomach now that Clem was taking an interest in her at last. For him it felt good to hold someone, someone warm and soft, vital and alive. He took Alice's hand and held it against his cheek and she snuggled in closer to him. A choir of tinkling water, chirping birds, and a breeze rustling through the trees, lulled them into a sense of peacefulness.

Alice turned inside Clem's arm to see if he'd fallen asleep. He met her eyes and rubbed the hand he was holding against her cheek then brought it back to his.

'We'll have to go soon, Clem.'

'When are you expected back?'

'I have no duties tonight. They are away at Sir Martin's, but Ruth and Esther will wonder where I am if I'm not back soon.'

'Five more minutes won't make much difference,' he said, placing his hand under her chin, very gently. He looked at her for a moment then kissed her with the lightest of pressure. The response from her lips was immediate and he pulled her into the circle of his arms. Alice moved against his body as she slid her arms, one behind his back, the other around his neck. Her movements brought his body to life with a shudder, every nerve quickening in exquisite pain.

Clem had thought this could not happen to him, not now. He wanted to kiss and hold Alice, he wanted her warmth, her nearness, he wanted her to bring life itself to his body, he wanted to drain her of her spirit and make him whole again. He had no power to stop the overwhelming force of his great need as he held her so tightly in his arms.

Alice panicked and tried to break free, but he soothed her with softly spoken words as he eased her down beneath him, misleading her with kisses of exaggerated lightness. His fingers found the laces of her stays and he pulled roughly at them.

'Don't, Clem,' she gasped between his kisses, 'let me get up.'

He didn't seem to hear her. His breathing came in short bursts, his mouth forcing hers open, passion overcoming his more sensitive feelings.

Alice struggled violently. 'No, Clem! No!' she cried out in fear. 'Not like this... please!'

Removing his hand from her bare flesh, he gave a cry of deep anguish.

'I'm sorry, Alice,' he moaned, 'forgive me. It's just that... I want you so much. Do you understand?'

'Oh, Clem,' she said softly, love and pity chasing away her fears. She reached up and brushed the strands of damp fair hair away from his forehead. 'I do understand what you've been going through. But I can't be Kerensa. She's lost to you forever. Just give me the chance and I will make you happy. Just let me try, Clem. Please let me try.'

He knew she would be willing now. It was almost dark. He could pretend in the dark. Pretend her hair was auburn red and curled under on her shoulders. Pretend her body was smaller, daintier, softer. Pretend she was finally his...

Alice raised her head to meet his next kiss, blissfully unaware, that Clem was making love to Kerensa Pengarron.

Chapter 9

Before leaving for an overnight stay on the occasion of Sir Martin's next supper party, Oliver showed Kerensa some of the Pengarron jewels. Earlier in the day he had selected the pieces he thought the most appropriate for her from the magnificent collection kept in the bank vault at Marazion. The collection had seen many additions with every passing decade until his mother's death. With no lady in the Manor house to wear them after that, they had laid incarcerated in the bank vault for years.

Kerensa was amazed by the jewels. Never before had she seen so many precious stones, many in large and elaborate settings. She had no wish to possess any of them but had always appreciated things of beauty and couldn't help but feel excited knowing that the sparkling gems, the gold and silver, laid out carefully in their wrappings on her bed, were for her exclusive use. She tried on various items of the jewellery, separately and in various groups. Then, when she was sure no one was about, except for a delicate five-stoned crystal necklace which she set aside, she tried them all on together. They felt heavy and she walked extra-cautiously and stood self-consciously in front of a full-length mirror to see the effect of all the finery at her throat, lying over the stomacher of her gown, reaching halfway up her arms, crowding every thumb and finger and even her head. She was overawed by the sparkle of the deep reds, blues and greens as the precious stones were caught in the candlelight as she turned sideways to view herself from all angles.

Becoming afraid she might lose one of these valuable baubles she laid them back on the bed, and spent so much time just looking that although he had no care if he kept people waiting, Oliver put his head round the bedroom door and chided her for making them late to leave for the night's entertainment. Kerensa did not care about his chastisement and didn't care if she was making them late. She had no fears about the forthcoming event. She hadn't asked to become Sir Oliver Pengarron's wife and felt no obligation to impress, or to fit in with, the people she was about to meet tonight. And as it seemed that Oliver had dropped the more unsavoury acquaintances he had previously associated with since the wedding day, perhaps some of them wouldn't be too dreadful. Anyway, if they didn't like her, it was Oliver's problem, not hers.

Kerensa had in fact decided to wear the crystal necklace tonight as a perfect complement to her gown of deep apricot and the discreet matching feather set in her gleaming upswept hair. Putting the other jewels back in their small chest and securing it in a locked cubby hole Oliver had shown her in her dressing room, she found she was unable to clasp the crystal necklace and ran downstairs to Oliver who was waiting by the main door for her. Cloaked and hatted already, he drummed his fingers on his arm as he looked at his pocket watch.

'Do you want Barney Taylor to take root on the carriage seat?' he said sternly.

'I can't manage the clasp,' she explained, unperturbed by his ill humour as she held out the necklace to him. 'Will you do it for me, please, Oliver?'

'Where is Alice?' he asked impatiently, breathing down her neck while he fastened the necklace.

Kerensa turned back to face him. 'I told her she could go to the Bible classes.' And with that she picked up her cloak and gloves.

'You did what! We are staying overnight at Martin's house. Alice was supposed to come with us.'

'I don't need her,' Kerensa insisted, 'and she looks forward to the classes,' she went on firmly, tying the ribbons on her cloak into a neat bow.

Oliver bit back a further angry remark. With her hair swirled on top of her head apart from two tiny ringlets nestling behind her ears, Kerensa looked so young, so full of sparkling youth and vitality.

'You are beautiful,' he said huskily, pulling on one of the ringlets. 'My mother favoured that crystal neckline too.' He held out his arm to her. 'Are you nervous?' he asked.

'No,' Kerensa replied as she took his arm. 'It doesn't matter to me whether Sir Martin's friends like me or not. I have no desire to mix with the gentry and if they find me common all the better, I'm not ashamed of my class and upbringing.'

'Really, my dear? I think, Kerensa, this should prove to be a most interesting evening.' Oliver's eyes held a twinkle of anticipation as he opened the door.

–

There were about ten people in the large plushly decorated drawing room when they entered, Oliver displaying Kerensa on his arm to the occupants. Fat Sir Martin hastened across the room to greet them.

'Ah, there you are Oliver. Late as usual, dratted boy. And Kerensa my little one, I may call you Kerensa, eh? I say, you do look ravishing tonight, it's a small wonder to me Oliver hasn't eaten you up yet!' The excited elderly gentleman planted a wet slurping kiss on the back of Kerensa's hand.

'Thank you for the compliment, Sir Martin,' she smiled at him as one would an amusing child, 'and of course you may call me Kerensa.' Oliver looked bemused at her confident reply but Kerensa was not surprised at herself. She was not going to allow anyone to intimidate her tonight.

'Good, good, and you must call me Martin. All my friends do, and I'm sure we will be friends eh, Kerensa?' he finished off with a loud bellow of laughter.

Some of Sir Martin's other guests had gathered round and he introduced them to Kerensa while slipping a sweaty podgy hand around her waist. Kerensa did not move out of Sir Martin's range, if Oliver found his arm around her permissible she would not object.

Oliver smiled down indulgently. He knew his late friend's father for a harmless old man of bawdy humour, incapable of actually participating in the subject he talked of more than any other.

The guests included Thomas Cole and his haughty looking wife Sarah, John and Alfred Sarrison, who were members of the mine consortium with Sir Martin, both grinned like puppets to reveal porcelain false teeth, and Ralph Harrt, a middle aged magistrate with a severe squint and the Master of the local Hunt. All greeted Kerensa courteously but with undisguised curiosity, but Ralph Harrt was very cool towards Oliver. Kerensa assumed the reason was Oliver's freetrading activities, since they were common knowledge, but others in the room could have told her it was because of Oliver's refusal to join the Hunt. On more than one occasion, he had been reported to have rescued a fox from its pursuers. Any fox that raided a Pengarron chicken house was tracked down and cleanly shot, rather than cruelly torn to pieces.

An elegant bewigged gentleman and his heavily pregnant wife were the next to come forward. Warm and friendly with their introductions, Kerensa was surprised to learn they were Sir Martin's son and heir William, and Rachael his wife. William was as short as his father, but as thin as the other was fat.

'It's a pleasure to meet you at last, Lady Pengarron,' he said jovially. 'I do hope you will enjoy your evening with us.'

'We were sorry to have missed your wedding, my dears,' put in the plain faced Rachael, 'but William was away in London on business and I,' she patted her swollen stomach in explanation, 'was not feeling too well on that particular day.'

'Well you are a picture of radiant beauty now,' said Oliver gallantly and he affectionately kissed her sallow cheek.

'You flatter me, Oliver. It's quite untrue, of course, for alas I never look my best when in this happy condition. Now,' she said to Kerensa, 'I'm sure we're all on first name terms, aren't we? May I suggest Kerensa we leave my disreputable father-in-law and our dear husbands to talk business or to play cards and retire somewhere comfortable to sit down.'

'You're not taking her away already are you? Damn me, Rachael, I've only just got my arm round her,' laughed Sir Martin. 'Go on then my little one, off you go to your gossiping, but I beg the pleasure of taking you into supper.'

'It will be my pleasure… Martin,' Kerensa said, delighting him with a smile and a curtsey.

Linking her arm through Kerensa's, Rachael led the girl to two chairs by an open window.

'That's better.' Rachael spread the full skirt of her gown as she sat down and unfolded her fan. She smiled understandingly as Kerensa copied her, the girl's movements coming naturally. 'Old Marty's quite fallen in love with you Kerensa, he'll speak of nothing else for weeks now.'

'I can see why Oliver is so fond of him, of Sir Martin,' Kerensa replied.

'You'll have to get used to it, you know,' Rachael said brightly.

'Used to what?' Kerensa was puzzled.

'Men falling in love with you of course, my dear, and desiring you. But I don't suppose you realise for a moment just how appealing to men you are,' Rachael informed, 'I never normally have any trouble keeping William in line, but he's hardly taken his eyes off you since you arrived.'

'I don't know what to say to that,' Kerensa said, looking awkwardly about the room. 'Is Captain Solomon expected tonight?'

'Not tonight, my dear. So you've met Hezekiah, have you?'

'Yes… after the wedding. He was the only person who was civil to me after the ceremony.'

Rachael's brow wrinkled with momentary concern. 'Don't expect that man to fall in love with you though, Kerensa. He's as cold as marble.'

Kerensa looked curiously at the other woman but Rachael had a mind to move on to something else.

'Don't take any notice of those two,' she said, having observed Sarah Cole tittering behind her fan to the only other woman in the room. 'Everyone knows Thomas Cole would not have married that ferret-faced Sarah Sarrison if she wasn't in a certain condition at the time.'

'Sarrison? Is she a relative of those two elderly gentlemen?'

'Their niece actually. Shares the same ridiculous grin if one is bored enough to watch her long enough to spot it. I don't care for her company myself, but poor Thomas has to cart her along with him every now and then. She probably found out you were coming here tonight and wouldn't be left at home.'

A footman approached them with a tray of wine glasses, but informed in advance of Kerensa's preference for not drinking alcohol, Rachael waved him away.

'Who is the other lady with Mistress Cole?' Kerensa asked. 'I haven't been introduced to her. Or to the gentleman standing behind Oliver at the moment.'

The gentleman in question was a young man in his early twenties, tastefully dressed in fawn and black.

'That's Josephine Courtis, the widow of a wealthy banker. She must hate you, my dear, she had an eye on Oliver for herself. Though I can't see why, she's most definitely not the sort to take his fancy. As you can see, she's a good ten years older to begin with. She was furious at not receiving an invitation to your wedding.'

'Does Sir Martin like her?' asked Kerensa.

'Marty can't bear the woman, but she's an enthusiastic card player and can afford to lose heavily.'

'I see. And the gentleman?'

'He's Josephine's half-brother, Peter Blake, and you can take it from me he is no true gentleman. He may possess a rather beautiful countenance, but I'd advise any lady, young or old, to avoid him.' Rachael gave a merry laugh and put her hand on Kerensa's arm, 'Oh my goodness. I sound more like a chaperone than a hostess. Well, I suppose I ought to introduce you to Josephine Courtis then you can make up your own mind about her, my dear.'

–

While Kerensa was being introduced to the widow, Peter Blake had managed to attract Oliver's attention.

'My congratulations on your recent marriage, Sir Oliver.'

'Thank you, Blake,' Oliver replied stonily, looking above the younger man's head.

Peter Blake had once served in the 32nd Regiment of Foot, the same regiment as Oliver. Oliver had resigned his commission eight years before to run the Pengarron Estate on his father's death, leaving with honour and distinction. Blake had been dishonourably discharged several years later over a scandal involving a serving maid of the royal court. As far as Oliver was concerned, Blake had disgraced all Cornish men, including Arthur Beswetherick, who had served King and country with fervent loyalty. He despised Peter Blake and made no secret of it.

Oliver had been proud to show Kerensa off to his friends tonight. From his earliest observations of her since their marriage he was confident she would not let him down in manners or appearance, that she would not set out deliberately to embarrass him and make a laughing stock of him before his peers. He was pleased to be able to flaunt her youth, grace and beauty as proof of his winning the better part of the bargain he had made with her grandfather, as well as enhancing his reputation of being the most unconventional gentleman in Cornwall. He was not only territorial about Kerensa, he felt protective towards her now. He didn't like Peter Blake mentioning her. If he had his way Blake wouldn't even be allowed to look at her.

'Your wife looks most charming, sir,' he said, looking across the room where Kerensa was talking to his half-sister Josephine Courtis, and another woman.

'She is,' Oliver snapped. 'Now, if you'll excuse me, Blake?' With that he stalked off, but Blake seemed unruffled by his ungracious behaviour.

At the earliest opportunity Rachael Beswetherick disengaged Kerensa from the other women and they took seats together. Kerensa was feeling hot and was grateful for the pleasant breezes drifting lightly through the open window, bringing with them the fragrant scent of spring flowers. She lightly waved her fan, and Rachael sent a footman to bring two glasses of cold spring water.

She squeezed Kerensa's hand. 'You did very well against those two's acid tongues. They don't come any worse than that.'

Kerensa said, 'I didn't expect to enjoy myself, but I am.'

'You don't seem at all nervous,' Rachael remarked, peering at her. 'I expected to find you a timid little thing, quaking in your shoes.'

'Marrying Oliver was such an overwhelming event, nothing seems daunting to me now.'

'Well, my old grandmother used to say all the airs and graces and fancy manners in the world doesn't make a real lady. You're a natural, my dear.'

Rachael moved in as close as her bulging middle would allow. 'Tell me, Kerensa, how did you get on on your wedding night?'

'Well, I…' Kerensa blushed furiously. She was not particularly shy or prudish by nature, but her Methodist-influenced upbringing had led her to believe you shouldn't discuss such an intimate thing, especially with someone you had only just met.

'Oh, my dear!' Rachael laughed and covered the girl's hand with hers. 'I didn't mean to cause you any embarrassment. It's many a year since I have felt such shyness. He's very good though, Oliver, isn't he? And so handsome. I've lain with him many a time, you know.'

Kerensa's eyes widened as her embarrassment turned to shock. She didn't know if Oliver was 'good' in the marriage bed, she had no previous experience to compare him with as Rachael had. She did not dread his approaches as she had on their wedding night, there was nothing about him that frightened her now, and she did not dislike the other times when he seemed only to want to show her a little affection. She supposed she ought not to be shocked to have met someone he had been with in the past, he had not stinted himself in the amorous side of life, but she looked with hostility at the two other women in the room and wondered if they were past conquests of his too.

'Before I married William, of course,' added Rachael, patting Kerensa's hand.

But although she had felt an immediate liking for this outspokenly risqué lady and was not unhappy to be in her company, as far as Kerensa was concerned Rachael's last remark didn't make it right that she had slept with her husband.

Left on his own Peter Blake moved slowly about the room, making a pretence of admiring the numerous ornaments and valuable paintings dotted about. He drank several glasses of wine, indulging in only the occasional scrap of small talk with the people around him. He stopped behind a towering green plant and pulled aside the foliage to observe the new Lady Pengarron. When Kerensa laughed softly at something Rachael Beswetherick said to her, Blake very slowly ran his tongue along his thin lower lip.

Kerensa left the supper party shortly after twelve-thirty. The aged Judith Teague had waited up for her, insisting on helping her out of her gown to prepare for the night's stay, saying it was a pleasure to wait on a lady again so long after Lady Ameline's death. Judith treated Kerensa as though she'd been born into the gentry. The next hour was spent in pleasant chatter with the old servant and her reminiscences of the Beswetherick family.

'Hasn't changed one little bit, Sir Oliver hasn't, m'lady. Always dashing about he was, getting everyone else in a proper dither the times he came to stay at Tolwithrick with young Master Arthur.' Judith sighed happily at the memories.

Kerensa was deeply curious about Arthur Beswetherick but had for some reason always felt it unwise to ask Oliver about his late friend. Judith Teague was the ideal person to put her unanswered questions to.

'How long is it since Master Arthur died, Judith?'

'All of ten years now, m'lady. He and Sir Oliver was away fighting the French alongside of the King, but only Sir Oliver came back,' Judith said, her expression faraway. 'I believe it was a worse blow to him than to the Beswetherick family. Thinking about it, perhaps Master Arthur's death changed something in Sir Oliver. Sometimes he'd look so lost and lonely.'

Kerensa nodded her understanding of this. There were occasions she had noticed when Oliver would gaze at nothing and a momentary look of pain would appear on his face from somewhere deep inside him.

'They must have been very close friends,' she murmured.

'Inseparable,' Judith agreed.

When the maid retired for the night Kerensa lay back on the sumptuous bed. Sir Martin's guest rooms were, like everywhere else in the recently built house, ornately decorated throughout. She mulled over the events of the evening, getting them clear in her mind so that she could tell Alice, Ruth and Esther all about them. How she had made a friend of the loud-voiced Rachael, the details of the gowns of the other ladies, their jewels, their wigs and their mannerisms. And the elegantly dressed men, some bewigged and powdered.

There had been a mountainous supply of food, and liquor enough to quench the thirst of every miner in West Cornwall, served by grave-faced, white-and-gold liveried servants. But the thing she had enjoyed most of all was the excellent performance of the band of musicians. When the gentlemen, with the exception of Peter Blake, drew aside to the card tables, Kerensa would gladly have stayed longer to listen to the beautiful sounds. But when Rachael had been forced to retire with rapidly swelling ankles, she had not felt compelled to remain in the company of Sarah Cole, or under the disquieting glance of the remaining young man.

She was still awake when Oliver came to bed. Surprised to see her eyes open in the candlelight, he whispered, 'I thought you'd be asleep. Are you ill?'

'No. I've just been lying here thinking,' she replied. 'Is it very late?'

'Only about two-thirty. Here, I have something for you.' He threw a leather pouch to land on the bed beside her. 'I managed only a modest win at the table tonight. As you had a very successful evening, it's yours.'

Kerensa sat up, picked up the pouch and pulled open the draw-strings. She tipped a pile of clinking coins on to the top bed-cover. 'There must be fifty pounds here!' she gasped.

'Fifty-three and seventeen shillings to be exact. Spend it as you will.'

Kerensa couldn't think of anything to say except, 'Thank you.' It was more money than she had ever seen before at one time and she had no idea what she would do with it. In a stunned silence she dropped the coins, one by one, back into the pouch and reached over to place it on a nearby cabinet. When she turned back Oliver was casting aside the last of his clothes to add to all the others he had previously strewn about the floor. Annoyed by this Kerensa fought the urge to jump out of bed, pick them all up and fold them tidily. He climbed naked into the bed beside her. She thought this most unseemly, particularly in someone else's house, but she knew he would only laugh if she spoke of it.

'So, my dear,' he said, settling himself back comfortably with an arm behind his head, 'you got on very well with Rachael. Martin was sure you would. She's a good woman, is Rachael. Actually she's properly Lady Rachael, her father being the Earl of Nansavellion.'

'She doesn't behave as if she's the daughter of an earl. That is, not as I would have expected. She made me laugh a lot. I like her. She invited me to stay at Tolwithrick.'

'Did she? Good. Every time I see Rachael she seems to be with child. Goodness knows how many this will make now, I've lost count.'

A feeling of disappointment welled up inside Kerensa. She wanted to have a child herself, to help her forget the loss she still felt over Clem. To obscure some of the overwhelming presence of Oliver in her life but also – somewhat contrarily – to provide him with the heir he so greatly desired to carry on the Pengarron name.

Very quietly she said, 'Nine. Rachael told me this child will be their ninth.'

'Ninth! As many as that, is it?' Sensing the change in her mood Oliver turned on his side. Resting on his elbow he looked down at her. In the glow of the candlelight and the silvery fingers of a pale moon stealing in through the window, he made out the tautness of her small features. 'You'll wrinkle up like Beatrice if you pull that face for long,' he teased her.

Kerensa met his gaze, catching her breath with a sense of wonder. At the far reaches of her mind she had always found him physically attractive, had unaccountably been drawn to him. Looking at him now, with the moonlight gleaming on his finely muscled body, perfect in its line and balance, the full realisation of these feelings swept over her. And for the first time she was not disturbed that she could be so easily overwhelmed by him.

He ran a finger down her cheek, then kissed her forehead. He kissed her eyes, the tip of her nose, the soft skin behind her ears.

Brushing his lips in gentle circles on hers, he pulled her nightdress from her shoulder then nestled his mouth into the well at the base of her neck. His hands traced the soft contours of her body, lingering in the places that made her tremble.

It pleased Oliver that she now seemed to find his attentions not unwelcome, with each succeeding time he came to her she tried to please him more and more, abandoning herself to his touch. Tonight he sensed something new in Kerensa and a thrill of pleasure ran through him at the thought that her desire matched his.

She stopped him suddenly with a restraining hand on his shoulder. 'Rachael said…'

But he kept kissing her and she spoke breathlessly in the short moments his mouth sought her elsewhere.

'…that… you… and… her…'

He took her hand from his shoulder and slid it round his neck. 'What did Rachael say?' He stopped kissing her long enough for her to tell him.

'She said that you and she had been lovers,' Kerensa got out at last.

Oliver grinned. 'Did she indeed?' He planted a tiny kiss on each of her parted lips. 'Well, that, my pretty love, was all a very long time ago.' Kerensa had given little thought to Oliver's past affairs, before tonight, but lying in a room next to one of his ex-mistresses, yet another new feeling, awesome in its intensity, grew inside her. Lady Rachael Beswetherick, her new friend and a woman she liked and felt comfortable with, became at that moment an object of distrust and animosity. It would have surprised and amused Oliver to know she was jealous – jealous of a plain sallow-faced woman almost twice her age, heavily pregnant, and safely married to someone else for a good many years.

He reached out to pull a candelabrum closer to the edge of the cabinet.

'Are you still interested in her?' Kerensa asked fiercely, watching his face closely in the clearer illumination.

'In Rachael! I've hardly given the woman a thought in years. Why do you ask?'

Kerensa didn't answer. She gripped the hair at the back of his neck with both hands and, pressing her body to his, raised her head until her mouth demanded his in an act of definite possessiveness.

–

Kerensa gave the greater part of Oliver's gambling winnings to the Reverend Ivey to distribute among the parish's poor and needy. She had listened to too many harsh warnings from the likes of Matthias Renfree, and indeed in the Reverend's sermons, on the evils of gambling to feel it right to spend the money on herself or on things for the Manor. With the remaining money she paid a visit to Mistress Gluyas' dressmaking shop to buy a wealth of materials, sewing silks and threads to make baby clothes.

In the daytime she took her needlework out into the gardens, either to sit under the cherry, apple and pear trees of the orchards, or on the steps of the large fountain with its naked cherub at the front of the house. At other times she sought out the company of Jake Angove in the potting shed or beside the flower beds where he would be giving attention to clumps of daffodils, tulips, grape hyacinths and the many other flowers and shrubs that grew in abundance under his care. Jake was always pleased to see her and have her chat happily to him as she sewed, Dunstan sleeping peacefully at her feet.

Alone in the evenings, when the daylight began to fade, Kerensa stitched and embroidered by the light of a myriad candle. She felt it prudent to keep the growing bundle of baby's clothes she was making away from Oliver lest he think they were for use at the Manor. Many times she held out a little garment to view her work critically then clutched it in her lap and wished it was for herself and not another woman. She would feel melancholy for a short time, then picking up her needle with a smile would resume her work. At least she could make new clothes for a baby who otherwise would wear nothing but ragged pass downs – and surely the day would come…

She chose a clear morning in late April to take a dozen of the completed garments over to Perranbarvah. On this occasion she rode on her own pony, Kernick, a sleek chestnut chosen for her by Oliver from the Ker-an-Mor stud quite recently. Kernick was solid and dependable and Kerensa held him at a slow trot as she rode to the little fishing village. The sun shone brightly in competition with the golden blaze of the gorse bushes. More gold came from the wide splash of celandines and dandelions. In sharp contrast, the purple heads of wild violets stood out against the subdued shades of yellow, pink and white sweetly scented primroses.

Under the patient instruction of Jack and Nathan, Kerensa had quickly become an able rider. She was in a light-hearted mood, and listened with joy to the caw of the rooks and carrion crows, the songs of the swallows and the soaring songflight of a skylark, gloried in the impressive aerobatic displays of a lapwing, as she trotted along. As she closed in on Perranbarvah her eye was caught by the flight of an elegant kittiwake and a fulmar gliding on stiff wings on soaring air currents.

As she arrived at the small stable of the Parsonage, Ben Rosevidney, the Reverend Ivey's only manservant, hurried forward to help her dismount. Ben, a shy bent-over man of fifty, deaf and dumb from birth, trebled up as a groom, gardener and sexton. He took his cap off to Kerensa and with his widest grin pointed up to the sun to remark on the day's warm weather.

'Yes, Ben,' she agreed, speaking clearly for him to read her lips. 'It's a really fine day. Is the Reverend at home?'

Ben shook his head.

'Is Mrs Tregonning in her kitchen?'

Ben pointed to the church which Mrs Tregonning had entered only a short time before to do her cleaning.

'I'm going down to the village, Ben,' Kerensa said, pointing down to the cottages. 'I'll be back quite soon.'

He nodded emphatically and handed her the parcel from Kernick's back. She thanked him heartily, and still grinning Ben led Kernick away.

Kerensa walked quickly down to the village with light springy steps. She'd decided against wearing her riding habit, dressing in simple clothes so as not to stand out amongst the fishermen's wives and daughters.

Arriving unexpectedly at the Drannock cottage she sent Jenifer into a whirl of agitated activity. She invited Kerensa inside at once. Despite the warm weather the inside of the cottage was dark, damp and chilled. The furniture was sparse and the building consisted of no more than two cramped rooms, which at night would be lit by cheap, ill-smelling candles.

Jenifer hastily tried to gather up discarded clothes and dirty dishes.

'I had no idea you would pay me a visit, my lady. I have been unwell of late and as you can see, I am rather behind with my housework,' she said, moving heavily about.

'Please don't worry on my account,' Kerensa said quickly. 'It was wrong of me not to ask you if I could call on you first, but I've made these things for little Jack and the coming baby, and wanted to bring them over straight away.'

Jenifer wiped her hands up and down her skirt. She hadn't noticed the parcel Kerensa was holding and eyed it with disbelief and anticipation.

'Well, I'm sure that's very kind of you, my lady. I… I don't know what to say.'

'You don't have to say anything. Please, just take them,' Kerensa said, as embarrassed as Jenifer was. 'I was always used to being busy… before… it's been good for me to be occupied.'

It felt strange to the girl to be giving charity to a woman who had once held a higher station in life than she herself, a criminal's granddaughter. Mrs Tregonning had told Kerensa that Jenifer Drannock was the daughter of Joshua Mildern, a ship's chandler at Marazion. When Jenifer, a once beautiful girl of whom Joshua had nursed high hopes, had fallen pregnant to Samuel Drannock, a poor fisherman, Joshua had turned his back on her for good. It was a sad story, but one Mrs Tregonning told with relish.

Kerensa held her breath. Jenifer had not spoken a word or moved for several moments, and she was afraid she had given offence. Then with a gracious smile Jenifer stepped forward and accepted the parcel.

'Please sit yourself down, my lady, if you have the time to stay. I'll call Bartholomew, my eldest son, to fetch fresh water to make tea. That is, if you'd care for some?'

Kerensa could not hide her delight. 'I'd like to stay very much. Thank you for inviting me, Mrs Drannock.'

'It's you that deserves thanks for your kindness. And, please, if you'd like to, call me Jenifer.'

Cautiously shooing a scruffy tabby cat from the chair nearest to her, Kerensa sat down. Shouting loudly at the door to summon her eldest son, Jenifer woke her youngest. Jack Drannock bawled from his wooden-box crib. Kerensa had not noticed him before, lying in the fresh air under the open window.

'Can I pick him up?' she asked hopefully.

Jenifer nodded, coming back from the door. 'He can be such a bad-tempered little mite. You are the only one I've known him to be good with.'

'Hello, Jack,' Kerensa said when she had the baby in her arms. 'Remember me?'

He stopped crying at once. He rubbed his eyes with tight fists and stared at her for a moment before a sunny smile spread across his thin puckered face in answer to her question.

While cooing to Jack, Kerensa looked ruefully at her hand.

'I'm afraid he's more than a bit wet.'

'He always is when he wakes up,' Jenifer smiled. 'Give him to me for a moment and I'll change him.'

'I'll do it for you,' Kerensa volunteered eagerly.

Jenifer smiled again. 'Have you done it before?'

'No, but I think I will manage all right.'

'There's some clean napkins there by your chair,' Jenifer said, sitting her heavy body gratefully down. Putting the parcel on her knees she unwrapped it, giving the clothes her full attention as she lifted them up one by one, so as not to embarrass the girl in her efforts to make the wriggling baby clean and dry.

Kerensa had laid Jack very carefully on the wide table. After a struggle to keep the active baby still she successfully replaced a clean tattered square of rough cloth for the soaking wet one between his thin white legs. Jack kicked and tugged at her hair throughout, at one time scattering items off the table on to the floor, before Kerensa triumphantly picked him up and settled him comfortably on her lap.

Jenifer glanced up and saw the happiness in the girl's face as Kerensa cuddled Jack closely against her and kissed both his cheeks.

'Well, that's your first napkin change,' she said kindly. 'I can't remember how many I've done.'

Kerensa's face was aglow. 'I'm hoping to put the practice to good use for myself,' she admitted.

Jenifer felt she had no right to ask the question burning in her mind. Instead she said, 'These clothes are lovely, and so well made. Did you sew them yourself?'

Kerensa nodded. 'I did most of the work on them. You aren't offended, are you? I mean, I didn't...'

'It's quite all right,' Jenifer answered kindly, 'I think it's very kind of you and I'm grateful. Some of the clothes will be big enough to fit Charles too. He and Jack, and my daughters, Naomi and Hannah, are all on the small side. Only Bartholomew is tall and broad-shouldered, like his father.' She frowned at the door. 'Now where has that boy got to?'

Rather unsteadily Jenifer got to her feet to peer out of the door.

'Bartholomew is being rather tiresome today. With my time being so near, his father makes him stay close to home in the event I need someone to run for Elizabeth King. She acts as midwife for all this area.'

'She's a good woman,' remarked Kerensa. 'She delivered me.' Kerensa had relaxed, finding Jenifer Drannock easy to talk to. 'I wonder who delivers the Pengarron babies? Doctor Crebo from Marazion, I suppose. I've met him at church, he seems a nice enough man.'

Jenifer looked at her thoughtfully. 'It was Beatrice who delivered all of Lady Caroline's babies, including Sir Oliver, so I've been told.'

'Of course.' This made Kerensa frown. 'I remember her telling me the first time I went up to the Manor house.' Jack jumped up and down on her lap, digging in hard with his tiny bare feet. 'Jack is certainly strong enough anyway.'

A beaming smile brought a hint to Jenifer's face of the once beautiful girl she had been before the weight of drudgery and constant childbearing had taken its toll.

'I lost two babies before I had Jack, and he more than makes up for them. Ah, here comes Bartholomew at last.'

Bartholomew Drannock pushed the door roughly aside on his way through it.

'So there you are, my son,' Jenifer said. 'You took your time as usual. See, we have a visitor, Lady Pengarron. Say good morning to her then be a good boy and fetch me a kettle of water, please.'

Not as tall as Paul King, but taller than the average nine year old in the village, Bartholomew Drannock was as his mother had described him, broad-shouldered, with dark eyes set in a deeply tanned face.

He viewed Kerensa with suspicion for several moments, then, 'G'mornin', lady,' he said sulkily. He turned abruptly to his mother before Kerensa could reply. 'Fetchin' water is girl's work,' he grumbled.

'I'll not have any of your tempers, Bartholomew. You know the girls are playing with Charles, and it won't do you any harm to do some work for me. Now off you go, quickly now.'

Bartholomew stood with grubby hands resting on his hips and looked as if he was about to argue further. He changed his mind, and snatching up the kettle he stamped outside.

Kerensa felt as though she had been struck by lightning. There had been something uniquely familiar in the last defiant stance Bartholomew Drannock had held. Coupled with the flash in his dark eyes she knew why he had reminded her of someone when he'd first pushed his way into the cottage.

'I am sorry,' his mother was saying. 'He has terrible manners and gets a bit out of hand at times. Bartholomew must get these moods from his father.'

'Yes,' agreed Kerensa, hiding her flushed shaken face behind Jack's little body. 'I'm sure he does.'

Chapter 10

Before marrying Kerensa, Oliver had spent a varying number of his days away from the Manor. This he still did. He did not volunteer information on his whereabouts and Kerensa did not ask him where he was going or how long he planned to stay away each time. When he did unexpectedly arrive home again it was usually evident with whom he had shared his company and time; Sir Martin, Hezekiah Solomon, or Adam Renfree on Ker-an-Mor Farm.

On this occasion he had been gone two days when he surprised her by his sudden appearance in their bedroom. Her hand flew to her mouth to stifle a scream.

'No need to be frightened, my love,' he said teasingly, holding his arms wide for her to come to him.

Kerensa remained still, her lovely face frozen.

'What is wrong?' he asked, dropping his arms and moving towards her.

'Nothing,' she replied, and nimbly side stepped away from him.

He watched dumbfounded as she pulled back the covers, climbed into the huge bed and turned on her side without further words. Sitting on the edge of her dressing table, he folded his arms.

'What have you been doing these past two days, Kerensa?'

'I rode over to Perranbarvah.'

'When was this?'

'Today.'

'To see the Reverend Ivey?'

'No.'

With nothing more forthcoming from her Oliver shrugged his shoulders and moved off to his dressing room. He pulled off his shirt, and not troubling to call for hot water, washed in the cold left in the pitcher beside the bowl. He would never be able to tolerate the stultifying life of an idle gentleman and had spent two satisfying days helping Rudd Richards and his family on Rose Farm to catch up with their tilling and hoeing. He had been looking forward to being with his wife again. Many reasons for Kerensa's strange behaviour passed through his mind as he prepared to retire.

She did not turn round. At the touch of his hand on the top of her arm he felt her body stiffen. Never a man to tolerate for long inexplicable moods in others, Oliver turned her rigid body round to face him.

'Just what on earth is the matter with you tonight!' he demanded.

Kerensa blinked at his sudden harshness, but she was angry too. Angry at this man who had fathered a child and abandoned the young mother to marry someone else and live in virtual poverty.

'There's no need to shout at me,' she retorted back.

'I wasn't shouting. I just do not understand why you are so cold towards me.'

Kerensa kept her mouth tightly closed and stared back at him.

Softening for a moment, Oliver smoothed her hair back from her face. 'Are you indisposed, is that what it is?'

'No.' Her answer was as blunt as her previous ones.

Oliver let out a sigh of exasperation as he took her in his arms. Kerensa didn't try to stop him making love to her, but for him the whole act was as unloving and uninteresting as it seemed Kerensa found it.

Later she said, 'I would like to go to Tolwithrick to take up Rachael's invitation.'

'You can't go anywhere until after the May Day celebrations. Pengarrons have a long tradition of attending the fairs.'

Kerensa sat up and appealed to his stern face. 'I would like to go straight away, Oliver.'

'You'll do what you're damned well told to, girl!' he snarled. 'Then you can stay at Tolwithrick for as long as you like.'

He turned sharply away. Kerensa's hand hovered over his shoulder for an instant, then she too turned away, tears welling up in her eyes.

Rising at first light Oliver rode Conomor long and hard across the cliffs in a vain attempt to dispel some of his black mood. He stared out to sea at Pengarron Point for a long time, the waters mirroring his restless feelings, and uncertain about what to do next. How could she do this to him? He'd never expected her to care for him. He'd never expected her to return his love in the way she had done that night at Sir Martin's house. But then, it wasn't love, was it? There had been no talk of love. It was only his right. Her duty. The joining together of any man and his wife.

'Just like a woman to use that to delight or injure a man!' he shouted at the black-backed gull circling out at sea. But you're hardly a woman, are you, Kerensa? he thought, while tapping his riding crop against his leg. Not you... not yet.

He moved closer to the cliff edge, kicking at the long damp springy tufts of coarse grass. She must be angry because I don't tell her where I go for several days at a time. But I can't... I won't be chained down to a life of routine, not for anyone.

Now it was full light the shapes and contours of the cliffs were clearly visible as far as the eye could see. He kicked a tuft of grass viciously. I should have wrung the truth out of her! He whirled around as if he sensed someone was watching him, reading his thoughts. Only me up here... and God... God and me... and my thoughts. Flinging his arms wide he looked upwards. All right, I suppose it is thoughtless of me not to tell her where I go...

Oliver sank down on the grass as in defeat. She might worry about me... perhaps she does care for me, after all? Pulling out his pipe and tobacco he was surprised to see how unsteady his hands were as he lit it. He put the pipe between his lips and held up his hands, studying them carefully.

All the things I've done, all the people I've known, he laughed to himself ironically, and it takes a slip of a girl to do this to me.

'Grandfather!'

The winds were raging all around her, tearing at her hair and clothes and chilling her flesh to the bone where she stood on the clifftop overlooking Trelynne Cove.

'Grandfather,' she repeated.

Old Tom was not alone. There was a boy with him…

'Davey!'

She started jubilantly towards them. Davey was not dead after all, and it was so good to see her grandfather again. But her joy quickly turned to horror and her agonising screams were lost in the howling of the wind.

'No! Please God! No!'

With hysterical laughter her grandfather had pushed Davey Trembath over the edge of the cliff…

Davey screamed out to her to help him as he desperately clung to the black granite, only his fingertips in sight.

Her grandfather disappeared but his maniacal shrill laughter could be heard, together with the wailing winds and angry sea and Davey's desperate cries.

She began to run towards him but each step was painfully slow, forced and heavy… could she reach him in time… she must reach him… Davey must not die! Her arms reached out to stop the terrified boy's death plunge into the churning sea below him. If only she could run faster. She must not let Davey die.

She kept her eyes riveted on the boy's hands… she must not lose sight of them… she must reach him soon… soon… soon…

'Davey! Hold on, I'll save you!'

Her own cries echoed with his inside her head, but new sounds were rushing up behind her, the ghostly thundering hoof beats of shrieking, snorting spirit ponies pounding towards her.

They were almost on top of her now… she must not let them reach the boy… she must keep them away from Davey.

Davey cried and screamed. 'Stop them! Stop them! Help me… Ted… Ted!'

She wanted to turn, to see what was bearing down on her, but she must keep her eyes on Davey's hands. She must or the boy would be swept away by the ponies, swept to his death.

Nearly there now… she must reach Davey before the spirit ponies. Nearly there. She must not let him die. One more painful step…

She got a grip on one bloodstained hand and then the other. She must pull him to safety, pull him up before they reached him and snatched him away from her.

Screaming his name, she pulled and pulled. She must save him… must pull him up.

Suddenly the boy's head shot up in front of her.

'Davey!'

But it wasn't Davey. It was the wilful mocking face of Bartholomew Drannock, scowling and spitting blood in her face. His hands were burning into hers… burning her flesh… his eyes, dark, dark eyes, burning into her very soul.

She fought to release herself from his painful grip, screaming at the child to let her go.

Suddenly he was gone. She was alone in the howling lamenting winds on the clifftop… alone and frightened, and so very lonely.

Desperately, she looked about for a shawl to cover her thin night-gown and trembling body and hide her impropriety. The usually familiar main street of Marazion now threatened and intimidated her as the crowd of people following her grew larger. There was laughter and jeering, faces pressing in on her from all directions. More people were up ahead, standing feet astride with hands on hips, laughing at her with their heads thrown back.

One by one they looked directly at her, each face holding a contemptuous expression, arms extended and pointing at her.

Her head spun as wildly she looked from face to face… Oliver… Sir Martin… Hezekiah Solomon… Sarah Cole… Peter Blake… Josephine Courtis.

Oliver again… then Bartholomew Drannock.

There was laughter, peals of mocking laughter. The faces whirled around her. She clutched her hands over her ears to drown out their derision, and ran. She must get away!

But where to?

More faces... more people to mock her?

No, it was Clem. Someone was with him. It was Clem and her mother.

She ran towards them, aching to reach the comfort of their arms.

But why were they receding further and further away from her?

'No! Come back. I need you...'

She screamed in anguish as their images faded.

'Come back! Oh, please, come back. Come back...'

—

Kerensa woke with a start, perspiration trickling down her face, her nightdress sticking to her body where she lay. She breathed heavily, relieved to see the dawn's light seeping in through the window where a curtain had been thrown back. She found Oliver had gone, the place where he had lain still warm.

The events of the past few months had crowded in on her, mocking and terrifying her in her sleep. Bartholomew Drannock's existence had placed a barrier between her and Oliver. In her dreams he had been an evil child, and with the nightmare still fresh in her mind she feared for the nature of any offspring she might have with Oliver. It seemed ironic that he wanted an heir when he knew he already had a son, one he had apparently spurned – but then, the result of a few minutes of pleasure with a lesser mortal meant nothing to the gentry, even the mighty Sir Oliver Pengarron who prided himself on his honour.

She had dreamt of Clem, of him disappearing, not able to help her. She'd needed him then and felt a strong need for him now, but there was nothing she could do about that. He had been with her mother and she felt the loss of them both in her life acutely. She had not mentioned her mother's death to the Reverend Ivey since that fateful, shameful day of the finding of Davey Trembath's body, not wanting to be reminded of that terrible event. But it haunted her still, like Oliver's memories of his friend Arthur Beswetherick's death. When she arrived back from Tolwithrick speaking to the Reverend would be the first thing she would do. But for now she lay back on her pillows and tried to empty her mind.

She lay awake until full daylight filled the room, trying hard not to think as she rose, dressing quickly before Alice made an appearance, and picking miserably at her breakfast.

'So there you are,' Alice said, entering the smaller of the dining rooms as Kerensa was feeding Dunstan with titbits of bacon.

'Good morning, Alice. I couldn't sleep so I got up early.'

'You spoil that dog,' her maid said reprovingly. Not satisfied with Kerensa's explanation she made no bones about scrutinising the other girl's face. 'Are you feeling all right?' she asked.

'Of course I am,' Kerensa replied shortly. 'Why?'

'Mmmm… you look a bit peaky to me. You're not with child, are you?' Alice rarely spoke with any sense of delicacy and the blunt question brought a wry smile to Kerensa's face.

'No, Alice, I am not going to have a baby. I have got some other news for you, though. After the May Day fairs we're going to stay with the Beswethericks at Tolwithrick. That is, you and I are. You should get on well with Lady Rachael… you're both outspoken.'

'Really?' Alice pouted. 'When will we be coming back?' She felt a little excited at the thought of staying at another grand house but at the same time disappointed at not being able to see Clem.

'We'll be leaving here on May Day evening and I don't know when we'll be coming back,' Kerensa said briskly.

'I see. Be glad to get away from him for a while, will you?'

'You mean Oliver?'

'Well, I didn't mean that daft old dog there,' Alice said, popping a bread crust into her mouth.

Dunstan seemed to understand the insult and growled under his breath. Alice fed him chunks of bread and butter.

'Like your master, aren't you, my old handsome?'

'Are you hinting at something, Alice?' Kerensa asked, smoothing a hand along Dunstan's back, while looking rather crossly at her maid.

'Oh… only that I heard his lordship went off in a huff this morning.'

'We've got packing to do, Alice.'

Kerensa led the way upstairs to her dressing room. 'Who told you Oliver was in a huff?' she asked.

'Jack. Poor little soul got a cuff round his ear, for no good reason too according to Nathan. And he played merry Hell with Barney over the state of the stableyard.'

'You shouldn't listen to gossip, Alice,' Kerensa said, pulling stockings out of a drawer.

'I was listening to something more about his lordship last night,' the maid said petulantly, 'but of course you won't want to hear about that now.'

'Hear what?' Kerensa looked up. 'Tell me, Alice.'

She made a show of being busy. 'Which gowns will you take, Kerensa? Tell you what?'

'You can be infuriating at times, Alice Ford!' exclaimed Kerensa, placing her hands on her hips.

'Sorry.' Alice smiled brightly. She knew she and Kerensa would always be friends and they often playfully teased one another. 'Well, Matthew King told Esther and Ruth that Oliver has taken to riding down to Trelynne Cove and spends ages just looking around.'

'And does Matthew think this unusual or something?' said Kerensa, looking puzzled. 'The Cove belongs to Oliver now… perhaps he has plans for it.'

Alice moved in close and spoke a good deal softer. 'The saying is that his lordship has a belief your grandfather could still be living somewhere around there.'

Kerensa's expression changed from interest to excitement. 'You pack anything that you think I'll need, Alice. Don't you drag heavy trunks about though, get Jack or one of the gardeners to do it. I need some fresh air. I'm going for a long ride.'

Quickly changing into her riding habit Kerensa waited impatiently for Jack to saddle Kernick, wondering why she hadn't had the good sense to ask him before she'd changed her clothes. She felt guilty about Jack's bright red ear, feeling it was her fault Oliver had been bad-tempered enough to hit the boy so hard. As it was, Jack was unusually quiet and while she waited she popped into the kitchen and brought him back a handful of freshly baked biscuits. By the time she left the stableyard he was his old cheerful self again, whistling between bites of biscuit.

Keeping Kernick at a steady gallop Kerensa quickly neared Trelynne Cove. All thoughts of her suspicions as to the paternity of Bartholomew Drannock were forgotten in the hope of seeing her grandfather again. If anyone could find out if Old Tom was living undetected in the cove, she could.

There were many nooks and crannies, in amongst the rocks, large enough for a small man to shelter in. She knew of many herself; some she had discovered in her natural explorations as a child, others Old Tom himself had shown her, and were unknown to even the oldest of the locals.

Kerensa pulled Kernick back to a trot as they closed in on the pathway leading down to the cottage. She jumped down from the pony to lead him down the winding path, not possessing the confidence to ride the rocky descent as Oliver did.

A movement on the cliff edge several hundred feet away captured her attention. Standing motionless was an unmistakable figure. Ted Trembath had his back to her and Kerensa knew he could hear no other sound save the roar of the waves where his brother had died fifty feet below.

Her heart pounding in her chest Kerensa hurriedly remounted, praying that Ted Trembath would not turn round until she was out of sight. She kept looking back but he remained motionless and she let out an enormous sigh of relief when she felt the danger of being seen was past.

If she had come across Old Tom with Ted Trembath about, what would have been the consequences? She would have to find out when Ted would be on core at the mine during the daytime and come back to the cove then, hoping that the next time, Oliver would not be there either.

–

Much later in the morning Oliver pulled up Conomor in the stable-yard to find Jack chattering to Alice Ford over a stall door. He jumped guiltily to attention and bolted out of the stable to take Conomor from the master. Oliver was feeling contrite at having cuffed him around the ear for no other reason than his own ill-humour. He did not reprimand Jack for idling away his time but was offended at the way Alice flounced off without acknowledging his presence. She had already rounded a corner of the yard by the time Oliver had dismounted and he quickly went after her.

'Just a minute!' his voice boomed out across the cobbles, bringing Alice to an immediate standstill.

She walked back and bobbed him a curtsey but her face showed no respect. 'You want me, m'lord?' she said pertly.

'Just where do you think you're going?' Oliver asked angrily.

'I'm on me way to the closet,' she answered, nodding at the relevant small building behind her, adding in an impatient tone that Oliver found outrageous, 'If that's all right with you, m'lord?'

'It is not! Whatever you may be doing or wherever you may be going, when you find yourself in my presence there is something you must do first, and at once!' Oliver's eyes narrowed and he bent his head level with Alice's. 'As you very well know.'

She pretended to look puzzled.

'You are not in the least bit stupid, girl. But,' Oliver warned, 'you would be very stupid indeed to deliberately cross me!'

Alice blinked but held her ground. She had her hands clasped in front of her but unlinked them and put them in the same manner behind her back. 'I'm very sorry, sir,' she said with false humility, then raised an eyebrow as if something important had just occurred to her, 'I think I forgot to show me manners when you rode into the stableyard?'

'You did it on purpose,' he said icily. 'Are you going to add to your misconduct by denying it?'

Alice shivered and finally flushed under his anger. 'No, sir.'

'Then explain yourself, girl,' Oliver ordered, his eyes on her like a bird of prey's.

Alice had been deliberately uncivil because of his treatment of Kerensa and unjust anger with Jack. She was nervous of her master now and she was not going to risk an explanation that would betray her feelings or bring more wrath upon her friend or the stable boy. She said, as jauntily as she could, 'I'm sorry, sir. I'm just as common as muck, sir. Don't know me manners, sir.'

'Then you had better learn some very quickly, hadn't you!' Oliver roared in a voice that threatened to shake the foundations of the Manor house.

Alice jumped back, her arms shooting straight down at her sides. It took all of her nerve not to turn and flee. Oliver's face was red with fury and she knew she had gone too far this time. 'Y-yes, sir,' she stammered weakly.

Oliver could cheerfully have put his hands around her neck and thoroughly wrung it. 'I'm not convinced that your explanation is a truthful one. But let me tell you this – if you ever act like that again, just once, I can promise you that you'll be out of the Manor and removed from your position without a reference. I will not tolerate any form of rudeness from my servants. Do you understand me?'

'Yes, sir,' Alice whispered, trembling and looking down at her feet.

'Look at me as you answer,' Oliver ordered, but his voice had dropped several decibels now. 'Is your mistress in the house?'

'No, sir. She went riding,' Alice replied meekly.

'Did she say where she was going?'

'Yes, sir. Trelynne Cove.'

'How long ago did she leave?'

'A while ago, sir. I reckon she will be back any minute now.'

'I see. If she wants to know where I'm spending the day, tell her I will be at Ker-an-Mor Farm.' With each succeeding sentence Oliver's voice had steadily dropped until he said quietly, 'Go about your business now.'

Alice stared at him for a moment; it was the first time he had left information on his whereabouts for Kerensa. Then she turned and hastened towards the refuge of the servant's closet.

'Alice.'

She turned back fearfully. 'Yes, sir?'

'Her Ladyship depends on you. It would be a shame if she were to lose you, don't you agree?'

'Yes, sir.' Alice nodded with a lump in her throat.

Chapter 11

The coolness between Kerensa and Oliver continued for the next few days, causing a feeling of tension to permeate the Manor house. Beatrice, who had managed an unusually long period of sobriety, drank two bottles of gin on the second day and clutched a third to her dropping bosom. Grumbling that she'd rather stay at Painted Bessie's with 'they blamed disgustin' drunkards than be in such a miserable place', she promptly took herself off.

Everyone was relieved when a warm cloudless morning heralded the first day of May. Kerensa and Alice completed their packing for the stay at Tolwithrick, ensuring that they were ready with the whole household and outdoor staff at eight o'clock for the journey to Ker-an-Mor Farm for the crowning of the parish May Queen. Oliver appeared promptly at the specified time, smartly dressed in comparison to his usual casual manner.

All those not riding on horseback piled into the back of a farm wagon. The subdued mood they had held for the last few days quickly changed to laughter and light-hearted banter as Oliver and Kerensa rode on ahead. Nathan O'Flynn on Derowen stayed close to the wagon, chatting to Jake Angove and the two undergardeners. Jack sat squeezed between Esther and Ruth, proudly showing them yet again the scrap of paper where he had written his name as Kerensa had taught him. The two women ruffled his hair and teased him about the names of the young maids he had his eye on for the Maypole dances.

'How about Alice here? Will she do?'

'If I find one as beautiful as her ladyship,' Jack said sheepishly, 'then I'll ask her to dance with me.'

This brought hoots of affectionate laughter and more teasing from the others in the wagon, particularly Alice.

'You'll have a hard job to find one as beautiful as her, I d'reckon,' said Jake Angove.

'Or as kind,' said Esther.

'Or as gentle,' added her sister.

'Aye,' agreed Nathan, 'or as sad as these past few days.'

The company fell silent and the farm hand driving the wagon looked round in surprise.

'Come on, you lot, what's the matter with 'ee? Tes May Day and there's fun 'n' games ahead of 'ee.'

'Perhaps things will be better when she comes back from Tolwith-rick,' said Jack, ignoring the farm hand and instinctively nestling in against Ruth's arm.

Jake turned his head, and taking his pipe out of his mouth, spat on to the dusty ground. 'Wonder what he did to her?' he murmured to himself.

Oliver crowned Moriah Andrew, a pretty fifteen year old from Barvah Farm, as the year's May Queen, a traditional task for the Lord of the Manor that stretched back more than two hundred and fifty years. Moriah blushed fiercely as Oliver placed the crown of may blossom and other wild flowers on her head and lightly kissed both her hands.

Nearly everyone in the parish and on the Estate was there and a roar of cheers and claps thundered around the field next to the farmyard. Kerensa congratulated the May Queen, kissing her cheek and presenting her with a posy of flowers from the Manor gardens. Amid more clapping and cheering she found herself surrounded by small girls offering her bunches of flowers tied with brightly coloured ribbons.

After that she wandered about among the people gathered there, talking to as many as she could and taking an interest in them all. Some she knew already, the others readily introducing themselves to her. She looked about for Clem, but he was not there. As all the other Trenchards were present, she assumed he was staying at home to be with Kenver, his younger brother, who had been crippled and housebound from birth.

She approached the Trenchards and Florrie's mother, Gran Donald, with apprehension, but there was no need to be worried. They were as warm and friendly as the last time she'd seen them, when she'd been Clem's future bride. Rosie, Clem's small sister, clung to Kerensa as she kissed her, presenting her with the largest bunch of wild flowers she had yet received.

Oliver stood in the shade of an old hawthorn tree talking with Adam Renfree as they drank mead and leisurely smoked their pipes. He looked around at regular intervals until he spotted Kerensa, unaware that Adam was taking in the admiring glances he directed at the girl's slender form. She wore a dress of russet brown that enhanced her natural beauty.

'I'm holding a local court tomorrow, Adam. I was hoping by now to have Colly Pearce up before me. I'd have him up to Launceston for the next County Assizes so fast he'd think Old Nick was on his back,' Oliver said passionately.

'A crafty old fox that one, sir. I'd like to see him caught in one of his own traps one of these days. Would serve him right,' said Adam, reaching for a jug of mead.

'Go easy on that, Adam,' Oliver teased. 'Your son and my wife are making their way over here.'

Adam pulled back his arm in a guilty movement. 'S'pose it is a bit too early in the day,' he commented with disappointment.

Matthias Renfree was waylaid by a worried-looking miner, and Kerensa joined the men under the hawthorn tree.

'Good morning, m'lady,' Adam said, taking off his cap. 'Um… not a lot of may blossom out yet.'

'A bit too early yet, Adam,' Kerensa agreed. 'Will you be going over to Marazion after the ox roast?'

'Not me, m'lady. I'll stay here to keep an eye on things, but I daresay Matthias will later on.'

Adam was somewhat surprised that after Oliver's admiring looks at the girl he now stared straight over her head with features set like cold marble. He glanced slyly from one to the other and it soon became apparent that Kerensa was ignoring her husband too. 'I trust you're getting on well with Kernick, m'lady?' he ventured.

'He's wonderful,' she assured him enthusiastically, 'we took to one another at once.'

'I thought you would. Told his lordship here, didn't I, sir, Kernick was the best choice for you when he picked him out?' Adam looked pointedly at Oliver who merely grunted an affirmative reply.

Kerensa and Oliver exchanged a brief unfriendly look then she bid Adam good morning and moved away to talk to Jenna Tregurtha.

Oliver swallowed a mouthful of mead. He looked at his farm steward's amused face. Adam moved round to face his employer, raising a curious eyebrow.

Holding out his glass for a refill, Oliver said drily, 'You can mind your own damn' business, Adam Renfree.'

When they arrived in Marazion during the middle of the afternoon, Oliver and Kerensa found the ancient market town packed with people enjoying the fair and festivities. Pilgrims on the spiritual journey to the castle on the Mount squeezed their way through the crowds.

Leaving their mounts in the stables of Sealey's Hostelry, Kerensa took the arm ungraciously offered to her by her husband, only to find herself having the greatest difficulty keeping pace with his long quick strides.

'Please slow down, Oliver. I can't keep up with you,' she told him breathlessly.

'Don't concern yourself,' he returned, his face displaying extreme annoyance. 'Martin should be somewhere near the maypole. You can walk with him for the rest of the day.'

Kerensa stayed quiet as she allowed herself to be pulled through the milling throng; Oliver's height, bearing, and ill mood ensured them a speedy passage to the western end of the town where the maypole was situated, near to a slipway running down to the sea. She was more miserable than ever before. If she was wrong in her belief that Oliver had fathered the Drannock boy then the hurt and perplexity, the subsequent strained atmosphere, all of her making, was unwarranted and cruel. Yet deep inside she felt it was more than a coincidence, a misunderstanding, more an intuition...

The maypole was adorned with brightly coloured ribbons and covered with flowers, including strongly perfumed white and pink may blossoms. As daintily as was possible in hob nailed boots or bare feet, bashful young men danced with radiant-faced girls, dazzling in their Sunday best dresses, posies and ribbons. Kerensa watched the streaming long ribbons flowing down from the rotating circle on the head of the maypole, as the skilful dancers passed in and out to form the pattern of a spider's web. Oliver looked about for signs of Sir Martin and their circle of friends, finding no interest in the cavorting pastimes of the working class.

He was not elated to be set on by Josephine Courtis, dressed as elaborately as the maypole, latching herself on to his other arm. She ignored Kerensa as she regaled Oliver with a tale about the unfortunate Mayor Oke, whose expensive new horsehair wig had been stolen clean off his bald head immediately after the opening ceremony. Oliver listened to the widow with a detached air but couldn't help making an unfavourable comparison between her sharply receding chin, small startled eyes, blemished skin and prurient appetites, and the simple good taste and beauty of the young woman on his other arm.

Spotting Matthew King proudly escorting Marazion's May Queen, Lowenna Angove the blacksmith's daughter, he called the lofty young fisherman over to him. It was easy to see Matthew regarded Oliver's invitation as an honour, and he guided Lowenna, a wisp of a girl, through the bustle with such care one might have believed he thought she would easily break in two.

'G'afternoon, m'lord,' Matthew said gaily, 'Tes a lovely day for the fair.'

'And you have the loveliest of May Queens with you,' said Oliver, treating Lowenna to one of his rare but striking smiles. 'Have you seen anything of Sir Martin Beswetherick, at all, King?'

'No, sir, but here comes the Mayor. He was talking to Mr Cole, the coroner, not so many minutes ago. He may know where Sir Martin is.'

While Oliver conversed with Matthew King, Kerensa talked to Lowenna. Josephine Courtis stood moodily silent, but held on persistently to Oliver's arm. Matthew and Lowenna moved off to wait their turn at the maypole as the town's Mayor, Jonathan Lanwyn Oke, approached in his gait-legged walk to welcome Oliver and his new wife to the festivities. Having had the good fortune to have regained his splendid new wig the Mayor was in jubilant spirits. A man of steady habits he lived by the philosophy of 'each to his own'. Although having at one time refused Oliver's offer of a half-anker of brandy, he thought no ill of the other's participation in freetrading.

The Mayor informed Oliver that he would find Sir Martin, and their mutual circle of acquaintances, in the upstairs lounge of the Commercial Inn, sipping ale and mead in the company of the St Aubyns from the Mount. When Oke drifted off to greet other important visitors to the town, he left the scent of warm lavender water on the fresh breeze blowing in off the sea.

Disengaging Josephine Courtis' clinging hand from his arm, Oliver eased Kerensa round to face him.

'I'm going to join Martin Beswetherick. You can remain here in Mistress Courtis' company,' he said curtly. 'If you avoid the inns, alehouses and alleyways, you'll be well able to look after yourself for the rest of the afternoon. Nathan O'Flynn will be outside Sealey's Hostelry to escort you back to the Manor at five of the clock.'

'Shouldn't we be together, Oliver?' Kerensa tried to whisper so the widow could not hear.

'Why?' he asked in undisguised hostility.

'Surely people will expect us to—'

He cut her short and pushed her hand away from his arm. 'You should know me well enough by now to realise I seldom do what anyone expects me to.'

Kerensa called after him as he stalked off. Oliver turned half round and looked at her coldly.

'Will I see you before I leave for Tolwithrick?'

'Perhaps.'

'He's in a bad mood today,' remarked Josephine Courtis as Oliver pushed his way through the crowds. 'More like his old self again. But then, your marriage is hardly a love match, is it?'

Kerensa did not reply, hiding her hurt as she acknowledged some of her Bible class friends with a wave.

'My dear, you must really feel at home here today… what with all these common working-class people about.'

Kerensa wasn't unduly bothered by the spitefulness of the remark but sadly realised how untrue the words were. There were few people she could feel comfortable with now apart from Alice, Jake, Jack, Nathan, Lady Rachael Beswetherick and the Reverend Ivey. Those from her old life for the most part were friendly and respectful, but too acutely aware of her changed position to shake her hand, kiss her cheek, or call her 'maid'. And goodness alone knew what the class she had married into thought of her. Though Josephine Courtis' comment was some indication.

It was still painful, her loss of Clem. He was never far from her thoughts and she looked around in the hope of catching sight of him. If she could rid herself of the disagreeable widow, perhaps the two of them might snatch a few words together in a quiet place somewhere. She had not seen him since the day of Davey Trembath's funeral, or received word of him, and Alice had of late become reluctant even to mention his name.

'Looking for anyone in particular, my dear?' Josephine said, a suspicious glint in her eyes.

'No. Shall we look at the stalls, Mistress Courtis?'

Josephine looked down her nose and bobbed up and down in her shoes. 'Well, I have no wish to purchase anything – but as you please. You lead the way.'

Kerensa did not push her way through the swelling crowds, but found most people willing enough to part a way through for her and the woman following close on her heels with a handkerchief crammed tightly to her nose. Kerensa stopped in front of a clothing stall. Pinching a garment between finger and thumb of one gloved hand, Josephine held it up and tossed it disdainfully aside. Refusing to rise to the bait Kerensa bought two serge shirts in a size she thought would fit Bartholomew Drannock; she knew the boy would not wear anything fancy and hoped Jenifer would accept them for him.

'Charity, my dear,' sniffed the widow. 'You'll end up like Oliver's late mother, Lady Caroline. But you'll know more about what to buy for these people than she did, won't you?'

Not taking her eyes from a small muslin dress she was holding as she examined its stitching, Kerensa said coolly, 'I am not ashamed of my background or my upbringing, Mistress Courtis, nor shall I ever try to hide it. I've no more wish for your company than you have for mine. And as for Oliver, I have it on very good authority that he had not the slightest interest in you. And, anyway, I believe he prefers younger women.'

The sharp-faced stall holder had listened in amazement as the girl he knew to be the new Lady of the Manor tongue-lashed the haughty doxy at her side.

Josephine turned bright red with rage, and hissed back, 'Why, you common little bitch! How dare you speak to me in such a manner!'

'I found it easy enough. If you insist on being rude and tiresome, Mistress Courtis, you must learn not to be surprised if you are treated in kind. Good day to you.' Kerensa had looked Josephine straight in the face and kept calm throughout the further tirade. She now turned to the stall holder. 'I'll take this dress, please, and another the same in a bigger size.'

'Thank 'ee, m'lady,' said the amused stall holder with a bow as Josephine Courtis stormed off to look for a familiar face with whom to share her outrage over the dreadful experience with Oliver Pengarron's common little wife.

'Shall I 'ave 'em sent up to the Manor for 'ee, m'lady?'

'No, thank you,' Kerensa said happily, glad to be minus the widow's company. 'I can manage. My pony is not far away.'

'Let me carry 'em for 'ee then,' offered the stall holder, tying a strong knot to finish off the neat parcel he had made from a square of bright red cloth for her.

'No, no, no. It's all right,' Kerensa insisted. 'You may miss another customer or have your stock taken. I'll be fine, truly. But thank you anyway.'

'As you please then, m'lady, an' thank 'ee very much for your custom.'

The stall holder gave another bow, longer this time, in a style not unlike that of Hezekiah Solomon.

As she passed through the crowds Kerensa looked keenly about for signs of Clem. From the various stalls in the bustling noisy market town she bought a tortoiseshell inlaid comb for Alice, lace handkerchiefs for Ruth and Esther, a neckerchief for Jack, a little white apron for Rosina Pearce, and even dared to buy a small bottle of cheap scent for Beatrice.

There was still no sign of Clem but as she browsed over a sweet-meat stall, pondering on whether to buy some sugared almonds for Lady Rachel Beswetherick's children, she caught sight of two of the people she had bought gifts for. Rosina Pearce was helping a highly intoxicated Beatrice through the crowd, and the old nursemaid was bawling out news of Kerensa's private life. She tried to rush to them as Beatrice's words clearly reached her ears.

'They git on me ruddy tripe, the pair of 'em! One minute they 'ate each other, then soon as they get t'like each other a little bit... well, whad'ya think? ...summat 'appens an' now they'm 'ardly talkin'.'

'Shush, Beatrice,' Rosina pleaded, 'let's just find a place and sit down.'

'Oh, 'e's an uppity sod, right enough. Don't know when 'e's well off! She's a dear little maid, sweet 'n' pretty, what more does 'e want? Eh? Eh?'

Beatrice wasn't mentioning any names but Kerensa knew the folk turning their heads to stare and listen to her could easily tell who it was she was shouting about. She almost knocked over a pottery stall in her haste to reach the old woman to shut her up.

'An' she,' Beatrice went on, 'she's a dear little maid but I don't know what she's got 'er nose up in the bleddy air for these days. What more do she want? Gotta a fine roof over 'er 'ead, food in 'er belly, an' a man who gives 'er—'

'Beatrice! Stop it at once!' Kerensa prodded the old woman with a fierce elbow and Beatrice rolled her piggy eyes at her.

'Oh! Tes you, me 'an'some, I wus jus' tellin' little Ro... Ro...'

'Be quiet, Beatrice,' Kerensa hissed angrily. 'Everybody's looking at us.'

'Didn't mean no 'arm.' Beatrice hiccuped, her eyes rolled again, and she looked as if she was about to collapse.

'I'm sorry, m'lady,' Rosina said. 'I've been trying to get her out of harm's way but she's so heavy and with me having only one good foot myself...' Rosina used her slight body as a wedge to hold Beatrice upright.

'There's no need for you to apologise,' Kerensa said, looking about for a suitable place to put Beatrice out of the way in. 'I thought she was going over to Painted Bessie's – it's a pity she didn't! Look, there's a barrel over there against that fence by the pig pen. Will you help me get her over there, please? I can't manage on my own with all these packages.'

'Of course,' Rosina said. Then, 'Hey!' Beatrice had stood up straight and scuttled off before the two young women had a chance to gather their wits and try to stop her.

'Oh, well,' Kerensa said to the startled Rosina, 'she's gone, and there's nothing we can do about it now. I only hope she makes it to Painted Bessie's in one piece.'

Rosina was smiling to herself now, seeing the funny side of what had happened, but she kept a straight face before Kerensa, who was most annoyed. She would not make any reference to what she had heard. 'I didn't know Beatrice could move so fast. She's a cunning old thing.'

'Yes,' Kerensa said, stung with embarrassment. 'Anyway, it's good to see you again, Rosina, we haven't spoken in months. How are you? I do miss you, and the Bible classes.' Like all the people who cared about Rosina, when meeting her Kerensa looked for signs of fresh bruises.

Rosina smiled serenely but hurriedly pulled a sleeve down to cover her wrist. 'I'm very well, thank you. It's a lovely May Day. How are you keeping, m'lady?'

'I don't expect my friends to call me "m'lady" when we're alone, Rosina,' Kerensa said brightly. 'Would you like to go somewhere and have a dish of tea with me?'

'I would like to, thank you, but if Colly got to hear of it... and I've got to be on my way soon.'

Kerensa always marvelled at how Rosina never sounded disappointed at not being able to do so many of the things she wanted to because of her selfish brother.

'Well, I've got a little something here for you, Rosina, I hope you won't be offended. It's just a little white apron. And I bought some perfume for Beatrice but I think it wouldn't be a good idea to give it to her now. She would be furious, I'm sure. I don't know how I had the nerve to buy it in the first place. Perhaps you'd like to have it too.'

'I'd better not, but thank you for thinking of me. I can't accept anything else, Kerensa. You've already been very kind to me, sending along things by Alice, but Colly gets jealous.' Rosina made the excuse, 'He would like to give me nice things himself, you see.'

'Well, perhaps…' Kerensa glanced down at her purse then coloured profusely, but Rosina put a hand on her arm.

'It's all right, I'm not offended. Perhaps you could oblige me with a few pennies to buy a bite to eat.'

Rosina had covered her friend's embarrassment again and Kerensa knew she would use the money to buy the first good meal she had eaten in ages.

'Have you had any news of your grandfather yet?' Rosina was also curious about Kerensa's new life as the Lady of the Manor but too tactful to ask in case her old friend was extremely unhappy.

'No, nothing yet,' Kerensa replied wistfully, 'I suppose he'll get in touch with me eventually.'

'Are you worried about him?'

'Well, yes and no. I'd like to know where he is and what he's doing, of course, but Grandfather can look after himself. He said he was going off on a ship to start a new life, but you never could believe a word he said. I think he's just lying low somewhere for a while… I do miss him.'

'I'm sure he'll turn up soon,' Rosina said to comfort Kerensa while gently pulling her out of the way of a man carrying a huge tray of pies on his head and earmarking his pitch for the place to spend the pennies she had been given. 'He'd probably cause a few problems if he was around at the moment.'

'Like turning up regularly at the Manor asking for money when he knew Sir Oliver wasn't there? Yes, I've thought of that.' Kerensa smiled fondly as she recalled Old Tom's character.

Kerensa managed to extract a promise from Rosina to send word to her via Alice if she required anything and was able to ask for it, then Rosina limped away to the pieman.

Kerensa moved on by herself, pleased that although she could not see Rosina as often as she wished there at least was one person she could still feel comfortable with.

She looked again at the stalls and wondered whether to buy something for Oliver. At first she decided she would not, then feeling guilty at being churlish, bought a long wide length of black velvet ribbon. In the event of her leaving the Manor for Tolwithrick before he returned home sometime later in the day, she mentally wrote a note to leave with the ribbon on his study desk.

So deep in thought was she as she began to leave behind the noisy hubbub of humanity, she did not see the man standing directly in front of her until it was too late. Her purchases were scattered over the dusty ground as she walked straight into him.

'Oh, I'm so sorry!' she cried out.

'No need for apologies, Lady Pengarron. It would have helped if I had stepped out of your way,' said a smiling Peter Blake. 'Allow me to be of assistance to you?'

He gathered up her parcel and other purchases but made no movement to hand them to her. 'Are you quite alone, ma'am?' he enquired of her. 'It seems to me that indeed you are, although I cannot understand why this should be the case. If I may say so, it's rather remiss of your husband to leave you unescorted with the town full of rogues, drunkards and cut throats. If you'll allow me, I'll feel it an honour to escort you to your intended destination, ma'am?'

For some reason this young man, whose face had qualities to turn the eye of a female of any age, with a smile full of charm revealing the whitest of straight teeth, made Kerensa instinctively feel uncomfortable.

'I thank you, Mr Blake,' she said, keeping her eyes on him rather distrustfully. 'My pony is in the stable of the Sealey's Hostelry.'

'So you know who I am, Lady Pengarron, despite the fact we were not introduced at Sir Martin Beswetherick's house a few weeks ago.'

'Lady Rachael told me your name, Mr Blake.'

'Did she, indeed?'

They turned the corner by a grocery shop where a group of dirty urchins were wrestling in their path, throwing up choking dust from the dry ground.

'Hey! You there!' shouted Peter Blake. 'Hold still till we're past.'

The children unwillingly pulled apart, scowling as the gentleman and lady walked past them. Blake tossed them a few copper coins and they sent up yet more dust in their scrabble for them.

Blake laughed. 'Practising for the day they will be able to take part in the wrestling matches, I fancy. Will you be watching the wrestling this afternoon, ma'am? This fellow King, the one they call the Barvah Giant, is reckoned likely to win again this year.'

'I will be joining my husband to watch the wrestling, sir,' Kerensa lied, afraid Blake would suggest she accompany him. She was in fact hoping to come across Nathan O'Flynn to escort her back to the Manor, having had enough of the May Day celebrations for this year.

She stumbled suddenly into a pot hole and Blake reached out and grasped her arm as she steadied herself.

'Take my arm, ma'am, before you have another misfortune today. Perhaps when…'

Kerensa looked up from the offending pot hole to see why Peter Blake had stopped talking. The reason was the way a tall, fair-haired young man, with a curly-haired girl clinging on to his arm, was coldly staring at them. A wave of shock coursed through her at seeing Clem and Alice together in such a manner, and Clem was making it obvious he didn't much care for her being in Blake's company.

It was she who broke the silence. 'Hello, Clem. Hello, Alice.'

Red-faced, Alice stammered. 'Oh, m'lady, I… I was on my way to find Ruth and Esther when I—I saw Clem. We thought they might be by the maypole…'

'They were not there a short while ago, Alice,' Kerensa informed her.

Clem's blue eyes were searching Kerensa's face. Blake looked with deep interest from one taut expression to the other. Recalling the information gleaned from his half-sister about the young Lady Pengarron, he quickly arrived at a correct understanding of the situation.

In a bitter voice, Clem said, 'If you'll excuse us? Good afternoon, m'lady. Sir.'

'Of course. Good afternoon to you both,' Blake said genially in his quiet voice. 'Enjoy yourselves at the fair.'

Clem walked quickly on, followed by the embarrassed Alice. Charity bounded after them, but not before she squatted to wet the dust in front of Blake's feet. Skirting the wet patch as they continued on their way, he raised one gently curving eyebrow.

'Friends of yours, are they?'

Kerensa tried to sound matter-of-fact. 'Alice is my maid. Clem is the son of one of the Pengarron Estate's tenant farmers.'

'Seems a disagreeable sort of fellow to me.' Two small girls running towards them stopped their progress again and Kerensa was relieved not to have to talk any more about Clem.

''ere, lady,' one of the girls said shyly, 'we picked some flowers for 'ee.'

Both girls held up a huge bunch of pale yellow primroses in grubby little hands.

'Why, thank you very much,' Kerensa said, taken with surprised delight, smiling at each of them in turn. 'It's very kind of you.'

With great care she placed her hands over the little girls', and one at a time slowly drew out the bunches of primroses until she was holding the floral gifts. She breathed in the delicate scent of the flowers, made strong and heady by the heat of the sun.

'They're really lovely. Thank you again. When I get home I'm going to put them in a crystal vase in my sitting room.'

'Up in the big Manor house, lady?' asked one girl, wide-eyed.

'Yes, that's right.'

'Will 'is lordship see 'em too?' the other girl wanted to know.

'Yes. And he likes wild flowers as much as I do.' Kerensa glanced down at the purse hanging by its drawstrings from her wrist. 'Oh, dear.'

'Is something wrong?' Peter Blake asked quickly.

'I want to give them sixpence, but my hands are not free,' she said, looking helplessly at the primroses.

'Well, that's no problem,' he said, and producing two silver coins from a waistcoat pocket, dropped one into each pair of eager hands.

'Thank you, sir, and you, lady,' they said excitedly, and skipped off to spend their reward among the crowds at the fair.

'You seem to be making a habit of coming to my rescue, Mr Blake,' Kerensa commented.

'Most willingly I assure you, ma'am,' he said pleasantly.

Blake was obviously aware of Kerensa's growing embarrassment. She felt him to be a sophisticated man, a calculating man, but not in any sense dangerous in the same way as Oliver.

He allowed them to reach Sealey's Hostelry without further conversation. It was quiet within, favoured only by a small number of the older gentlefolk at that moment, who were eager to be out of the hot sun and the noise and bustle.

Kerensa looked around the unfamiliar surroundings and wondered who to approach for assistance. A serving maid came forward and offered to relieve her of the primroses.

'Thank you for your help, Mr Blake,' Kerensa said drily. 'There is no need for you to be detained any longer.'

Blake smiled with all his charm, a small dimple appearing at each corner of a rather sensuous mouth.

'Oh, I have nowhere in particular to go, ma'am, or nothing in particular to do. May I not ask you to take some refreshment with me?'

As Rachael had remarked, he was quite beautiful; not tall like Oliver or Clem, but many women might think him more attractive than either with his cornflower blue eyes. Most women would be flattered and delighted to be receiving his attention, but Kerensa distrusted him, even feared him a little, the reason why this should be so, completely eluding her.

'My husband has taken a room in the hotel for the day,' she said determinedly. 'I wish only to withdraw and rest for a while.' She opened her purse and took out a silver coin. 'Your shilling, Mr Blake.'

He took the coin and kissed her hand. 'I hope to have the pleasure of your charming company again very soon, Lady Pengarron.'

'In church perhaps, Mr Blake?' she said mischievously.

'That, I fear, will never be, ma'am. Myself, I am an unbeliever. I thank you for the shilling, but I did not want it returned. Your servant.' With a bow, he turned and left the hotel.

Kerensa felt a chill spread inside her. She had not told such lies to anyone as she had to Peter Blake. What was it about him that caused her to act that way? He was a perfect gentleman. Too perfect perhaps, and according to Rachael, not a gentleman at all. What exactly did that mean? She was at least glad it was not a lie about Oliver taking a room for her convenience here in the hotel.

On entering the building Blake had placed her purchases on the clerk's desk. Retrieving them, she asked to be shown to her room and to be informed at once if Nathan O'Flynn made an appearance outside.

She followed the same serving maid wearily over the worn carpet as they climbed the staircase. It would be a blessed relief to be a good distance tomorrow from Oliver and his dark moods, from the fishing village and the Drannocks. She would miss Dunstan… but why did Oliver have to insist she take her maid? At that moment she was bitterly jealous of Alice.

Why had she been holding on to Clem's arm like that?

Outside in the hot sunshine Peter Blake looked up at the sky and smiled contentedly. He pressed the shilling coin to his lips before slipping it into a waistcoat pocket, then made his way to the nearest brothel.

Chapter 12

High up on a sloping valley of Trecath-en Farm, Clem Trenchard was sweating heavily as he cut furze to be used for fuel in the winter. It was a job that required skill and vigilance and he knew his father would be scornful of his discarding the shirt which offered some protection against the harsh spines of the drying gorse bushes. In the mood he was in Clem could easily have been tempted to cast off the heavy thick leather gloves he wore and allow his hands to be ripped to shreds. As it was, the long scratch marks and the droplets of blood resulting from them on his arms, neck, and shoulders, purged some of his despair as he worked at a furious pace.

To add to his frustration Alice had not gone to Tolwithrick with Kerensa. On her return to the Manor on May Day, she had been taken violently ill. Kerensa had delayed her departure for Tolwithrick until the following morning but Alice had been too ill to get out of her bed. Ascertaining that her maid had no serious malady, Kerensa had left the Manor on her own. She had never felt the need for a personal maid and the Beswethericks would have more than enough servants if she did find she required one.

Clem had secretly watched Kerensa leave in the stately refurbished Pengarron coach, driven by Barney Taylor, with Jack sitting self-importantly at his side. To Clem it brought some small comfort to his aching soul to know that for as long as she was away, Kerensa would not lie in the arms of Oliver Pengarron.

Immediately following the disturbing meeting with Kerensa and Peter Blake, the lack of a reason for her being in Blake's company adding to his worries for her, Clem had tried to end his association with Alice. Cleverly she had sidetracked his every attempt, encouraging him to drink too much ale in an effort to lift his rapidly failing spirits. The outcome had been yet another sinful union between them, and it was getting harder and harder to face his parents and grandmother in the mornings. Why couldn't she realise that her presence only served as a painful reminder of the girl he loved and had lost, and still couldn't get out of his mind?

Prickles embedded in the knee of his breeches pierced deeply into his flesh as he knelt to retrieve the sharp hatchet which had spun out of his hand in his careless hacking.

'Bloody girl!' he swore angrily. 'Why did you have to be hanging on to my arm when we came across Kerensa with that man Blake? Only the Lord knows what she must be thinking now.'

Charity was restlessly hunched on all fours, close by. She got slowly to her feet and ambled uncertainly towards her master. Clem took no notice of her and glared down the empty valley.

'Hell and damnation to everything!' he screamed at the top of his voice.

Charity jumped back and darted her head in each direction while the young man himself looked about to challenge anyone who might have heard his outburst.

He returned to work, crying out with an oath as a group of barbarous spines raked across his chest. His father would have told him it served him right for swearing and harbouring such uncharitable thoughts.

Charity edged back closer to Clem, but he ignored her. He worked on until the furious stinging across his chest and arms made him straighten up, and pulling off his gloves, he reached for his water flask. The water he poured over his wounds was warm and soothing. Charity wriggled across his feet and whined appealingly to him as he gulped down enough warm liquid to quench his thirst.

Contrite at his disregard, he ruffled her ears and sought comfort for them both in hugging her warm soft body to him. Mechanically, he poured water into a cupped hand for the dog to lap from.

As he stood up the river below glittered across his line of vision. There was an elm tree on the opposite bank. It was under that tree he had first made love to Alice.

'Now, with Kerensa away to stop you feeling guilty about us,' he murmured, his body slouched in an attitude of defeat, 'you'll bother me all the more.'

He pulled his shirt on over his head grimacing when the rough material dragged over the deep scratches in his flesh. He carried on with his work, taking more care but without easing up on his pace. When he'd cut enough furze he tied large bundles securely into faggots. A farm labourer was expected to cart back fifty faggots of furze in a good day's work, to be dried off and later ricked near to the farmhouse. Clem was likely to complete fifty, and another ten, and with them several deep painful scratches on his body as proof of his rage and foolhardy speed.

–

Oliver Pengarron was in no mood for company either that day as he toiled with the heat of the sun burning down on his back. He was butchering half of a pig he had just killed. Before leaving the farmyard to ride out on his daily rounds of the busy Estate farm and stud, Adam Renfree had stopped to give him a report on the latest dairy yields and had offered to send him some help. Oliver had bluntly refused, saying the farm hands would be more usefully occupied in the fields than getting in his way.

He arranged the expertly butchered half of the pig into barrels of salt for consumption in the coming winter. The other half he loaded on to a cart to be taken to the butcher's shop in Marazion. Pumping up plenty of fresh spring water, he filled several buckets to swill and scrub away the pig's blood and other evidence of the slaughter before washing himself thoroughly clean.

For propriety's sake he put on his linen shirt to return the sharp knives he had used to their places on a rack on the kitchen wall. As he passed the dairy on his way back to the yard a young dairymaid at the window held his attention for a few moments. She glanced up from the large stone sink at which she was smacking butter between wooden pats and blushed under his steady gaze before looking away. Although she possessed no other physical resemblance to Kerensa, the dairymaid had the same tender build.

Oliver sighed heavily and walked off briskly. Why does every wench I set eyes on remind me of something about her? he thought crossly.

Perching on the side of a water trough he kicked stones and pieces of straw at his feet. What's got into her these days anyway? And why did she become as cold as ice overnight?

Wiping sweat from his brow he reached for his pipe and tobacco. Whatever the reason, I can't think it's because of anything I have done.

He lost interest in his pipe when half a dozen black puppies spilled out of a barn and raced over to him. Oliver knelt to gather them up in both arms, the squirming bundle of fur fighting one another to lick his face, neck and hands while wetting his breeches in their excitement. Some of the farm hands ignored the puppies, some seemed to like them, while others still were likely to kick them aside, but from this particular man they were always sure of receiving a warm welcome.

'Women,' Oliver said to the puppies. 'Why can't they be more like men? Or animals? Or the seasons of the year, each coming in turn, one after the other? Even the sea is less unpredictable and easier to understand than they are.'

Jenna Tregurtha, who spent more time on Ker-an-Mor than on her brother's farm, came to the kitchen door and shook breadcrumbs off her large apron on to the cobbles. All the puppies save one struggled out of Oliver's arms to scramble off to snap up the unexpected titbits before the fowls who were bent on the same notion.

Oliver stroked the remaining puppy and lifted it up to look under its belly. 'Well, little fellow, I think I know someone who would very much like to have you for her own.'

He pulled the black velvet ribbon that Kerensa had bought for him from his long hair. He had stayed the night of May Day at Sir Martin's house and arrived home late the next day to find the ribbon on top of a note left on his desk. It was written in Kerensa's girlish hand and was now folded up inside his breeches pocket.

'There you are, my boy,' Oliver told the puppy as he tied the ribbon firmly around its neck. 'Adam will know which one of you I want kept aside by this.'

Digging the note out of his pocket he read it through very slowly again, savouring each word, hoping it would provide an answer to the mystery of Kerensa's attitude towards him.

'Dear Oliver,' the note read, 'I Hope you will Like this Ribbon I Bought for You at the Fair.' It was signed simply, 'Kerensa'.

Once more he felt a pang of disappointment at not having reached home to say goodbye to her before she left for Tolwithrick. Folding the note carefully he put it back in its place. The puppy licked his face and playfully bit his hand with needle sharp teeth as his thoughts wandered far away.

After putting in a satisfying day's work, Oliver welcomed the appearance of Hezekiah Solomon at the farmhouse. Adam Renfree immediately brought out a pack of cards in the parlour but instead of the friendly game enduring until the small hours of the following morning as Oliver hoped, Hezekiah left precisely at nine o'clock to keep a mysterious assignation with an unknown lady. From the looks Adam cast in the direction of the kitchen, where Jenna Tregurtha could be heard preparing supper for them, Oliver perceived his farm steward also desired female company. After eating he tactfully with-drew from Ker-an-Mor Farm.

He was undecided where to go at first, riding off in no particular direction, but very soon he had been drawn towards the Manor house. Kerensa might not be there in his bed tonight, but her things were in the room. Her primroses were in her sitting room, her fragrance still lingered throughout the house.

He wondered what she was doing at Tolwithrick. Probably making herself busy with Rachael's eight children. Eight children… He would be content with only one, a son or a daughter, if she turned out to be like her mother. Kerensa would make a good mother.

Rachael would be spoiling her, of course. Making sure she was waited on hand and foot, giving the girl more than she could possibly want or need, and probably trying to fill her head with silly notions.

Well, Kerensa was too sensible to allow Rachael to influence her unwisely. As for William, he'd been captivated by Kerensa from the first moment he had seen her, but he was a man a husband did not have to worry about. He lacked the imagination to have affairs. If his brother Arthur had still been alive, however, he would have taken some close watching.

The last of the daylight was fading when Oliver reached the Manor grounds. Movement not far in front of him caused him to narrow his eyes as he made out the figures of Clem Trenchard and Alice Ford. The two were involved in a heated argument and neither heard his approach until he was nearly on top of them. Clem looked up sharply and muttering something to the girl, abruptly walked off in the direction of his father's farm without acknowledging Oliver's presence.

Anger flared up in him. He was offended by the youth's lack of manners. Ignoring his landlord was something Morley Trenchard would never have done. He watched Clem's back until he disappeared out of sight then looked to Alice for an explanation of what had occurred between them. She had one hand held to her throat, the other clutching her stomach. His displeasure with Clem Trenchard was forgotten as Oliver quickly dismounted.

'What is it, Alice?' he asked gently. 'Are you ill again?'

'I… I just feel…' she managed, before a severe wave of nausea filled her whole being. With both hands to her stomach she doubled over, only just turning her head in time to prevent herself from vomiting over Oliver's feet.

Alice moaned between each spasm of retching. Her vision left her for a moment, ringing filled her ears, and she would have sunk to the ground if Oliver had not supported her.

It was several moments before she could speak again. 'I'm sorry, sir. I…'

'It's all right, Alice,' he said, thrusting his handkerchief into one of her hands before helping her move a few steps away. 'Have you finished or is there more to come?'

'Yes… I mean, no. I'm sorry. I'll be all right now, sir.' She wiped her mouth with the handkerchief, then turned it inside out to dab at her eyes. 'I'll be all right now,' she repeated. 'It… it just comes over me any time of the day or night.'

Releasing his firm grip on her only when he was sure she was steady on her feet, Oliver whistled for Conomor.

'When you're ready, Alice, I'll lift you up on my horse and get you quickly into the Manor house. You're shivering. I'll get one of the King sisters to make you a hot drink and help you into bed. It's a pity Beatrice has not come back from Painted Bessie's yet, she would have a remedy to get you well in no time at all,' Oliver's tone was one of kindness and concern.

'Please, sir,' Alice sounded panicky, 'I don't want Ruth and Esther to know about this. I don't want anyone fussing round me.'

'Very well. If that is what you want,' he said soothingly. 'I wish I had something to keep you warm.'

He lifted her up to ride side saddle as though she were as light as thistledown.

'How long is it that you have been unwell like this, Alice?' he asked, taking the reins and walking beside her.

'A few days now. I'm that sorry, sir, and sorry I couldn't go over to Tolwithrick with her ladyship.'

'I should think the company you've been keeping of late is enough to make anyone sick,' Oliver remarked, still rankled by Clem's abrupt departure.

'You mean Clem, do you, sir?'

'Yes, I do. He was fortunate not to get his head blown off tonight. I keep a pistol in my saddle in the event of meeting undesirables on the road… or on my property. If you want someone to pay you court, Alice, I'd have thought there were more suitable young men attending your Bible meetings than him. If you'll take my advice, you won't see Trenchard again.'

Alice's lip trembled and her eyes filled with tears. 'He doesn't want to see me again anyway. He was just telling me when… when you rode up to us, sir.'

Oliver stopped walking. 'I see. Are you fond of him, Alice?'

'Yes,' she blurted out through her tears.

'In that case, I'm sorry. We haven't much farther left to go now. Hold on tightly, I'll soon have you warm and comfortable.'

—

It was well past midnight when Clem lay on his bed in the cramped room he shared with his brother. He'd stayed out late purposely to ensure his family would all be sound asleep when he returned. The anguish he'd suffered at having to be so forceful with Alice still remained with him. The girl had been determined not to make what he had been trying to say easy for either of them. Quite deliberately she had misconstrued everything he had said in an effort to end their relationship as painlessly as possible.

'You're just a bit tired, Clem,' she had insisted, 'only a bit off colour. Perhaps you're coming down with the same sickness as me.'

At the last he had been so brutal with her he believed even high and mighty Sir Oliver Pengarron himself could not have achieved a better job of it. When Alice finally had to admit she understood what he was saying she had become almost hysterical, accusing Clem of being selfish and cruel, of wanting her for one thing only, and now he'd got it, no longer wanting her at all.

If she had allowed him to finish, Clem would have explained that he needed time to be by himself, to sort out his feelings, to see which direction his life was to take. They could have stayed friends and perhaps sometime in the future…

What future? he thought wretchedly in the darkness. He thumped his pillow then looked hastily across at his crippled brother to see if he had been disturbed, but Kenver slept peacefully on.

All Clem could see of his brother was the back of his fluffy fair hair. He almost envied Kenver at that moment. Paralysed from the waist down from birth, he had no aspirations towards marrying or producing a family, content to craft useful or more exotic items from wood, stone, shells and driftwood, or to sculpt them from blocks of granite. Florrie regularly sold the finished articles at the marketplace in Marazion, and at fifteen years old Kenver was contributing well to the family coffers. He was no liability to them, a term Morley Trenchard had used concerning Clem more than once in the last few months.

His thoughts were brought back to the sixty faggots of furze he had cut and tied that day; he had made up for the necessity of that remark. But the relentless stinging of his scratches was a more than uncomfortable reminder of the price he had paid while doing so.

Turning restlessly, he stared out of the window at the indigo star-speckled sky, and very soon the stars merged into a glimmering haze as tears of hopelessness brimmed over in his eyes.

–

Dunstan plodded back into the kitchen after his last visit to the garden for the night. He took his reward of a biscuit gently out of Oliver's fingers, then nuzzled his master's leg as a thank you, before taking it to eat at his leisure in his bed next to the fireplace. He was licking up the crumbs when the sound of a light step brought his old head up expectantly. But it wasn't the girl he'd hoped it would be, and grumbling like the sound of low thunder over Perranbarvah, he settled himself down to sleep.

Alice hastily pulled her shawl tighter over her nightdress. She had not expected there to be anyone in the kitchen this late except Dunstan.

'I'm sorry, sir…' she began, then broke off miserably.

'It's all right, Alice,' he said, moving over to her with a hand held out in case she became faint. 'Are you ill again?'

Despite being uncomfortably hot, Alice shivered. She couldn't meet her master's eyes and looked down at the stone floor beneath her bare feet. 'I've just got a bit of a headache, that's all,' she answered shyly. 'I couldn't sleep so I came down for a sip of water.'

The grandfather clock in the hall chimed a quarter hour past one o'clock. The night was oppressively close and stuffy. The mixture of smells, the yeast, herbs, game, smoke from the smouldering fire and Dunstan's own peculiar odour, was suddenly overwhelming to Alice. The kitchen walls and ceiling seemed to close in on her, bile rose in her throat and acid burned at the base of her stomach. It wasn't until

Oliver asked her if she was about to be sick that she realised she was rubbing her stomach in circles with the flat of her hand.

'Um... no,' she murmured in confusion. 'I don't like the smells in here. If I could just have some water... lie down...'

'A little brandy would do you more good,' he suggested.

'I don't drink anything like that, sir,' she told him, her teeth beginning to chatter as she shivered more and more.

She made to move past him to the water pump at the huge stone sink, but he stood his ground and barred her way.

'A small drop of brandy won't hurt you, Alice.'

As she would not look up at him Oliver bent his head close to hers to encourage her. Alice turned her head from him but he took her chin in one hand and raised it as he eased her back round to face him.

'It will settle your stomach. St Paul rendered similar advice – 'But use a little wine for thy stomach's sake' – and even your Preacher Renfree can't argue against that.'

There was no fight left in her, Alice nodded meekly and allowed Oliver to lead her to his study.

He poured a small measure of brandy, topped the glass with water and gave it to Alice, ensuring both her hands were clasped firmly around it. As he poured a drink for himself she moved over to a window, pretending to look out of it as she sipped the sweet-tasting liquid, her hands shaking in uncontrollable spasms.

Oliver warmed the bowl of his glass between his hand, glancing only occasionally at her so not to increase her distress. He finished his brandy slowly. Alice had hardly touched hers.

He called softly across the room, 'Alice?'

'Yes, sir.'

'Do you feel any better?'

'Not really. I...'

With an effort she placed her glass down safely on a small circular table at her side. Sobs racked her body as she put her head in her hands. Oliver reached her quickly. Alice sensed him there. She turned and cried wretchedly within the comforting warmth of his strong enfolding arms.

The next day found Oliver and Clem in Perranbarvah's parish church to attend a funeral. William and Lamorna Sampson of Polcudden Farm were bereaved of their son Henry, his neck broken when he had been thrown from a pony trap. It was a particularly sad tragedy for the Sampson family. Two sons had already predeceased him, and his death left his parents with three small daughters and no son to take over the lease of Polcudden Farm in later years.

The whole farming community of the Pengarron Estate, along with many an interested onlooker, was gathered for the funeral. It had been thankfully cool inside the church, but the sun was stifling hot as the plain wooden coffin was lowered into the ground to rest in the family grave with the two other Sampson sons. As the mourners moved off, Ben Rosevidney moved respectfully out of sight to collect his shovel. He would return the earth to the grave only when the last mourner had left the churchyard.

After offering a few comforting words to William and Lamorna Sampson, and promising to arrange for a suitable labourer to help on Polcudden in their son's place, Oliver walked over to the Trenchard family.

Morley took off his cap as he approached them. 'Sorry business, all this, m'lord,' he said with a resigned sigh.

'Indeed it is, Morley,' Oliver agreed, looking from him and nodding a solemn greeting to Florrie and Gran Donald before resting his eyes on Clem. 'I want a word with you,' he said coldly. 'Now, if you please.'

Clem said nothing. Morley and his wife exchanged worried glances. Gran Donald took the initiative. 'We'll make our own way over to Polcudden for the funeral tea. Clem can catch us up later.'

The Reverend Ivey watched the two men left alone by the retreating Trenchard family. With an expression of deep concern, he gave Lamorna Sampson his arm and led her gently to the farm cart that was to convey the remaining members of her family back to their home. He threw worried glances over his shoulder every few steps until the two men were out of his sight.

'I don't think we have anything to say to each other,' spat Clem, the moment his family were out of earshot.

'Well, *I* have a good deal to say to *you*, Trenchard,' Oliver returned, moving in closer to gain a more dominating position. 'About Alice Ford.'

'My friendship with Alice has nothing to do with you.' Clem made a move to follow his family. 'Just keep out of my business.'

'Something has happened to make it my business. You either listen to me, Trenchard, or I'll shout loud enough for everyone to hear what you've been up to.'

It was enough to bring Clem to a halt. 'Well, what has happened? Alice is all right, isn't she?'

Oliver looked around. The churchyard retained one or two groups of quietly conversing people, and the beach at the bottom of the steep hill was busy with fishermen preparing to launch their luggers. With the over-inquisitive Mrs Tregonning off to the funeral tea, and Ben Rosevidney waiting to fill in the grave, the Parsonage garden afforded the best chance of privacy.

'Follow me,' he ordered.

'What's this all about?' demanded Clem, when they were standing on the Reverend's neatly cut lawn.

Oliver stood no more than six inches away, his feet planted firmly apart, hands on his hips. He began speaking slowly. 'I don't like you, Trenchard. I don't like your surly moods or your bad manners. Furthermore, I don't like the way you worry your parents. A worried farmer may produce poor crops and livestock, neglect his farm.'

Clem attempted to interrupt but was stopped by a raised hand.

'But what I particularly dislike about you is the way you've seduced one of my servants, made her pregnant, and have now cast her aside.'

Clem's face paled. 'Alice, pregnant! She's said nothing to me about it. What makes you so sure?'

'Don't be a fool, man! Why do you think she's always being sick? No one else at the Manor is, and we all eat and drink the same food and water. You don't deny making love to her, do you?'

Clem stayed silent for several moments, trying to take in this new development in the muddle of his life, then said stonily, 'I'll go and

216

see Alice at once, and you needn't worry – I'll do what I have to do, to put things right by her.'

'You most certainly will, Trenchard! There will be no question of your ducking out of your duty to her. Alice is a fine girl, she'll make you a good wife.' Oliver folded his arms and deliberately lowered his voice. 'And perhaps it will stop you hankering after mine.'

It was all too much for Clem. To be told of Alice's pregnancy by this man, of all people. To be practically accused of wanting not to marry her when he had made it clear he would offer to, and then to be taunted over losing Kerensa to him, was more than he could bear. All the hatred and loss he had suffered because of this man's actions erupted with the vicious strength of a freak wave over a jagged rock.

With all his might he aimed his fist at Oliver Pengarron's jaw.

Always alert in a confrontation, Oliver brought up his forearm to ward off the blow and plunged his tautened fingers into the pit of Clem's stomach.

Clem staggered backwards. 'You bastard, Pengarron!' he gasped, 'You rotten, pig-headed bastard! I could kill you!'

'Don't be fool enough to try, Trenchard. I doubt if you're a match for me,' Oliver threatened. 'But if it's a fight that you want, I'll be more than happy to oblige you.'

'If it makes you happy,' Clem retorted, throwing off his coat, 'it will give me the greatest of pleasure.'

Oliver raised his eyebrows, his expression disdainful as slowly he unfastened his coat. He held it out by the collar with the tips of his fingers before letting it slide to the ground.

Clem rushed forward but Oliver was not unprepared for the fresh onslaught. Although Clem's fist hit home this time, bruising Oliver's cheek just to the side of his left eye, Clem received another sickening blow in the gut, followed by one powerfully driven under his chin. As he was hurled backwards he snatched a good grip on Oliver's shirt, pulling the taller man with him as he lost his foothold and hit the ground.

They grappled over the full expanse of the dry grass of the lawn, indiscriminately crushing flower beds and knocking over the

Reverend's bird table, each man warding off as many blows as he received.

Oliver got to his feet and, clutching the youth by the collar of his torn shirt, dragged Clem up with him, only to be surprised by a blow to the jaw which sent him staggering back heavily against an apple tree. Both were now somewhat out of breath. Oliver allowed the tree to support his weight while at a safe distance Clem crouched down, breathing in deeply. But this respite lasted only for a moment. The two men paced the ground, sizing up the other for signs of weakness.

Spots of blood had appeared on the front and sleeves of Clem's shirt, the scratches from the gorse spines pulled apart in the tussle. He had no sensation of pain, he was enjoying this battle and did not want it to end. He relished every punch he delivered to the other man's body and took sadistic pleasure at the sight of the cuts and bruises suffered at his hands. But he knew he was unlikely to inflict the kind of damage he wanted to unless he adopted more subtle means.

Oliver Pengarron was bigger and broader than he, stronger too, with the added advantage of more years and the experience of close fighting as a professional soldier.

Clem allowed Oliver to advance almost upon him, and at the last moment butted his head hard into his stomach. As Oliver's head was brought down Clem ploughed his head in again, this time directly at Oliver's mouth and nose. The baronet's teeth cut into his head as Clem grasped Oliver's legs and plunged him to the ground.

Oliver ended up in a sitting position. Clem, nimbly running behind him and encircling his neck with one arm, used his other cruelly to heave Oliver's head to the side. Gagging and choking, Oliver reached behind and clenched two fistfuls of Clem's shirt. The shirt was ripped out of Clem's breeches but Oliver was strong enough to toss him cleanly straight over his head. Clem's body struck the ground with a tremendous thud and he lay still on his back, gasping in deep lungfuls of the warm air.

Wiping blood away from his mouth and nose, Oliver said breathlessly, 'Give it up, Trenchard. This is getting us nowhere.'

Clem raised himself up on one elbow, panting heavily as he spoke. 'I'll kill you first, Pengarron.'

'You most certainly will not! I will have an explanation for this outrageous behaviour, and why the two of you think you have the right to fight on my lawn!'

The Reverend Ivey was furious. It was distressing enough to bury the body of a young and fruitful soul. To come across this immediately afterwards was almost unforgivable.

'At first I could hardly believe what Ben was frantically trying to tell me,' the Reverend continued, while the two adversaries pulled themselves shakily to their feet. 'Clem Trenchard, go and wait by the Parsonage door. I'll speak to you presently.'

Panting like an old dog Clem snatched up his coat, gave Oliver a look of pure hatred, and made for the Parsonage door, slightly bowed over as he clutched his painful gut.

Oliver watched him derisively but his expression turned to one of shame when the Reverend held his own coat in front of his eyes with the bland statement, 'I think this belongs to you.'

'I… um…'

'Have not set a very good example?'

From his great respect of the old gentleman parson, whom he saw as a father figure, Oliver took the chastisement. 'I offer you my apologies, Reverend. I'll send someone over immediately to clear up and repair the damage.'

'That won't be necessary, Oliver. Ben doesn't like anyone but himself to touch the garden.' The Reverend Ivey looked down at his hands. 'I suppose I don't have to guess the cause of the altercation?'

'No,' Oliver replied softly.

'Oliver, if I may be so bold… there are times when your kindness and charity go unnoticed and unthanked. There are other times when your impatience and pride rise to unacceptable levels and you are every bit as rude as the people you condemn for it.' The Reverend gave a small cough and plunged on, 'I would even go as far to suggest it is time you stopped behaving like a spoilt child.'

Oliver's face darkened, but only for a moment. With a wry smile he waved his hands in submission.

'Good, then that's got that out of the way. Kindly give my regards to Kerensa when you see her next.'

The Reverend Ivey was surprised at the way the baronet had accepted his remonstrances and hoped the chastisement he was about to give to the lovelorn Clem Trenchard would be just as well received.

–

Florrie Trenchard was alone in her kitchen when her son showed himself at last. She was not pleased with him. 'What have you been up to, Clem? And why didn't you come over to Polcudden? The Reverend Ivey drew your father aside over there and told him he'd had words with you. You seem to have no thought for anyone but yourself these days.'

'It's a long story, Mother. I'm going to change for milking.'

'Just a minute, my son. Change, you say? From what is left of your one good shirt, is that what you mean? You're not going anywhere until you tell me what his lordship wanted with you, what the Reverend Ivey said to you, and have explained how you came by those cuts and bruises.'

Clem put a hand to his face. 'That's nothing much, Mother,' he said blankly, all emotion drained from him. 'Sir Oliver didn't want anything of importance and the Reverend Ivey told me off about my behaviour.'

'Oh, what did he say? What have you been doing?' Florrie Trenchard pointed to a chair but her son did not intend to stay and give a lengthy explanation.

'He just said my behaviour hasn't been fair to others. After that he was quite understanding, said I ought to go and talk to Matthias Renfree – but that won't do any good.' Clem made for his bedroom and paused at the door. 'I, um, have been over to the Manor house to ask Alice to marry me.'

'I see,' Florrie Trenchard said quietly. 'What did she say?'

Clem's face was vacant. 'Yes. She said yes.'

–

Sinking down in an armchair in his study, Oliver closed his painful black eye. Alice knocked and entered with hot water and towels.

'What's that for?' he said, opening his eyelid slowly.

'I saw the state you were in as you came across the yard. Clem left not long ago in a similar condition. Was it me you were fighting over? He wouldn't tell me anything.'

'Yes… among other things.' He stayed quiet as she cleaned and dabbed at his swellings, cuts and bruises, and finally wrapped the freshly laundered handkerchief he'd given to her the night before around his grazed knuckles. 'You will not be needing this again, I take it?' he asked her, holding up his hand.

'That's a nasty cut on your lip,' Alice remarked, then looked into his eyes. 'No, Oliver,' she said, now, in private, on first name terms with her master as she was with her mistress, 'I won't be needing it again.'

Chapter 13

Tolwithrick, the grand country seat of the Beswethericks, was roughly the same size as Pengarron Manor. It was more stately in appearance and furnishings and built a century later than the Manor, and did not possess the same atmosphere of history and continuity. There was, however, an abiding atmosphere of contentment throughout Tolwithrick, with children playing noisily up and down the staircases, in and out of the rooms, and all over the gardens, orchards and stables. Kerensa looked forward to each new day there.

Most of the gossip in the kitchens of Tolwithrick for the past week that she had been staying there had centred on her, as Sir Oliver Pengarron's new young wife.

'I'd never thought he'd get married,' the housekeeper remarked.

'She may not have noble blood but she's just the sort of little wife young Master Arthur would have liked,' put in the cook.

One footman nudged another. 'Do 'ee reckon Sir Oliver will be keeping someone else's bed warm at the moment, do 'ee?'

'Dunno,' the other answered, 'but we all know his reputation.' He moved closer to whisper, 'Bet he's missing her anyway. I know I would, and I wouldn't mind gettin' my—'

'Ahem!' A stinging look from Polly Berryman, the maid from Rachael's household who had been assigned to wait upon Kerensa, and who had come into the kitchen to collect her breakfast tray, brought the smutty conversation to an end. But when her back was turned, a nod and an earthy grin from the first footman informed the other his views were shared.

'I'll take this up to Lady Pengarron, then,' Polly Berryman said to the cook, keeping an indignant eye on the two footmen who busied

222

themselves about their duties. 'I'll inform her that Lady Rachael was delivered of her baby last night.'

–

'Babies always seem to be born through the night, don't they, Polly?' Kerensa said, sitting up in bed and settling the tray across her lap. 'Is it a boy or a girl?'

'A little small boy, m'lady. I've heard this one is the image of old Sir Martin himself.'

'Last night Lady Rachael told me she had a feeling the baby would be born before I returned to Pengarron Manor,' Kerensa said, unable to hide her excitement. 'Polly, do you think I'll be able to see the baby today? And to think I slept soundly and knew nothing about it! You say Lady Rachael is perfectly well?'

'She's fine, m'lady, and I'm sure you'll be able to see her and the baby later today,' Polly answered with a warm smile.

Polly Berryman was a second cousin to Daniel Berryman of Orchard Hill Farm, and had been in service at Tolwithrick from the age of twelve.

Now a sober woman of twenty-five, she had at first been reserved about being called on to wait on a baronet's wife from a low working-class background. But Kerensa's friendly simplicity had soon brought a smile to brighten Polly's pleasant face. Kerensa assumed no false airs like others Polly had known who had married above their station, and was content to allow the maid to help and advise her on what gowns to wear and on how to have her hair arranged. On one occasion she had sought advice on how to behave now she was staying in a conventional noble household.

Kerensa liked Polly too, and as she sat propped up against white silken pillows, chattering like an excited child as she ate her breakfast, she was unaware of the growing loyalty her temporary maid felt towards her.

After breakfast she slipped out into the gardens. Rain showers through the night had refreshed the air and ground. The sun was bright and friendly as she ran with a light step to Elwyn Trethowan,

Tolwithrick's head gardener. A carbon copy of Jake Angove, he gave her a toothy grin as he straightened up from the hydrangea bush he was attending to, and offered her a small fork.

'Mornin' to 'ee, ma'am,' he said. 'Ready to get yer back into it again, are 'ee?' Like Jake Angove, Elwyn Trethowan did not stand on ceremony.

'Good morning, Elwyn,' Kerensa smiled back. 'Have you heard about the new baby?'

'Ais, but it's not an unusual occurrence round these 'ere parts. See you got summat more suitable to wear today then.'

'Yes. Polly found this dress from somewhere for me,' she said, swinging the skirt of the simple light brown dress she was wearing instead of one of her new gowns, the only ones Alice had packed for her.

Kerensa worked with Elwyn for most of the morning in either companionable silence or pleasant conversation, carefully removing weeds that had escaped earlier tending. It was like being at home with Jake, but without the added company of old Dunstan. In fact there were no dogs at all to be found at Tolwithrick, and on enquiring from Elwyn what the reason was for this lack of canine company, she was told Rachael feared them, having been badly bitten by one as a child.

After a hectic luncheon with the five elder children of Rachael and William, Kerensa, now in a green muslin day gown, was ushered into Rachael's large bedroom. She was sitting up in bed as lively as a young girl at her first ball, belying the fact that she was a woman in her late thirties who had given birth less than twenty-four hours before.

'Kerensa, my dear,' she said gaily, holding out both her hands. 'You do look pretty. Come and sit down here on the bed beside me.'

Kerensa sat carefully on the edge of the creaking bed that had seen the birth of many generations of Beswethericks.

'How are you, Rachael?' she asked, marvelling at how her friend's complexion had changed overnight from sallow yellowness to clear pink softness. 'You look radiant.'

'I feel radiant, thank you. But then, I've always found childbearing easy enough. Do you know, if we go on at this rate, William and I will end up producing more children than all the brats in Perranbarvah?' At this Rachael hooted with laughter and received a disapproving look from the stern-faced nurse who was in the room folding clean linen.

Kerensa laughed with her and asked hopefully, 'Can I see the baby today, Rachael, please? Will it be all right?'

'Of course you can see him. He should wake up soon. He's in the small nursery in the next room. I'd rather have him in here with me, but she insists it will disturb my rest.' The last sentence was aimed in the direction of the nurse's back.

William put his head around the door. 'All right to come in?' he whispered. 'I've got Martin and Ameline with me.'

Rachael glanced at the nurse to see if she would raise any objection. With none forthcoming, William and his two elder children tiptoed into the room.

'You may as well bring the baby in now, Nurse,' Rachael said.

'Very well, m'lady,' replied the nurse, her disapproving look set harder.

Martin and Ameline, the image of their father and mother respectively, gazed down at their tiny new brother with awed wonder for some time after the nurse passed the baby into their mother's arms. Ameline asked if she could hold him and was told she could in a few days' time. Martin tried to show that as an almost grown-up thirteen year old he was hardly interested in any baby, but couldn't hide the look of pride on his young face.

The nurse bundled the children out of the room ten minutes later, and Rachael handed the baby, snugly wrapped in a woollen shawl, to Kerensa.

'He's beautiful. What a lovely family you have,' Kerensa said, smoothing the baby's soft, downy red cheek with a finger. 'You must be very proud of them.'

'Yes, we are proud of them all,' Rachael said happily. 'We've been lucky too. It's unusual to have a large family and not lose one or two of them.'

'Us Beswethericks have always had a houseful of brats,' William put in, 'not like the Pengarrons at all. They usually only manage one or two at a time, you know. You must have noticed by now Oliver has hardly any relatives.'

Chuckling to himself he went on, 'You should have seen him when he was a small boy, Kerensa. He was the most dreadful child! Always up to mischief he was, with Arthur, my youngest brother, in the thick of it too. They got many a beating for Oliver's daredevil schemes. Poor Lady Caroline had six children, but Oliver was the only one to live past two or three years. He was very precious to his mother and father and they spoiled him dreadfully. Oliver was determined to have his own way in everything, always determined to be top dog. And the energy he had! When he came over here to stay with Arthur, he'd have the house in turmoil within an hour. It was almost as if he was making up for not having brothers and sisters, as if he had all their energy as well as his own.' William sighed, his face shining at his reminiscences. 'When I think of the things those two used to get up to...'

Kerensa had taken it all in with deep interest. She looked up from the baby. 'It sounds as though Oliver and your brother were quite a handful,' she said, wondering if William knew of her husband's past association with Rachael.

'They certainly were, my dear. Oliver still is, wouldn't you say? It's as if there's something driving him ever onwards. He works harder than anyone I know. I believe it's nothing unusual for him to rise well before dawn, work hard for several hours with his horses or on the farm, then sit down to his paperwork. Then he'll perhaps visit a tenant farm, then a friend, check up on all his injured animals, follow it up with a party, and spend nearly the whole night at the card table. To top it all, he'll be up bright and early the next day and begin all over again. I'm sure I don't know where he gets all his energy from.'

Kerensa nodded. It was a good description of the man she was learning more about with every passing day.

'Then of course there are all his other activities,' Rachael said wickedly, a twinkle in her eyes.

'If it's the ladies she means, my dear,' William told Kerensa hastily, not sure if the girl understood his wife's humour, 'Oliver's left them alone since he married you.'

'Yes, but do they leave him alone?' asked Rachael, teasing William now.

'Um… not really. But they soon give up when they realise he's not at all interested.' William became embarrassed. Kerensa smiled at him and he squeezed her hand. 'Well, I'd better be off and get on with some work… plenty to do.' Kissing Rachael, then his son, he was relieved to be able to leave the room. 'I'll be up to see you after supper, dear,' he said as he closed the door.

Rachael turned to the nurse. 'It's all right if you leave us, now, Nurse. Lady Pengarron will call for you if you're needed.'

The nurse sniffed her disapproval before reluctantly leaving the bedroom again.

'Anyone would think I've not had a baby before and knew nothing about them,' Rachael remarked, 'but I suppose she means well, poor old sourpuss.'

'If he were mine, I wouldn't let anyone else look after him,' said Kerensa, almost fiercely, cuddling the sleeping baby closer to her body.

Watching the girl closely, Rachael said, 'I suppose you will be hoping to give Oliver a child fairly soon?'

'Yes,' Kerensa answered quietly, 'Oliver talks about it from time to time.'

'And you? Do you want children, Kerensa?'

'Yes, of course. I just wish something would happen.'

'Give it a little more time, my dear,' Rachael said soothingly. 'You've only been married a few months.' She leaned forward and touched Kerensa's arm. 'Do you miss Oliver?'

She looked defensive. 'I suppose so.' She was glad to be getting on well with the Beswethericks, especially Rachael. It was good to be on friendly terms with some of Oliver's friends, would give her someone to talk to at any social events he took her to. But would it be wise to confide in Rachael, could she be trusted? She might pass on to Oliver any confidences she was told.

'You've hardly mentioned his name since you've been here and you look so sad when you think no one is looking at you,' Rachael said, sounding concerned. 'Oliver's not cruel or demanding to you, is he?'

'No, it's nothing like that, Rachael. It's just that, that...'

'He's impatient, stubborn, childish and self-centred?'

It brought a smile to Kerensa's face, 'Yes, no... well, he's not as bad as that.'

'What is it then? Don't you want to talk about it? Or am I seeing something that doesn't exist?'

For a few moments Kerensa thought about telling Rachael of her suspicion about Bartholomew Drannock and the strain it had caused in her relationship with Oliver. She wanted to live peaceably with him, she was his wife and that fact would never change. She didn't want to spend the rest of her life living in a situation fraught with bad feeling. Rachael had a successful marriage, she was an experienced mother, her advice might be invaluable; she might say the very thing to help her put Kerensa's feelings into perspective and point a way to a brighter future. The baby stirred in her arms and she decided against speaking out.

'I'm just finding it hard to adjust to my new life, that's all. The baby is lovely, have you chosen a name for him yet?'

Rachael stayed quiet for a moment, studying Kerensa, then said, 'If you ever want to talk, Kerensa, you'll find I have a willing ear.' Then she added straightaway, 'He's to be baptised Sebastian Pawly Richard James. Quite a mouthful, isn't it? We've sent word to Oliver, by the way, and invited him over for the baptism in the family chapel next week.'

Kerensa was surprised to find that the thought of seeing him was not unwelcome to her. Perhaps by then the time apart would have diminished some of their ill-humour towards each other, and if he was in a sympathetic mood perhaps she could find the courage to confront him about the Drannock boy and they could resolve the matter in some way.

'Will he come, do you think?'

'Oh, yes, he is godfather to all our boys. Takes it all very seriously too and shows great interest in them all. Martin is particularly fond of Oliver, believes him to be quite a hero and follows him about everywhere when he comes to stay with us. Come to think of it, he hasn't stayed overnight for several months. The last time he was here was a few hours on last Christmas Day. Old Marty ended up roaring drunk, the poor dear. Funny, though,' Rachael said, pursing her lips, 'Oliver seems to drink a lot but I can't ever recall seeing him in his cups. Have you?'

'No,' Kerensa said. 'But all that alcohol can't be doing him any good.' She looked at the baby again. 'Sebastian's gone to sleep.'

'So you do worry about him?' Rachael watched for a reaction to her remark.

'Sebastian?'

'Now, you know I meant Oliver. I'd like to ask you something, Kerensa, but I don't want to upset you.'

'What is it?' the girl asked quietly.

'You were going to marry someone else, weren't you... a farm labourer or something?'

'You're talking of Clem, Clem Trenchard. His father is one of Oliver's tenant farmers.'

'Did you love this Clem, Kerensa? Do you still love him?'

With downcast eyes she answered, 'Yes. I feel so bad about losing him and hurting him, Rachael. Clem is kind and gentle and considerate, he's very handsome too, but now he looks so lost and helpless. I'm sure we would have been very happy together.'

Rachael reached out her hand and turned Kerensa to face her.

'It is a shame about that, my dear, but no one should live in the past. I wanted to marry an attractive young curate I met in London before it was arranged for me to marry William. I suffered agonies at the time, like you are now, but I quickly grew to like William and I have been content over the years. I have to say, Kerensa,' Rachael said seriously, 'you do not sound to me as if you have an all consuming love for this farmer's son. You are probably feeling guilty more than anything.'

'Now I'm more confused than ever!' Kerensa sighed in exasperation.

Rachael smiled as one who knew best. 'There is a lot of good in Oliver if you take the time to look for it, it's your duty as his wife to do so, and I believe you are not totally unhappy with him.'

'Now you sound like the Reverend Ivey, Rachael.' Kerensa smiled. 'He has a great liking for Oliver and often talks to me about his good points.'

'Well, there you are, my dear. If a man of God can see the good in him, it can't be far below the surface, can it?'

As Kerensa changed back into the simple brown dress before rejoining Elwyn Trethowan in the garden, a jumble of impressions vied with each other for the dominant place in her mind. One was Clem's face, sullen and heartbroken, one Oliver's proud and impatient, yet kindly. The other was Bartholomew Drannock.

A long shadow fell over Kerensa as she struggled to tie back a straggling hydrangea bush.

'I can't quite manage this one, Elwyn,' she gasped, panting in her efforts.

'Try tying the knot other than at the back of the bush.'

She jerked her head around at the unexpected voice. 'Oliver!'

'Rachael seems to have turned you into a grubby little urchin,' he said drolly.

A light tingling sensation made its way quickly through her. She had left the Manor under the cloud of her suspicions and his ill-humour, but it was good to see him again. To look up at his dark face, to gaze back into his dazzling eyes and know, without feeling any shyness, that he desired her.

Kerensa took the hands he offered to help her to her feet, feeling their warm roughness as he held on to hers. Oliver looked on his wife with pleasure. She had bloomed during her absence from him. Her cheeks were tinged a warm pink, her eyes sparkled more than before, and he wanted to linger over her full red mouth.

'I enjoy working out here,' she said simply.

'Mmmm… you look well enough on it.' He looked down at her plain dress. 'Were you not expecting me?'

'Yes, but not until later tonight.'

'Well, now that I'm here, you can show me William's latest brat.'

Kerensa became animated as she talked about the baby. 'Oh, Sebastian is lovely, he doesn't cry very much and has such soft fluffy hair.

Rachael lets me hold him any time I want to. She's been up and out of bed for days, much to the annoyance of her nurse.'

Oliver took her arm and tucked it inside his as they walked to the house, only half-listening as she chattered on about the Beswetherick children and how excited young Martin was at the prospect of going trout fishing with his godfather. Then she was eager to know how the people at the Manor were.

'How's Alice? Is she any better? And Jack, how's…'

He stopped walking and held her firmly by the shoulders.

'I'll tell you about everyone later. I would like to know how you are, Kerensa. Are you still in the ill-humour you were in when you left the Manor?'

She flushed but did not move away from him.

'Did you miss me at all?' he asked sincerely.

'Yes,' she said very softly. 'I've missed you, Oliver.'

He leaned forward and took her face in both hands and brushed her lips with his. She made no attempt to escape from him so he gathered her in close and kissed her with some of the passion that had been growing steadily inside him for her since she had gone away.

Kerensa slid her arms inside his coat and clasped her hands behind his back. When Oliver raised his face from hers she buried her cheek against his chest. Stroking her hair with gentle fingers, he kissed the top of her head and rested the side of his face against it.

Watching them from an upstairs window, Rachael Beswetherick nodded and smiled to herself.

–

'Now what are you doing?' he demanded impatiently from the bed.

'Picking up your clothes. You're not at home, Oliver.' Kerensa gathered them up and folded them neatly over the back of a chair.

'Never mind all that. Get into bed, will you? As it was I thought that woman was never going to finish with you.'

Kerensa looked at him squarely. 'Rantings and ravings,' she said, reminded of what Jake Angove had said about him; and Beatrice: 'Tempers 'n' tantrums.'

'What's that?'

'You should learn to be more patient, Oliver. If I was a long time with Polly, it's because she likes to be thorough.'

'Are you deliberately being difficult, girl? Perhaps I should get out of here and drag you into this bed.'

'If I'm being difficult maybe it's because I've had a good teacher in you,' she returned pertly, 'but I'm coming now.'

She blew out all the candles but the ones in a triple sconce on Oliver's side and climbed into bed beside him. 'I thought you were going to stay down and talk with William,' she told him, as he pulled her against his bare chest.

'I don't recall that I was,' he said moodily, 'and I'm not sure I approve of this new you. Has Rachael been encouraging you to be rebellious towards me?'

Kerensa pulled away a little from him and looked him in the face. 'Are you cross with me then?'

'No,' he laughed. 'It's good to see you gaining in confidence.' He kissed her neck then added in mock threat, 'But don't let it get out of hand or...'

'Or what?' she whispered.

'Oh, I'll think of something,' he said, untying the ribbons down the front of her nightgown.

Kerensa held his hands still. 'You were going to tell me about Alice and the others,' she teased him.

'Not now,' he said, roughly pulling the nightgown off her shoulders, 'not now...'

He had spent one of the most trying days of his life. The four-mile ride over to Tolwithrick had seemed much longer than it usually did that morning. The time spent with the new baby and his older brothers and sisters had been a torment to him. Even the hours he'd spent fishing for trout with young Martin in the nearby Withy river, because Rachael had insisted on Kerensa joining her for the afternoon, had dragged interminably, instead of proving as enjoyable as they normally would have been. He felt as though a worm was relentlessly chewing into his gut with every hour he endured, longing to be alone with his young wife.

Promptly at four o'clock, with William and Rachael, they'd eaten a plentiful dinner of goose and roasted lobster, plum pudding, jellies and custard. Oliver had hoped Rachael would lie down for a rest before supper when it would have been easy enough to suggest to William that he might like to take himself off to his study for an hour or so. But Rachael, starved of society for too long at the end of her pregnancy, kept them all occupied with gossip and the playing of the harpsichord, while each of them were required to take a turn at singing to its accompaniment. Kerensa's voice was sweet and clear, but he had only wanted to take her in his arms.

Tea was brought in at eight o'clock and Rachael had poured out several rounds with irritating ceremony, her gossip persisting until almost eleven. Oliver had very nearly loudly exhaled the sigh of relief he felt inside when she announced that she must retire to bed if she was to look her best for the baptism the next morning. Kerensa retired with her, William kissing them both and Oliver following suit before the ladies left the room.

'Father will be arriving with Judith early tomorrow,' William said, 'he'll be delighted to see Kerensa here. Will you join me in a glass of cognac, Oliver?'

'I'll have one, thank you, but very quickly,' he'd answered.

'You sound as if you're going somewhere in a hurry.'

'While I'd like to stay and chat with you, William, right now my wife will make better company.'

'I thought she might,' William grinned across the room.

Now at last Oliver was relaxed. Kerensa had loved him with all the responsiveness and affection he could have wished for. It had been a long lonely two weeks. His home had been empty without her, even worse than before their marriage when there had been no reason to go home at all. Even if she made him suffer with more of the inexplicable moods like the one she had been in when she came here, or became a terrible nag, or even bad-tempered to the point of screaming abuse at him, he would not mind too much. Kerensa at home in any circumstances was better than no Kerensa at all.

Kerensa stroked Oliver's hair, while still floating on an aftermath of silken waves from their passion. She had been as impatient for these moments as Oliver had been, and had found it harder to wait, much too shy to reveal her eagerness to be in the arms of her handsome sensual husband again. It had been lonely here before, lying in this enormous bed without him close to her. He had been different this time. He had wanted her not just because it was his right to take her but for herself, for who she was. If Oliver accepted her as a person in her own right and not just an appendage who was expected to obey his every whim, she might just be able to ask him about Bartholomew Drannock.

A small pang inside warned her that it might cause his mood to swing sharply again and ruin the wonderful intimacy they shared. What if he knew about the boy and could not care less about him? And if the boy turned out to be Samuel Drannock's son in the end, what would Oliver think of her for believing him to be the boy's father and abandoning him and his mother?

'You're quiet, my love,' he said dreamily.

She took a breath. 'Oliver?'

'Yes.'

At the last moment she decided the question of Bartholomew Drannock would be better left alone, at least for a short while, to see if she could live with the knowledge without resenting Oliver. She might even end up opening a can of worms – perhaps he didn't realise he was the boy's father, if he was, and Jenifer was passing off Samuel Drannock in his role. Instead she said, 'You were going to tell me about Alice and the others, remember?'

He moved to look down on her, his face serious. Kerensa smoothed the network of tiny fine lines gathered at the corners of his dark eyes.

'Is something wrong at home?' she asked. 'The rest of the servants are well,' he told her, 'but Alice has left the Manor and has gone home for the time being.'

'But why? Has someone upset her?'

'The girl is getting married, Kerensa. She's pregnant.'

She could not hide her shock. Oliver had to move aside so she could sit up, swallowing hard as she murmured, 'To Clem... is it Clem?'

'Yes. I made sure he'll do the honourable thing by her. His parents are relieved in a way, I think, and his grandmother told me that with a wife to come home to, and a child on the way, perhaps the boy will pull himself together at last.'

'I hope they will get on all right with each other,' Kerensa said doubtfully.

'Why? Is there a reason that they should not?' he asked, a trifle sharply.

'Well...'

'Well, what?' Oliver's tone was much harsher now, and the warm pleasant feeling inside Kerensa was beginning to subside. It was a good thing she had not mentioned the Drannock boy if he could become bad-tempered and suspicious so easily.

'It's just that when I used to go to the Bible classes with Clem, Alice used to hang about us a lot and he would get quite annoyed,' she explained. 'He thought her rather childish and once said a bal-maiden would never make a farmer's wife. She used to hang about Henry Sampson too, you see, and he's reckoned to be a good catch, being the next in line for Polcudden Farm.'

'Well, Trenchard will have to make her a farmer's wife now, won't he? If he didn't want to take a chance on it he shouldn't have rolled her in the hay in the first place. As for Henry Sampson, that poor soul won't be taking any maid to wife.'

Kerensa flinched at the outburst. 'Why? Has something happened to Henry Sampson?' she demanded, dreading the answer.

When he confirmed her fears, tears sprang to Kerensa's eyes and she turned her head away. Oliver was angry with himself for hurting her, and the memory of Alice's fears served to make him feel worse.

'I'm sorry, my love,' he said contritely, 'I didn't mean to sound so cruel.'

She turned back, wiping her tears away crossly with the side of her head, then jabbed a finger at the fading bruises on his body and the cut healing on his lip.

'How did all this happen?' she demanded of him. 'It was no accident from the looks of it. Who were you fighting with?'

'No one of any concern to you,' he told her quietly.

The flashpoint was over. Cupping her small oval face in his hands he kissed her fiercely, and with almost the same intensity they made love again.

Neither slept well that night. A sudden thunderstorm lashed the skies overhead, a counterpoint to their unease. Oliver got out of bed, wrapping a sheet around his waist. He threw a window open to cool the stifling heat of the room and, resting his hands on the sill, watched Nature's nocturnal entertainment.

Cries from some of Rachael's less hardy children soon filled the house, and thankful for the opportunity to slip out of bed Kerensa retrieved her nightgown from its crumpled heap on the floor and left the room to offer comfort to the fearful little ones.

Seeing the slight form of his mother's guest heading for the nursery, young Martin Beswetherick knocked and entered the room she had just left.

'Can I come in, Oliver?' he had to shout above the thunder.

'Yes, Martin. The storm keeping you awake too, is it?'

The boy joined the man at the window. 'Father told me once that you and Uncle Arthur would get out of bed and play outside in a storm when you were boys,' he said.

'We used to get up to all kinds of things,' Oliver said. 'We received a lot of thrashings, Martin, but we had a lot of fun.'

'With women too?'

Oliver gave the boy a sideways glance. 'Lots of women,' he said, winking an eye.

Martin moved closer to his godfather. 'Did you have your first one by my age?'

This brought a laugh from the man. 'No, of course not… but not long afterwards.'

They watched the sky light up at rapid intervals, their faces illuminated with each flash of lightning.

'I think Kerensa is very beautiful,' Martin said. 'Can you get me a wife like her when I'm old enough, Oliver?'

He pondered on this as a streak of lightning lit the length of the Withy river, turning it from a stretch of darkness into an irregular shimmer like a huge silver fish struggling out of water.

'I doubt it, Martin,' he said. 'I know of no other woman quite like Kerensa.'

'Do you think she's beautiful?'

There was no hesitation. 'Kerensa is the most beautiful person I've ever known.'

Chapter 14

Alice was sitting on the bed in the lean-to built on to Trecath-en Farm. She was taking in everything slowly and with meticulous care, trying to familiarise herself with its shapes and shadows, furniture and fabric, its size and smells, to help give her the feeling of belonging there.

The narrow bed was only just big enough for two people to share and was covered with a patchwork quilt of green and blue, sewn in squares by Gran Donald. At the side of the bed stood a sturdy round table that Kenver Trenchard had made for her and Clem. A single candlestick and candle rested on its top beside a chipped crock of field campion, honeysuckle, broom, dog roses and yellow turnip flower, a touching tribute of welcome from young Rosie.

She smiled at the rickety straight-backed chair in the corner. Alice knew it wouldn't even bear the weight of one of the farmyard cats but supposed it looked better there than an empty space. The floor of stamped earth was covered with mats of woven rush and plaited strips of rag, and she wondered why her own mother had never thought of doing the same to add warmth and comfort to the draughty cottage on Lancavel Downs.

Her eyes next moved to a solid oak linen chest situated on the other side of the bed. This had been produced from timber supplied by Nathan O'Flynn and cut and carved by Kenver. Getting up, Alice moved around the foot of the bed and, kneeling down, admired the carvings on the outside of the splendid piece of furniture. The sides of the chest displayed the figures of the twelve apostles, on the top were birds of the sea, the moors and the fields. It must have taken several months to plan and complete, Alice thought poignantly, originally meant as a wedding gift for another girl, and now ironically containing a generous quantity of the finest household linen available in Marazion sent over for her and Clem by Kerensa herself.

Lifting the lid with great care Alice moved aside a pile of the linen in one corner and pulled out a dull wooden box inlaid with damaged pictures of mother-of-pearl fishes and sea creatures. It was the only thing Alice owned that she valued, left to her long ago by a deceased aunt. She opened one of its many compartments and taking out the coins lying inside, let them trickle through her fingers on to her skirt. Ten guinea pieces, given to her by Oliver Pengarron on the day she left the Manor house. He had insisted on her taking them, saying she might well have the need of a sum of money one day. Alice was grateful for the feeling of security it gave her, whilst at the same time knowing she could turn to that quarter if she needed moral support in the future.

She returned the coins, then the box to its corner, and replaced the linen. Closing the lid of the chest she looked rather crossly at the much smaller article of furniture beside it. It was a baby's cradle, used last by Rosie Trenchard, and Alice believed it was tasteless for it to be placed in the room on the day of her wedding. But as she tried to imagine the tiny face of her own baby lying there, with the blue eyes and silky hair of the Trenchards, a bright maternal smile lit up her face and she rocked the cradle from side to side. She didn't hear Florrie Trenchard open the door and come to stand behind her.

'I used to do that,' Florrie said with understanding, 'before each of mine were born. I would gaze down in that cradle for ages and wonder what they would look like.'

'I hope my baby will have hair like Clem's,' Alice said, rising to her feet. 'Not these dreadful curls of mine.'

'Oh, don't say that, Alice,' Florrie laughed kindly, 'You've got the prettiest hair I've seen.'

Alice didn't look convinced.

'Well, are you feeling better now?' asked Florrie, feeling sorry for the girl who had looked uncomfortable all day and then had become faint on top of it. 'Everyone's getting ready to leave and I thought you'd like to see them off.'

'Yes, of course. Thanks. I'm feeling much better now.' Alice placed a hand on her stomach and looked seriously at her mother-in-law. 'I love Clem, Mrs Trenchard. I'll do my best to make him a good wife, but farming is new to me, it's like nothing I'm used to. I'll need your help.'

Florrie Trenchard looked pleased and gave Alice a motherly smile. 'Don't you worry, maid. You're a willing worker and Gran and I will make sure you know the difference between milk and manure by the end of the year!'

The small number of wedding guests had all left to make their way home by twilight, after disposing of a plain but tasty tea made up mainly of farm produce. Owing to the cramped condition of their miner's cottage, the Fords had readily agreed to hold the wedding tea at Trecath-en. Nothing stronger than tea and coffee was drunk following the quiet ceremony at St Piran's church, as Methodism preached.

Ruth and Esther King had sat in the spick-and-span farmhouse parlour with Alice, her mother and three younger sisters, Florrie, Gran Donald and a very excited Rosie. The women had talked about the wedding ceremony, the hot weather, the prices of tea and materials, and childbearing. Although Alice had tried to keep her pregnancy a secret it was common knowledge by the time she stood beside Clem at the altar. As more than half of the local brides were like so on their wedding day, it caused no more than the odd raised eyebrow. But she still had been acutely embarrassed when Gran Donald had informed her that her sickness attacks would stop soon, now she was nearly three months along.

Although no one had actually suggested it the menfolk had gathered outside in a swilled down part of the farmyard, gossiping every bit as much as the women inside. Clem had fixed up a cart with clean dry straw and blankets and had carried Kenver outside to join them. Except for the occasional friendly word to his brother, Clem stayed quiet and slightly apart from the rest of the masculine company. His father, Matthias Renfree and Nathan O'Flynn had cast knowing glances at one another from time to time, but Alice's father and twin ten-year-old brothers were too interested in the farm and the animals

240

to notice the gloominess of their new relative. The conversation of the men included the urgent need for prolonged rainfall, the price of grain and tin ore, and the different aspects of their modes of livelihood. A lot of time was spent admiring the work Clem and Morley had put in on the completion of the lean-to for Alice and Clem to live in.

Left alone now with her new family as she and Clem waved farewell to the last of the guests, Alice felt shy and rather lonely. Florrie moved behind them and put an arm around each of their waists.

She said to them, 'Gran, Rosie and I are going to have a good tidy up. Now why don't you two go off for a little walk.'

'Oh, but I really should help you...' Alice began.

'I've got the milking to do,' Clem countered his mother.

'Father can do the milking and we can manage inside.' Florrie shooed them on their way. 'Stay out as long as you like.'

'We'd better not go too far,' Clem said, after only a short time.

'Why not?' Alice was concerned by this.

'Because you're pregnant. You might be sick again, and Gran said your ankles swell up in the evenings.'

'Oh, Clem.' Alice stopped walking and slipped a hand in his.

'What?' he said, quite puzzled.

'It's nice of you to care about me, Clem, that's all.'

'Why shouldn't I care about you, Alice?'

She took his other hand and looked up earnestly at him. 'I won't pretend you wouldn't have married me if I wasn't going to have your baby.'

'Alice—'

'Please, let me finish, Clem. I... I know you're still in love with Kerensa. You could hardly be expected to feel any different after such a short time. I want you to know, Clem, that I won't put you under any pressure. I... I'm just happy to be your wife and...'

'Alice, Alice, I know what you're trying to say.' He pulled her close to him. 'I'll look after you, don't worry. I know my duty as your husband.'

Morley Trenchard changed into his working clothes and sought out his wife who was by herself clearing away dishes in the parlour. Morley nibbled on a piece of cheese.

Florrie knew her husband had something to say. 'What is it, dear?' she said quietly, continuing with her clearing up.

'Do you reckon they'll be all right, Mother?' he asked, after a long pause.

'We can only hope and pray,' she sighed, 'but unless the boy gets that other little maid out of his mind, it's not going to be easy for either of them.'

—

Oliver had left Tolwithrick immediately after baby Sebastian Besweth-erick's baptism in the family chapel. Kerensa had followed him two days later, taking with her, at Rachael's suggestion, Polly Berryman as a welcome replacement for Alice. At Kerensa's wish Polly became the Manor's housekeeper instead of her personal maid, and quickly struck up a favourable working relationship with Ruth and Esther who were somewhat relieved to have a more experienced woman to help run the huge building.

Kerensa was glad to be home. With Oliver she lived in an uneasy truce, but it was far better than the stony atmosphere before her two weeks' absence, and he still spent most of his time elsewhere. It was good to be out in the gardens again with shaggy-bearded Jake Angove, checking on the development of the seeds and plants she had put in and the health of the convalescent wildlife in Oliver's hut. She raised no objection when Beatrice suddenly appeared, seemingly more sober than drunk, and crushed Kerensa in welcome against her large smelly bosom before shuffling off on her way again.

For many long hours Kerensa rode around the Estate and the farms and through the bluebell-strewn woodland high above the Manor. Suitably scrubbed clean, and with his long hair licked back, Jack often accompanied her. At times Nathan joined them; at others they met him about his work in forest, dell or river, and Kerensa and Jack watched, amused, as the gamekeeper's interest in Polly Berryman began to rival his interest in his livestock.

Kerensa kept herself as busy as possible, mainly to mask her mixed feelings about Alice marrying Clem. She very much missed Alice's presence in the Manor; she had no one to confide in now, and worst of all no one to cheer her up and make her laugh. Kerensa had had no idea that there was anything going on between Alice and Clem until she'd seen them together on May Day. At first she had felt betrayed by Alice's secrecy but on thinking it through Kerensa had understood that her friend couldn't have spoken to her about it. She remembered her maid's reluctance to talk about Clem, and knowing of Alice's loyalty to her, Kerensa realised she must have been torn inside about the association she had formed with him. And why shouldn't another girl set her cap for Clem? He had always attracted a lot of female attention and Kerensa herself had left him unattached. Why shouldn't he turn to someone else in his loneliness? He must have had many a woman wanting to comfort him, and, in the end, Kerensa was glad it was Alice, who would be good and faithful to him. But now it seemed Alice's friendship was lost to her and Clem even further away.

Kerensa was happiest in the company of old Dunstan. They sat together under the trees in the orchard and in her sitting room in the warm, increasingly light evenings. He waited for her to come down each morning for breakfast, to come back from church and her riding excursions. The old dog followed her about the gardens as she worked with Jake or picked armfuls of flowers to fill every vase she could find in the house. He slept at her feet while she ate her meals, or sat with her as she sewed and embroidered, and if Oliver sounded impatient or raised his voice to her, Dunstan would growl at him with distinct menace. And on the day of Clem's and Alice's wedding, he had kept her company in her loneliness.

It was several days after that before Kerensa left the Estate. She rode over to the Parsonage to keep an appointment with the Reverend Ivey, but first took a mixture of wild and garden flowers and filled the granite pot she'd had made in Marazion specially for her mother's grave. She lingered there awhile in silent thought and prayer, then pulling off her hat, she walked to Mrs Tregonning's kitchen.

'Ooh, m'lady!' Mrs Tregonning rushed to greet her. 'How lovely you look. It seems ages since you were here last. My, you do look well.'

'It's good to see you too, Mrs Tregonning. The Reverend's not expecting me till three so I came over early to see you first. I brought some Congo tea over for you, I know the Reverend likes it.'

Mrs Tregonning wiped flour off her hands. 'I hope you don't mind me asking where it came from?' she said, eyeing the package the girl put on the table with suspicion.

'I brought it back from Tolwithrick with me actually,' Kerensa smiled, seating herself at the table.

'Humph! Probably came from him up there, all the same. How is he these days? No improvement in his temper or manners, I'll be bound.'

'Sir Oliver's well,' Kerensa told the woman patiently.

'Well, is he?' said the housekeeper, pouring out the tea. 'If he had his way, the poor Reverend wouldn't be. Messing up his garden like that indeed! Disgusting, that's what I say.'

Kerensa frowned. 'I don't think I know what you're talking about, Mrs Tregonning.'

'You don't know about it? That's typical! He and Clem Trenchard, it was, fighting like tom cats all over the flowerbeds and lawn. Shameful it was, shameful, and right after poor Henry Sampson's funeral too, rest his soul.'

'I see,' said Kerensa, not knowing what to think or feel about this revelation. 'When Sir Oliver came to Tolwithrick, I noticed he had fading cuts and bruises. Now I know why. Was Clem hurt?'

'Came off a bit worse than he up there did, but no, not too badly. Serve they both right if they get aches and pains for the rest of the year because of it, that's what I say.'

Holding her cup tightly in her hands, Kerensa asked in a closed voice: 'Have you any idea why they were fighting?'

'I don't know for sure, but some do say, not that I know anything about it, you understand,' Mrs Tregonning said in the tone of one involved in a conspiracy, 'that Alice Ford was in a delicate condition when she married Clem. Could be something to do with that, I s'pose. Anyway, the poor Reverend was really angry. He was the one what caught them at it. Gave they a proper telling off, I can tell you.'

'Good for him,' Kerensa said, mainly to herself. She didn't want to talk about it any more, knowing the Reverend would give her a truthful uncoloured account of the incident later. She asked, 'Has Jenifer Drannock had her baby yet?'

'A little small maid, she had. Born on... let me see... on the eleventh, I believe. Yes, that's right, the eleventh. I remember now because it was a Friday, and I always bake a fresh batch of bread on a Friday, and I was up to my elbows in flour when that tiresome boy Bartholomew came running for me to give Elizabeth King a hand. Jack, the baby you brought here that day, wouldn't stop crying and...'

Kerensa let the woman prattle on to herself. The eleventh of May. The day before the birth of Sebastian Beswetherick. Guilt welled up inside her. Since her return to the Manor she had checked every thought of Jenifer and Bartholomew and little Jack Drannock. Even now her reason for being in Perranbarvah was only to question the Reverend Ivey about her mother's death.

'Are they both all right?' she interrupted Mrs Tregonning's steady flow of speech. 'Jenifer and the baby?'

'Jenifer's better than she was. Had a bad time of it, she did. Won't pay her to have another, if you ask me. That husband of hers should keep himself to himself, if you get my meaning. Not that he will, mind. You know what men are like now you're married yourself, don't you, m'lady?'

Kerensa didn't answer but asked another question. 'And the little girl, how is she?'

'Aw, a weak little mite she is, what with the difficult birth and all. Reverend baptised her the day after her birth. She wasn't expected to live for long, you see.'

'I must go down and see them after I've seen the Reverend. If I'd thought of it before leaving home, I would have brought some things over for them.'

'I was going down later myself with some bread, hevva cake, butter and eggs. You can save my old legs up and down the hill, if you like,' Mrs Tregonning said, pointing to a basket on the end of the table. 'By the way, m'lady, how's this Polly Berryman getting on at the Manor? Been over to see her cousin yet, has she?'

'Yes, she's—'

A knock on the door was followed by the appearance of Ben Rosevidney. By his signs and gestures they quickly ascertained that he'd been given a message by someone sent by the Reverend Ivey. He sent his apologies, but would be delayed for an hour. Lady Pengarron was welcome to wait, or he would call on her himself tomorrow at the Manor house. Kerensa decided to see the Reverend the next day, and thanking Ben picked up the basket of food from the table. She would go down into the village at once, relieved to get away from the plump housekeeper's wagging tongue.

Jenifer shouted out, 'Come in!' to her knock on the door, and Kerensa took in the mess and clutter inside the gloomy cottage with one glance.

'Good afternoon, Jenifer,' she said. 'How are you and the family?'

Jenifer looked up from changing Jack's tattered napkin. 'Good afternoon to you, my lady. We're all quite well, thank you. It's good of you to call again. I hope you'll excuse the mess but I'm afraid I never seem to get around to clearing everything away. If you'd like to hold Jack when I've finished with him, I'll get the little one for you to see.'

The tiny pink wisp that Jenifer held swamped in a scrap of blanket looked as if she would fit into a man's hand.

'But she's so tiny,' Kerensa breathed, having difficulty holding Jack as he wriggled about in her arms.

'She only weighs about four pounds. We thought she wouldn't survive for long so we asked the Reverend Ivey to baptise her on the day following her birth, but I know she's going to be all right now.' Jenifer kissed her newest daughter's forehead. 'She's a born fighter.'

The tiny baby was half the size of Sebastian Beswetherick, and the life and circumstances she had been born into could be in no greater contrast. Jack grabbed at Kerensa's cheek and jealously tried to receive all of her attention.

'Look at your baby sister, Jack,' she cooed to him. 'Isn't she pretty?'

Jenifer laughed. 'Sam says she looks more like a rat than a human being, but he'll soon be doting on her, like all our others.'

'What does Bartholomew think of her?' asked Kerensa slowly.

'Bartholomew? Oh, he was cross at first that she wasn't another brother for him, but when we thought we were going to lose her, I'm sure I saw tears in his eyes. Now I think he's quite proud of her, but it's always difficult to know what is going on in Bartholomew's mind.'

Kerensa nodded. 'I can understand that.'

Jenifer looked at her curiously and Kerensa said quickly, 'Is there anything I can do for you? Anything at all? You must be rushed off your feet, and here's me with nothing in particular to do with my time.'

Jenifer saw the sincerity in the sad young face and at that moment felt more sorry for Kerensa than the girl did for her. 'Very well,' she said, 'I won't stand on false pride. How much time have you got to spare at the moment?'

'Hours really. Sir Oliver is away on business all the way over at Penzance for a few days. As long as I'm back at the Manor by twilight the others won't worry about me. Have you something in mind?'

Jenifer spread her hands to indicate the condition of the room. 'I've known better times than this., and you've known something similar, although I'm sure nothing quite as bad. You say you're happier when you're busy, when you're doing something useful, so if I ask Mrs King to have Jack for a while and keep an eye out for my others, if you're agreeable we could clear up some of this mess together.'

'That's a marvellous idea, Jenifer,' Kerensa said, her face aglow with the prospect.

When Jack was unhappily settled in with Elizabeth King, and Kerensa had an apron tied around the dress of her riding habit and a scarf around her head, she and Jenifer set to work to give the dingy room of the cottage a thorough cleaning. They dusted, washed and scrubbed, discarded a great deal of rubbish, and collecting up all of Bartholomew's treasured pieces of driftwood, birds' eggs, pebbles and shells, put them in an old disused kindling wood box. After that they polished everything in sight and finished off by rearranging the furniture. They had worked without a break for over two and a half hours, shooing away the other curious Drannock children more than once during their time.

'I've still got some of that tea left you brought over the last time,' Jenifer said breathlessly, when finally they were satisfied everything possible had been done. Pushing back tresses of light-coloured hair she reached for a big tin kettle now cleaned from the blackening of the fire.

'I'll make the tea,' offered Kerensa, 'I don't want you to be tired out.'

'Oh, you are a dear,' Jenifer said, and on impulse gave the girl a warm hug. 'And just look at the state of you. You've got dust streaked on your arms and face. You look more like one of my little ones than a married woman.'

'Well, I haven't enjoyed myself like this for a very long time,' Kerensa smiled as she ladled out water from a heavy bucket by the door into the kettle.

They had just sat down with their tea when Kerensa looked up at the sound of a noise no louder than the mewling of a kitten. 'Is that the baby waking up?' she asked, jumping to her feet and going to the crib. 'Yes, her little eyes are open. Do you know, I haven't asked you her name yet.'

'Her name is Cordelia,' Jenifer told her.

Kerensa lifted Cordelia with extreme care. 'She feels as light as thistledown. It's hard to believe anything so small can be alive.'

'She's the smallest of my brood and I don't mind admitting I hope she will be the last. But I do marvel at the sight of a newborn baby, just like you're doing now. Each one seems a miracle in their own right.'

Cordelia began to wail and Kerensa handed the near weightless baby to Jenifer to feed.

'She'll grow some hair later on,' Jenifer remarked, 'but I think she'll be dark like Bartholomew.'

'He is dark, isn't he?' Kerensa agreed, and mention of the boy was easier now she had put her feelings on the matter aside. And one thing she had learned today was that even if Oliver was Bartholomew's father, the child was well looked after and lived in an obviously happy home.

'Samuel is going to see about some goat's milk for her. I don't think mine is good enough for her to thrive on.'

'There's goats all over the estate, Jenifer. If you like I could arrange for some to be sent over tomorrow for you, for as long as you want it.'

'Thank you. It's very kind of you. You've been good to us. The girls were thrilled with the dresses you sent over for them and even Bartholomew has been glad to have a decent shirt to wear to church. Thank you again for the goat's milk. Samuel will be pleased not to have to spend time away from his precious boat.'

Jenifer looked happier and less tired despite all their hard work. The clean and tidy cottage had had a definite therapeutic effect on her.

–

Kerensa headed back up the steep hill, smiling happily to herself all the way. When she reached the lychgate a tall man stood barring her way. Although she had never seen him before he somehow looked familiar. He nodded politely before speaking.

'Lady Pengarron, I hope you don't mind me stopping you like this. I'd like to talk. I am Samuel Drannock.'

They went into the church, which was cool and dark inside except for two carved pews on opposite sides which were bathed in a shaft of bright sunlight. Kerensa sat on the end of one of them, the sunlight giving her an aura of insubstantiality. Samuel Drannock seated himself on the other, facing her. The fisherman had a confident air about him. Kerensa felt uneasy, wondering what the reason for him wanting to talk to her might be.

'Why do you want to see me, Mr Drannock?' she asked, wanting to get this interview over with quickly.

'First of all, to thank you for what you've done for Jenifer and the children,' he replied, his voice firm.

'It was nothing really. I'm only too glad to help in any way I can.'

'I don't hold with charity,' Samuel Drannock said coolly.

249

'Oh!' Kerensa was taken by surprise, the man's keen stare making her feel guilty. 'I didn't mean to give offence.'

'Not from the gentry,' he went on, 'or my own class even. But particularly not from a Pengarron. It's only because I know you to be sincere, ma'am, that I've allowed you to, that and the fact that before Jenifer married me she was in the position where she did the same. Some folk feel the same as me, some don't. What I can't provide for my family I believe they should go without, same as I did when I was a boy.'

Kerensa lapsed into silence at the rebuff. Samuel Drannock smiled at her, a smile full of ready charm. He was not an unattractive man, his frame slim and broad-shouldered. Kerensa guessed he was roughly the same age as Oliver. She could see no reason to return his smile.

He said, 'I love Jenifer very much. Accepting the clothes for the children made her happy and I like to see her happy, but—'

'But now you don't want me to give anything more to your family,' she finished for him.

'That's right, ma'am. Do you understand why?'

'To be truthful, Mr Drannock, no, not really,' she said very quietly. She understood male pride but kept the thought to herself. 'Thank you for telling me how you feel. I was going to arrange for goat's milk to be sent over for little Cordelia. Can I at least do that?'

Samuel Drannock thought for a moment. 'Yes, that will be all right. I thank you, ma'am. But after that no more, please.'

Kerensa rose to go, wishing only to reach Kernick and be on the road home. Helping Jenifer had helped her in turn to feel useful and wanted, and now this too was to be denied her.

Samuel Drannock rose with her. 'There's something else.'

Her throat was too dry for words but she raised her head to meet any challenge.

'My wife said you looked shocked the first time you saw Bartholomew. We think perhaps you saw something in him most others fail to see.'

Kerensa held her breath.

'Do you believe Bartholomew is your husband's son?'

'I… I don't know… Is he?'

'No, ma'am, he is not. Bartholomew is most definitely my son. I've been worried you've been thinking along those lines. You're close enough to your husband to have noticed the same darkness in Bartholomew's eyes, the same bearing and at times the same wilful expression, aren't you?'

'Yes,' Kerensa said, 'but I don't understand.'

'My son's Pengarron traits are inherited from his grandfather, Sir Daniel Pengarron. He was my father.'

She sat down again, quite stunned, partly with relief, the rest shock. Samuel Drannock resumed his seat on the pew.

'You do see that I couldn't let you go on thinking my own son isn't mine, and Jenifer knew any man but me?'

'Of course, and I'm very grateful you've told me,' Kerensa said, having grasped the full meaning of his confidence, 'but that makes you Sir Oliver's half-brother. I've wondered for weeks if he knew he had a son, now I'd like to know if he knows he has a half-brother.'

'I'm quite sure he doesn't, and he must never know. Although we grew up about the same time I resemble my mother, so there was nothing to cause anyone to suspect the truth.'

The fisherman crouched down so they were face to face. 'My mother only told me who my real father was just before she died. She realised when she found herself with child that Sir Daniel could offer no more than financial support, but when she told him, he wouldn't even provide that. Flying into a rage, he called her a whore and challenged her to prove he was the father of her baby. A quiet simple man, Caleb Drannock, who fished out of Newlyn, offered her marriage. My mother accepted and they settled down well enough. Caleb was lost at sea not long after my birth and my mother came back to her family in Perranbarvah. She kept her secret for nigh on eighteen years, till her death, and only I and Jenifer, and now you, ma'am, share it. You see now, don't you, why I want nothing from a Pengarron?'

'I understand how you feel,' Kerensa said, 'but the Pengarrons owe you so much. You shouldn't have to endure hardship while they live in comfort and plenty.'

'I'm happy enough as I am, ma'am,' Samuel Drannock said, getting to his feet. 'Forgive me if it hurts you to hear me say this, but I want nothing from the Pengarrons, not ever. To me, your husband is little more than a rogue. He's immoral, and to my way of thinking, cruel and selfish. He's probably hardly set eyes on me anyway because I don't go to church with Jenifer, preferring to find my faith at sea, and I don't get myself involved in his smuggling ventures. Jenifer and I may be poor but we're content with each other and our children, despite the seeming drudgery of our lives. We don't need anyone to feel sorry for us. Will you keep my mother's secret with us, ma'am... please, I beg you?'

'You have one thing in common with my husband, Samuel Drannock,' Kerensa said curtly. 'You both say exactly what's on your mind. Yes, I'll keep your secret, but it will be a burden to carry it alone.'

'I have often wished I did not know it myself. I'm sorry, but I felt I must tell you to save you at least one agony at your husband's expense.'

Kerensa stood up and faced the fisherman squarely. 'Agony? My husband is not the monster you think him to be, I can assure you.'

He studied her deeply for a moment. 'Ma'am,' he said with a polite nod, then without another word, left the church.

Kerensa was left bringing to mind everything that she could in Oliver's defence. His better points and good humour. All the acts of kindness to others she had come to know about that he performed willingly. She felt guilty that she had ever believed for a moment that he was the sort of man who could cast a pregnant woman aside and prayed silently for forgiveness, while making up her mind to make it up to him. She wished with all her heart that she did not know the Drannocks' secret, that she had not promised to keep it from Oliver. If he ever found out, and got to know that she knew...

Chapter 15

A cold numb feeling remained with Kerensa as she journeyed home. She knew she would have to forget about the Drannocks if she was ever going to be content in the future, but it was difficult for her to lose the bad taste in her mouth after the encounter with Samuel Drannock, a seemingly honest, good man.

She had wanted Jenifer for a friend and he had put a stop to it without giving his wife any say in the matter. Kerensa had a feeling he ruled over his family in a way that even Oliver would not insist upon. He had never stopped her from having a friend, she thought sulkily. As far as she could see Samuel Drannock was a bigot.

When they were about halfway home Kernick suddenly lurched and threw off a shoe. Kerensa jumped down on the dusty track, picked up the shoe and gave the pony a few words of comfort before setting off again, holding on to the reins as she walked along beside him.

She wanted to walk and walk forever, glad this would delay her reaching home, glad to be alone with only the pony for company in the countryside where no people or cottages could be found. She took the longest route back to the Manor, following the twisting rutted cart track running between Rose Farm and Polcudden, and skirting wide around the hamlet of Rosudgeon.

The sun sank low in the sky, and the further she walked the more her spirits lifted. She was thinking of nothing but the walk now, the regular motion of step after step, the cooling breeze of the early evening. The feeling of oneness with Mother Nature soothed away her melancholy. Everything and everyone else was forgotten, there was only here and now. Kerensa wanted to walk and walk and walk.

By and by she became aware of the dull thud of approaching hoofbeats, and stopped walking and slowly turned around. She still had no desire for company, but resigned herself to the certainty that whoever it was riding up fast behind her, a Richards or a Sampson most likely, would insist on escorting her safely home.

It was not a farmer, however. She was surprised to make out the figure of Peter Blake astride a handsome chestnut mare.

With a pleasant smile he reined in beside her. 'Good evening to you, Lady Pengarron. It appears once again I come upon you in need of a rescuer. A task I am more than happy to perform, with your permission?' Blake dismounted and bent down to look at Kernick's raised foreleg.

'It's only a thrown shoe,' Kerensa told him haughtily, holding it up for his inspection. She was in no mood for the light-hearted banter of this member of the gentry so soon after the forthrightness of the blunt fisherman.

'Ah,' he said, straightening, and flashing his brilliant white teeth at her. 'Are you quite well, ma'am? If you'll forgive me being personal, you seem a little pale. You weren't thrown from your pony, were you?' He was most handsome in his gallantry but it was lost on Kerensa.

She accepted the offer to ride his mare back to the Manor, feeling it would save time in the end because he would feel bound by honour to insist upon it. Blake indulged in chit-chat as he guided the hobbling pony along beside her.

'Why are you on this track, Mr Blake?' Kerensa asked, as soon as it crossed her mind to enquire.

'I was out putting my mare through her paces. I only acquired her at the weekend and wanted to see what she can do. It was a happy accident to come across you in your time of need, ma'am.'

'I wasn't concerned, Mr Blake. It's not far from here to the Manor.'

As they entered the stableyard Jack ran over to meet them. 'What 'appened, m'lady?' The boy held out his hand to help Kerensa down. So did Peter Blake. Kerensa accepted Jack's hand.

'Kernick has only thrown a shoe, it's nothing to worry about, Jack,' she told the boy, giving him a warm smile. 'This is Mr Blake. He was kind enough to offer me his horse to ride home on.'

Jack ran his hand down the chestnut mare from neck to belly. 'What a beautiful piece of 'orseflesh, 'is lordship 'imself would be proud to 'ave 'er in 'is stable. Shall I give 'er a drink, sir?'

'Thank you, boy, she could well do with one. I've had her out most of the afternoon.' Blake tossed the boy a sixpence which Jack deftly caught and put inside a grubby waistcoat pocket.

Blake was perfectly relaxed as he looked about the stableyard and Kerensa knew she had no choice but to offer him some refreshment, but for once she wished she had Oliver's lack of manners when the occasion suited. Blake accepted with an element of feigned surprise, saying he would be most honoured. Kerensa led the way inside, giving her hat and gloves to Polly and after explaining the reason for Peter Blake's presence in the Manor, asked for tea to be brought to the drawing room.

–

Polly entered the kitchen in a flurry. The King sisters looked up curiously from the vegetables they were preparing for the late evening meal.

'You should see the gentleman with her ladyship,' Polly said in a confidential tone. 'He's really quite handsome, and his clothes look as if they've been made in France. He's not tall like his lordship, and is a few years younger, but he's really nice-looking in a different sort of way.'

'Here, I'll tell Nathan about this,' teased Esther.

'And what is this really nice-looking gentleman doing with her ladyship?' Ruth wanted to know. 'Is he a friend of Sir Oliver's?'

'I don't know who he is,' answered Polly as she poured boiling water into a white, bone china crested tea pot. 'Her ladyship's pony threw a shoe on the way home and this gentleman, a Mr Peter Blake, came across her walking back and offered assistance.'

'Peter Blake!' gasped Esther and Ruth together.

'You know him then?' asked Polly, holding a saucer in mid air.

'We certainly know of him,' said Ruth. 'His lordship would never have invited him into the house for a start.'

'He lives in Marazion,' said Esther, taking up the tale, 'owns some of the shops there and is half-brother to a dreadful wealthy widow called Josephine Courtis who's had designs on Sir Oliver ever since her husband died.'

'Yes, she even came over to the Manor twice while her ladyship was away at Tolwithrick and I'm glad to say both times he wasn't here,' went on Ruth.

'So why doesn't Sir Oliver like this Peter Blake, then?' asked Polly, anxious now to learn more.

Esther carried on. 'Rumour has it he was dishonourably discharged from his regiment, the same one as what his lordship was in. It must be true too, because he returned to Marazion all of a sudden and after a while no one called him captain anymore.'

'And he's an atheist,' put in Ruth. 'Some do say he's involved in witchcraft even.'

Polly grinned a little wryly at Ruth.

'Well, there's been some funny goings on around the holy well up on Lancavel Downs these past years.'

Blake looked across the drawing room, his expression one of kindly concern. 'You look a little better now, ma'am,' he said.

'I am really very well, Mr Blake,' Kerensa said emphatically. She was hoping she would soon be rid of this man. Then she would change out of her riding habit and go out into the gardens before dark and try to recapture the feeling of calm that had grown inside her before his unwelcome appearance.

'This is a most pleasant room, very tastefully decorated and furnished,' Blake commented, but keeping his eyes on Kerensa's face rather than looking around the room as he spoke. 'Are you responsible for any of it, ma'am?'

'No, Mr Blake. I believe Sir Oliver's late mother was.' Kerensa was relieved to hear footsteps. 'Here comes Polly with the tea,' she said with a suppressed sigh.

When the housekeeper had left the room Kerensa poured the tea. Blake rose from his chair to take his cup and saucer from her and brushed her hand as he did so. He remained standing, staying close by her chair.

'Shall I have the pleasure of meeting your husband before I leave, do you think, ma'am?'

'I shouldn't think so. He has business at Penzance—' She stopped abruptly, cross with herself for telling Blake even that much.

'Indeed? I wasn't aware Sir Oliver's business interests stretched that far.'

She was spared having to find an answer to the question by an urgent scratching at the door. Blake looked at it with something akin to anger. 'It's only Dunstan, Sir Oliver's old dog,' Kerensa explained. 'He likes to keep me company.'

'Would you like me to let him in?'

'Yes please, if you will.'

Blake opened one of the double oak doors but ignored the old black dog who plodded into the room and flopped down heavily at Kerensa's feet. Dunstan placed his head on her lap, looking at her with reproachful watery eyes, softly growling a complaint at not being invited in sooner. Kerensa laughed at him and stroked his head as she fed him a placatory biscuit.

Blake did not return to his former place. He moved about the room, looking at anything that caught his interest, but only for a moment at a time. Reaching a section of wall upon which several miniature enamel portraits were mounted, he stopped and pointed to one in particular.

'May I ask who the lady is in this portrait?' he said. 'I've a fancy I've seen her somewhere before.'

He was blocking all but the top row of miniatures from her view, so Kerensa crossed the room to look where he was pointing. 'It's likely you may have seen that lady before, Mr Blake. She is Sir Oliver's mother. She died many years ago.'

'I remember now. Lady Caroline. She used to attend feast days and the fairs at Marazion when I was a child. Well, that is, I barely remember her, I was only an infant at the time. She was very beautiful.'

'Yes, she was,' Kerensa agreed. 'I'd like to have known her myself.' She bent forward a little to study the enamel of her long dead mother-in-law closely for a moment. When she moved back Blake had moved in closer to her than was comfortable.

'Seems to me the Pengarrons have a fondness for beautiful women,' he said, his softly spoken voice lower than before. 'In your case though... a beautiful girl.'

The way Peter Blake was looking at her was not unlike the way her husband had done the day he'd arrived at Trelynne Cove to bargain with her grandfather. It was a look no decent woman found welcome on a man's face and it whipped up a fury within her.

'If you'll excuse me, Mr Blake, there are some things I have to attend to,' she said acidly.

'You're asking me to leave?'

'Yes, I am.'

'Are you sure you want me to go?'

'What do you mean?' Kerensa said angrily. She took several steps away from him but he matched every one with a movement forward.

'You can't tell me you're happy in this arranged marriage of yours with a man twice your age, even if he doesn't look it. If you'll allow me to, my lovely, I could provide some... light relief in your lonelier moments.'

Pure rage flashed in her grey-green eyes. 'Get out! Get out of here at once!' She edged away until her back hit a heavy bureau and she was trapped as Blake swiftly placed an arm either side of her.

'Come now, my lovely. Don't tell me you're as innocent as you look. Even if Pengarron was the first, I'll warrant I know a thing or two that he doesn't.'

He closed in on her like a predatory cat, muffling the scream in her throat with his mouth pressed over hers. He sought to hold down her arms with one hand while with the other he tightly gripped the hair at the back of her neck.

Kerensa felt she was suffocating. Reaching wildly behind, her hand searched about and found a pewter tankard. She snatched it up by the rim and swinging the tankard round, smashed it viciously on the side of Blake's head. He staggered back from her, and from somewhere deep inside Kerensa let out a high-pitched scream.

Although he had little hearing it was enough to alert Dunstan. He snarled menacingly at Blake who held a hand up to his head where drops of blood were trickling through his fingers over his ear and spattering on to his smart buff-coloured dresscoat. His face reflected not handsomeness now, but evilness and lust.

'You spiteful little cat,' he said in a low inhuman voice. 'I can play rough, too, if that's what you want.'

As he took a step forward the dog bared his remaining teeth. Blake took another step and cried out in pain as Dunstan sank his teeth deep into his ankle.

'Call off this animal or it will be the worse for him!' Blake threatened.

'Leave Dunstan alone!' Kerensa hurled herself across the room, wielding the bloodstained tankard at Blake.

He savagely kicked Dunstan in the ribs before she reached him. She managed a blow to his shoulder but Blake delivered a violent slap across her face, sending her reeling backwards and knocking over a small table and a vase of flowers with a crash. He turned back to the old dog and Kerensa screamed out at every kick he sank into the dog's body and head until his ankle was free at last. Dunstan's yelps had turned to whimpers when Blake looked again at Kerensa.

'Keep away from me!' she cried, picking up a piece of broken pottery from the vase.

'Oh, I can't do that, my lovely,' he said, with a salacious smile.

Kerensa was shaking with anger and fear. It wasn't his violence that frightened her, however, but the quietness of his voice. She felt the piece of vase cut into her hand as her grip automatically tightened as he moved towards her.

The doors suddenly crashed open. It was Jack and Polly. The boy was visibly shaking as he held out one of Oliver's firearms in his small dirty hands.

'Get away from her,' Jack uttered nervously, 'move right away from them both.'

'You wouldn't dare fire that gun, boy. You'd be tried and hanged for murder,' Blake mocked him.

Jack gulped. The firearm wavered as he tried to fix his eyes on Blake's face. 'I will... if I have to. Now get away!'

'Very well,' Blake said, moving away from his victims and advancing quickly on Jack. 'Now just put that gun down, boy, if you don't want to get yourself into trouble. It wouldn't do, you know, to shoot a member of the gentry.'

'Stop! I'll use this... stay where you are.' Jack's hand shook, and wildly he looked about for help.

'Put the gun down, boy,' Blake mocked in his low soft voice, 'or you'll have your neck stretched to twice its length.'

'Polly!' Tears sprang in the boy's eyes. 'Don't listen to him, Jack—'

Polly didn't get to finish her sentence. Another person rushed into the room and snatching the firearm from Jack, trained it squarely on the middle of Blake's forehead.

'You won't get the better of me, you swine,' Clem Trenchard muttered between gritted teeth. 'I'll give you ten seconds to get out of here.' Fear mixed with anger played on Blake's face for a fleeting moment, then he turned to look at Kerensa, still sprawled on the floor. He smiled pleasantly at her and gave a small bow as though he was saying goodbye on any normal occasion. Running his tongue slowly across his lower lip he shook his head and said, 'Pity.'

Pushing his way roughly past Clem and Jack, despite the injury to his ankle, Blake passed quickly by Polly who jumped back out of his way. She scurried over to Kerensa and with Jack's help they got her to her feet, but she shook them off and knelt down beside Dunstan.

Clem put a gentle hand on her shoulder. 'Kerensa,' he said softly, 'are you hurt?'

She shook her head, her eyes on the whimpering dog.

'I have to make sure Blake has gone, Kerensa,' he went on. 'I won't be gone long. Will you be all right?'

This time she nodded and he wanted to stay with her but it was more important at that moment to be certain her attacker had left the grounds.

'Come with me, Jack.' He turned to the boy and put his hand on Jack's bony arm in a comforting gesture.

A shiver ran the length of the boy's body before he followed Clem outside to the stableyard. They were just in time to watch Peter Blake ride out of the yard at a gallop. Jack took the sixpence out of his waistcoat pocket and hurled it after the disappearing figure.

The King sisters moved tentatively into the drawing room. Polly snapped orders at them. 'One of you go and fetch a blanket, the other fetch hot water and clean linen. Go on. Run!'

Esther and Ruth rushed off as though springing to life from a daydream. Polly knelt down beside Kerensa and looked at Dunstan. 'My lady,' she said gently, 'he's very badly hurt. He'll have to be...'

Kerensa looked up sharply. 'No,' she murmured, 'no!' Her body rocked in shock and grief as she looked back at the pitifully whimpering, blood-streaked animal. 'No... no... no...' It went on and on.

Polly tried to pull the girl close in a bid to comfort her, but Kerensa held her body rigid and wouldn't be moved.

Esther returned first with the blanket which Polly took and wrapped around Kerensa's shivering body. When Ruth rushed into the room with the hot water and linen, Polly motioned to her to place them on a table.

'Wring out a cloth,' she whispered to Ruth, 'we'll wrap it around her hand.'

Nathan O'Flynn was with Clem and Jack on their return. 'Has he gone?' Polly asked.

'Aye,' Clem answered her. 'Blake's gone.'

Polly glanced anxiously at Nathan and he knelt down beside her and Kerensa. Pulling the girl's stone cold hands away from the dog's head, he clasped them in his. Now was not the time for social niceties.

'Kerensa, my dear. Dunstan is badly hurt. He's suffering.' Nat turned her frozen young face to his and forced her to meet his eyes. 'I'll have to take him outside and... and put him out of his misery. Do you understand?'

It seemed an age before she answered. 'Do it quickly, please, Nat.'

Clem had moved around behind the pathetic kneeling trio. He pulled Kerensa to her feet to lean against his chest. Polly had watched keenly. So this was the fair-haired young farmer's son whose heart had been broken by the girl's marriage to Sir Oliver? She wondered what he was doing at the Manor, but other things demanded her attention now.

'Ruth, Esther,' she said. 'Take Jack to the kitchen and make yourselves some tea.'

All his young life Jack had taken care of himself and was competent and near self-sufficient, but never before had he faced such acts of brutality and evil in one afternoon. The two sisters took his arms and the white-faced boy let them lead him out of the room.

'I'll help you with the dog, Nat,' Polly said when they had gone.

Nathan met her eyes, and they silently agreed that, for now, Kerensa would be best left alone with Clem. As gently as they were able, they lifted up the old dog, Polly supporting his head. Dunstan yelped once and Clem held Kerensa tighter to him.

They stayed still until the shot rang out. Kerensa groaned and turned swiftly to be in Clem's arms.

'Not Dunstan... not Dunstan,' she cried painfully, 'how will I bear it?'

Clem held her as tightly as he could without hurting her. He caressed her cheek and placed his own against it, feeling the wetness of her tears.

'You will bear it, my dearest love,' he said very softly, 'because I'll always be here for you... always.'

—

A woman with long straggling hair left the Star Inn in Marazion holding on tightly to the arm of Peter Blake. She shrieked as the suddenness of a hard shower of rain stung her face and the full bosom that was barely contained by the stuff of her dress.

'C'mon, m'dear, we'll be darned drowned in this 'fore I get 'ee back to my place,' she squealed.

Blake nuzzled her neck and directed his eyes down to the escaping white flesh. Pulling the dress off her shoulder he ran his tongue round and round in circles on the uncovered skin. 'You were going to take this off anyway,' he said lewdly.

Farmers, hawkers and shoppers in town for the market scurried for shelter as the shower gained momentum, ignoring the couple hanging on to one another as they ran laughing down the muddy street and turned off into an alleyway. Out of sight of pedestrians and travellers Blake yanked the woman towards him and kissed her with abandon. The woman was pleased. She'd been hoping to get this well-heeled, good-looking gentleman as a customer for many weeks. If she satisfied him she'd heard he would pay well. A lot more than the few pennies the odd farmer, fisherman or miner could spare, and more than the most generous sailor moored up on the Mount.

Blake too was pleased. He could tell she was well experienced in her profession and judging by her eager response to his kiss would perhaps allow more than just a quick outlet of his pent up lust on her, and be willing to indulge in some of the things he'd learnt with his military acquaintances from the more dedicated harlots of London and France. He pulled her close.

'Blake!'

The shout roused him from his amours. The sight of the tall man standing, feet astride, at the other end of the alley cleared the look of anticipation from his face.

'Who the 'ell's 'e?' squawked the prostitute, indignant at the untimely interruption.

Blake threw the woman aside so roughly her body hit the wall, painfully winding her. 'Get out of here,' he hissed, not even giving her a look. 'What… what do you want?' he blurted out nervously to the man who had called his name, his hand straying down to the small pistol he carried hidden in the waistband of his breeches.

The prostitute looked from one man to the other. Blake's face had paled considerably, a blue vein twitched on his temple, and it was obvious he was afraid of the man now advancing steadily towards them. When he was close enough the expression on the man's face brought fear creeping up her spine. She had seen him before, she had even propositioned him once and he had turned her down. Then, he had been irritated; now it seemed hatred was his companion.

The face of strikingly fine, clear dark features was set as hard as the granite of the Cornish cliffs. And looked as dangerous as those rocks, that appeared so innocent above the water but in reality lay in wait with their jagged, bulky shapes hidden beneath the depths to ground and crush unfortunate sailing vessels.

The prostitute stayed to see no more but ran back the way she had come, her legs and skirt becoming splashed in the muddy pools of rainwater.

The two men were now only two feet apart. Blake trembled. Oliver Pengarron's voice was pure venom.

'You ask me what I want, Blake? Your life, and no less. You tried to force yourself on my wife. You killed my dog. You frightened my servants and dared to invade the peace of my house. You, Blake, are scum, and scum such as you cannot treat anything of mine in such a manner without answering to me afterwards.' He had spoken quietly, too quietly for Blake to muster up an ounce of courage or self-defence.

'You... you can't mean... to actually kill me,' Blake blustered.

'That's exactly what I mean to do.'

Blake walked backwards. 'But, look... wait!'

Oliver advanced on him. 'What's the matter, Blake? No guts for a fight unless it's a woman or an old defenceless animal you're kicking to death?'

The first blow, delivered powerfully to Blake's jaw, sent him straight back against the same wall as the unfortunate prostitute, but with greater severity. Clutching Blake by the throat, Oliver slammed him again and again against the wall until his breathing came in laboured gasps.

'How does it feel, Blake? How does it feel to experience what you put my wife through? The same pain you made my dog suffer, eh? The only thing in your favour is you didn't try to deny it. Or were you going to?' He punched Blake deep in the belly. He doubled over. 'Well, were you? Were you?'

Another punch in the same place, followed by a further slamming against the wall, ensured a gasp of an answer. 'No.'

Oliver suddenly let go of Blake. He sank slowly to his knees before keeling over and writhing in the mud. The rain washed blood off his face and patterns of narrow red rivulets ran over his dresscoat and on to the ground. Oliver pushed dripping hair back from his eyes. Only a small part of the anger, hatred and pain raging inside of him since the news had reached him in Penzance, had abated.

Blake struggled to a sitting position, gripping his stomach and feebly moaning. Oliver bent and grasped his coat by the collar with both hands, but Blake had managed to slip the small pistol out of his waistband and thrust it into the other's ribs.

He felt Oliver's body go rigid, and spitting blood in his face, Blake jeered, 'Looks like… the tables… have turned, Pengarron.' With two quick movements Blake released the safety catch and pulled the firing mechanism.

Oliver braced himself to receive the bullet in his chest.

Nothing happened.

Their eyes met for a second before Blake panicked. Squealing in fear he wildly brought the firearm down in ineffective thuds on Oliver's arm. He was hauled to his feet and shaken like a child's rag doll, biting his tongue in several places.

For the first time in his life all reason seemed to have escaped Oliver Pengarron. He punched and struck the other man unmercifully, until his fists were bloody. Hezekiah Solomon and two of his seamen who had entered the alleyway, ran up and were forced to use all their combined strength to wrest him away from his act of violent fury. 'Leave him, Oliver! Leave him!' Hezekiah shouted. 'You'll kill him!'

'It's no more than he deserves!' Oliver shouted back. 'Let go of me!'

Hezekiah held on tightly to his friend's arm. 'He's not worth hanging for, whatever he's done. Hit that man once more and I'll swear it's you who will have to answer to the Almighty. I'd be no friend of yours if I stand by and let you beat him to death.'

Some of the fierceness in Oliver's dark eyes had drained away. 'All right, have it your way if you must, but order these men to let go of me,' he snarled.

'Only if you give me your word you'll come with me straightaway for a drink to help you calm down.'

Oliver fixed his eyes on Hezekiah's pale smooth face. 'Very well. Now get your hands off me and tell your men to do the same.'

As the three men loosened their grip on him Oliver shrugged them off like an old coat. Sounds of everyday life in the market town reached his ears again and he realised it had stopped raining. The two sailors moved over to Peter Blake, now lying in an inert heap on the ground.

'Leave him be!' Oliver shouted angrily at them.

The sailors looked at their Captain for further guidance.

'Do as he says,' Hezekiah told them. 'Go on to the alehouse and talk to no one about this.' He tossed them a shilling coin each, and with a nod of understanding they took the same way out of the alley as the prostitute had done.

'Let's go, Hezekiah,' Oliver said tightly. 'The very sight of that scum lying there makes me feel sick.'

Striding back down the alley Oliver didn't wait to see if Hezekiah was following him. He glanced around to check if anyone was coming through either end of the alleyway or whether the scene of violence was being watched from a window. There was no one that he could see, and sweeping a hand back through his white hair he followed the back of his rapidly disappearing friend, leaving the beaten Peter Blake to his fate.

–

'You were going to tell me what that business in the alleyway was all about,' Hezekiah said. He had waited a good twenty minutes before asking the question on arriving outside Painted Bessie's kiddleywink some time after Oliver. The pony Hezekiah had hired could not keep pace with Conomor, and knowing Oliver lacked the patience to wait he had suggested they race on ahead and purge their mutual restlessness.

Oliver had washed the blood off his hands in a pool of rain water in a deep rut near the kiddley's front door. Conomor had quenched his thirst in the horse trough then had followed his master's lead by wandering off a short distance alone. Hezekiah had found them, man and horse, alike in their colouring, pride and temperament, looking out to sea. The sun was blazing down with no competition from any clouds, the springy coarse grass beneath their feet already drying out.

Keeping his eyes on a point across the Bay that was the fish market village of Newlyn, Oliver answered Hezekiah's question. 'Blake tried to rape Kerensa,' he said tonelessly.

Hezekiah looked up from the bejewelled fingers of the hand he was studying. 'When was this?' he asked, keeping his voice low.

'Early last evening. He was also responsible for the death of Dunstan.'

'Then he most certainly deserved the beating you gave him, Oliver. How is Kerensa now?'

'Shocked, upset. More for Dunstan than for herself. I was over at Penzance. If it hadn't been for Jack, and Clem Trenchard…'

'Trenchard? Isn't that the fellow—'

'Yes,' Oliver interrupted, swinging round to face his friend.

Hezekiah knew the discussion was over, but couldn't help wondering why Clem Trenchard had been at the Manor in Oliver's absence.

'I'm ready for that drink now, Hezekiah,' Oliver said gruffly, leading the way to the kiddley.

Inside the gloom of the shack, Painted Bessie rushed her gross body over to greet her two superior customers. She wiped her nose in her dirty apron and patted her waddling hips as she approached them.

'Afternoon to 'ee, sirs. Always glad to see such exalted persons as yerselves 'ere. What's it to be, then? Brandy? I've gotta good supply in, thanks to you both, if you sees what I do mean,' she said, winking a heavily painted eye at them.

Oliver pushed past Bessie and took a seat in a secluded corner, leaving Hezekiah to confirm they would indeed take brandy. As Hezekiah seated himself a group of miners coming off the morning core from the Wheal Ember trudged into the shabby alehouse. One of them, Colly Pearce, looked nervously away from the pair. He took a huge battered pewter tankard of cheap ale, served to him by a wafer thin girl of about ten years, as far away as he could to sit with his back to them.

Bessie served Oliver and Hezekiah herself with two large glasses set on a clean tray and a bottle of good French brandy she'd obtained from a secret cubby hole in her own private room. She placed the tray down on the table after rubbing away spills from the previous customers with the sleeve of her dress.

Jerking her head towards Colly Pearce, she said, 'Want me to gets t'ridst of 'im, sirs?'

'No, he's welcome to drink alongside of me,' answered Hezekiah grimly, 'if he keeps his mouth shut.'

Oliver threw an assortment of coins on the table which Bessie gathered up rapidly.

'Thank 'ee, sirs. Enjoy yer drink, stay as long as you like, and give a shout if 'ee wants anything else.'

'That woman is grotesque,' remarked Oliver, looking as though he'd eaten something bitter. 'Even Beatrice is better by comparison.'

Hezekiah laughed as the proprietress of the alehouse resumed her usual post, sitting at the end of a large table. Picking up her knitting she puffed away on a dirty clay pipe. 'She'd make a good mate for Old Tom,' said Hezekiah.

'Yes,' Oliver agreed, pouring two generous quantities of the dark red liquid.

'Any developments in that quarter since I've been away, Oliver?'

'Not yet. I've been down to Trelynne Cove many times and looked around. I'm convinced he's to be found somewhere about there.'

'Maybe he really has gone off for good? Could even be dead.'

'Maybe, but I don't think so. Ted Trembath shares my suspicions too, I think. He spends a lot of time up on the cliff above the cottage.'

'What's he doing there, do you know exactly?'

'He just looks wistfully out to sea, Hezekiah. Says it helps him to feel close to Davey.' Oliver shrugged. 'Anyway, I'd better drink up and set off for home.'

'Of course,' Hezekiah nodded. 'Kerensa will be needing you.'

'Perhaps,' Oliver said, causing his friend to look at him sharply. 'The Reverend Ivey has been with her all the morning but I ought not to leave her alone with only the servants for too long.'

'I was thinking,' said Hezekiah.

'About what?'

'Old Tom. If he is still around, Peter Blake could well receive a knife in his back one dark night for attacking Kerensa.'

'Good,' Oliver said between clenched teeth, before draining his glass.

Chapter 16

'I don't... believe... in heaven... so you... can't... be an angel,' Peter Blake murmured deliriously between bouts of coughing and choking. The small face peering down anxiously at him told his eyes it was Kerensa Pengarron, but his mind reasoned it couldn't possibly be her.

'I'll try to help you... help you... help you...'

The words echoed through his head as he tried to grasp their meaning, and it took a tremendous effort to focus on the speaker's face.

'Try to put your arms around my shoulders,' the girl said.

'I... can't.'

'Try, please try. You can't stay here in the mud,' she encouraged him.

Pain racked every part of Peter Blake's body. His head whirled and flashed like a crazily spinning maypole, while his lungs felt as though they would burst with every breath. As though in a weird dream, he managed to put an arm around the girl's thin shoulders and clutched at her shawl. With Blake using his other hand to push against the wall, they got him to his feet. Nausea flooded through him before everything became black again, and desperately he clung to the girl's small body. She couldn't hold his dead weight and they sank down together.

'I'll have to go for help,' she gasped, trying to prop him up in a sitting position against the wall.

'No, please.' He blinked his eyes again and again. 'Just round... the corner... to Angarrack's. I live... over the shop.'

The girl got him to his feet again, struggling to move him down the alleyway. It was not easy, she having a limp herself. They made

270

three steps before nausea overtook him again and he slumped forwards, dragging the girl down.

'Hold on, Rosina. I'll help you!' a shout came from behind them. Matthias Renfree reached them quickly. Disentangling Blake's arm from the girl's shawl he helped her to her feet, while preventing Blake from slipping further into the mud and potholes.

'I'm really pleased to see you, Preacher,' Rosina Pearce said when she'd regained her breath.

'It's fortunate I decided to come this way, Rosina. What happened to him? Do you know?' Matthias pulled a handkerchief out of a pocket and dabbed at Blake's swollen face.

'I've no idea. I found him like this lying in the mud. He asked me to take him to Angarrack's, the shoemaker. Do you know who he is, Preacher?'

Rosina knelt down and wrapped her shawl around Blake's shoulders. He was shaking violently between intermittent periods of consciousness; the shawl didn't help but Rosina could think of nothing else to do for him.

'We'd better get him home quickly,' Matthias said, looking at the girl. 'If he lives over Angarrack's he must be Peter Blake. Are you all right?'

'Yes, of course, but can you manage him on your own?'

'Don't worry, he's no great weight to me.' Matthias put one of Blake's limp arms around his shoulders and lifted him easily to his feet. Blake slumped backwards with a groan, and realising the injured man would not be able to help himself, Matthias eased him over his shoulder and carried him. A fairly tall but stocky man, he found lifting Blake's body no greater burden than the tasks he carried out on Keran-Mor Farm.

Rosina picked up the wicker basket she'd dropped when she'd first come across Blake's unconscious body. It contained only two brown eggs, a slither of pale yellow cheese, and three rashers of thinly cut bacon bought from the market stalls. She straightened the white muslin bonnet that held her long fair hair tidy, then followed Matthias Renfree out of the alleyway.

Passersby looked curiously at a young man carrying the swaying unconscious body of another, and the girl limping along beside them, mud and blood on her clothes. Some, on recognising the injured man, passed by with a nod to Matthias and their faces grimly set. James Andrew, the tenant farmer of Barvah Farm, the smallest on the Pengarron Estate, was the only person to offer assistance.

'Here, young Preacher, I'll take him from you,' he offered in his deep voice. 'Some wouldn't bother to help this man. Tis all round the district what he did to young Lady Pengarron yesterday.'

'Some haven't bothered to help, James, just like you said. What is Mr Blake supposed to have done to warrant such an uncharitable beating? It's all right, I can manage to carry him the rest of the way, but I'll be glad to have a hand to get him up the stairs.'

James Andrew glanced at Rosina who was listening attentively. 'Here, maid,' he said, smiling at her as they neared the shoemaker's noisy shop, 'be a dear and go up they stairs beside the shop there, and knock up Mr Blake's housekeeper.'

Rosina smiled shyly and passed the three men quickly, her lame right foot of little hindrance to her.

When she was out of sight James Andrew jerked his head in Blake's direction. 'I didn't want to say anything in front of the little maid, Preacher. Seems he here, early last evening, tried to… you know, to Lady Pengarron, Old Tom's granddaughter I mean. And after that, tis said he kicked Sir Oliver's old dog nigh to death, and it had to be shot. And everyone knows how Sir Oliver loved that old dog.'

'How do you know all this, James?' Matthias said, having to walk around two stern-faced matrons who refused to move out of his path.

'Beatrice! She's going all round the town saying she'll kill this bleddy sod – sorry, Preacher – Mr Blake,' James Andrew replied rather heatedly, prodding the inert body from where Matthias couldn't see him. 'She said the poor little maid up in the Manor's in some dreadful state. Smacked her round the face he did, terrified her out of her wits. And she loved that old dog too. Apparently, she's taking his death really hard. Tis a crying shame, young Preacher, that maid's had a Hell of a year so far as it is. Folk are outraged about it, and no wonder.'

'I see. That's terrible,' said Matthias coldly. The strong smell of leather filled their nostrils as they hauled Blake between them up the narrow wooden staircase of the shoemaker's, their feet scuffling noisily on each step. 'And presumably that's the reason for him being in this state now?'

'Wouldn't be at all surprised. I saw Sir Oliver myself riding out from town not half hour since with that strange white-haired sea captain friend of his. No, Sir Oliver's not the sort of man to take a thing like that lying down.'

'I don't hold with this sort of behaviour though, James,' retorted Matthias, sadly shaking his head, 'and some of this mud on Mr Blake is drying off already so I wouldn't be surprised if other people left him lying in the alleyway before Rosina came across him.'

They had reached the top of the stairs and came up behind Rosina who was knocking loudly on a door. 'Shall I try one of the others? There's two more on this landing.' Peter Blake moaned and rolled his head. James Andrew took all of his weight from Matthias. 'Knock on 'em all, young Preacher, this man is getting proper poorly.'

'Wait a minute,' Rosina said, putting her head closer to the door. 'It's all right, I can hear someone at last.'

'All right, all right, I'm coming,' a shrill voice called out within. Peter Blake's housekeeper opened the door no more than a crack and peered out short-sightedly at the slight figure of the girl standing there in shabby clothes. 'Yes, what is it, m'dear? Did Mr Blake tell you to come up and wait for him?'

'Open the door, woman!' shouted James Andrew impatiently. 'Me and the young Preacher have got your master here and he's hurt bad and needs a doctor.'

The housekeeper opened the door wide and screamed at the sight of Peter Blake, covered in blood and caked mud, supported by the two men.

'Calm yourself and run and fetch Mr Blake's doctor. Quickly now,' ordered Matthias in a more kindly tone.

After a moment's dithering the woman collected her bonnet and shawl, and with a scrap of lace-edged handkerchief stuffed against her gulping mouth, pitter-pattered down the dark shadowy staircase.

Moving about inside Blake's rooms, Rosina had located his bedroom and beckoned to the others to bring in its unfortunate occupant. Holding Blake's limp form upright, the men pulled off his dirty, stained dresscoat and waistcoat, and laying him carefully on the bed with the covers pulled back, they each dragged off a leather boot. They asked Rosina to turn her back as they pulled off his breeches and the rest of his clothes. Placing the covers gently over Blake's shivering and jerking body, they stood back and looked down on him. Rosina turned around and stood between them.

James Andrew announced he must be on his way and Matthias thanked him for his help. 'It's all right, young Preacher,' James said, with a deep sigh, 'but after what he's done, and even lying there like that, it don't bring the Good Samaritan out easily in a man, I can tell you. I'll say good day to you then.'

He gave Rosina a warm smile. 'You take care of yourself, maid. Pity about your shawl. It's all muddy and bloodstained, and it won't wash easily out of that tartan twill. That daughter of mine left one behind when she took off with that tinker fellow. You're welcome to it, maid. I'll get the missus to bring it up to Jeb Bray's tonight for the Bible class.'

'Thank you, Mr Andrew. It's kind of you to think of me,' Rosina said, straightening the bed covers.

'It's him who needs to thank you, maid,' James Andrew said seriously. 'I'll be off then. I wish you both well of this affair.'

The housekeeper returned with the doctor in his gig and was of no use at all. She sat and sobbed in the kitchen, drinking endless cups of tea and leaving Rosina to boil water and find clean linen to tear up for bandages.

Doctor Charles Crebo was an efficient surgeon and physician, well versed in the treatment of broken ribs, broken jaw bones, major and minor cuts and contusions, split lips and crushed hands. He worked for over an hour, stitching, cleaning, prodding, bandaging, and regularly listening to the heart and lungs of his patient.

'There you are, my dear,' said Dr Crebo, as he fastened the last piece of bandage on Blake's hand, to Rosina on the other side of the bed. 'You make an excellent nurse.'

'Thank you, Doctor,' she said softly. 'Will Mr Blake be all right? He looks an awful mess.'

Ugly bruises and swollen lips had transformed Peter Blake's handsome face into a bloated ugly mass. The top of his body and one arm were swathed in bandages. Matthias Renfree came and stood beside Rosina. He looked at the figure beginning to stir in the bed, and repeated her question.

'By and by,' said Charles Crebo, 'he should be, as long as no complications set in the next forty-eight hours, and if he fights off infections. Master Renfree, you can tell me something. It's obvious to me how Mr Blake came by his injuries, but have you any idea why someone should do this to him? He's not a popular fellow I know...'

'I have my thoughts on the matter, Dr Crebo,' Matthias replied soberly, 'but for the time being I'd rather keep them to myself.'

'Very well. As you please. Do you reckon there could be another injured party about somewhere?'

'That, I think not.'

'Well,' said the doctor with a long sigh, 'someone could easily find himself facing a murder charge over this.'

'Excuse me for butting in,' Rosina said, 'but I want to show you something.' From a deep pocket of her skirt she produced a small, ivory-handled pistol.

'May I?' Charles Crebo held out his hand. Rosina passed it to him. 'Where did you find it, my dear?' he asked, scrutinising the pistol closely.

'Beside Mr Blake,' Rosina answered quickly. 'Has it been fired?' she added anxiously.

'No, the firing mechanism is jammed, thank God. There are two initials on the handle. P.B. It looks as if Mr Blake's adversary may have had a lucky escape.' He put the pistol down on the bedside table and looked again at his patient. 'I suppose that accounts for his crushed hand. Probably been stamped on by a heavy boot. Well now,' he said brightly, rubbing his hands together, 'where is that hysterical woman with the tea?'

The housekeeper obliged them with a fresh pot. Clutching her handkerchief to her mouth to stifle another scream, she ventured over to the bed to look down at her employer.

'Poor Mr Blake,' she squeaked between sobs. 'What a terrible thing to do to him, it's the work of the Devil himself. Did you bleed him, Doctor?'

'Don't be ridiculous, woman,' said Charles Crebo airily, disappointed there was not a slice of madeira cake or a shortbread biscuit to go with the tea. 'Don't you think he's lost blood enough already?'

Rosina shuddered and Matthias reached back to the chair where he had thrown her shawl. He frowned at the stains on it, but they were mainly dry, having been close to the hearty fire he had lit to keep the bedroom warm.

'I'm afraid this will have to do for now, Rosina,' he said kindly, wrapping it round her shoulders. 'Are you all right?'

She became embarrassed by his sudden concern, and the smiling fatherly looks Dr Crebo was aiming at her at regular intervals. 'Yes. Thank you. But who's going to nurse Mr Blake over the next few days?' she said, looking doubtfully at the housekeeper.

'Well?' the doctor turned to the woman who clutched her bosom in alarm.

'Oh! Not me. I couldn't… I just couldn't!'

'How about you, my dear?' the doctor said to Rosina. 'I'm sure Mr Blake's family will pay you well.'

Rosina's gentle face coloured. 'No,' she blurted out, 'my brother wouldn't like it.'

'Oh?' said Charles Crebo curiously.

'I know!' interrupted the housekeeper, 'Mistress Courtis! Mr Blake's half-sister. She'll arrange something, I'm sure. I'll go and call on her at once. She ought to be told about this anyway.'

'I'll drive you there myself,' said Dr Crebo, collecting up his bag, coat and walking cane. 'Lives over Trevenner way, doesn't she?'

'Yes, that's right, Doctor. It's very kind of you,' simpered the woman gratefully. 'But what about Mr Blake? These good people can't stay here all day, but I can't leave him alone. I wonder if Mrs Angarrack will come up from the shop, but she isn't too good on the stairs at her age.' She ended with a panicky attack of biting her nails.

Rosina had been thinking about her brother. It had been the last day of May, the day before, and Colly had received his monthly wage, so she could almost be certain he'd be holed up somewhere in an alehouse well on the way to getting roaring drunk. It was about four-thirty and he wouldn't arrive back home for several hours yet.

'I can stay a while longer, if you like,' she said quietly.

'Why, bless you, my dear, you're an absolute angel,' declared Peter Blake's housekeeper, looking overly relieved. 'I'll get my shawl and bonnet,' she squawked at Charles Crebo. 'Oh! And bless you too, young man, it's nice to know there are a few good Christian people about these days. Did I hear the doctor call you Master Renfree?' She gave Matthias a short-sighted false smile.

'That is right, Mrs...?'

'Mrs Blight,' she told him with a silly giggle. 'I believe I've heard about you. Hold Bible meetings or something, don't you? I'd come along myself only Mr Blake wouldn't approve, you see. Says it's just a lot of silly nonsense put about by people from a holy club or something he heard about when he went to Oxford University. He's a very clever man, you know, is Mr Blake. Anyway, I can't get out much myself these days, it's my nerves, you know.'

Matthias had not seen Mrs Blight before. Indeed not many people in Marazion had. She was content to stay in her room and indulge herself in a glass or two of gin when her master entertained a visitor, invariably of the gentler sex, or to occupy herself with her household duties.

'Don't worry about Blake, Mrs Blight,' Matthias said, not looking at her but the patient who had begun to moan and curse. 'I'll stay with Rosina until you get back with Mistress Courtis.'

Dr Crebo watched Blake until consciousness slipped away from him again, then he left a collection of bottles, jars, salves and ointments, all labelled with neat, clear instructions for their usage, on the highly polished bedside table. What Mrs Blight lacked in fortitude, she made up for with cleaning abilities.

When Dr Crebo and the squeaky housekeeper had left, Matthias put more logs on the fire. 'There, that should keep it going for a while, Rosina,' he said, when satisfied with the blaze.

'Thank you, Preacher,' she said, her voice as soft and clear as the morning dew. 'Mr Blake is sleeping now, I'll sit and watch over him.'

Hammering was heard on the outside door. Matthias smiled and said, 'I'll go and see who that is.'

Rosina pulled up a chair by the bedside. Between anxious glances at Blake she took delight in noting the beautiful ornaments, pictures and furniture in what she considered a very grand place. A bracket clock in an elegant marquetry case, its square face, handle, and finials on the top all of gleaming brasswork, fascinated her the most. After a while she got up to see who was keeping Matthias so long talking at the door and saw Seth Angarrack from downstairs who had come up anxious to know what had happened to his landlord. Rosina had a quick closer look at the bracket clock before returning to her post.

She was startled by the deep, cornflower blue eyes watching her movements.

'Who... are... you?' Blake gasped painfully.

'My name is Rosina,' she answered him, 'but you shouldn't try to talk. You need all the rest you can get.'

He tried to lick his dry lips, but having bitten his tongue in several places when he was shaken, it was too sore and he gagged and choked. Rosina rushed forward and raised his head until the unpleasant moments passed and he was relaxed enough to be lowered back on the pillows.

'Water...' he murmured with an effort. 'Will... you... get... me...'

'Yes, Mr Blake,' she said, smiling to encourage him. 'I'll only be a minute.'

In the kitchen she filled a small basin with cold water and searched out a piece of clean cloth. 'Here you are, Mr Blake,' she said on her return. 'I'll squeeze a few drops of water out of this cloth for you.'

The drops of water moistened his split lips and he just had enough strength to use the tip of his tongue to take some into his mouth. It was only a short time before he was panting with the effort.

'Don't go,' he said breathlessly.

'I'll stay with you until your sister gets here,' she reassured him, 'your housekeeper has gone to fetch her.'

Matthias had finally relieved himself of the ageing shoemaker and come to stand the other side of the bed. Blake did not realise anyone but the slightly built golden-haired girl was there.

Rosina glanced at Matthias with a look that conveyed her sympathy for Blake's plight. She squeezed more drops of water for Blake, he all the time looking at her like a frightened child. He watched her as she put the cloth and basin down and sat on her chair. When he couldn't see her face Blake became agitated so she moved closer and looked directly down into his eyes.

Matthias moved to another chair, a short distance away, and bowed his head in silent prayer.

'Don't leave... me... please...' Blake tried to raise his bandaged hand to Rosina but did not have the strength to do it.

'Don't worry, I won't,' she said soothingly.

The agitation left his eyes and Blake slipped into unconsciousness again, his breathing coming in regular laboured gasps. Rosina gently stroked his hair and sang softly in the hope it might comfort him somehow. Matthias sat and listened, quite enchanted by the girl's lilting voice, until a key was heard in the door heralding the return of Mrs Blight and the arrival of Blake's half-sister.

Chapter 17

The interment of three miners crushed to death by a rockfall down the Wheal Ember mine saw the presence in Perranbarvah's churchyard of the Reverend Ivey and Matthias Renfree. Such a gathering was not an uncommon occurrence, with accidents on the land, at sea, and the many local tin and copper mines, as well as the weak, the young and the old being snuffed out at frequent intervals by a variety of fevers. Attending a burial was part of the normal way of life for the whole community.

The rockfall had claimed the life of another of Ted Trembath's brothers, this time Curly. With him in death was Amos Bawden, son of Carn and sister to Heather, the little girl who had carried the news of the discovery of Davey Trembath's body. Richard Astley was the third, leaving behind him a widow and four young children to fend for themselves in a harsh world.

Like the day of farmer's son Henry Sampson's funeral, the sun blazed down in a cloudless sky, making the children restless and the mourners tug in discomfort at the unwelcome heat in their black clothes.

'We meet too often like this, Matthias,' the Reverend Ivey said, shaking his head sadly after the last of the large number of mourners had left the churchyard.

'Yes, Reverend. I suppose we should be thankful it was only three dead. Apparently Ted Trembath and Colly Pearce were among those who were able to scramble to safety. If Ted had died, his mother would no doubt have made up a fifth burial today,' remarked Matthias, stooping to pick up a fallen wild flower dropped by a female mourner.

'I didn't notice Colly Pearce paying his respects among the mourners, or giving thanks for his escape,' the Reverend commented drily.

'That was only to be expected, of course, but what I did notice were fresh bruises on Rosina's face and throat, even though she did her best to conceal them. I am greatly concerned about her welfare.'

'That poor girl. I wish something could be done about her dreadful situation, but it's difficult to think of any that would not make the matter worse.'

'Actually, Reverend, I've had an idea about that.'

'Oh, really?' said the elderly parson in a hopeful voice. 'And what might that be?'

'Well, I thought... I... um... could offer Rosina marriage.' Matthias kept his flushed face on the wild flower he was twirling between finger and thumb. 'I know we're not in love or anything, but I'm very fond of her. She's quite the sweetest little thing... and... and I suppose I could do with a wife, and I'd really look after her and... and...' Matthias' rapid speech finally petered out.

The Reverend Ivey was partly amused, partly serious. He kept his eyes on a pile of dry earth dug for one of the graves to allow Matthias' embarrassment to subside.

'You don't think it's a good idea then, Reverend?' he asked awkwardly.

'I really don't know, Matthias, I'll have to think about it. Mind you, it would be wonderful to think of the girl safe and sound away from her brother. If you can spare the time, come into the Parsonage for tea. There's something I would like to talk over with you.'

'I can spare a little more time, Reverend. I hope Mrs Tregonning will have a fresh batch of her yeast buns just out of the oven. I wouldn't tell Faith Bray, of course, but I've tasted none better.'

The delicious warm smell wafting out through the kitchen window as they neared the Parsonage told Matthias his hope was not in vain. Settled in the parlour he and the Reverend discussed the families of the recently deceased men.

'There are other wage earners in the Trembath and Bawden families,' the Reverend said, 'but Richard Astley's widow and children will

281

have to leave their cottage and she will have to find some form of employment.'

'Perhaps they need someone at the Manor,' Matthias suggested.

'That could be a possibility. I'm going to see Lady Pengarron tomorrow. I'll ask her about it then.'

'Sir Martin Beswetherick sent Mrs Astley two guineas,' said Matthias, absent-mindedly crumbling a piece of yeast bun. 'Not a lot of help in the long run, but better than what most of the mine owners would do.'

'I'll inform you if she can be taken on at the Manor. If not, we'll see what else we can come up with.' The Reverend's voice took on a grave tone. 'Actually, the thing I want to discuss with you, Matthias, concerns Kerensa Pengarron.'

'The attack on her by Peter Blake, you mean?'

'No, not that. Although the effect on her of that distressing incident has been worrying me a good deal, this could be even worse.' The Reverend ran a hand over his bald pate and through the wisps of surrounding grey hair. 'It's about Mary Trelynne, Kerensa's mother.'

'Oh?' said Matthias, baffled and intrigued at the same time.

'You won't know anything about her death, of course?'

'On the contrary,' Matthias broke in. 'I know the exact circumstances of Mary Trelynne's death. My father told me about it when we were discussing Kerensa's decision to go through with the marriage to Sir Oliver. I must have been about fourteen at the time of her death and remember feeling then there was something odd about the whole affair. When I mentioned it to Father he told me about the other terrible thing Old Tom was responsible for. Makes me shudder just to think of it. Why has all this come up now?'

'On the day of the attack Kerensa came over to see me concerning her mother's death. I was delayed that day and didn't see her, but she is bound to ask me again soon. It seems Kerensa has always been curious to know all the details of how her mother died, and knowing that I was present at the time she wants me to tell her of her mother's last moments. I'm afraid Kerensa has no idea of the dreadful circumstances behind them. She has told me she wants to put the past behind her so she can look more firmly to the future but of course hearing the truth will only distress her, not comfort her in any way. What I fear now is, if she broaches the subject again tomorrow, will she be able to bear up under the present strain she is going through? I'd be interested to hear your opinion, Matthias, you knew her quite well before her marriage.'

Matthias sipped thoughtfully from the cup he'd been holding between mouth and saucer. He said, 'She could hear about her mother's death from another source if she's been questioning others about it. I would say the sooner she knows the truth the better, and the sooner she could put it behind her too. Of course it will be very distressing but I see no reason why she should go to pieces, if that's what you mean. No, Kerensa has deep strength of character to go with her gentleness and beauty.'

'Thank you, Matthias. Do you know, I believe there's more than a touch of the romantic lying hidden in you,' the Reverend said fondly. He'd known the young man all his life, schooled him, and watched with approval the way he'd turned out. He had not been perturbed at Matthias' keen interest in the rapidly expanding Methodist movement, not sharing the fierce opposition of the majority of Anglican clergymen to it. He smiled warmly at him. 'I seem to have embarrassed you, Matthias.'

'No, it's all right,' he said, smiling back boyishly for a moment. Serious again he went on, 'I have a lot of thinking to do about Rosina. But I don't envy you, Reverend, having to tell Kerensa about her mother.'

Gloom descended in the parlour like a sudden heavy shower of rainfall. The Reverend slapped a hand down heavily on a large fly walking across a nearby book. It slipped through his fingers and flew to safety high on an enclosed bookcase.

'No,' he sighed, inwardly relieved at the fly's escape. 'It won't be easy...'

On the same afternoon the two men were discussing Kerensa's late mother, Alice Trenchard turned up at the Manor house. Knocking on the kitchen door she entered self-consciously to find Esther kneading dough, Ruth sewing at the end of the table, and Beatrice drunkenly asleep in her chair.

'Alice!' exclaimed Esther in surprise. 'Come on in and sit yourself down. Her ladyship will be really pleased to see you, won't she, Ruth?'

'She will,' said Ruth, putting down her work and pulling out a chair beside her. 'Come and sit down here. I'll go tell Polly you're here in a minute.'

Alice was thankful to sit down after her long walk. Pregnancy was not coming easily to her; her ankles were swollen, her back cramped. 'Are you sure, Kerensa, I mean her ladyship, will be pleased to see me?' she asked rather anxiously. 'I've been wanting to come over ever since she came back from Tolwithrick, but didn't know whether or not to... what with me marrying Clem. But I haven't been able to rest for a minute since I heard what happened to her. How is she?'

'It's hard to say for sure, Alice,' Esther replied. 'One minute she seems her normal self, then off she goes to be alone and when she comes back it's obvious she's been crying her eyes out.'

'As it was on the day, before... before what that dreadful man did. Polly said she was looking vexed,' put in Ruth.

'Do you know why that was, Ruth?'

'No. None of us does. She had been to Perranbarvah. All we can think of is she didn't like that man's company on the way back.'

'Poor girl,' murmured Alice. 'Anyway, what's this Polly Berryman like? Do you all get on well with her?'

'Of course, you don't know Polly, do you?' said Ruth. 'She's a good woman, is Polly. Been in service for years and has taught us a lot about what goes on in a big house. She stays with her ladyship as much as possible to stop her from moping, and has even given up her evening walks with Nathan since it happened.'

'Nathan?' Alice raised her eyebrows. 'With a lady friend? This Polly must be worth having a look at, then.'

'So you've showed up, 'ave 'ee?' rasped Beatrice, waking from her slumbers.

Alice turned round to greet the crone. 'Hello, Beatrice, and how are you?'

Beatrice coughed indiscriminately into the room and wiped the back of a hand across her chins to remove an outpouring of dribble. 'I'm right enough,' she answered, bending forward to peer closer at the girl. 'Yourn 'ave to watch yerself though, maid, yourn all puffed up, jus' like 'is lordship's mother was when childbearin'. See it's another babe conceived before the weddin' 'n' all.'

Alice pulled a face but Beatrice promptly grunted herself back to sleep.

'Well, I'll go find Polly, then,' Ruth said, rising from the table, 'and tell her you're here, Alice.'

When Ruth had gone Alice looked all around to be sure no one else was about. 'How are things between her ladyship and Sir Oliver, Esther?' she asked, barely above a whisper.

'He's been very good to her, kindness itself at times, and hasn't been staying away so much as he used to. We don't think he's been… um… bothering her either, if you take my meaning.' Esther's face coloured deeply at her last sentence.

'I see. Is Sir Oliver here at the moment?'

'No, gone over to Marazion to see Cap'n Solomon, I do believe.'

'I heard what he did to Peter Blake. Clem went to market last week but didn't find out how he is now. Have you heard anything?'

'Last I heard, that sister of his had him moved to her house over Trevenner way. If you ask me,' Esther said, putting lumps of dough on baking trays, 'that man was lucky to get away with his life.'

'You're probably right,' agreed Alice, massaging her aching back. 'He always made me feel quite cold, for all his fine looks.'

'Well, his looks aren't so fine now.'

'Of course he can never bring charges against Sir Oliver. If he did, what he did to her ladyship and poor old Dunstan would come out in the open and make an even bigger scandal. He'd be hated more than ever then.'

Ruth returned shortly with Polly Berryman who warmly shook Alice's hand. 'It's nice to meet you at last, Mrs Trenchard,' she said pleasantly. 'Her ladyship talks about you quite often. She's in her sitting room at the moment. Would you like to come along with me now?'

'I'm glad you've come,' Polly said, as they made their way through the house. 'I believe her ladyship misses you, and you may be able to cheer her a little.'

'I'll do my best,' Alice promised, but she felt rather nervous about seeing Kerensa again.

Polly opened the door to Kerensa's sitting room. 'Mrs Trenchard for you, my lady,' she said, and withdrew at once.

Kerensa was half-heartedly arranging flowers by a window. She stared at Alice with a wide-eyed look of disbelief for several moments, then letting flowers fall from her hands, rushed across the room and hugged Alice tightly, tears running freely down her face.

'Alice! Oh, Alice, thank you for coming to see me.'

Tears insisted on leaving Alice's eyes too as she murmured, 'I wasn't sure if I should come or not, Kerensa. Now I wish I'd come sooner.'

Stepping back, Kerensa took Alice's hands. 'If only you knew how good it is to see you again,' she said, beginning to laugh through her tears. 'Oh, I hope you can stay for ages and ages. Come and sit down and tell me everything you've been doing since I saw you last.'

'Mother, Mrs Trenchard that is, said I was to stay as long as I like,' Alice said, easing her thickening body down on a comfortable sofa, 'if you were at home.' Florrie Trenchard had in fact said 'if you are received'.

'And Clem. Will he mind how long you stay? I suppose he's looking forward to the baby coming.'

'Clem won't mind as long as I'm back before he comes in from the fields. He doesn't take much interest in the baby. A bit too early yet, I expect.' A dark shadow slid across Alice's face as she went on, 'I'm sorry about what happened to you, and poor old Dunstan. I should have been here, Kerensa, I should...'

'There was nothing you could have done, Alice.' Kerensa reassured her, fighting back a shudder at the memory. 'Jack was very brave, I'm so proud of him.'

'So Clem told me. It was a good thing he came over to see Nathan that day, or only the Lord knows what might have happened.'

286

'Yes, only the Lord knows,' Kerensa said softly. 'I'll always be grateful to Clem. Oliver will be too, I'm sure.'

'Sir Oliver actually wrote to Clem to thank him. Matthias Renfree read it out for him properly. Clem didn't say anything about it, but Mother and Father Trenchard, and Gran Donald, were overwhelmed. I thought it was very good of him.'

Kerensa smiled at her friend. 'It sounds as though you've settled in well with the family. How's Kenver and little Rosie?'

'With the others fussing about me not being on my feet for long, I spend a lot of time sitting with my work and chatting to Kenver. Did you know he's very good at poetry? Preacher Renfree comes in now and again to help him write it down, but paper's scarce, of course.'

'I'll get you some from Oliver's study for him, he's got plenty in there. And Rosie?'

'Well, she's such a dear little maid, isn't she? Likes to hold on to my hand, and talks about you and the Manor all the time. She was really excited when she knew I was coming up here today.'

'You must bring her with you next time. We'll show her all over the house and she can play in the gardens and see if there's any injured animals in the hut.' Kerensa's face brightened as she talked, for a moment eliminating the trace of deep tragedy behind her eyes, before she became earnest. 'You will visit me regularly Alice, promise me you will? It wouldn't do for me to go to Trecath-en, but you can come here as often as you like.'

'I'd like that, Kerensa,' Alice said. 'I promise to come as often as I can.'

She gave an audible sigh of relief. 'Good, that's settled. I'll not have you walking in your condition though. I'll send Jack or Barney over in the trap for you and you can ride home later today.' She sprang up happily and pulled the bell rope beside the mantelpiece. 'I'll ask Polly to fetch us some of Beatrice's delicious cold fruit and spiced cordial,' she said, smiling.

'That sounds good,' Alice said. 'Do something for me, will you, Kerensa?'

'Yes, of course, anything.'

'Then keep smiling. It takes away the dark shadows under your eyes. And start eating again. I've never seen you so thin before, and with me putting on weight it looks even worse.'

'Dear Alice,' Kerensa laughed, 'as blunt as ever.'

When Polly left the refreshment tray she was pleased to see the two younger women chatting and laughing together. She closed the door after her with a satisfied smile.

Taking her glass from Kerensa, Alice said meditatively, 'Strange, isn't it? I used to bring in the tea trays not so long ago. And last Christmas we would never have believed you would marry Sir Oliver and become a lady.' She added, looking less sure of herself, 'Or that I would marry the man you were going to.'

Alice still felt on edge. Since she had left her employment at the Manor to marry Clem it had nagged at her as to what Kerensa really thought about it. She told herself often that Kerensa had no claim on Clem after she had married another man, but she knew Kerensa would dominate the greater part of Clem's heart for the rest of their lives, and Alice believed love had a way of winning through in the end. The thought that Kerensa and Clem might end up together eventually and she would be left out in the cold was a distressing one. Like the feeling she could not shake off that she was an infiltrator in the Trenchard household.

'You don't mind too much – me marrying Clem?'

'It felt strange at first, Alice,' Kerensa admitted. 'I know I had no right to, but I kept wondering what it would have been like if I had married Clem. I was very jealous of you. But now I'm pleased for you both… I think you will be good for Clem. I'm glad he's settled down.'

It was an uncomfortable and embarrassing topic for them both and they were relieved it was done with. A look of deep understanding passed between them that said there was no need for any more words. Alice was cheered inside. She felt certain that Kerensa would not take any course of action that could threaten her marriage.

As Kerensa sat down, Alice took her hand. 'How are you? I mean, how are you really feeling inside?'

She looked dreamily into space then met Alice's searching eyes. 'I'll be all right, Alice, don't worry about me. It wouldn't be half so bad if it wasn't for Dunstan, of course. I miss him so much. If I hadn't invited that man into the house, he would still be alive. But Oliver says I'm not to blame myself. How can we know what anyone else will do... I can't help feeling it's all my fault though. I will have to try and put it all behind me and look forward to the future.'

'Will that be very difficult for you, Kerensa?'

'I won't let it be,' she said defiantly. 'Come on, drink up your cordial and then we'll take a stroll round the gardens.'

Alice relaxed back into the sofa's plump cushions. It was good to see some of her friend's old spirit returning to her again.

–

Alice's visit did much to bring vitality back into Kerensa's mournful soul and salve her aching heart. With Dunstan gone and so few people to call a friend in this new life, and practically no one to visit her in her new surroundings, it was like being given a lifeline to have Alice's friendship back again. Now that Clem had someone else in his life to turn to, some of her guilt at hurting him lifted from her shoulders. With his child to look forward to, there was something for him to build a new life for. The Reverend Ivey was pleased to find her in a lighter mood than he had anticipated.

They strolled in the warm sunshine, her arm wound around his, and he resting a fatherly hand over hers.

'A truly lovely day, Kerensa,' sighed the Reverend, as a light breeze playfully teased his wispy strands of hair. 'I congratulate you on the beauty of your gardens.'

'Oh, the credit must go to Jake and the other gardeners, not to me. I do admit though that I'm pleased with everything.'

'You shouldn't be so modest, my dear. I detect more than a touch here and there of yours.'

'The wild flowers, you mean?' Kerensa said, looking about. 'I couldn't bear to live without them growing close by. I was surrounded by wild flowers in and around the cove. Wild madder, thrift, sea kale.'

'Not forgetting the chicory with its lovely blue petals.'

'That usually opens only in the morning,' she added. 'And stinking iris and storksbill, and kidney vetch as golden as the gorse.' Kerensa laughed gaily, and the Reverend thought it was a shame the information he had come to impart would no doubt distress her more than anything that had yet happened.

'Of course,' she chattered on, 'many of those won't grow very well here away from the coastline, but most of the roots and cuttings I've taken from the hedges and wayside will.' Wanting to delay the subject of Kerensa's mother for as long as possible, the Reverend spoke on many different topics. 'Do you think you might have the opportunity to hear Mr John Wesley preach in this part of the country later in the summer?'

'To be honest, Reverend, I haven't give it much thought. Ruth and Esther are going to, they asked me about it ages ago.' She stopped walking to sniff a lilac bloom. 'Perhaps I will go to hear him. Jack could come with me, and Oliver probably wouldn't mind.'

'I'm sure he wouldn't, my dear. You go. It will do you the world of good.'

'I admire you for your liberal approach, Reverend.'

'Oh, I see eye to eye with anyone if they preach the true word of God, Kerensa. It's a pity more of my contemporaries couldn't do the same.'

Leaving the formal gardens they strolled round the back of the Manor house to the hut for injured animals.

'There's a lot of rabbits in here today,' remarked the Reverend.

Kerensa picked up a young one and checked the bandage on its foot. 'This one was found in an illegal trap. Most of them that are found are too badly hurt to save. There's been a lot caught this year in this cruel way – because we had such a dry spring and many more young rabbits have thrived. A lot die if we have a cold wet May, you see.'

'Really?' said the Reverend, suitably impressed. 'You're such a little mother.'

'Becoming a true mother is my greatest hope at the moment, Reverend,' she said, snuggling the rabbit into the straw of its box.

'I'm sure you will be, Kerensa. You've plenty of time yet. You're very young.' The Reverend passed her a jug of water and Kerensa refilled the animal's supply. 'If you'll forgive a frank question, my dear,' he said, 'how are you getting used to living with Sir Oliver?'

Kerensa pondered on this for a moment. 'I really don't know. I seem to know so little about him at times. At least I feel more comfortable than I did when we first married. I'm beginning to see through Oliver's little games now.'

'Little games?' said the Reverend, frowning. 'I don't think I like the sound of that.'

'It's nothing to worry about, Reverend,' she said, smiling as proof of her assertion. 'I can't explain it, it's just one of his idio... idio...'

'Idiosyncrasies?'

'Yes, that's the word. Oliver says Mrs Tregonning has them,' she whispered, like a child telling tales.

The Reverend looked at her fondly. 'Shall we take a walk through the orchards next?' he suggested. 'I do enjoy the smell of apple blossom and there is still plenty left on the trees this year.'

'You were going to ask me something when you first arrived,' Kerensa said, when they were outside again.

'Oh, yes. I was going to ask you about Richard Astley's widow. I buried her husband yesterday and I'm hoping there might be a position for her here at the Manor.'

'I know the Astleys well from the Bible classes, they were a close-knit family. It's so sad. We need no one here, but Oliver told me last night Lady Rachael is to offer Mrs Astley work cleaning at Tolwith-rick.' Kerensa fell into a melancholy silence.

'Well, that is good news.' The Reverend left her in her quietness for a while, then gently asked, 'What are you thinking about?'

She sighed deeply. 'The Trembaths, the Bawdens, the fatherless Astley children. There's so much tragedy in the world. It makes me feel guilty to be living in a grand house, wearing fine clothes and having servants to do everything for me if I want them to. I would like to do something useful, feel my life is worthwhile.'

'I happen to know you have been very good to Rosina Pearce,' the Reverend said.

'But there's so little I can do even for Rosina. She can't accept much help because Colly objects.'

'Why don't you tell Sir Oliver how you feel, my dear? At the least, I'm sure he'd be interested.' The Reverend stopped, and pulling down the branch of an apple tree drew in a deep breath of sweetly scented blossom. 'Kerensa, perhaps I should have mentioned this earlier to you. It may help you to know there is one burden you don't have to bear alone.'

'Oh?' She looked up expectantly.

'You see, I know what passed between you and Samuel Drannock in the church.'

'You do? Did he tell you?'

'No, it was Jenifer. She was deeply concerned that you were hurt by Samuel's blunt refusal to allow you to give them any further help. She also told me of his true parentage.'

Kerensa leaned her back against the trunk of the apple tree. She closed her eyes for a moment and let out a deep breath. 'Oh, Reverend, it's such a relief to be able to share it all with someone. I thought Oliver had fathered Bartholomew and cast Jenifer aside, and I treated him so badly. I haven't been able to explain my behaviour or ask his forgiveness. I suppose the best thing is to try to forget it and look towards the future, and do what I need to get everything cleared up from the past. Then perhaps I will be able to settle down here and give Oliver that child we both long for. I've come to terms with Clem marrying Alice and my own guilt at hurting him so much. There's just one thing left and that I simply have to know. Reverend, I want you to tell me exactly how my mother died...'

—

While she waited impatiently for the writer of the letter she was holding, Lady Rachael Beswetherick held it close to her powdered face and read again for the umpteenth time. As far as she was concerned the letter's contents were all very mysterious, a suggestion of a secret meeting, but she was apt to allow the simplest of matters to grow out of proportion.

As she reached the bold signature at the bottom of the last page again, she cried, 'Ah, at last!' and waved away the servant who was proceeding Sir Oliver Pengarron and about to announce him. 'Where have you been? How can you be so cruel as to keep me waiting for so long? I'm simply dying to know what you want to see me about!'

Oliver kissed her on both cheeks and sat down, perfectly relaxed, at the small round table set for two out on the immaculate sweeping lawn at the rear of Tolwithrick house. He teased her impatience by gazing lengthily all around them, then said, 'I'm not late, Rachael.'

She snatched up the letter, her sharp nose almost on the paper as she searched for the time mentioned on it, then pursing her ruby red lips she tucked the letter down into her bosom. 'You can be an absolute beast at times, Oliver Pengarron,' she said, sounding aggrieved. 'I've a good mind not to grant you this interview you desire with me.'

'You won't do that, Rachael,' he replied confidently.

'Oh! And what makes you so certain of that?'

Oliver slowly helped himself to a tall glass of barley water, then drawled, 'Because you are too nosey.'

'Well! Of all the—'

'Shut up, Rachael,' Oliver said, in the same lazy tone. 'Facetiousness does not become you. I've written to you, you've read my letter, you're desperate to know why I've asked to speak to you alone, and here I am. So let's not waste any more time.'

Rachael threw back her bewigged head and let out a most unlady-like laugh. 'I've a good mind to slap your handsome face, just for the pleasure of kissing it better.'

'Be my guest,' he said, putting it close to hers.

Rachael couldn't resist giving him the kiss. 'You'll never change, dear-heart, and who would want you to?'

Oliver's face changed with a remarkable speed to become straight and deeply serious. 'Kerensa might.'

'Well, that gets straight to the point,' Rachael said, also becoming subdued. 'And I thought it would be her you wanted to see me about. How is she these days? Coming to terms with her double ordeal?'

'Yes, she is slowly, I think. She's been much better since the girl who was once her maid turned up one day out of the blue to visit her.'

'Oh, the one who married the farmer's son?'

'Yes, the farmer's son to whom Kerensa was betrothed. Thank you for being tactful, but I've come here today for some straight talking. That was also a shock to her – Clem Trenchard getting married. I want your advice, Rachael. Kerensa is very young, she's led a sheltered and protected life, and thanks to her grandfather, myself and others, this year has been spent in turmoil. Now, after the attack on her, I'm not sure what to do about her. I want her to be happy.' Oliver looked a little unsure of himself, then continued. 'Rachael, despite the many differences between Kerensa and me, in our ages and background, I want our marriage to work. I don't want to do anything to hurt her. I was hoping you, as a mature woman, could advise me on what approach to take from now on.'

Rachael smiled. 'You're getting very fond of Kerensa, aren't you?'

'Am I?' Oliver asked self-consciously, sipping his barley-water.

'You know you are, Oliver. You dote on the girl.'

He looked down the length of the long lawns but didn't see the clipped privet or formal rose trees at their end. His mind was back at the Manor. 'She's given purpose to my life, Rachael, she's brought not only life to the Manor but the whole Estate, and hopefully, one day when we have children, there will be someone to pass all my hard work on to.'

'It's made me very happy to hear you say that. William and I had often talked in the old days about how lonely you were. Now you have Kerensa, and as far as I can see you are doing all the right things by her. You're patient and caring and have been staying at home more often.'

'I don't like leaving her for too long in case she starts brooding. I planned to come over here today because I knew the Reverend Ivey was calling on her.'

'You only need to give her time now, Oliver, to get over her hurt, let her mourn for the dog. Everything will be perfectly all right in time, I'm sure of it.' Rachael put a hand over his. 'You know, Oliver, I believe Kerensa's rather fond of you too.'

'Oh, I don't know about that,' he returned quickly. 'She may tolerate me, perhaps she doesn't feel too badly about me now... but she must still be somewhat in love with Clem Trenchard.'

Rachael took her hand away and cast down her eyelashes, putting her fingertips to pouting lips. She gave a small shake of her head. 'Well, only time will tell about that.'

Chapter 18

The moment the Reverend Ivey left the Manor Kerensa rode straight to Trelynne Cove. Jack had been worried about her rigid white face as he'd saddled Kernick, and had wanted to ride with her, but she'd insisted on being alone. She stood on the shoreline of her old home, her heart rent into pieces, her mind hardly able to take in what the elderly parson had told her.

Waves licked at her feet, over her shoes and day dress; she had not bothered to change her clothes. She didn't realise she was getting wet until the sea water reached her knees. She turned numbly. Her legs would hardly carry her as she waded back on to dry land.

Her head spun as her eyes darted around the cove, picking out spots where she had sat and climbed and played. 'All this time,' she whispered, 'and I didn't know.'

Her eyes stayed on one particular place: a dark triangular crevice up in the rocks. It looked a deceptively small opening, but she could crawl through it. So could a small man. Old Tom had hidden his smuggled booty through there. He had even made a little hidey-hole out of a shallow cave to hide in in the event of trouble. She had been going to squeeze through the crevice and look about for signs of the old man on the day she had seen Ted Trembath up on the cliffs. His presence had stopped her. Since then there had always been something to keep her away. But not now. Now she would go and look.

'Grandfather!' she seethed, and ran across the beach, her heart thumping wildly, face burning in pure rage, mind almost exploding. Pebbles scattered under her feet. She tripped, fell, cried out in anguish, pulled herself up and carried on with fists clenched, hair flying in front of her eyes. She clambered up to the crevice, stayed still a moment, breathing gasps of salty air.

Kerensa got down on her hands and knees and, heedless of the rough edges of the rocks, crawled through the crevice, scratching and bruising herself as she hauled herself through to the other side.

The surge of the sea was stronger on this side of the rocks. Several feet away it crashed over the granite, and high up above was the spot where Davey Trembath had been dragged to his death. Kerensa looked up and pushed anguished hands to her cheeks, her body shaking with the agony of the things Old Tom had done, and was thought to have done.

There were not many rocks to climb over to reach the old man's hidey-hole. Kerensa did this nimbly despite the rigidity of her body, her dress tearing as it dragged behind her. She had to be more careful getting around a chunk of rock jutting out several inches across the only safe path through to the hidey-hole. Around that and she was facing the hidey-hole. And that was not all.

She let out a strangled whimper and clutched her hands to her breast. She edged forward, one tiny step at a time. Her grandfather was sitting huddled at the entrance of the little cave. Strewn around him were a few things from the cottage; blankets, a mattress, a stool, a tin kettle and mug, and his sack of belongings. A fire had been lit. Several empty gin bottles were scattered about. Kerensa could go no closer because of the stench, Old Tom had been dead for some time.

She stared at the grisly sight. There was nothing left that she could recognise of the man who had brought her up and loved her – and sold her – who had done so many terrible things, one being the worst thing you could do to a child.

'How could you, Grandfather?' Kerensa whispered to his corpse. 'How could you take my mother away from me?'

And then her tortured heart, mind and soul gave vent to all the shock, pain and outrage she had suffered at the old man's actions, in one almighty scream.

–

Not long after Kerensa had left the Manor, Oliver arrived back in the stableyard to find Jack preparing to leave on Meryn. Jack cantered up to him.

'I was just going after her ladyship, m'lord. She went out on Kernick not long since, insisting on going alone, but I didn't like the look of her and she didn't change for riding.'

'You were doing the right thing, Jack,' Oliver said, brow furrowing. 'Did she say where she was going?'

'No, sir, but I was going to try Trelynne Cove first.'

'I'll go there myself. You hurry along towards Marazion in case she went that way, and if you catch up with her, whatever you do, and no matter what she insists, don't leave her alone.'

Oliver galloped all the way to Trelynne Cove and found Kernick hitched to the cottage door. He peered all around but there was no sign of Kerensa. He entered the cottage and searched the two rooms but nothing had disturbed the dust since his last visit. He shivered in the empty gloom, the cottage long since scavenged of all its furnishings and fittings.

He ran up and down the beach, calling her name, looking behind outcrops of rock, glancing into every opening and crevice he had found on his frequent visits. It might have been from instinct, but he climbed up to the place where Kerensa had crawled through and stopped. Anxiety gnawled at him. He put his hands on his hips and bit his bottom lip. If Kerensa was, or had been, in the cove, there was no sign of her now. He put his hands to his mouth to call her name again and heard the long agonising scream. It froze his entire body.

'Kerensa? Kerensa! Where are you?' He looked about wildly in every direction. Had the scream meant she had gone over the cliff as Davey Trembath had done? 'Kerensa!'

Panic rose inside him, then he heard her call back.

'Oliver!'

'Kerensa! I'm over here, I can't see you!'

The knots in his stomach twisted again until a movement down low to his right attracted his attention. From a triangular-shaped crevice a small hand appeared, followed quickly by the auburn head, shoulders and top half of his wife. Springing into action, Oliver knelt and pulled Kerensa out. He tried to hold her at arm's length at first but once her hands had clutched his shirt she clung to him tighter than a limpet.

'I'm so glad you're here,' she sobbed wretchedly. 'I'm so glad it's you.' She repeated the words over and over and he gathered her to him like an infant, stroking her hair and gently rocking her.

'It's all right, my love,' he soothed her. 'I'm here now, and whatever it is can't hurt you any more.' He waited for her sobs to die away and her body to become still against his. She felt hot to his touch and her tears had soaked his shirt.

Oliver held on to her, thinking how well her small body fitted into his arms. When she fumbled for her handkerchief he loosened his hold, and searching inside her sleeve he found it for her and placed it in her hand. She wiped her eyes and clung to him again.

Caressing her cheek with a finger he said, 'Can you tell me what it is now.'

'He's dead,' she whispered, her voice choked with tears.

'Who's dead, my love?' Oliver asked gently.

'Grandfather.'

'You've found him? Old Tom?' he said incredulously.

'Yes. He's through there.'

'The crevice you crawled out of?'

'Yes. He's dead!' she shouted. 'He's dead and I'm glad!' Her sobbing started again and he held her as before.

'Shh, shh, my love. You'll make yourself ill.'

'I'm glad he's dead!' Kerensa cried viciously, suddenly pulling away from Oliver. 'I hate him! I hate him!'

Shocked by her outburst he let her slip from his arms. He caught hold of her before she could stumble far. She struggled violently to get away.

'Let me go! Let me go!'

Gaining her other arm he held her tightly and felt sickened as his fingers dug into her flesh as she struggled. 'Stop it!' he shouted. 'Kerensa! Stop it, will you!' Taking her by the shoulders, he shook her.

'Now stop it or I'll be forced to slap you. And, please, my love, don't make me hurt you.'

The outburst stopped as suddenly as it began. 'Oliver...' she said feebly. 'I'm sorry.'

He pulled her close. 'You have nothing to be sorry for, my love. Now tell me slowly what this is all about.'

'He killed her,' Kerensa told him very quietly. 'He killed... my mother.'

Oliver thought back to the time of Mary Trelynne's death but he had been with his regiment then and knew of nothing unusual about it. 'How did he kill your mother, Kerensa? What happened?' he said gently.

'It was when I was about seven years old. Grandfather... he... he raped her. My father had died not long before and up till then... he... he'd never touched her. When I think of what Peter Blake tried to do to me... he is young... handsome... Grandfather... old and dirty.' She swallowed hard and fresh tears appeared as she continued.

'Mother became pregnant. She was very ill. One day she was so ill she begged Grandfather to fetch help... but he refused.'

Kerensa broke off and Oliver, his face drawn tight at what he was listening to, tenderly kissed her tear-stained cheek.

'And then?' he said softly.

'And then, apparently, when Grandfather was out,' Kerensa picked up the thread of the tale again, 'Adam Renfree and the Reverend Ivey, who had been suspicious that there was something wrong, turned up just before my mother died. She... she bled to death... from a miscarriage. It was too late to save her.' She cried quietly and Oliver took her hand and held her closer.

'Who told you this, Kerensa?'

'The Reverend Ivey, earlier today. He didn't want me to know, Oliver, he hoped he would never have to tell me, but I've been making enquiries about my mother's death and he thought it better coming from him. I can remember now my mother being ill, two men turning up one day and later taking my mother away... they buried my tiny half-brother in the churchyard that night. Only they and Ben Rosevidney know where. They told everyone my mother died of pneumonia so as not to disgrace her name. No one bothered to question the word of a parson and a respected man like Adam, and it would have remained a secret if I hadn't been curious. They couldn't be sure that someone else might not know something about it and tell me one day.'

Oliver sighed deeply. 'What a dreadful thing to have happened. Your poor mother. And what a terrible shock for you, my love. I thought I knew all there was to know that had happened in the parish but this dreadful affair is a complete surprise to me. What I can't understand is why on earth the Reverend Ivey allowed Old Tom to raise you.'

Kerensa pressed her face closer to his tear-wet shirt. 'It was my grandfather... he turned up at the Parsonage where the Reverend was keeping me overnight and caused a big scene. He said he was my next-of-kin and was responsible for me, that he wouldn't let me be thrown on the mercy of the parish and that wherever they put me he would only take me away. Grandfather said if they were intent on hushing up the true facts of my mother's death, then folk would be curious if he wasn't allowed to raise me – everyone knew he doted on me. The Reverend Ivey was far from happy about it and he told Grandfather he would keep a careful watch over him. All those years, Oliver...' she sobbed again. 'All those years he brought me up and was so good to me, and I didn't know what he'd done!'

Oliver rocked her as she cried out her distress. Time passed and still he held her.

Eventually he said, 'I had a strong feeling Old Tom was somewhere around the cove but I couldn't find him. When you feel able, will you show me the way to his body, my love?'

She nodded against his shoulder and whispered, 'We'll do it now.'

He helped her to her feet and she shook all the while as they returned to the huddle of rocks through which she had appeared.

'There,' she said. 'Grandfather showed me the way through when I was a child. It's where he kept his contraband. It looks much smaller than it really is, set back like that, but a small man can just about squeeze through.'

Oliver crouched down to examine the triangular opening. 'I can't get through there myself. I'll have to move some of these rocks out of the way.' He pulled aside two huge granite boulders, making an opening big enough for him to squeeze his large frame through. 'I won't be long, my love,' he said, wiping sweat from his brow. 'You stay.'

'I'm going with you,' she said firmly.

'Are you sure, Kerensa? It will only upset you again.'

'Please, Oliver. I don't want to be alone.'

'Come on then,' he smiled at her. 'I'll go through first.'

He wriggled and squeezed himself head first through the short opening where all he could see were more rocks of the same size and shape with deep blue water beyond. Helping Kerensa through, he held her hand as they climbed carefully over rocks for a few feet, until he felt her nails dig painfully into his palm.

'Are we nearly there?'

'Yes. He's… he's just round that rock jutting out over there.'

Oliver followed her pointing finger and was relieved when Kerensa sat down on a flat rock behind her. She said nothing, her eyes large and wary, while her fingers pulled agitatedly at a tear in her dress.

'I'll be as quick as I can,' he said gently, stooping to kiss her forehead before leaving her.

Oliver put a forearm across his face against the putrid smell of Old Tom's body. Crabs, insects, and a multitude of tiny creatures were feasting on what little had been left by the seagulls and other scavengers. Old Tom's jaw was wide open, as if he had been about to shout at the moment of his death, the one long yellow tooth standing tall like a landmark. In one skeletal hand he grasped a leather pouch, in the other a red neckerchief. Oliver gingerly tugged both away, hurriedly shaking off a swarm of scurrying insects. He stuffed the kerchief deep into his breeches pocket before returning to Kerensa.

Sitting motionless and keeping her mind numb she jumped to her feet and rushed to be back in his arms. 'What have you got there, Oliver?' she asked, looking at the pouch.

With his arms still around her he undid the knot and pulled open the drawstrings, tipping some of the contents of the pouch into his hand.

'The hundred guineas, or most of it, that I paid Old Tom with for the cove,' he said. He met her eyes frankly. 'I couldn't abide your old grandfather, Kerensa, but I don't regret him talking me into that agreement, you know.'

She leaned against him, drawing comfort from the strength and warmth of his body. 'I didn't mean it when I said I hated him, but after this I can never think of him the same way again. My poor mother...'

'Come on, I'm taking you home. I'll send someone for Old Tom's body later.'

When they reached their horse and pony, Kerensa suddenly took her husband's hand. 'I'm so glad it was you who was here, Oliver.'

–

Towards the end of July, Peter Blake, sitting stiffly upright on his mare, trotted over Lancavel Downs. His silk shirt clung uncomfortably to his body. He pulled off his neckcloth and, his shirt open at the neck, fanned himself with his hat in an effort to keep cool. The continuing lack of rain was causing great concern to the farmers for their coming harvest, but Peter Blake did not share their worries as, at regular intervals, he pulled the mare to a halt and with one hand shading his eyes peered across the landscape.

The ground was hard and dry. Tall brittle ferns were grouped together beside massive granite boulders arranged meticulously in interesting shapes by nature's giant hand. White and purple heather mingled with gorse bushes and pinkish-purple marsh woundwort. The light held a clear brilliance, bringing forth the vibrant form and colouring unique to the vast sweeps and distant horizons of moorland and sky.

To Peter Blake, accustomed as he was to closely built shops and houses and the life of a busy market town and sea port, it was like wandering about in another world. At times he found himself over-awed by the loneliness of the large expanses all around him and had

303

difficulty shaking off the longing to see just one other living soul. He rode past the deserted, lichen-covered workings of an abandoned tin mine where no one but the knockers, or underground imps, could be heard making mischief to the tune of the wind as it whipped and whistled through the ruins.

Stopping to drink the sparkling cold water of an ancient holy well, Blake soaked his necktie in the tiny trickle of water to mop the sweat from his neck and brow. He regretted not bringing a tot of rum to help deaden the pain of his slowly mending ribs.

It was not to seek solitude that Peter Blake had come to the downs on the three occasions in the last week he had ridden there. He was looking for Rosina Pearce.

From the time his eyes had focused on her gentle face in the alleyway after his beating, the girl was never from his mind. He had kept a vision of her throughout the pain that had filled his every conscious moment. At first he had lingered betwixt a world of physical torment and one of silent black nothingness. As he recovered the bitter pain remained, but the other world became relentlessly filled with terrifying nightmares and only the girl's serene face could chase them away.

Matthias Renfree had called on him frequently, and many times in his delirium Blake had called out for 'the girl'. Once Matthias had said, 'You must mean Rosina,' and the name had whirled round inside his head and played on his lips. When he could hold a reasonable conversation Matthias told him of Rosina's circumstances, and on Blake's stating his wish to send thanks to her for her help on the day of his beating, begged him to be very careful about what he did, fearing that she might suffer yet more brutality at her brother's hands.

It had worried Blake to think of Rosina being left hungry while he had more than enough food to eat and no appetite for it. He sent a hamper of food to her via Matthias Renfree. She had received it with gratitude and promptly shared it among the miners' children, telling them it was from an unknown benefactor. Matthias had refused to do the same every week as Blake had wanted, knowing that if Colly Pearce found out about it, trouble would inevitably ensue. However, he got Matthias to accept money to buy food for Rosina and this he passed on to Faith Bray, she in turn keeping Rosina supplied with pies, pasties, fruit, eggs and milk when Colly was on his core. The supply of food was always generous and most of it found its way into the children's bellies and helped to keep their rickets and scrofula at bay.

To Blake it was a small thing to do for the girl, and the thought of seeing and talking to Rosina again hastened his recovery. In the knowledge he could go nowhere near the cottages on Lancavel Downs, he required his half-sister Josephine to make discreet enquiries for him as to where Rosina might otherwise be found. He learned she very occasionally came into Marazion for the market, as she had on the day she'd found him, but he feared Colly would find out if he approached her there. The information that Rosina was apt to spend time alone in some secret place on the downs suited him well. A loner by nature himself, he waited until he could bear to ride, then began to search the downs for sight of her. Peter Blake was a patient man. He was sure if he searched long enough, he would eventually come across Rosina, if not in this secret place of hers, then on her way to or from it.

He had ascertained that Colly Pearce was on the afternoon core that week, and Rosina working as a bal-maiden in the early morning till two. If she was out on the moorland it would be in the afternoon or evening. Blake glanced at the sun. It was high enough to allow another hour's search. Whistling to the mare he stood on the ruins of the well to mount, his ribs still too tender for him to swing himself up in the saddle. He rode south in as straight a line as obstacles permitted, spotting a swooping kestrel, scuttling lizards, the rotting carcase of a straying sheep, the red flash of the back of a secretive running fox, creatures on the rocks, creatures on the wing... but no girl with long corn-coloured hair.

On his return to the holy well he reined in again to quench his thirst. Splashing water over his face and neck, he gasped at its icy cold- ness despite the burning heat and pulled his shirt out of his breeches to dry his wet skin. The mare moved forward and Blake cupped his hands for her to drink from. As he straightened up his eye caught the sunlight highlighting a girl's long golden hair.

'Rosina,' he uttered quietly. She was only a few feet away from him.

'Hello, Mr Blake.'

Her voice was exactly as he remembered, soft and harmonious. And there she stood, an image of radiant innocence.

'I've been looking all over the downs for you,' he told her.

'I saw you riding out here earlier this week, but I had no idea you were looking for me,' she said.

He followed her gaze to his hanging damp shirt. 'Forgive me,' he said hastily, pushing it back rather self-consciously into its proper place. 'I've been wanting to thank you personally for a long time, for helping me that day.'

'I did no more than anyone else would have done, Mr Blake, and I'm glad to see you looking so much better now. I thank you for your generosity with the food you sent me.'

'Thank you for receiving it.'

'I think we have run out of all the thank yous now, don't you?' she said, with a smile.

'Yes. Yes, indeed,' he replied. Now that he had found Rosina, or rather now she had found him, he was unsure how to proceed. 'Do you... ah... know why I received that thrashing from Sir Oliver Pengarron?' he asked, becoming fearful the question would make her bolt from him and disappear like a wraith among the rocks and ferns.

But she remained. 'Yes, Mr Blake, I do know. It's common knowledge now.'

He sat down wearily on the remains of the well. His ribs ached as did his head. His legs felt weak, and the heat was stifling.

'Are you afraid of me?' he asked, after clearing his throat.

'Do I have reason to be?' she returned.

'No, I promise you. Please, I am hoping you can stay and talk...'

Rosina limped closer and sat on a low boulder in front of him, wrapping her arms around her knees. She seemed so frail and small in her ragged grey dress, her feet bare and her hair flowing long and free.

'You believe me then? That you have no reason to be afraid of me?' Blake sounded incredulous and hopeful.

'Yes.'

'I'm glad about that. You are the last person on earth I would mean any harm to.' Blake could sense that she was not much of a talker and was afraid she would soon leave if he didn't keep her interested. 'How do you feel about me… knowing what I've done?'

'Are you truly sorry for it now?'

'Yes, I am. Truly sorry. One can't talk to that Renfree fellow for long without having some of his enthusiasm for facing up to one's sins rub off.'

'Good,' Rosina said simply. 'Then there's no need for anything more to be said.'

'Is that it?' Blake gasped. 'If I say that I'm sorry, then all is forgotten? Most people hate me for what I did to that girl and the dog.' People like Rosina and Matthias Renfree were new to him, the forthrightness of the girl's words and her attitude unexpected.

Rosina kept her straight gaze on him. 'I thank God, Mr Blake, that I have never felt the need to hate.'

'You probably wouldn't know how to hate anyone,' he remarked in his naturally low voice.

When Rosina had found Peter Blake in the alleyway, his face was so badly beaten it had the appearance of a grotesque mask. Now, with the swellings gone, the bruises fading and the many cuts nearly healed, his fine looks had returned. His eyes were the same cornflower blue as hers, his hands delicately moulded and well manicured with a long scar marring the one on the right; a reminder of the retribution for his misdeeds. Perspiration had dampened the hair which edged his face and fell across his brow, and he sat with his chin resting in one hand.

They studied each other for a long time while the sun turned to bright orange-red and travelled halfway down the sky. Then without warning Rosina rose to her feet.

'I must be going.'

Blake stood up quickly and moved closer to her, keeping his hands behind his back in a silent statement that he had no intention of touching her.

'Don't go yet. Stay a while longer,' he pleaded.

'We must both go, Mr Blake. While we've plenty of daylight left,' she pointed out.

'I'll take you part of the way on my horse, if you like,' he offered.

'I will get home much quicker by taking short cuts over the downs. It's a long way round by horse.'

'But I've so much to say to you, Rosina,' he said earnestly, looking crossly at the sinking sun and knowing she was right. If he didn't go soon he'd have difficulty getting safely back on to the tracks and then the roads. 'Will you meet me here tomorrow?' He held his breath for her answer.

'It's Sunday tomorrow,' she said, 'I will be going to church and then a Bible class.'

'The following day, then. Please.'

'I won't be spending any time on the downs for the next few days. Mr John Wesley is preaching in West Cornwall at the moment and I'm hoping to get the chance to hear him.'

Blake was desolate. Was she giving him excuses because she didn't want to see him again? He could hardly blame her, of course. He was hardly suitable company for any female alone and particularly one with such strongly held Christian beliefs. His reputation lent him no moral standing in a decent woman's eyes. Perhaps he should have asked her permission to call her by her first name as one did a lady of the gentry. Crossing his fingers behind his back, he tried again.

'Will you consider meeting me here by the well one day of the following week?'

'I'll think about it, Mr Blake,' Rosina offered. 'Goodbye.'

She moved quickly, heading in the opposite direction to the sinking sun. He followed her a few steps and shouted after her: 'I'll come back after three days, every afternoon, until I see you again.'

He felt sure she heard him but she did not turn round. As she moved through the ferns and foliage and over the giant stones, her hair swayed like a field of ripening corn, and then in a moment she was gone.

Chapter 19

'He's looking at 'ee again, maid,' Faith Bray told Rosina.

'Who is?' asked the girl.

'Young Preacher, of course.'

At Rosina's puzzled look, Faith gave Hunk Hunken's wife standing beside her a knowing look.

'You don't mean to tell us, do 'ee, maid,' teased Lou Hunken kindly, 'that you haven't noticed him giving you the glad eye these past weeks?'

'Yes,' Faith chuckled. 'One of these days he may pluck up the courage to speak to 'ee.'

'A little bit of encouragement would help, you know,' Lou went on, smiling to include the other women nearby in her remark.

Rosina looked across to where Matthias Renfree was cheerfully talking to the group of small children who had clustered round him outside the Brays' cottage after the Bible class. He promptly smiled back at her and raised his hand in a friendly wave.

'Well, that won't come amiss,' remarked Carn Bawden amid a group of men lighting up their pipes.

'Make a good match they would,' Jeb Bray agreed with him. 'The missus reckons the little maid hasn't noticed young Preacher's attentions. Judging by the look on her red face, she has now.'

Taking in the rather silly looks aimed in her direction, Rosina quietly excused herself and hurried away from the unwelcome attention she was drawing. She chose a path unlikely to be used by the Perranbarvah fisherfolk or the Methodists among the farmers and farm labourers of the Pengarron estate on their way home. She had walked along a narrow footpath singing softly to herself for nearly ten minutes before Matthias Renfree hailed her. She stopped walking to let him catch up with her.

'Would you like some company as you walk along, Rosina?' he said awkwardly.

'I'm not going far, Preacher,' she replied, 'but you're welcome to come with me.'

'Um… Colly at home?'

'No. In an alehouse probably.' It was a hot airless day. Rosina was holding the shawl James Andrew's wife had given to her in one hand, the end trailing over the hard sunbaked ground behind her.

'Everything all right with him, is it?'

'The same as always, Preacher.'

They walked on discussing things like the hot weather, miners' paltry wages, Hunk Hunken's chickens, and Mrs Trembath's increasing bouts of apparent insanity. When Rosina stopped to herald her journey's end, Matthias looked around everywhere else but at her.

'Are you going back now?'

'I thought I'd sit here for a while, but you may go on.' She laid her shawl on an area of dry springy grass and heather and sat down, hugging her knees as she had done the day before in Peter Blake's company.

Matthias stood about awkwardly before he sat down a short distance from her. He stared at the ground and selecting a large red-tinged dock leaf, rolled it into a cylindrical shape between the palms of his hands, quite unable to meet her eyes. Although perfectly happy to discuss Godly subjects, Matthias was finding his first attempts at courtship far from easy.

'I was wondering…' he began.

'Do you think…' she started at the same time.

'You first, Rosina,' he said, with a self-conscious laugh.

'I was going to say, do you think there will be a good crowd at Newlyn tomorrow to hear Mr Wesley preach?'

'Oh, yes, I'm sure there will be.' Matthias' face lit up and his awkwardness vanished. 'A goodly number from our meetings are going, and I'm sure many will turn out from all the neighbouring hamlets, with a plenteous supply of curious onlookers.' He was looking at Rosina now and she was smiling.

'I'm so looking forward to it,' she said. 'Mr Hunken says Mr Wesley can move people to tears by his preaching.'

'It's true. I've heard him before and I was certainly moved by what he said. I was going to say something to you, wasn't I? Oh, yes, I was wondering if you'd care for me to escort you tomorrow. Newlyn will be full of strangers and there may well be thieves, pick-pockets and the like roaming about.' His face had steadily reddened and he looked down at the squashed dock leaf and the green stain it had left on his palms.

'I shall have plenty of company, Preacher. Faith Bray, Lou Hunken and the other women. I shall be quite safe with them.'

'Of course,' Matthias said quickly. 'I... I thought I'd offer.'

'Thank you for the thought, Preacher. I must go back now in case Colly gets home early.'

Matthias rose and offered her his hand. She took it and he helped her to her feet, but didn't release her hand immediately.

'Rosina, I want to ask you something,' he said haltingly.

'Yes.'

She had a disconcerting habit of looking people straight in the eye and speaking directly at them. This was one of those times and it was too much for Matthias. He couldn't bring out what he was striving to say.

'I... um... I... it doesn't matter. It's... um... not important.'

He let go of her hand and Rosina picked up her shawl, shaking it free of dust and bits of foliage. Matthias turned his head away, sighed and swallowed hard at the same time, making himself cough and wipe moisture from his eyes. He wondered if the mixture of disappointment and relief he was feeling showed in his face and was careful to keep it hidden.

On the way back they talked only of the evangelist preacher, John Wesley, his brother Charles, the prolific hymn writer, and the effect their hard work and messages of hope and salvation had had on the ordinary man and woman.

'I'll see you tomorrow then, Rosina,' he said quietly, at her cottage door.

'Good day to you, Preacher,' she said, before lifting the latch.

Inside the cottage, as she expected, there was no sign of Colly. Beelzebub, his vicious mongrel, was tied to a table leg and growled at her every time she moved near him. Early that morning Solomon King had called and left a large mackerel, already gutted and headed. Rosina cut the mackerel into pieces, and putting them into a large black pot, added a small amount of diced turnip and potato and wild herbs to make a fish stew.

While the meal simmered over the fire she tidied up then sat down by the open window to enjoy the cooling breezes on her face. She would have liked to have had the door ajar but her brother's dog barked and snarled at anyone who passed by and it frightened the children. She was resigned to putting up with the stuffy atmosphere inside her home.

Colly Pearce crashed through the door as Rosina was preparing to go to the monthly evening prayer service at Perranbarvah. He glared at her suspiciously.

'Off to yer Bible bashing again, are 'ee? Can't 'ee get enough of it?' He was drunk and leaned heavily against the wall to stay upright.

'I'm going in a little while,' Rosina said. 'I've made fish stew for your supper. I'll fetch you some hot water to wash.'

'Never mind that,' he shouted, lurching towards her, 'get the darned food on the table first.'

'All right then, Colly. Sit yourself down.'

'Must you always talk so bloody sweetly!' he said into her face.

Rosina turned her head at the stench of alcohol on his breath, stepping aside to get to the cooking pot. Her brother grasped a handful of her hair from behind and yanked her back towards him. She put up a hand to try to ease the pain.

He twisted her roughly round and snarled, 'Where have you been this afternoon? Eh?'

Her heart began to beat faster and her breathing came in tight gasps in the effort to pull her head away. 'I've been here all afternoon, Colly,' she told him, trying to sound as natural as she could, hoping it would calm him, 'Now sit down… and I'll put your supper on the table.'

But Colly wasn't satisfied. 'Where did you go after that Goddamned meeting in Bray's cottage, eh?'

'Only… for… a walk.' She was gasping to breathe properly.

Putting a filthy hand on her shoulder, he squeezed his fingers tightly.

'Please, Colly!'

'Alone, eh, little sister?' he jeered. 'Did you go for your walk alone, eh?'

'Preacher Renfree… kept me company… part of the way… ahh!' Rosina cried out.

Colly viciously tightened his grip on her shoulder and yanked her head well back. 'Whore!' he screeched. 'Preacher Renfree! Preacher Renfree! Preacher indeed. He's no bloody preacher! Got no right to be called preacher! Fornicator! That's what he is. That's what your bloody Preacher Renfree is. A bigger fornicator than the devil himself if ever there was one. You're a whore, little sister. A holy whore! Was it good with him, Rosina? Was it good with your filthy rotten Preacher Renfree? Eh? Eh?'

Tears streamed down her face. 'Let… me go… oh, please, Colly… please…'

The dog was barking fiercely now and Colly hurled an obscenity at it. Thrusting his sister away from him, he kicked Beelzebub in the ribs, then the head.

'Shut up, yer blasted mongrel!' he shouted before sitting at the table. The dog yelped for some time then settled down with a rumbling growl, baring its yellow teeth. 'Shut up!' Colly shouted again.

He looked up from his chair at Rosina who was trying to hold back more tears and trembling as she rubbed at her shoulder and the back of her neck. For just an instant a change of expression flickered across his face, making him look less of a drunken bully.

'I'll have my supper now,' he said, much quieter, 'and hurry up about it.'

313

Rosina's hands shook as she spooned stew into a bowl and placed it in front of Colly. She moved back quickly out of his reach. He gulped the food down noisily before speaking again.

'You had yours?' he said, without looking up.

'Yes, Colly,' she answered, and knew he was sorry for hurting her. But soon the sorrow would turn to relentless guilt and the only thing to give him peace and forgetfulness would be more alcohol.

'Well,' he snapped at her, 'get yerself off to your blasted praying and caterwauling, and leave me to eat in peace.'

Snatching up her shawl, Rosina made her way to the door. 'Goodbye, Colly,' she said, drying her face with the back of her hand.

He waved a hand tersely in the air and returned to his meal.

Outside Rosina walked dejectedly to the back of the cottage where no one could see her and leaned her trembling body against the cold dirty wall. She wiped away a solitary tear, drawing in deep breaths of warm evening air until her thin limbs became still. Minutes later, when she met the Bray family outside their home for the walk to Perranbarvah, her face was serene and smiling, as they had come to expect it to be.

–

Old Tom Trelynne was quietly buried in an unpretentious grave in Perranbarvah's graveyard. Thomas Cole, the coroner, was in agreement with Oliver's declaration that the old man undoubtedly drank himself to death, while the location of his body ruled out the possibility of a second person being involved. Kerensa was not surprised few people offered her their sympathy. She was the only one expected to remember Old Tom for long, or with any affection at all.

From the time they had spent together in the cove on discovery of her grandfather's body, Kerensa's relationship with Oliver took a new turn. When all formalities for the recovery of the body had been completed he had joined her in her sitting room. He'd found her shivering, and after lighting a small fire had drawn the curtains and held her closely until she had grown pleasantly sleepy.

Kerensa had enjoyed the tender little kisses he'd snuggled behind her ear and into her hair, and his soft circular caresses with the tips of his fingers on the top of her arm and cheek. She had lifted her face to him.

'You all right, my love?' he'd whispered.

'Mmmm,' was her only reply.

Oliver had not made love to her since Peter Blake's attack, and although Kerensa had not wanted this to continue for both their sakes, she had been too shy to make advances to him. But now, winding a hand around his neck, she raised herself in the circle of his arms to kiss his mouth. He had made the kiss short, but keeping her eyes closed she sought his lips again.

Oliver needed no second invitation. His body shuddering, all the feelings he had been holding back broke in a crescendo of ardent desire. With skilful hands he'd pulled loose the laces of her dress, and tossing cushions on the thick carpet in front of the fire, lowered her gently down. They made love until the tall flames turned to glowing embers.

–

Kerensa followed the Reverend Ivey's advice and spoke to Oliver about her wish to do something more useful with her time. She fully expected to be told being his wife, and mistress of the Manor house, and subsequently bearing his children, was more than enough to keep her suitably occupied. He in fact listened attentively and even agreed with her. Kerensa was again reminded her husband was a remarkably unconventional man. He suggested she take Polly with her and call on the young Richards family on Rose Farm with fruit and goat's milk for the children.

Moriah and Rudd Richards were a likeable couple with six children under the age of nine years. They were shy and awkward with Kerensa and Polly to begin with, but the housekeeper was also fond of children, and it was through the four small girls and two lively boys that they gained the family's trust. All the children were under-sized for their ages; the whole family, like so many of their working-class counterparts, badly undernourished.

Kerensa took them fresh food – eggs, cheese and goat's milk – and with Polly she rolled up her sleeves to scrub the shabby farmhouse into a more sanitary condition, leaving Moriah more time to help Rudd in the fields. Kerensa greatly enjoyed the time she spent with the Richards and it wasn't long before the first tentative requests for help from other needy folk turned into a fervent rush. She became settled and content for the first time in many months.

To keep Kerensa further occupied, Oliver invited Sir Martin and William and Lady Rachael Beswetherick to the Manor. They stayed for a week, Rachael leaving baby Sebastian in the care of a wet nurse.

Their visit was a great success. Kerensa enjoyed her position as hostess to their friends, Oliver providing fishing, shooting, riding and cards as entertainment, while Sir Martin regaled the company with his famous tall stories.

Shortly after the Beswethericks' visit, Hezekiah Solomon appeared at the Manor with baggage and hired pony. Kerensa had no knowledge of him being invited but she gave him a warm welcome, while secretly hoping it would provide the opportunity to penetrate a little of the intriguing mystery in which the man deliberately shrouded himself. Most of his time was claimed by Oliver, and Kerensa saw little of Hezekiah, who also inflamed the burning curiosity of Polly, Esther and Ruth as he greeted them with his impeccable manners in his exquisite clothes, dazzling white hair and a variety of strong French colognes.

They plied Kerensa with questions about their master's unusual friend. Where did he live? Was he married? How wealthy was he? How old was he? And did she believe the rumours of him killing in cold blood and actually enjoying it? Only Beatrice asked no questions about Hezekiah Solomon, exhorting all to, 'Keep away from Cap'n Sol'mon, 'cus 'ee do 'ave the evil eye, and no good'll come of any of 'ee gettin' mixed up with one of the Devil's own.'

When Kerensa told Oliver what Beatrice had said, he laughed heartily. 'If you ask me,' he said, imitating Beatrice's rasping voice, 'I d'come from a long line of soothsayers, me 'an'some.'

'But don't you find Hezekiah a great puzzle, Oliver?' she asked him after plying him with all the questions the servants had urged upon her. 'You say you only think he lives somewhere on the Channel Islands, you don't think he'd ever been married, and you've no idea how rich he is, and what Beatrice said about him is a load of old rubbish. Don't you know anything else about him? Why he dresses the way he does and splashes scent all over himself.'

'No, I've got better things to do, but at least I don't believe him to be a sadistic murderer.'

'Beatrice said that some people are terrified of him,' Kerensa persisted.

'The man's a fop, my dear, he couldn't frighten—'

'He stuck a knife through Colly Pearce's hand a few years ago,' Kerensa interrupted. 'Colly's terrified of him.'

'Well, of course he is. It wasn't a very pleasant occurrence, I was there, and witnessed it happen.'

'And that doesn't worry you?'

'The man deserved it, Kerensa,' Oliver said, as if he was talking to an inquisitive troublesome child.

'And you don't find Hezekiah at all frightening?'

'Of course not!' he scoffed. 'Do you think I'd have him under my roof if I thought he'd do away with us all horribly in the middle of the night? You aren't nervous of him, are you?'

'No, I just want to learn something more about him. The only thing we seem to know is that he owns his own ship, likes to dress in a most pretentious fashion, and has a Biblical name. You must want to know something more about him, surely, Oliver?'

'No. I'm not tarred with the same brush as you bunch of gossipy women are.'

Kerensa had found Oliver's attitude maddening. She watched Hezekiah closely and he seemed flattered by her attention, but as the days went by she realised she could tell the servants no more about the Manor's guest than what they could see and hear for themselves. On two occasions towards the end of Hezekiah's stay she did learn more about him, but kept the knowledge to herself. Her discoveries only served to make him more of an enigma to her.

The first occurred on a late morning. Oliver had been abroad for several hours and Hezekiah had expressed the desire to lay abed and not be disturbed until noon. Passing by his room as she carried a vase of flowers to her own bedroom, Kerensa heard sounds of anguished moans. She listened at the door for long moments and the sounds continued. Placing the flowers on a window sill in the long corridor, she tapped on the bedroom door and went into the room.

'Hezekiah,' she breathed softly, 'are you all right?'

The room was darkened by the curtains but she could see him well enough. His long white hair was splayed across the pillows as his body convulsed from side to side between groans and unintelligible utterances. The atmosphere in the room was overpoweringly stuffy, his cologne creating an odour of sickly warmth. Kerensa paced quickly over to the window, throwing back one of the curtains and pulling up the sash to let in several inches of bright daylight and fresh air.

She then moved to the bed and took Hezekiah's hand and called his name again to wake him. He did not waken, even when she raised her voice, so stretching out her other hand she shook him quite forcefully.

'Hezekiah… wake up, everything will be all right.'

He woke with uncontrolled violence, sitting upright in an instant and pulling Kerensa down to him. 'Don't leave me alone,' he gasped, his voice heavy and choked, 'don't leave me…' He gripped her hand painfully tight, clinging to her with his head pressed to her bosom.

Kerensa was alarmed as his body shuddered against hers, his breath coming like a man drowning and fighting for his life. At the same moment she decided to call for help, Hezekiah became still. He didn't move for several moments then murmured against the muslin of her bodice: 'Give me a moment more, please, Kerensa.'

She held him with a motherly instinct while stroking his hair. When he sat back from her he kept his face close, retaining the hand that held his.

'Will you be all right, Hezekiah?' Kerensa asked, her face creased with concern. 'Are you getting a fever or something?' She could read nothing in his eyes, but asked herself if, just for a moment, she saw fear on the surface of the steely blue.

'It was only a bad dream,' he told her, moving his fingers over her hand. Kerensa looked down at the movement, at the hand so unlike Oliver's, much smaller, softer, whiter.

When she looked back at Hezekiah he was composed, only beads of perspiration betraying his recent distress, but his eyes were cold and distant now, and she shivered at the thought that she had strayed into a trap.

'If you were anyone else's wife but Oliver's…' He left the sentence unfinished and let go of her hand.

Kerensa jumped up and stood back from the bed. 'What were you dreaming about, Hezekiah?' she asked, her voice unmistakably shaking from the implication of what he had said.

'It was nothing, Kerensa,' he replied, reaching across to the bedside cabinet to glance at his pocket watch. 'All best forgotten.'

The other incident also occurred in Hezekiah's bedroom. Kerensa was putting away freshly laundered shirts in a chest of drawers. Ruth had put other garments in the same drawer shortly before, neatly enough for most people's standards, but Kerensa was doubtful if it would suit Hezekiah's fastidious expectations. She pulled all the garments out including a silk-embroidered satin bag, the contents of which spilled out on to the floor.

With a small cry she bent down to retrieve the articles and picked up a rosary made of jet beads and a Bible tract—the gospel of St John.

'They are not mine,' Hezekiah said, from behind her shoulder, quite unexpectedly.

'I'm sorry,' Kerensa told him, whirling round and looking guilty like one caught in a sinful act. 'Whose… whose are they?'

'Someone I knew a long time ago.' He took the things from her and returned them very carefully to the satin bag. Although he knew Kerensa was hoping to learn more, he was not going to enlighten her further. Instead he put the satin bag inside his toilet box and locked it with slow deliberate actions.

'Be careful, Kerensa,' he said, looking at her with his angelic smile, 'You are innocent of this world. Take care someone like me does not destroy you. There will always be someone who may try, not necessarily an enemy either. Perhaps someone who loves you.'

Kerensa was the same height as Hezekiah and his face was but two inches from hers. She refused to be intimidated and said coolly, 'I'll get Ruth to replace the things in the drawer for you.'

'You don't understand me, do you, Kerensa?' Hezekiah moved to bar her exit from the room. 'But never mind that now. I will never harm you... but I will not go without a kiss either.'

Kerensa was surprised at the soft warmth of his lips on hers the next instant. It was neither the embrace of a friend nor the kiss of a lover and when he raised his head the expression on Hezekiah's ageless face held no clue to his real feelings. She was not offended by his taking this liberty but from then on was careful not to have occasion to enter his bedroom alone.

When Hezekiah left two days later to sail for the Channel Islands, Kerensa knew she would remember his stay with affection, her curiosity about the mysterious, seemingly effeminate gentleman unresolved. Indeed, considerably increased.

Chapter 20

Rosina met Peter Blake as he had asked on the Friday afternoon after their first meeting on the moorland. He was sitting on the ruins of the holy well as she light-footedly approached him. He rose to greet her.

'You came then?' He smiled at her.

'Did you think I would not?' she returned.

'I could think of no reason why you should want to see me again. I just hoped that you would. You look pretty today,' he added admiringly.

'It's this,' Rosina said, holding out the skirt of a deep blue muslin dress with both hands. 'Lady Pengarron was kind enough to give it to me.'

'That was good of her. It matches the colour of your eyes.'

Rosina always seemed to have a glow about her and his remark, which he had quickly regretted for fear she might think it over familiar of him on their short acquaintance, brought a sparkle to her young face.

'Why do you look so serious, Mr Blake?' she said.

'What? Do I?' He stood up and his smile returned. 'I was wondering what you would like to do. Stay here, or walk somewhere else perhaps?'

'People come past from time to time,' she said. 'It's better my brother doesn't find out I'm here with you. I know a quiet place not too far away.'

She moved over to Blake's chestnut mare and stroked its smooth forehead, the horse nuzzling its head on her shoulder.

'Would you like to ride on her, Rosina?' Blake said, coming to stand beside her.

'Yes, I would. I've never been up on a horse before. Does it have a name, Mr Blake?'

'She's called Vanity. Shall I lift you up?'

'Vanity,' she repeated. 'Yes, she does look rather proud of herself. Lift me, you say? But can you lift me? What about your ribs? They haven't mended yet, it might hurt you.'

'You look as light as a dandelion clock, Rosina. I'm sure my ribs will cope very well, but how did you know they aren't mended completely as yet?' Blake instinctively rubbed one side of his chest.

'They were sticking out of your chest when Dr Crebo was attending to you. He said it would take longer than usual for you to mend, and I noticed you rubbing yourself there the last time we were here,' she said, pointing to the area in question. 'You're doing it even now.'

'How observant of you,' he smiled, 'but I can lift you all the same. Put your foot in the stirrup and I'll help you into the saddle.'

'I won't be able to manage that,' she told him. 'I can't rest my weight on my foot... my lame foot. You get up first and I'll stand on the ruins, then you can easily lift me over in front of you.'

Blake looked stunned. 'You mean, ride Vanity together?'

'You can't walk far yet, Mr Blake,' she said, scrambling up on the low wall of granite still remaining of a long-forgotten hermit's sacred drinking place, 'it's by far the best way.'

'I'm not sure whether to feel shocked by your suggestion or to wonder if you're being bossy,' he said wryly.

'Not bossy,' she smiled at him, 'practical.'

'Well, as it happens, Rosina, I'll have to use the ruins to mount myself,' he informed her.

When he was settled in the saddle Blake stretched out his arms to her. He had touched a great many women in the years since his youth, but felt boyishly reserved as he lifted this girl to sit astride the mare in front of him. Leaning carefully forward he reached for the reins and placed them correctly in her tiny hands. Her hair smelled of herbs and he breathed in the fresh outdoor scent.

'As you do not mind my calling you Rosina,' he said, 'will you call me Peter?'

'All right,' she replied, pointing west. 'We need to ride this way.'

Blake shook his head unbelievingly at her simple trust. He placed his hands on the tops of his legs and pressed his knees into the mare's sides to urge her on. Blake was not tall, but Rosina reached no more than five feet, and he could look straight over her head as they moved slowly along.

'I had a fancy you had a secret place on these downs, Rosina,' he said.

'I have more than one secret place that I've found as I've wandered about. I reckon I know every inch of the downs, and I like to be alone sometimes. It looks even more beautiful from here on Vanity, I can see for miles and miles,' she said, unable to hide the sense of wonder in her voice.

'I found it a bit too lonely at times when I was searching for you. It was a strange feeling I found hard to shake off even when I got back to my rooms.'

'Oh, I've never found it lonely on the downs, but then I believe we're never totally alone. I need the quietness... it's good to be around people, but good also to be away from the noise and bustle of Wheal Ember and the cottages.'

And good to be away from your brother, no doubt, Blake thought. 'Rosina?'

'Yes.'

'I hope you don't spend a lot of time by the holy well.'

'Why is that?' she asked, half turning round to look at him.

'I've heard there are pagan ceremonies, witchcraft, and that sort of thing going on there,' he explained, 'I don't want you getting hurt.'

'Oh, that.' She smiled. 'Nothing like that has gone on by the well for years and years now. If it had the heather would be heavily trampled down. No, I spend a lot of time on the moors and I've never seen evidence of the like anywhere.'

'Well, if you're sure,' Blake said doubtfully. 'There must be something of the kind going on somewhere... I'm rumoured to be involved in it myself, which is quite ridiculous. I'm an atheist, I don't believe in any god, devil, or spirit, so therefore have no need to worship one.'

'I have nothing to fear up here,' Rosina said, gesturing towards the scenery then turning to face forward. Five minutes later, she said, 'This is as far as we can go on horseback, the track peters out here.'

Pulling the mare to a halt she passed the reins to Blake and slipped nimbly down to land on her good foot. He dismounted with care to stand beside her.

'Have we far to walk, Rosina?' he asked, brushing flies away from his face. 'It's so hot today,' he added, pulling at his neckcloth.

'It's only about half a mile. A linen shirt would be more suitable than a silk one on a day like this,' she remarked.

'I'll remember that,' he said, pretending to be chastened. 'You lead the way, I'll follow with Vanity.'

They walked through heather and short grass. Blake stumbled on hidden rocks and Rosina slowed down and pointed out a clear path for him to follow. Once, Vanity threatened to bolt as an adder slithered its way across in front of her, and Blake was relieved when Rosina told him they had reached their destination. In front of them was a formation of rocks shaped not unlike the letter 'N'.

'There?' he said.

'Just round the other side. The ground drops to the side here and the rocks will provide shade from the sun when we go around.'

'That will be more than welcome,' he said emphatically. 'These rocks look as if they've been deliberately placed like this,' he continued, peering up at the granite formation when they had finally stopped. 'They look like a huge table.'

'I believe they were put there,' Rosina said, 'by human hands long ago. They were even higher once, but you can see they've sunk down over the years.'

'Yes, over the centuries. The whole thing would be quite a land-mark otherwise.'

'It's a cairn, a stone chamber for the body of an ancient king. It's strange to think of other people standing here, perhaps in this very spot, hundreds of years ago.'

'Makes you feel small and insignificant, doesn't it?' Blake smiled at her. 'I've brought a flask of water with me, Rosina, would you like some?'

'I'll get it,' she said, 'you sit down and rest.'

Blake sat down at the foot of the cairn where clumps of dry ferns four feet in height swayed in a light breeze and provided a welcome respite from the heat. Rosina joined him with the water flask she'd taken from the mare's saddle.

'Vanity's a beautiful creature, have you had her long?'

'Only a few months.'

Her long fair hair rested on his arm and he touched a strand gently between thumb and finger. She looked at him and he met her eyes and they smiled easily at one another. Without a word they acknowledged the rapport growing rapidly between them. They shared water from the flask and both leaned back against the warm stone of the cairn to look up at a sky adorned with only the occasional cloud.

'It's pleasant here,' Blake said. 'I can see why you like to spend time alone in this spot, Rosina. Your brother is a miner, I know. Do you work at the mine too?'

'Yes. I sort the tin ore from the rock with the other women and small boys. Can I ask you what you do for a living?'

'You can ask me anything you like. I have a good income from rents on properties I inherited, and from dues on various seine fishing boats and luggers I own.'

'Seine boats? They're the ones that go out to sea with the huge nets for the pilchards, aren't they?'

'Yes, I believe you're right,' he replied.

'You can watch them at work from the cliffs under Wheal Ember when the shoals are round that way,' Rosina said, eyes shining. 'It's so exciting to watch.'

Blake smiled at her happy memories, pleased that she at least had some. 'I must make a point of watching them myself sometime. I also have money in the Wheal Ember mine where you work and one or two other mining ventures. I've been fortunate to have had good returns on them. I don't suppose I am a particularly wealthy man, but then I only have myself to spend money on. An easy life compared to the one you live, Rosina.'

'Yes,' she agreed, without envy, 'but it is what I'm used to.'

'So, tell me about your Mr Wesley, Rosina. Did you see him?'

'Yes.'

'And?'

Rosina sat up straight and put her delicate chin in her hands. 'It's hard to explain how you feel on hearing Mr Wesley preach. Crowds and crowds of people turned out to listen to him. He seemed to speak for hours and hours and yet it wasn't long enough. I could have stood and listened to him for a whole day and night without moving. He's not very tall, you know, and he stood on a high wall so we could all see him.'

'I can imagine. Like a big black rook in clerical collars.'

'He didn't look well actually. He had the flux so I've heard since, and it was very brave of him to stand up for so long in the heat and preach so powerfully.' Rosina looked towards the mare and watched her long brown tail flick away tiresome flies.

'I have offended you now. I'm sorry,' Blake said quickly, worry creasing his handsome face. 'Please go on. I want to hear, really.'

'I was offended for myself, Peter,' she said quietly, using his Christian name for the first time and facing him again. She went on. 'Although Mr Wesley was not well he looked contented, at peace with himself and the world. The peace of knowing God, Preacher Renfree called it. I had the honour of speaking to Mr Wesley afterwards and he was very polite. I shall never forget what he looked like. He had a high forehead, a long nose, bright eyes... and he wore a long white wig.'

Rosina seemed to glow as she talked and Blake thought if he reached out and held a hand close to her, her small body would radiate a comfortable warmth, like a well-tended hearth on a winter's night.

'What did he say to you?' he asked.

'Bless you.'

'Bless you,' Blake repeated slowly. 'Do you really believe in all the things he preaches, Rosina? In a God, a creator... all that sort of thing?'

'Yes.' She looked at the stone walls of the long forgotten tomb. 'If I did not,' she whispered, 'I could not bear to live.'

Oliver felt it was better to have the cottage pulled down in Trelynne Cove and have the small area of coastline returned to its natural dignity. He rode there early one morning after an hour of solitude at Pengarron Point to examine the labourers' work of clearing away all debris. He'd galloped Conomor for several miles across his land and clifftop before reining in at the top of the cove where the silhouette of a big stocky man showed clearly against the lightening sky.

Leaving Conomor to wander at will, Oliver strode over to the other man and joined him as he gazed out over a still-dark restless sea.

'Good morning, Ted,' Oliver said quietly to the miner.

'G'morning, m'lord.'

'Looks like it will be another scorching hot day.'

'Aye. Reckon you'll be right.'

Oliver took a step forward and looked down at the sea where it raged and boiled over the rocks below in the place where Davey Trembath had plunged to his death. He moved back to Ted's side.

'It won't bring him back, Ted.'

'No, sir, I know that, but it helps… coming up here helps me to set my mind straight. Mother and Will rely on me now, what with Curly gone to his rest too.'

Oliver pulled a large square of cloth out of one pocket. 'When I know I'm coming over to the cove I bring this with me. I want to return it to its rightful owner.'

Ted looked across to the bright red piece of cloth in Oliver's outstretched hand. 'My kerchief,' he said in surprise. 'Where did you find it, sir? Begging your pardon, but why are you bothering to return a scrap of cloth to me?'

'I came across it, Ted, clutched in the dead fingers of Old Tom Trelynne.'

A look of enlightenment slowly appeared on Ted Trembath's haggard face.

'You know it was me who killed him, then?' he said, without expression.

'I suspected you might have had something to do with the old scoundrel's death.'

'And you said nothing?'

'As far as I'm concerned, you and your family have suffered enough at that man's hand. I understand, Ted. It was not so long ago I almost killed a man for hurting someone dear to me...'

Ted took the kerchief from Oliver and passed it back and forth between his fingers, then returned his gaze to the sea.

'I would like to know what happened, Ted.'

'I came back here most days,' he began. 'I felt compelled to... at least until Davey was found. Like you, sir, I had a strong feeling Old Tom was somewhere hereabouts. It was only a week after Davey went over when I saw someone moving down by the cottage. It was Old Tom, right enough, no mistaking his build. I'm not a light man on my feet but I crept down the path and followed the old man from the cottage and over those smooth rocks on the east side of the beach. He was carrying something from the cottage and was roaring drunk so he didn't notice me following him. I watched him disappear through a small opening in the rocks. It was too small for me to crawl through but I moved some loose rocks out of the way until the opening was big enough.'

Ted stopped for a moment and licked his dry lips.

'It didn't take me long to find the old man on the other side, and when he saw me I d'reckon he became stone cold sober in that same instant. I killed him, Sir Oliver. There and then I choked the life out of that evil little man with my bare hands. I didn't give him the chance even to finish off a scream. It's strange though, I don't mind him pulling off my kerchief. It never occurred to me once after I lost it, it would be there. If anyone but you had come across his body, I might well have been hung for it by now.'

'It was my wife who found the old man's body, Ted,' Oliver said, 'but I don't think she noticed the kerchief. Most other people around here would remain silent about it, anyway. No one is going to grieve over Old Tom Trelynne.'

'Except for your wife, sir. She's a gentle soul and loved her grand–father, for all his bad ways,' Ted sighed. 'I'm sorry for her sake. I thank you all the same for keeping your peace.'

'I only wish I could do something for you, Ted. I feel partly responsible for Davey's death myself.'

Oliver recalled often the harsh statement from Clem Trenchard on the clifftop on the night of the tragedy. 'It's your fault the boy's dead.' It hurt every time it entered his mind, even more so standing beside Davey's grieving brother. It was also partly true, if he had not agreed with Old Tom's terms over this insignificant cove below them, there would never have been a landing there.

'No need for you to feel any blame, sir. It was me who let young Davey come along that night. It's for me, and me alone, to have to live with it.'

'If there is anything I can do for you at any time, Ted,' Oliver said, pressing his hand on the miner's shoulder for a moment. 'When you can no longer go down the mine, I hope on that day you will come and see me. There will be work for you and a cottage for your family then, or whenever you may wish to have it, on my estate.'

'That's very civil of you, sir.'

Sensing that Ted only wished to be alone, Oliver left him, and made his way down into the cove.

Ted Trembath remained still for several minutes. With tears pricking his eyes he moved to the edge of the cliff and let the kerchief fall from his fingers. He watched it flutter down to be finally swallowed up by the lashing white spray.

'Goodbye, Davey boy,' he whispered, then turned to head for home.

–

Clem settled his back comfortably against a wheel of the haywain in the middle of the field. His face was heavily streaked where he had wiped away sweat and dust, his upper body itching from the bits of chaff trapped inside his shirt and rubbing at his skin. Alice came and knelt beside him and handed him a pasty and mug of water, her body providing welcome shade from the scorching sun.

'Father says you're to have a proper rest,' she said, 'or you'll wear yourself out.'

'Huh,' Clem grunted, after gulping down the contents of the mug. 'There's not enough wheat in this field to wear out an old man of ninety. Tis no higher than a hare's back. You brought a dish for Charity?'

Alice took a large shallow bowl out of the basket she had with her and filled it with water from a flask. Taking the dish from his wife Clem put it down in front of his dog. He ruffled her dusty black ears as she noisily lapped up the water.

'It's the lack of rain, isn't it, Clem?' Alice said. 'The reason for the poor harvest.'

'Aye, but we're better off than some of the other farms. At least we have a deep well in the yard and can water our garden vegetables, and the river at the bottom of the valley hasn't quite left its banks yet.'

'What will happen, Clem? Is there any need for us to be anxious?'

'Well, it will mean the price of grain going up... tithes, rates and rents will be harder to find for all the farmers.'

Straightening her white muslin bonnet, Alice settled herself closer to him. 'There's such a lot to learn about farming,' she said, smiling at him and hoping he would approve of her interest, 'and I want to learn it all. I wish I could do more now. It don't seem right to see Mother, Rosie, and even Gran, working in the fields and there's me doing nothing much.'

'Nothing much?' Clem said, with an irritable sigh. 'You've learned how to make butter, cream and cheese, and how to milk the goats.' He went on, tapping a finger on the palm of his other hand, 'You help Mother in the farmhouse... Gran in the garden... you keep Kenver company so the others can get on with other things... you do most of the family's sewing. Stop selling yourself short, Alice.'

Her face looked stricken. Clem's temper had been getting shorter and shorter of late, and he seemed to look for opportunities to be quarrelsome. She said nothing about it to him, making excuses to herself for his unreasonable behaviour; he was still getting used to the added responsibility of a wife and coming child; he was worried about the poor state of the harvest; or he was simply over tired. She dared not give even one single thought to the real reason behind his uncaring attitude towards her; that he still loved Kerensa Pengarron and resented Alice for trapping him into marrying her.

'I'll be getting back to the farmhouse then,' she said, her voice tight and controlled as she used the side of the haywain to help her to her feet. 'I promised Rosie I'd finish the hem of her new dress for her birthday tomorrow.'

'I won't be home till late,' he told her, without looking up as he fed Charity his pastry crust.

The word 'birthday' ran through his head as Clem picked up his sickle to return to his work. It was another girl's birthday the same day. The twenty-second day of August. Rosie's thirteenth birthday... Kerensa's eighteenth. If they had married they would now be happily working side by side in the fields. He would have planned something special for her birthday. A present would have been bought secretly in Marazion and placed proudly on her pillow beside his in the morning. He would have picked an armful of her favourite wild flowers. They would have strolled hand in hand through the meadows and he would have made dozens of daisy chains to crown her rich auburn hair. Later they would have laughed and laughed as he teased her and playfully chased her round the field, Charity running beside them and barking excitedly to join in. Then he would have gathered her up in his arms and carried her to the haywain, and laying her gently down on the soft, sweet-smelling hay they would have made love again and again...

'You all right, boy?'

'What!' Clem snapped, angry at having his daydream disturbed.

'You were miles away,' his father said, 'been standing here, still as a statue, these past ten minutes.'

'I was just thinking,' he said moodily. 'Better get on with the reaping.' He stalked off, leaving Morley to stare after him, shaking his head.

Clem stayed much longer in the field than his father and the womenfolk of his family, piling dried sheaves on the haywain and lingering long enough for cooling breezes to soothe the skin on his face and arms burnt by the heat of the sun. By the time he had driven the haywain, pulled slowly along by the family's ageing carthorse, into the farmyard, he had worked off most of his bad temper and was feeling sorry at the way he had deliberately deflated Alice.

She was trying so hard to fit in with her new life and his family, to be a good wife to him. If only she didn't try so hard! If she would just take her time getting used to everything and give him a little breathing space to get used to her. It wasn't easy for her, he knew, the change from bal-maiden to farmer's wife. And she couldn't talk about the few months she had spent living at the Manor because he didn't like her talking about Kerensa, or more particularly Sir Oliver Pengarron.

'Poor Alice,' he told Charity, sitting up beside him with her long pink tongue hanging out in anticipation of her meal, as they pulled up in the farmyard. 'Nothing of what happened is her fault.'

Giving Charity a large bowlful of scraps and fresh water, he sought Alice out by the pigsty where she was giving the grunting animal a trough of skimmed milk.

'Hello,' he said, making an effort to sound genuinely friendly. 'Need any help?'

'I've finished here,' Alice said, looking up warily at him. Barring the sty's gate, she walked off.

Clem walked beside her. 'Where are you going with that?' he asked, peering into the pail she carried. 'You've still got skimmed milk in there.'

'It's for the cats.'

'Let me take it for you,' he said, reaching for the pail's handle.

'It's not heavy,' she said, rather defensively.

'Come on, Alice,' he gave a short laugh. 'Don't be so independent.'

She obediently handed over the pail, putting down the old chipped crocks one at a time for the cats as Clem filled them.

'You're as bad as Gran is with them,' he said, as they stood back and watched the motley creatures appear from different directions to lap up the skimmed milk greedily. Some had large knots of fur in their matted coats but the cats were far too spiteful to be groomed by human hands. 'They're vicious brutes, every one of them,' he continued, 'but I suppose they earn their keep. We hardly ever see a rat or mouse.'

'I've never had an animal of my own,' Alice said quietly, putting her head on one side as she watched the cats.

'You'll never make a pet out of one of these, Alice. Be careful not to touch any of them… a scratch could give you blood poisoning.'

'I had a rabbit once,' she went on sadly, 'but after two weeks it ended up in a stew.'

Clem put an arm round her shoulders. 'Tell you what, these cats deliver their litters all over the place. The next time I come across one, what say we take a kitten into the house and try to tame it?'

'Could we, Clem?' She was instantly cheered. 'That would be lovely. I saw you limping a bit when you came into the yard. Have you hurt your leg?'

'Oh, it's nothing. I got carried away and knocked it with the rulling hook.'

'Rulling hook?'

'What we use for pulling the sheaves together.'

'Is it bleeding?'

'Just a bit. After supper, will you bathe it for me?'

'Of course I will,' she said, happy now Clem's mood was a pleasant one and he'd asked her to do something for him, instead of asking his mother, grandmother or sister as he usually did. 'Come and see Rosie's new dress. I've got it hidden in the lean-to. She should have a nice birthday tomorrow.'

'Yes, she should,' Clem agreed, staying quiet for a minute now he felt he had done enough to make things up to his wife. 'Let's go inside for supper.'

Chapter 21

On the day of her birthday Kerensa was out riding alone. She called first on the Richards with fresh fruit, bacon and bread, saddened to find despite her and Polly's efforts to help the family to a cleaner, healthier way of life, the inside of the farmhouse dirty and smelling of humans and animals both. All six of the children had the flux.

Kerensa stayed to help Moriah Richards change the children's bedsheets; the linen she had made for Clem and herself had been gratefully received here but now the sheets were so soiled it was unlikely they would be returned to their former condition. After giving the children cooled boiled water with added sugar and a pinch of salt, she left. She promised to take over the next day some of Beatrice's strong camomile tea to settle the children's stomachs, and bunches of lavender to hang up to discourage the plague of flies that abounded everywhere you turned inside the insanitary building.

Kerensa was relieved to leave the dusty cluttered farmyard and breathe fresh clean air into her lungs. She rode at a canter with the intention of going straight to Ker-an-Mor Farm to help Jenna Tregurtha prepare food and ale for Oliver, Adam Renfree, and the labourers in the fields. Instead, she found herself trotting along the side of the hedgerow that divided the greater part of Trecath-en from Ker-an-Mor, and when the hedgerow came to an end at the top of Trecath-en's valley, she allowed Kernick to wander over on to Trecath-en soil.

She rode slowly down to the river at the bottom of the valley where the water was progressively vanishing in the summer's prolonged heat. Dismounting and tossing her straw hat aside to land among a mass of stinging nettles, she left it where it fell and looked across the river where on the other side a small flock of skinny sheep were grazing at a distance from the elm tree with its summer finery of wavy leaves and fuzz of small twigs.

For a while she walked beside the water, listening to its subdued singing and gurgling over the stone-covered bottom. Then on impulse she pulled off her shoes, and hitching up her skirts she slipped off the bank into the water. It was not refreshingly cold, but warm. She paddled awkwardly over the freely shifting stones that stubbed and hurt her feet, but she was enjoying the experience with the heedlessness of a child. She was singing cheerfully and splashing water over her arms and face when someone spoke to her from the same side of the bank she had lowered herself in.

'I did not expect to find a waif and stray here.'

Kerensa looked up guiltily, her hands falling to her sides, water dripping from her fingertips.

'Clem! I'm afraid you've caught me trespassing.'

'Mmmm. Perhaps I should pull you out of there and keep you locked up somewhere secretly for the rest of your life. What do you think?'

His expression was serious and Kerensa was for the first time ever unsure of what he might be thinking or feeling. He gazed at her steadily and she felt herself blushing.

'There's not so much water in the river as last year,' she said, rubbing her wet hands in the folds of her skirt. 'Do you think it will get much lower than this?'

'No, whatever happens this river has never been known to dry up,' he replied, then closed his lips in a tight line.

'Well,' she said, 'at least that's good news.'

'I suppose it is,' he said, non-committally. 'We don't get droughts in Cornwall like other parts of the country.'

'That's what Oliver said last night.' Kerensa tried a small smile on Clem but he did not return it and made no further comment. It was easy to see he had not liked her mentioning her husband. Perhaps he was annoyed at finding her uninvited on his father's land? She waded towards the bank, stumbling over the stones to stop in front of him. Before leaving the water she decided to test his mood again.

'Um… where's Charity? It's unusual to see you without her.'

'She caught her paw in the barn door. I left her back in the yard.'

'Poor Charity. How's Alice? I enjoy her visits to the Manor.'

'Alice is all right. She was out in the yard spinning a short time ago… I think she enjoys visiting you.'

'Does she tell you about her visits, Clem?'

'No.' This was said sharply. 'I don't want to hear anything about your life… with him.'

Her face flushed, Kerensa looked down into the water. 'I'd better get out of here,' she muttered, 'my feet are going numb.'

'Take my hand,' Clem ordered her. He stooped until their eyes were on the same level, his face wearing the serious expression it had to begin with.

Kerensa held out her hand to his, but as their fingers touched she stumbled. 'Ouch! My toes!'

Clem hauled her out beside him and Kerensa gripped his arms, hopping about on one foot.

'Sit yourself down,' he said, 'we'll look at what you've done to your toes.'

He did not sound sympathetic. Lifting her foot he inspected the damage inflicted by the shifting stones on the river bed.

'Oh, it hurts,' Kerensa complained, trying to push his hands away so she could see for herself.

'Keep still,' Clem said gruffly, 'and don't be such a baby.'

'What?'

Ignoring the puzzled look on her face, he said. 'You've cut three of your toes. Nothing serious, but they'll be sore for a few days.'

Forgetting her toes Kerensa caught a fistful of Clem's shirt at his shoulder. 'Will you please tell me why you're such a crosspatch today, Clem? I haven't had one civil word from you so far.'

He didn't answer at once, but placing her foot gently on the ground as she released her grip, sat close beside her.

'I'm sorry, Kerensa. It's just that I've had so much on my mind today, with it being Rosie's birthday. I couldn't forget it's yours too. I really missed you today, more than any other day, and seeing you there enjoying yourself in the river in the same way we did together last year... oh, I don't know.' He shrugged his shoulders. 'For some reason it made me angry rather than pleased to see you.'

'I'm sorry. I shouldn't have come here. I had no right.'

Kerensa made to rise but Clem put a restraining hand on her arm. 'No, don't go. I'm glad you did. I'm glad you're here.'

Settling back down again, she said earnestly, 'I'd hate it if I thought you were no longer my friend, Clem.'

'Friends.' He sighed heavily. 'I suppose I'll have to settle for that. Why did you come here today, Kerensa?'

'I don't know. I had nothing to do and was just out riding and wandered across the boundary at the top of the valley,' she told him with a smile.

'I see. Do you ever think of me?' he asked abruptly, his face still serious.

'Yes, of course,' she replied, meeting his direct look.

The hand he had placed on her arm to stop her leaving moved to take hold of hers tightly. 'I think of you all the time, Kerensa. Never stop. I didn't know I could hurt this way. All the plans I had for our future together are gone, and nothing seems worth the bother any more.'

'Oh, Clem, I'm sorry. I wish... Are you so unhappy, even with Alice?'

'Alice, poor Alice,' he said, taking in the pained look of Kerensa's face. He ran a finger along the contour of her chin. 'I'm not making much of a job of making her happy. I think she's lonely... she was on about having a pet animal of her own yesterday. I've promised to try taming a kitten from one of those mangy cats for her.'

Kerensa put her other hand over Clem's and said in a serious tone, 'You must not feel sorry for yourself, and you must make the best of the situation you're in.'

'Hark at you,' he said. 'Trying to talk like a matron but still looking no more than a child.'

'If you're going to go on like this,' she said crossly, pulling both hands away, 'I'm going to leave right now.'

Rising quickly to his knees, Clem put his hands on her shoulders. 'Still the same as ever,' he said, 'sticking out your precious little chin when you get angry.'

'You've given me good reason to be angry with you, Clem Trenchard!'

'Then I might as well add to my sins.'

He kissed her full on the mouth then sat back on his heels.

Kerensa put the back of her hand against her lips and looked up at him under her eyelashes.

'Now you look even more like a little girl,' he said, laughing softly. 'Want to slap my face?'

'Not for kissing me,' she told him huffily, kneeling up to face him. 'But for laughing at me, I could beat you willingly.'

'I'm not laughing at you, my little sweet,' he said, smiling at her.

'My little sweet... you always called me that, Clem,' her anger swiftly dying.

'Yes, I did, didn't I? You will always be that to me.'

Kerensa returned his smile. 'Are you in a better mood now?'

'Yes. Shall we start again? Pretend I've only just found you in the river?'

'Only if you tell me you won't have me thrown in gaol for trespassing,' she teased.

'You are Trecath-en's honoured guest,' he said, in the same humour.

Exchanging a friendly hug they sat down again, Kerensa massaging her foot above her sore toes while Clem threw stones and bits of grass into the sparkling water as they talked.

'I hope you do get a kitten for Alice,' Kerensa said. 'There aren't any cats at the Manor. Oliver comes out in a rash and gets runny eyes if they're about.'

'Does he?' Clem gave a short mocking laugh, tossing away a last stone and sinking to his side to rest on an elbow. 'He's not as perfect as he likes to think he is, then.'

'I don't think he does believe he's perfect.'

'Do you, Kerensa?'

'Oh, he's hardly that, Clem… but he's not quite as bad as he would have people believe. He's had a different upbringing to us, has different expectations, a different way of looking at life.'

Kerensa was surprised at Clem's next question. 'Do you like him?'

She was careful how she answered. 'Most of the time.' She didn't want to hurt him by what she might say so turned the conversation round. 'Do you like Alice?'

Clem thought for a moment, plucking a blade of grass and biting it between his front teeth. 'Silly, isn't it? It's not crossed my mind before to wonder if I like Alice or not… yes, I think I do. I suppose if I hadn't been obliged to marry her I might have gone mad.'

'I'm pleased you like her. Alice is the only friend I can really turn to.' She reached out and stroked his cheek. 'Don't hurt her, Clem, please.'

They stayed still, looking at one another without talking for a long time, happy just to have been given one unexpected secret hour together. They got up at the same moment, Clem taking Kerensa's arm to help her along so she could keep the weight off her sore foot, and stooping to pick up her shoes on the way. On reaching the patch of stinging nettles he retrieved her hat, then fetched Kernick and handed her the pony's reins. Then, with a whispered 'Goodbye', he kissed her cheek, turned and walked away from her.

When she reached the top of the valley Kerensa looked back and watched Clem moving further and further away, his fair head standing out clearly against the dull landscape, but not upright and proud as it had been. A feeling of guilt and longing welled up painfully inside her and she wiped away the threat of tears. She had no desire to go to Ker-an-Mor now and rode off in the direction of home.

–

Daylight was fading when the harvesters on Ker-an-Mor Farm had finished washing themselves down at the pump in the farmyard and were ready to call the hard day's work finally at an end.

Oliver clamped his hand on Jack's scrawny shoulder, the boy almost asleep on his feet.

339

'You've put in a good day's work again today, Jack. Here,' he said, taking a coin of large denomination from his pocket, 'treat yourself the next time you're in Marazion.'

'Phew, thank 'ee, sir,' Jack said brightly, before his eyelids drooped again.

Nathan came over to them, neatly tucking his shirt into his breeches.

'I'll be off then, if that's all right with you, sir.'

'Thank you for your help, Nat. Make sure Jack gets back to the Manor all right, will you, please?'

'Aye, sir, that I will,' Nat said, sweeping back his thick hair with both hands. 'Come on, Jack, don't hang about,' he threw at the sleepy boy.

'Nat in a hurry, is he, sir?' Adam Renfree asked at Oliver's side. 'He can't get the boy on that horse fast enough.'

'I think he wanted to pay a call at Orchard Hill first, Adam,' Oliver grinned broadly, a wicked glint in his eye.

'How's that then, sir?'

'A certain woman happens to be paying her cousin a visit there today.'

'On Orchard Hill? Oh! Polly Berryman, Daniel's cousin, is that what you're on about?' Adam's grin was wider than Oliver's. 'So that's the way the wind's blowing, is it? Well, I never. I thought O'Flynn had time only for his trees and pheasants.'

When all the farmhands, and the hired help of rovers looking for casual work, miners working before and after their cores, and those without work at all like the men who were too old and those with lung diseases making them too sick to go down the mines but who missed the company of working men, had all gone home, Oliver and Adam relaxed their aching backs in the farmhouse over a glass of mead.

Settled comfortably in the parlour with his pipe, and his feet raised on a stool, Adam relaxed. 'Thought to see your wife here today, sir.'

'I thought she would ride over myself, Adam,' Oliver agreed with him, 'but it's hardly surprising, with you making it so plain you don't approve of women in the fields unless they're working hard or bringing food and ale and leaving again at once.'

'Some of them get in the way and distract the men,' Adam said, unrepentant. 'Besides which, it's no place for a lady.'

'Kerensa comes from working-class people, Adam. She doesn't mind getting her hands dirty.'

'Maybe so, but surely you wouldn't approve of her ladyship pulling sheaves together, sir?'

'Of course not, but she likes to feel useful,' Oliver asserted, 'and I like for her to be content.'

Adam thoughtfully moved his pipe to the other side of his mouth. 'She's done a lot to help the Richards and it's a shame they don't appreciate it. They have no idea how to keep anything clean. You'll not find a dirtier family, or a less efficient farmer than Rudd Richards, I do reckon. It's only a matter of time before they lose some of they children to one of the fevers.'

'I'll agree with you there, Adam. They will be affected far worse than the rest of us by the poor harvest.' Oliver eased himself back in his chair and massaged the areas of stiffness in his neck, arms, and shoulders. He not only liked to work as hard as the other men, he drove them on in their labours at a fearsome rate.

'There will be hardship this winter,' he went on. 'The price of grain will soar well beyond the ordinary man's pocket. Make sure there's plenty left in the fields for the labourers and locals to glean, Adam. It will provide a little more in their larders for the winter ahead.'

'I'll see to that, sir. I'm afraid the ricks won't be so high and round. The grain flailed on the barn floor'll be paltry compared to last year. Still, it's better than the old days now we're growing more clover, sainfoin, lucerne and turnips for animal fodder to see us through.'

Oliver sighed and swallowed a mouthful of mead. 'I suppose you're right, Adam, but fewer crops means more reliance on salted food and I hate to see the cereals so dry and brittle, the potatoes green and bitter.'

'Tis a crying shame, sir,' Adam said, leaning forward to pull stubborn corn stalks out of his stockings. 'I've never known a summer like it. My grandmother used to say you can't get too much rain before mid-summer or too little after. Well, we haven't had any rain since mid-summer, but we could've done with plenty before it… even the storms we had were only thunder and lightning, with barely a drop of rain to be seen or smelled.'

'Yes,' Oliver said, getting to his feet and walking towards a small built-in cupboard in the wall and taking a small key from a pocket to unlock it. 'Beatrice keeps on saying, "There be evil abroad, me 'an'some, evil. Jus' 'ee wait an' see."'

Adam chuckled at Oliver's excellent imitation of Beatrice's words and mannerisms and watched with keen interest as his master took a small, but longish box out from behind some papers in the cupboard and brought it over to him.

'Take a look at this, Adam. Tell me what you think of it.'

The box contained a pearl necklace, consisting of three strands with a larger pearl set in the centre, and a tiny diamond-encrusted clasp.

'Well, I don't know much about jewellery and the like, sir,' Adam said, rubbing his stubbly chin, 'but it's a fine-looking piece, right enough.'

'It's for Kerensa,' Oliver said, 'to mark her birthday today. Do you think she will like it?'

'Aye. It's not too big or fussy for the little maid's taste, I do reckon.' Adam looked up quickly at Oliver but couldn't help smiling. 'Sorry, sir, no disrespect meant, but her ladyship don't seem much older than a young'un at times, begging your pardon.'

'No offence taken,' Oliver said. 'I didn't want to wake her early this morning when I left her before dawn, so I brought it with me, thinking I could give it to her sometime during the day. Well, I'll be on my way home so she can have the necklace before the day is over.'

'She'll like that, right enough,' Adam said, pointing to the box as Oliver picked it up.

'I hope you're right,' he said, as he put the box carefully inside his shirt for the ride home. 'Goodnight to you, Adam.'

Chapter 22

Peter Blake sat at the foot of the cairn, playing a game from his childhood of making out shapes of animals, ships and faces in the scudding clouds, while he waited for Rosina. They had now met several times, either there beside the tall ferns or one of the other secret places Rosina had taken him to. Varying the location for their meetings each time, they approached from different directions to afford less chance of their association being discovered.

A slowly passing half hour went by and Blake pulled open the hamper of food and drink he'd brought with him and took a long draught from a bottle of white wine. He wasn't unduly concerned over Rosina's non-appearance yet, she came when she could and stayed as long as she was able, but as always he was longing to see her.

She limped towards him when he was busy replacing the wine bottle. He looked up, and the smile he had ready for her vanished in an instant. He saw the pain that etched its presence in her features and dulled the radiance of her face. He hurried to meet her.

'What's wrong, Rosina?' As he lightly touched her shoulder the girl winced. 'Have you hurt yourself?' he asked her. 'Or has that brother of yours been beating you again?' His face was coloured with concern for her and anger at Colly Pearce.

'Please, Peter,' she said wearily, 'could I just have a drink of water?'

Blake led her to where he was sitting and gave her water from the hamper in a small pewter tankard. Her hands were trembling and he held the tankard steady for her to sip from.

'Enough?' he said, when she pushed the tankard away.

She nodded, staring out across the still, now ominously silent, scenery.

Turning her face round to his, he said quietly, 'It was Colly, wasn't it?'

Her tears fell heavily and without warning and she leaned against him, wrapping her arms around his neck. Blake held her close. He had wanted to take her in his arms so many times but had not dared to, fearing he would drive her away from him. He closed his eyes, drinking in her warmth and softness, glorying in her trust, but shocked at her frailty.

'I can't bear to see you like this any more, Rosina,' he said, 'you must come back with me. I'll take you to my sister's house where Josephine and I can look after you.'

'I can't do that,' she said in a small voice.

'If you're worried about not being accepted, Rosina, I can set your mind at rest. Josephine has always adored me and I'm the only family she has. Whatever I like, she likes. Whatever I've wanted, all through my life, she's gone out of her way to obtain it for me. She'll like you very much, Rosina, she'll only be too pleased to have you stay with her, and I'll see you every day.'

'It's not that. I wish I could come with you, Peter,' she said, wiping away her tears, 'but I have to go home. I can't leave Colly. He needs me.'

'But I can't allow you to go back and receive more of this brutality, Rosina. I fear for your life,' he said, in all seriousness. 'I know what it's like... the pain... the humiliation...'

Brushing aside her long hair as he held her he pulled her dress away from her back, grimacing at the ugly, purple bruises discolouring her skin. She looked up at him, blinking away more tears and revealing further bruises under her chin and down her throat. Blake glanced down at her arms, bare between elbow and wrist. There were bruises of the same ilk there, too.

'Colly doesn't mean to harm me, he's always sorry afterwards.'

'That's no comfort to me, Rosina, seeing you beaten, starved, and so unhappy.'

'He wasn't always like this,' she informed Blake. 'Colly loved me dearly once... a long time ago.'

Blake wasn't convinced. 'So what happened to change him into a monster?'

She took a deep breath. 'Colly's a lot older than me, and while our parents doted on me, he could never seem to do anything right for them. Poor Colly, he tried so hard to please them, but he was clumsy, always breaking things and getting into trouble.'

'And presumably beaten?'

'Yes, he was. When I was old enough I used to cover up for him and say it was me who broke things, or did all the other things that upset our parents. Colly and I loved each other so much, we'd spend hours holding hands just wandering over the downs. I was all he had.' She stopped talking for a moment and pressed her face into Blake's chest.

'Then one day, when clearing a patch of ground our father wanted Colly to dig over to make a garden, he dropped a large block of granite on my foot. It wasn't Colly's fault,' she said, her voice rising, 'I'd run up behind him and tapped him on the back in play. He turned around in surprise, dropping the rock...'

'On your foot,' Blake finished for her, 'and that is why you are lame?'

'Yes. I was about five at the time and my right foot was badly broken. Colly could hardly bear the guilt he felt and Father beat him until he could no longer stand up. He couldn't go down the mine for a week and that caused more arguments. They just wouldn't leave him alone, Mother or Father. They shouted at him day and night about his loss of wages... about his clumsiness... telling him he was ugly and useless and hopeless.' Rosina looked up at Blake imploringly. 'But he wasn't, Peter, honestly he wasn't.'

'I know, I know,' he said soothingly. 'What happened after that?'

'At the end of the week our father was killed and Mother blamed Colly for the accident. Father fell off the ladder on the way down the mine and she said it was because he wasn't concentrating, because Colly had upset him too much. Dear Colly, he had all that to bear, and as my foot didn't heal properly it was a constant reminder to him... Oh! it's not fair!' she cried, pressing yet closer to Blake for comfort. 'It was me who tapped him on the back, it was my fault, not his. After that he became more and more remote from me, resenting every kind word Mother gave me and blaming me for every angry word to him. Colly took to drinking, refusing to go to church any more with us, and getting himself into fights and terrible rages.'

'It seems to me that it was your mother who shouldn't have gone to church, not your brother,' Blake commented. 'Do you know why they hated him so much, your parents?'

'I often asked my mother but she'd only say I wouldn't understand. When she died, Colly told me in one of his rages one day that he had a different father to me.'

'Well, that would account for your father's hatred of him, but what about your mother's?'

'While my parents seemed to love me, they were cool to one another. Perhaps my mother resented Colly because my father wouldn't let her forget he wasn't the first man in her life... something like that.' Rosina looked at Blake to see if he could answer his own question.

He nodded. 'Yes, it sounds likely.'

'When our mother died three years ago,' she continued, 'I hoped Colly and I would be close again, but it was too late. He'd been bitter for too long to change. He... he first hit me the day of her funeral... and...' She couldn't go on.

'And he's been hitting you ever since,' Blake said grimly, 'only now he's become dangerous, too dangerous for you to go home again, Rosina, my dear.'

She bowed her head. 'Can we talk about something else now? I want to enjoy being with you, Peter.'

'Yes, of course,' he said, suddenly becoming enthusiastic. 'I've got something for you, Rosina.'

She sat up straight while he pulled a folded piece of silk out of a corner of the hamper. 'You're always giving me things,' she protested.

'That's only food and stuff. This is for you to keep,' he said, taking her hand and putting the piece of silk into it.

Rosina glanced at Blake and gave him a simple, 'Thank you.' She carefully pulled each fold of the deep red material apart until she came

346

to a delicate piece of jewellery, a tiny piece of circular granite with a perfect white cross in its centre formed from crystals of felspar.

'Peter! It's beautiful!'

'I'm pleased you like it,' he said, glad to have been responsible for causing her radiant smile to appear. 'I bought it from an old man in the market and had it put in a setting and on a chain for you.'

'I've never been given anything like this in my whole life,' she breathed. 'It's very rare to find the Cross, you know. It's highly prized, and people search for it for years and never come across it.'

'Like looking for a four-leafed clover?'

'Oh, it's nothing like that, that's only superstition. Finding the Cross, which represents the Lord's suffering and victory, means such a lot more if you're a believer.' In wonder Rosina touched the pendant with a fingertip, the white crystals standing out against the black granite as clearly as her gentle disposition contrasted to her brother's cruelty. 'Will you put it on for me, please, Peter?'

Smiling, he took the pendant from its silk bed, and lifting her hair to the side where it fell over his arm, joined the clasp at the back of her neck.

'There you are,' he said, 'you'll be lucky from now on.'

'That's supposed to be for the one who finds the Cross in the rocks,' she said, laughing. Her face became serious and he looked curiously at her. 'I don't need luck, Peter,' she whispered. 'God has given me you.'

Her words overwhelmed him. 'Oh, Rosina,' he said, his low voice husky. He reached for her, then checked himself.

'It's all right,' she reassured him.

'I'm almost afraid to kiss you.'

She brought her delicate, gentle face in very close to his. 'We don't have to be afraid of anything.'

She closed her eyes. Blake placed a hand either side of her face and lightly touched her lips with his. When he moved his head slightly back, her eyes were still closed. He kissed her again, this time more firmly, his soul singing out at her tender response. When their lips parted she rested across his lap... and gradually drifted off to sleep.

Blake stroked her hair, marvelling at the way just knowing Rosina had changed his life. Before, any young female crossing his path had meant only sexual gratification, or the hope of it, to him; falling in love no more than a myth. He had not believed he could find so much love, trust and absolute faith in someone who suffered so much, someone who cared for others more than herself.

No one had ever cared for him except for his half-sister who had treated him from infancy as much as an amusing plaything as a brother she loved. She had been the main influence in his life, and she was a selfish, money-grabbing, shameless woman who indulged in a wild social life with the most unsavoury kind of people. She cared nothing for her servants or the poor of the parish, saying life was mainly what you managed to snatch away from others and who you could keep down. It had taken Rosina's purity and honesty for him to see there was another side of life, a better way to live. Rosina knew all about his sordid past, he had told her, and she had been willing to give him a chance to prove he could act like a man of honour, believing there was some decency in him.

As he held her gently against him insects buzzed in the heavy warm air and Blake allowed himself too to be lulled into a peaceful sleep.

He woke when Rosina sprang up in a panic.

'I must go!' she cried. 'Before Colly gets home!'

'No, Rosina!' Blake took hold of her. 'You can't go back there again.'

'I have to. Colly needs me. Let go of me, Peter, please let me go!'

'I need you too, Rosina. I love you. In the time you've known me, I've never tried to restrain you or do anything that might upset or offend you, but I'm taking you to my sister's home today... by force if I have to.'

He was right, he had never once said or done anything to suggest he was the same man who had once attempted to force himself on another girl. The light in his blue eyes showed a determination to protect Rosina, to be her champion, but she could not allow this. Colly must come first. First over the man she knew loved her, the man she loved with all her being, who was struggling to hold her and claim her forever.

'No! I'm sorry, Peter. I won't let you do this!'

She was thin and wiry and surprisingly strong. Blake lost his grip for an instant and she was free. She darted away from him, and running through the ferns, made her way around the cairn and along a route he was not familiar with.

Blake knew if he moved quickly he stood a chance of reaching the miners' cottages at the same time as she did. He leapt on his mare, crying out as pain seared through the tender spots on his ribs, riding as swiftly as was safe through the springy foliage laced with hidden rabbit holes, and dodging round granite boulders.

–

Twenty minutes lapsed before a breathless Rosina made it to her cottage door. People looked on anxiously as she ran past without greeting them. Beelzebub, dozing by the door, jumped up and snarled at her.

'Go run and fetch young Preacher from Mrs Bray's,' Lou Hunken ordered one of her children. 'Tell'n to come here urgently.'

Worry creased Lou Hunken's brow as she hurried off to gather her husband and the other menfolk not on core. She'd seen Colly Pearce slam drunkenly into the cottage but ten minutes or so before. She had assumed Rosina was inside at the time, and now icy fear breathed its way uncomfortably into the pit of her stomach. It was well known how angry Colly would get if the maid wasn't home when he turned up, and his violence had noticeably increased lately.

'Where the hell have you been!' Colly hurled at her accusingly as Rosina shut the door behind her. She leaned against it, panting to regain her breath, and swallowed hard.

'Just out for a bit of a walk, Colly,' she said, trying to keep her voice natural. 'I... I'm sorry if I'm a bit late getting back.' She saw a pile of dry twigs smouldering in the fireplace. 'I see you've lit a fire. I'll just cheer it up and—'

'Lazy slut!' he shouted, making her jump. 'Get me something to eat. You got no damn' right, out prancing on the downs when you should be getting my meals. Lazy slut! Bitch!'

'There's some bread and cheese,' she said, moving to the food cupboard. 'I thought you wouldn't be back yet. You said this morning—'

'Never mind what I said this morning! If you won't look after me properly I'll throw you out, and get in a woman who will. Not one who's got bloody religion either.'

He slumped down in a chair and drummed his fingers on the table as she put down mugs and plates and a board with the end of a loaf and a small piece of cheese.

'What's this?' he said irritably, pointing a dirty finger at the food.

'It's all we have,' Rosina said shakily. 'I... I'm not hungry. You have it all.'

'Why don't you go over to they Brays then and get yourself a nice big pasty, eh?' he jeered at her, his expression turning his eyes to slits and making his nose seem more bulbous.

'What do you mean by that, Colly?' she asked, redness creeping up her face.

'You know bloody well what I mean!' He thumped his fist on the table, making the tin plates clatter about. 'While that fat bitch is feeding you nice 'n' full, I get nothing but stale bread and mouldy cheese.'

'Colly, I...'

'Shut up! Just you shut up! I want none of your bloody lies.'

Rosina moved to the door.

'Where do you think you're going?'

'I'm going outside to give you a chance to calm down, Colly.'

She kept her eyes on him all the time as she moved in small sidesteps. She had read the warning signs, knowing he was about to reach bursting point at any moment. Rosina had tried to sound matter-of-fact, but he did not miss the note of fear in her voice.

'You're going nowhere to tell your Bible-thumping friends I ill treat you,' he snarled, pushing his chair back so harshly it crashed to the floor. 'Just you come here.'

'Please, Colly... I... I just want some fresh air.'

Rosina managed to get halfway through the door before Colly yanked her viciously back, making her scream out. Beelzebub began to bark, jumping and scratching at the door after Colly Pearce slammed it shut. He threw his sister back across the room, thrusting the wooden bar across the door.

'It's high time you were teached a real lesson,' he said, with the eyes of the deranged.

Slowly he pulled off his belt. Wrapping it around his hand he advanced towards her. Rosina backed away, her eyes bright with fear, a hand to her throat. Too late she realised she was still wearing the pendant Peter Blake had given to her.

Colly was on her in a moment, snatching her hand away and ripping the chain from her neck. He dangled it in front of her eyes.

'Well, what have we here? Very pretty,' he taunted. 'Who gave you this?'

'A... a... friend,' Rosina stammered, staring at the white cross on the pendant as it swung to and fro.

'A friend, eh? Looks as though it was a close friend, a gentleman friend, if he can afford gold. Got yourself a gentleman friend, have you, little sister? What did you have to do to get this, eh? Who's been laying on you in the heather?' He threw the pendant across the room behind him. 'Well? I'm waiting for an answer.'

His face was evil, his body stank of the rottenness that ran through to his very core.

'Colly, please, for the love of God!'

The mongrel was still barking and trying to get inside as Colly gripped Rosina by the throat and hurled her slight body violently across the room. She fell heavily close to her cross and clutched it in her hand at the same time as the heavy belt slashed across her back. She heard a scream but didn't realise it was coming from her own throat.

A loud hammering started on the door, followed by a single yelp from the dog.

'Open this door, Pearce, or we'll break it down!' It was Jeb Bray in the company of several others.

'Go to Hell you bastards!' Colly shouted back.

'We've killed your mongrel, Pearce!' Hunk Hunken was the next to shout. 'Now let the maid go or it'll be the worse for you!'

Colly Pearce gave a horrible laugh. He looked down at his sister who was peeping up at him through the fingers of one hand. A glimmer of compassion showed in his eyes before it disappeared under a glaze of insanity. Rosina took her hand away from her face to plead silently to her brother. A mighty kick from the tip of his boot left her stunned.

Peals of laughter from Colly drowned out the battering on the door, and the threats and shouts of the angry miners. He crossed the room, grunting like an imbecile, and picked up a full bottle of gin. Gulping down a mouthful he sprinkled the rest over the floor and sparse furniture before smashing the bottle against a table leg. Some of the men outside began to pound on the door with their shoulders in the effort to break it down. At the same time Peter Blake threw himself off his mare and pushed his way through the gathering crowd, startling miners and wives at his sudden appearance.

'What's going on?' he demanded, taking in the dog's body and the scene before him. 'Where's Rosina? Where's Miss Pearce?' he went on fearfully. 'Is this where she lives?'

'She's in there,' a miner said, 'her brother's gone mad.'

'Rosina! Rosina!' Blake's shout was near to a scream.

There was no answer but now he could hear the demented laughter coming from inside the cottage.

'Look! Smoke!' screeched Lou Hunken, standing back from the crowd and pointing to the window.

'Get that door down!' Blake urged the miners. He made to help the men pounding on the door but Matthias Renfree pulled him out of the way.

'Let them do it,' Matthias told him, 'they're stronger than you are. You will have your ribs broken again.'

'What's going on in there, Renfree? Is Rosina all right?'

'We don't know for certain, Mr Blake… look, the door's about to give way.'

It splintered and cracked, then fell in under the miners' combined weight. Pulling himself free from Matthias, Blake roughly shoved them aside to plunge through the doorway first. He came face to face with Colly Pearce.

'So,' Colly sneered, 'my sister really 'as got 'erself a gentleman.'

Blake coughed in the smoky room. 'Get out of my way,' he said icily.

'You won't find 'er,' said Colly, laughing horribly again. 'She's dead, she's dead, she's dead, she's...'

A scream tore from Peter Blake's throat as he found the strength to push the crazed man back into the room and out of his way. Colly went staggering back to the fireplace. He had put Rosina's shawl on the twigs which had finally caught alight. It was smouldering and filling the room with smoke. As he righted himself his hand caught the shawl and he dashed it to the ground. A small flame from it was enough to make the gin he had splashed around flare up. Panicking like a terrified animal, Colly ran but slipped backwards, the flames setting his shirt ablaze. Somehow he scrambled to his feet and, screaming in agony, dashed out of the cottage, scattering the crowd back from the doorway, his back, hair and arms well alight. Women and children screamed in horror and Matthias and Hunk Hunken ran after him to put out the flames.

By now Blake had located Rosina's motionless form. Gently lifting her up, and choking on the thickening smoke, he carried her outside, pushing away the helping hands he encountered. He knelt with her in his arms a good distance from the cottage. Gasping in fresh air, he pushed the hair back from Rosina's brow.

'Rosina!' He shook her gently then placed a hand over her heart. Panicking when he could feel nothing, he put his head on her chest, almost crying with relief at the faint heartbeat he could just hear.

Kneeling down beside them, Faith Bray rubbed the girl's wrists between her hands.

'Poor little maid,' she said, 'just look at her forehead.'

An ugly bruised swelling covered Rosina's temple, while blood trickled into her hair. An old woman pushed forward and tapped on Blake's shoulder.

'Here, Mr Blake. Put this blanket round the little maid. Tes a hot day, but she be in shock.'

Peter Blake looked up and met the old woman's encouraging smile. 'Thank you,' he said, his voice made husky by the smoke. 'I'll make sure it's returned to you.'

Not all those gathering round were to prove as friendly.

'You get your hands off she there,' a miner piped up suddenly, 'the likes of thee got no right to be touching her.'

Murmurs of assent went round the crowd and they pressed in closer to the group huddled on the ground. Faith Bray looked on worriedly as Peter Blake wrapped the ragged grey blanket around Rosina's limp body. Faith stood up when he rose, the girl held firmly in his arms.

'You, Peter Blake, you're not taking that maid anywhere,' Carn Bawden said, standing directly in front of him and folding his arms.

Peter Blake was not afraid or intimidated. He held his head high, looking from face to face. The miners who had tried to extinguish the fire in the Pearces' cottage had given up the task as hopeless and had joined their neighbours at the back of the gathering.

'Are you any better than me? Any of you?' Blake said in quiet anger.

The crowd fell silent to listen to what he would say next. They were joined by Matthias Renfree and Hunk Hunken who had returned, unsuccessfully from trying to catch up with Colly Pearce.

Blake included them in his next sentence. 'Did one man here among you ever try to stop what was happening to Rosina?'

Heads dropped and feet began to shuffle amidst the guilty silence.

'I thought not,' he continued. 'I've met Rosina many times on the downs during the last few weeks. I've not done a single thing to harm her and she's been happy with me. When she was with me today I determined not to let her return here again, but she slipped away from me. And look what happened. Her damned brother nearly killed her!'

Blake looked down at the girl in his arms. Rosina's eyes were open and she was looking back at him, bewilderment in her pale, pinched face.

'It's all right, my dearest,' he said tenderly. 'I'm taking you to my sister's house.'

Rosina closed her eyes with the merest trace of a smile, but as Blake took a step forward, a few miners stood their ground. Their faces were stern and unyielding, their whole stance threatening. Blake was not afraid. He would not leave without Rosina. He opened his mouth to speak but Matthias Renfree also had something to say and was a word ahead.

'Let Mr Blake through. He's right in what he said, and Rosina will receive better attention and medical care at his sister's house than we can provide for her here.'

Their young preacher had spoken and had an edge of authority in his voice enough to win the argument. The miners moved reluctantly aside and Hunk Hunken brought forward Blake's mare.

'Here, sir,' offered Jeb Bray. 'I'll hold the maid while you get on your horse.'

Blake looked doubtful and held Rosina a little tighter. He was not going to lose her now. Matthias moved forward and held out his arms.

'You can trust me,' he said. 'Rosina's place is with you now. I trust you to look after her.'

After another moment's hesitation Blake passed Rosina to him, taking her carefully into his arms again when mounted.

'May I call on you later today?' Matthias asked.

Blake nodded. 'What will you do about Rosina's brother?'

'We'll send a search party out for him... try to help him.'

'Don't tell him where Rosina is, Renfree. If I see him anywhere near her again, I'll kill him. I swear it.'

'I think he's too badly hurt to cause her any further trouble, Mr Blake,' Matthias said, sadly shaking his head.

'I have money in the mine,' Blake said, looking across to the stark black silhouette of the Wheal Ember engine house on the horizon. He cast his eyes over the ragged skinny children staring at him with huge eyes in skull-thin faces. 'Look at them... all too thin, all malnourished. Like Rosina. I'll send food and milk over every week for them. Will you oblige me, Renfree, by seeing they get it?'

'Indeed I will, Mr Blake, and thank you for your thoughtfulness.' Matthias said.

Blake quickly quieted the murmurs of dissent from the mining folk. 'Don't think of it as coming from me,' he said harshly. Then softening his voice, 'Think of it as coming from Rosina.'

Matthias Renfree felt guilty and ashamed as he watched Peter Blake lovingly wrap the blanket closer around the girl's unconscious body. Matthias had only made a half-hearted attempt at the one thing he could have done for Rosina, and even then she had seen right through him. Oh, he had prayed fervently for her deliverance, but hadn't the Good Lord given him a tongue and two good legs and arms to go to her aid as well?

Turning his back on the couple on horseback he said to the few miners who had not drifted off with the main body of the crowd, 'Let's go and find Colly. He'll need help.'

The Pearces' cottage was an inferno as Blake rode away with Rosina nestling close to him. She was fully awake now and held up the hand clutching the pendant.

'Peter,' she said in a whisper. 'It's broken.'

'Never mind, my precious angel. I'll have it repaired for you.' He smiled down at her. 'And as long as I have breath in my body, no one will harm as much as a hair on your head, ever again.'

–

For two days Colly Pearce, driven on only by pain and madness, had scrambled across the downs and on to the edge of the clifftop. He could make no distinction between light or darkness, night or day. The burnt flesh on the upper part of his body was putrid and stinking, and feasted on by a swarm of flies. By now he was dangerously dehydrated.

He had slept through the second day after the fire, unseen, only a hundred feet from Painted Bessie's kiddley. He woke to wander wildly about as twilight fell. The light was fading, the sea a restless marble green. A sliver of cloud cut the orange-red sun in half as it neared the horizon.

Colly loped and stumbled along the cliff edge, not seeing the beauty in the short stubbly gorse and heather in a patchwork cover of gold and purple stretching away inland. At times he cried for Rosina, one moment wanting to kill her, the next convinced he had and weeping wretchedly. Other times his mind regressed to his childhood and he was running happily over the heather on the downs holding his little sister's hand.

Slugs, and snails in patterned shells, slithered in abundance over the damp surface and Colly slipped on the wetness and stumbled in the deep rabbit holes repeatedly. Each time he managed to get to his feet he looked behind, thinking someone was following him. But his wavering vision could detect no movement, his ears, buzzing and whistling, no sound behind or to the side of him.

Colly loped on, singing a bawdy alehouse ditty, one breathless word at a time.

'If ever there was a comely wench, Tis sweet Annie Pol—'

He swung round and rubbed his eyes, listening hard for the sound of footsteps or the rustling of clothes. He could see nothing but cliff landscape, sky and sea, he could hear nothing except the sounds of the waves below and the wind whistling in his ears. Turning, he stumbled on.

'She's twice the woman now.'

Colly swung round again. The next word died in his throat, fear made his eyes bulge. His body lost control of its basic functions.

'YOU!' he gagged on the word, backing away with trembling hands held out in front of him, the scar on the palm of his right hand covered by a blister the size of a hen's egg.

The sun sat like a red disc on the horizon. A sound cut through the evening air and a straight line slashed across Colly's throat matched the fiery redness of the sun. He leaned forward, his blood gurgling in his throat and splashing on the extravagant white layers of lace that spilled from his attacker's coat sleeve.

Hezekiah Solomon wiped his blade on the front of his victim's shirt, his ice-cold eyes burning comfortlessly into Colly's until the miner's eyes rolled back in his head.

Colly Pearce died on his feet, and before his body could crumple, Hezekiah Solomon pushed the lifeless form over the cliff edge. Dressed as immaculately as ever, Hezekiah ripped off his blood-splashed cuffs and watched them flutter after Colly as he fell down the sheer edge before hitting some rocks in the savage water below. White froth

357

covered the broken body as waves crashed against the black granite. It moved at crazy angles at first, then slid into deeper water that held it up for a while, bobbing about as if in farewell to the world, before finally the sad remains of Colly Pearce were sucked out of sight for ever.

Hezekiah Solomon bent to wipe his bloodied hands clean in the wet grass and rose to breathe a contented smile. He looked out across the silvery sparkling sea and watched the red disc of warmth and light bid farewell to the day, before walking back to the kiddleywink. His white face was lit by a wide angelic smile.

Chapter 23

Kerensa was absorbed with arranging flowers in Oliver's study. Humming contentedly to herself, she didn't hear her husband creep up behind her.

'I've got something for you, my love,' he said proudly, almost in her ear.

'Oh!' A startled hand to her bosom, she turned round. 'Oh,' she said again, this time with delight.

Cradled in Oliver's arms, with bright appealing dark eyes and a black velvet ribbon tied in a bow on its collar, was a friendly-looking black puppy. Holding out her arms to take it, Kerensa laughed as it wriggled about excitedly while trying to lick her face.

'He's lovely, Oliver. Is he really mine?'

'Yes, he's all yours, my love. A descendant of old Dunstan. He's several weeks old now and could have left his mother a lot sooner. But I wanted to be certain you'd got over Dunstan's death before I brought him over from Ker-an-Mor for you.'

Gently stroking the puppy's velvety head, her face aglow, Kerensa said, 'Thank you, Oliver, he's wonderful.' And added with a shy smile, 'Like you.' She raised herself on tiptoe and tilted his face up to his.

Oliver thought if his gift warranted him as being 'wonderful' he deserved more than a peck and he kissed his wife soundly.

'Ah,' she said, a trifle breathlessly, fingering the animal's collar, 'now I see what you did with the ribbon I bought for you on May Day.'

'That's right,' he said, untying the bow and pulling away the length of velvet. 'He won't be needing this now. We don't want him looking effeminate.'

Kerensa studied the puppy's small square face. 'He's definitely no Hezekiah.'

Oliver laughed. 'A scruffy individual, this one. Nathan will show you how to train him, but make sure he's kept out of my study. I keep some important papers and documents in here.'

Kerensa put the puppy carefully down on the floor where he chewed at the hem of her dress before whimpering to be picked up again. Happy to indulge him, she crouched down and cuddled the warm squirming body to hers.

''e went be as spoilt as you are,' uttered Beatrice, flapping into the room.

'Who, me? Spoilt?' Oliver said, pointing to himself.

'Jus' 'ee look at un, maid,' Beatrice puffed on. 'Pretendin' 'e don't knaw what I be on 'bout. Bin spoilt, 'e 'ave, by ev'ry female in 'is life.'

Lifting the puppy, Kerensa moved over to Beatrice so the old woman could stroke him.

'Isn't he lovely, Beatrice? Did you know about him before today?'

'Fust I knawed of un, maid,' Beatrice rasped back, making watery guttural noises at the puppy. ''e never did tell nothin' to nobody. Deep 'e is… gettin' deeper, if 'ee asks me.'

'Well, he can sleep in Dunstan's old basket. I'll find him a new blanket after I've showed him to Polly, Ruth and Esther. Oh, and Jack will love to see him.'

'Ais, be proper luvly to see 'is 'an'some little small body in that em'ty basket.'

'I'd better find something for him to eat…'

'Ahem,' Oliver said loudly. When he had their full attention he continued, 'Now if you two ladies will take yourselves off and carry on your conversation elsewhere, I have work to do.'

'Of course,' returned Kerensa, walking over to him. 'I'll have to think of a name for the puppy. Have you any ideas, Oliver?'

'No,' he replied, shrugging his shoulders. 'Call him anything you care to, my dear, as long as it's not Tom.'

Oliver was halfway between standing and sitting when a stinging slap sent him hurtling to the floor and knocking over his chair.

'What the hell…?'

'I wouldn't dream of calling him after my grandfather,' Kerensa said crossly, looking down on his startled face. 'If you'll excuse me, I'm busy too. The Richards children have the flux again so Polly and I are going over to Rose Farm. Jack can look after the puppy until I get back. Oh, and another thing. I'll be grateful, Oliver, if you would not swear in the house.' With a toss of red hair Kerensa flounced out of the study with the puppy in her arms.

Beatrice laughed and laughed, tears streaming down her screwed-up face as she held her sagging stomach.

As he got to his feet Oliver ruefully rubbed his stinging cheek. 'What did I say? Why did Kerensa do that?' he appealed to the old woman.

'Looks… looks like 'ee've come… across,' Beatrice managed to get out through bouts of uproarious laughter, 'a female at last… who… who went spoil 'ee, me 'an'some.'

Righting his chair and picking up a pile of papers from his desk, Oliver shuffled them tersely until all the edges were neat and equal.

'I d'reckon 'ee'd best not be so free with they sarky words of yourn in future, boy.'

Beatrice wiped her grotesque wet face with her dirty apron and headed for the door, unable to stop herself from breaking out into fits of hearty chortles.

'And you had better not mention this to anyone else, Bea, not to *anyone*,' Oliver warned her, sitting down and reaching for his goose quill.

–

Finding Nathan O'Flynn waiting for her in the stableyard, Polly Berryman called out, 'Good evening,' to him.

'Good evening, m'dear,' he answered with a ready grin. 'All set for a nice long walk in this welcome cool breeze?'

Polly took Nat's arm. 'Not too far this evening if you please, Nathan,' she said as they walked off, 'I'm not feeling too good at the moment.' Peering at her downcast face, he said, 'Now you come to mention it, you don't look at all well, Polly. We'll go no further than halfway to the oaks, how about that, then?'

'A quarter of the way would be better.'

'In that case, just here will be fine,' said Nat. 'I'll not have you making yourself ill on my account.'

Stopping in the orchard they sat close together on the garden seat Kerensa had set near to Dunstan's grave.

'Are you sure you're all right, m'dear?' Nat asked kindly. 'Would you rather not go inside?' Polly smiled at his worried face. She was pleased and proud with Nat's courtship of her. The son of a poor immigrant farm labourer, he had received no good looks at birth or later in life. He had none of the social graces and was often awkward and clumsy away from his work, yet he was kind and caring, loyal and sensitive, with a delightful optimistic nature.

Ruffling his bushy dark hair Polly said, 'I'm just feeling a bit dizzy, that's all. It'll pass by the morning.'

'Lean yourself on my shoulder and close your eyes and take in a deep breath of this lovely fresh air,' Nat told her.

Settling comfortably against his shoulder she murmured, 'I can't remember such a hot dry summer for years. Thank goodness for a cool evening.'

'Aye, with such a harvest it means more hardship for the poor, and things are bad enough for them as it is.'

'At least the Pengarron Estate farmers and workers will fare better under Sir Oliver than others will under some landlords.'

'That's right enough.'

A chuckle escaped from Nat's throat and Polly sat up straight at the unexpected noise.

'And what's the matter with you, Nathan O'Flynn?'

'Oh, nothing really.'

'Well, it must have been something. You don't usually laugh when we're talking about something serious.'

'You mentioning his lordship made me think of something, that's all,' Nat said, kissing Polly's cheek.

'Made you think of what? I'll burst if you don't tell me,' she said, becoming keener by the moment to know the answer to this seeming mystery.

'Well,' he chuckled again. 'I couldn't help thinking about that little girl hitting his lordship to the floor. How I wish I'd been there to see it.'

'How do you know about that?' Polly was shocked. 'And where's your sense of manners? It's her ladyship, not "that little girl"!'

Nat was always somewhat amused at Polly's insistence on propriety.

'Sorry, Polly, but she'll always be that to me. When I first met her, I thought her too young to be attached even to Clem Trenchard. As to how I come to know about her slapping Sir Oliver, it was Beatrice who told me. Anyway, if I'm not supposed to know anything about it, how come you do?'

'Oh, that's simple enough,' Polly said, beginning to smile. 'I was looking for her ladyship to tell her her pony was saddled ready for our journey to Rose Farm.'

Looking all about them she leaned closer to whisper in Nat's ear, 'Actually, I saw it all from the open doorway.' She burst out laughing. 'It was so comical, Nathan. I had to go away and hide for ten minutes to stop myself laughing. If only you could have seen his lordship's face! It's a picture I'll never forget as long as I live.'

They laughed together and Nat said, 'I'd give a year of my life if I could see it. Fancy that though, Polly, a tall, muscular man like Sir Oliver being knocked off his feet by a slip of a girl.'

'Shh,' she said, looking around to be sure they were not being overheard. 'Don't forget you're not supposed to know anything about it, nor am I. His lordship warned Beatrice very firmly not to tell anyone what she saw and heard.'

'Then he should have warned her not to hit the gin bottle as well. She was well gone when she sang out the news to me, Jack and Barney, and on her way out to Painted Bessie's she stopped to tell Jake.'

'So it will be all round the parish by morning,' Polly said, holding her sides at a new outbreak of laughter.

'Aye, that it will. I reckon some will say Sir Oliver's young wife has got her own back on him at last.'

363

'Oh, my head,' murmured Polly, putting a hand to her brow. 'All this laughter is doing me no good.'

'Well then,' he said, placing a strong capable arm round her shoulders, 'close your eyes and settle down again, m'dear.'

Nathan brushed away a dozy wasp, then had to do it several times more before the insect flew away elsewhere.

'You… um… thought over the question I put to you the other evening?' he said.

'About becoming your wife you mean, Nathan?' she replied, smiling like a young girl.

'Aye, that's right enough. Well?'

With her eyes still closed Polly took his large hand between both of hers.

'I didn't come looking for a husband when I left Tolwithrick, nor did I ever really expect to get married, but… if it's all right with her ladyship, it's all right with me.'

Nat smiled, and resting his head against hers, he too closed his eyes under the coolness of the apple trees.

Chapter 24

Wide awake when Oliver came to bed in the night, Kerensa shaded her eyes from the glow of the candles he was holding.

'Still awake?' he said quietly, moving closer so he could read her face and ascertain her mood.

'I can't get to sleep,' she answered him, sitting up with one hand over her eyes and the other rubbing her neck.

'The light's bothering you,' Oliver remarked.

Putting the candles down out of her line of vision he sat on the bed beside her and touched her forehead.

'You're hot and freely perspiring, my love. Can I get you anything?'

'Polly left me some water on the table over there,' she said, pointing to the middle of the room. 'Will you pour me a glass, please?'

He did this, glancing at her often. As she took the glass from him Kerensa caught hold of his hand.

'I'm sorry I hit you, Oliver,' she said contritely.

'So am I,' he said, rubbing his cheek and giving a small laugh. 'You can slog with the best of them. I'm thinking of putting you up against Matthew King at his next wrestling match. I've not beaten him and Nathan O'Flynn made no impression on him, but I'm sure you would stand a good chance.'

'Mmmm… perhaps I'm not sorry after all, Oliver Pengarron. You thoroughly deserved it.'

Kerensa sipped from the glass. Oliver kissed the top of her head and, moving away, pulled off his boots and quickly undressed.

'Is it safe for me to get in bed,' he teased her, 'or are you going to hit me again?'

Kerensa pulled back the sheet, the only covering over the bed, and he got in beside her. She took another sip of water.

'I believe you are a good deal more of a baby than the baby's going to be,' she said dryly, as Oliver was winding his pocket watch.

'What! Are you…?' He dropped the watch on the bedside cabinet.

'I think I'm going to have a baby, yes,' she went on in a matter-of-fact voice. 'It's why I'm not feeling well.'

'Good, good,' he said enthusiastically, while throwing his arms about her and almost yanking her hot body against his. 'I mean good that you are pregnant, not that you're unwell. You deserve a big kiss for this, my precious love.

'You are hot, aren't you?' he said, taking his mouth from hers. 'You must take life easy for the next few months. We'll ask Beatrice for advice, she's an expert on childbearing.'

'Beatrice will probably say there's no need to take things easy, Oliver. Anyway, I'm fit and strong, always have been, and have always been active.'

'Even so, I won't allow you to expose yourself to other people's illnesses. You must not go over to Rose Farm again, at least until you have delivered the child. I don't want you taking any unnecessary risks, Kerensa.'

'There's no point in trying to help the Richards family,' Kerensa sighed, 'unless to send food over for the children. They have no real desire to keep themselves or the farmhouse clean, so they will always suffer from the fevers.'

Oliver kissed the top of her head in consolation. 'There will always be people like that in the world, my love.'

'I do fear for them, 'specially the children. They look at me with such big trusting eyes, and there's nothing I can really do, with their parents the way they are.'

'You did your best, my love, be content with that for now.'

Kerensa sighed and rested a hand protectively on her stomach. 'Oliver, did your mother have a doctor to attend her?'

'Certainly not. Pengarrons have never approved of doctors. Concoction-giving charlatans, the lot of them.'

'You are huffy about doctors, aren't you? I must admit I've always found the thought of them rather frightening... like magistrates.'

'And titled wealthy men?' he asked teasingly.

'Those particularly,' she replied, smiling while finishing her drink of water.

Oliver took the empty glass from her. 'Have you decided yet what you will call the puppy?'

'Yes. Bob.'

'Bob? As a derivative of your father's name?'

'Not really,' Kerensa said sleepily, snuggling under the sheet. 'The Richards children chose it for me... and they never need slapping...'

She was restless all night keeping Oliver awake in the process. When he rose at five she was sleeping fitfully, and felt much hotter to the touch of his fingers on her brow. After dressing he decided to seek out Beatrice and get her to make up an infusion of herb tea to bring down his wife's temperature. He was fortunate to find the old crone asleep in her chair in the kitchen and not to have to go searching for her. It took a long while to rouse her from her drunken slumbers. She grumbled profusely as Oliver got her unsteadily to her feet, but calmed herself quickly when he sternly told her what he required her to do. She shuffled off, grunting like an old sow, to her well-stocked, pungent-smelling medicine cupboard.

Oliver was bringing the puppy in from the garden when he startled Esther as he came through the kitchen door. Settling Bob in his basket, he asked her to give the puppy a drink of milk and to bring his own breakfast to the smaller dining room in an hour, then headed for the stables for his morning ride. He made straight for Pengarron Point to ponder on the prospect of becoming a father. On his arrival back he struck Jack with wonder by tossing him Conomor's reins and singing happily on his way into the Manor house.

He ran up the wide staircase to check on Kerensa and was met with confusion.

'Oh, sir!' cried Ruth, meeting him halfway on her way down. 'Her ladyship is that sick. Polly too.'

Esther appeared next, rushing up behind him, carrying a large pitcher of steaming hot water.

'What's that for?' Oliver demanded to know.

'To clean up her ladyship, sir. She's been that sick.'

'She wasn't that bad when I left her an hour ago!' he exclaimed. Dodging around Ruth, Oliver took the stairs three steps at a time and burst through the bedroom door. He found Beatrice holding Kerensa up as she retched over a bowl.

'I'll take her, Beatrice,' he said at once.

'Be gentle with the poor cheeil,' the old woman said in a whisper, struggling to get her massive weight back on her feet, as they changed places.

'How long has Kerensa been like this?' Oliver asked, as her body heaved violently and she gulped for breath after each bout.

''cordin' to Ruth it musta started as soonas 'ee went fer yer ride an' I wus sortin' through me cupboard fer somethin' fer the poor little maid.'

Clutching her stomach Kerensa groaned as the vomiting stopped. She looked mournfully at Oliver but could not speak. She fell back into his arms, her body visibly shaking, her nightgown soaked in perspiration. Esther wrung out a towel and washed Kerensa's face, neck and hands.

'I'll get her a clean nightgown, sir,' she said quietly.

'Thank you. Has someone been to see Polly?' Oliver asked her.

'Yes, sir. She's been sick, but doesn't seem nowhere as bad as her ladyship is,' Esther answered, searching in a chest of drawers. When she found a nightgown she looked distastefully at the contents of the bowl. 'If you can manage with this, sir,' she said, holding out the garment towards him, 'I'll take that away. There's another one by the bed if it's needed.'

'Thank you, Esther,' Oliver said gratefully. 'It certainly doesn't help having that in here.'

Covering her nose and mouth with her apron, Esther picked up the offending bowl and hurried out of the room.

Kerensa moaned, her head rolling back on Oliver's arm, so weak now she had lost consciousness.

'Get that maid out of that wet gown 'fore she catches 'er death of cold,' Beatrice instructed him. 'I'll 'elp 'ee.'

They pulled the gown over and off Kerensa's burning hot body. The movements brought her round and she moaned feebly.

'Leave... me... be...'

'It's all right, my love,' Oliver said tenderly, 'we'll soon have you dry and comfortable.'

Rapidly, Beatrice towelled down Kerensa's damp skin and Oliver pulled the fresh nightgown over her head. Together they eased the cool linen garment down to cover her decently, then Oliver lifted Kerensa and held her while sitting on the bed.

'I'll get the other bowl ready,' the old woman said.

Oliver took note of her worried face. 'You think there is more to come, Beatrice?'

'I'm 'fraid so, me 'an'some. This is no ordinary mornin' sickness. I bin thinkin' 'bout Polly too. They wus both over to they Richards yes'day.'

'You think they ate something bad over there?'

'Or drunk somethin' mebbe.'

'Beatrice,' Oliver said, his brain working fast, 'tell Jack to ride over to Rose Farm to see how the Richards are faring. Tell him not to eat or drink anything while there, and if they are very ill to go on to Perranbarvah and inform the Reverend Ivey and Mrs Tregonning. She may be able to help the family, and the Reverend can check if there's an epidemic breaking out.'

'Right away, me 'an'some, don't 'ee worry now.'

Beatrice hastened to the door then Oliver called her back.

'Do you think Kerensa is pregnant, Bea?'

'She may be, I s'pose, boy, but I can't see no signs of nothin' and I'm never wrong.'

'No, you're never wrong about that,' Oliver said to himself, when she'd left the room.

Esther returned with the bowl, emptied and clean. She raced over and pushed it under Kerensa's chin as the retching and vomiting began again. This time nothing was left in the girl's stomach to be brought up and she cried out miserably, making the other two in the room wince each time. When the spasms were finally over she slipped away into total unconsciousness. Her breathing was laboured, the fresh nightgown already showing signs of dampness.

'It would be better if you laid her ladyship down,' Esther said, 'You'll only make her hotter holding her like that, if you don't mind me saying so, sir.'

'You're right,' he said, and reluctantly laid Kerensa's still form on the bed sheet, covering her loosely with the top sheet only up to her waist. Oliver and Esther stood side by side for many moments, staring down on the girl in the huge bed.

'She looks so small,' Esther murmured to herself.

Glancing at the tall woman at his side Oliver said grimly, 'Too small, too pale, and far too young to be ill like this.'

'She'll be all right, won't she, sir?' Esther grew more alarmed as he remained silent. 'Sir? Sir?'

'She must be… she must be,' he whispered finally.

Beatrice, Ruth and Esther took turns to sit in the bedroom throughout the day with their sick mistress. Oliver refused to move outside the door to eat, to drink, or for any other reason. He paced the bedroom carpet, stopping at intervals to look down at Kerensa or to touch the things laid out neatly on her dressing table. Picking up her gilt-edged mirror he looked at his own reflection for a moment, then putting it down he picked up the tin fish-shaped brooch she often wore, turning it over and over in his hand and wondering why she treasured it.

The top drawer of the dressing table had been opened, presumably by Kerensa to take something out before her sickness overwhelmed her. Oliver lightly touched the items of her underclothes, shifts of soft white material, silk stockings, handkerchieves, things all very personal to her. His eye caught a small bundle of cloth in the corner of the drawer. He pulled it apart, and at once recognised the contents as Clem Trenchard's love tokens. The discovery made him catch his breath. So Kerensa was still in love with the blond farmer's son? She cherished his lock of hair, his kerchief, his flowers, given to her from out of his love. Oliver put the find back exactly as he had found it. He went to the bedside and looked down at his ailing young wife. Her eyes were open but she did not know he was there.

He knelt, took her hand and stroked her hot damp forehead. He said in a husky whisper, 'So there's more than just this fever that could take you away from me.'

She rallied occasionally but only to retch dryly. Oliver held her and helped to dab her burning hot body with cool water.

The Reverend Joseph Ivey was shown into the bedroom close to mid-day, bringing with him the awful news that all the Richards family, with the exception of Rudd, were taken with the same malady, two of the children seemingly close to death. An epidemic of typhus or something of the kind was thankfully not apparent elsewhere from his enquiries, the sickness appearing to be confined to the tenants of Rose Farm and its two visitors of the previous day.

Sitting unobtrusively in a corner of the darkened room the Reverend quietly prayed. He was afraid for Kerensa's life as Oliver and the servants were. He wanted to know why, just when it was becoming apparent that Oliver and Kerensa were getting along well together, had something like this happened?

His guilt at performing the marriage ceremony had reached a comfortable level after Old Tom's funeral when he had seen the close-ness Oliver and Kerensa shared. With Clem Trenchard now married to Alice Ford, and with the invaluable, unstinting help Kerensa was giving to the needy folk of the parish, the Reverend had begun to believe it was not after all an unfortunate thing she was married to Oliver. Kerensa was good for the parish, the Pengarron Estate, and seemingly for its proud master.

The Reverend Ivey had sat in many a sick room, attended many a deathbed, giving comfort to the patient and the relatives during each harrowing occasion. But if Kerensa died, he felt he would need as much comfort as the others who would be bereaved. He stayed for twenty minutes, standing beside the bed, before going to Rose Farm. Before leaving he lifted Kerensa's moist limp hand and sighed deeply.

'I do wish you would let me send to Marazion for Doctor Crebo,' he said.

'No,' Oliver retorted. 'There's been more people died at the hands of those wretches than have lived. Kerensa will fare better in the care of Beatrice... and God.'

371

'I beg you to reconsider, Oliver. It's ten years since Arthur Besweth-erick died from neglect on the battlefield and the Army surgeon responsible was drunk at the time.'

A vision of his closest friend bleeding to death on Dettingen soil, and he having to watch helplessly while it happened, made Oliver shudder and become angry. As Kerensa moaned he turned sharply away from the Reverend and whispered soothing words to her, placing the square of damp linen on her forehead.

'I beg you to think hard about it,' the Reverend persisted. 'Doctor Crebo is not of the old school of thought – leeches to cure everything and endless bleedings when it is obvious it will only cost the patient his life. He's dedicated to his skills and he… did an excellent piece of work patching up Peter Blake. And you know only too well he was most seriously hurt.'

Fury flared within Oliver. He was sitting on the bed and stood up slowly to tower above the parson.

'Did you not hear me clearly say no, Reverend Ivey?' he asked through gritted teeth, his full temper only kept under control because he was in a sick room.

But the Reverend remained unruffled. 'I heard you distinctly, Oliver, and I'm sorry to bring up the subject of Peter Blake, knowing how hurt you were at what he did. But, remember, it is Kerensa that we are concerned about now. I'm very, very fond of her and I want her to have every opportunity of making a full recovery.' Oliver was forced to think deeply, but was still torn when he made his decision.

'Ask this Doctor Crebo to come and observe if he'd care to, but I'll not guarantee to allow him to touch my wife.'

Kerensa's condition changed to one of severe delirium about the same time Ruth informed Oliver that Polly had not been sick for over two hours, her fever was abating and she had asked for a drink of water.

'I take it she is well enough to tell us about their visit to Rose Farm now,' he said soberly.

'She has already, sir. Seems they sipped a little water to encourage the children to drink. Polly only sipped with one child while her ladyship, bless her, sipped with all of them. It's got to be the reason why she's so much worse.'

'And they ate nothing?'

'No, sir.'

'Then it has to be the water supply on Rose Farm, it must be contaminated,' Oliver said. 'Is Nathan O'Flynn about?'

'Yes, sir,' Ruth replied. 'He's downstairs asking if he can see Polly. Will it be all right, sir?'

Oliver nodded. 'Tell him to keep it brief, Ruth, then to get over to Rose Farm and locate the source of the trouble, and to take fresh water from here for the Richards.'

'Yes, sir.' Ruth curtsied. She threw a worried glance at the girl writhing and muttering gibberish on the bed, and wiped tears from her eyes when she left the room.

A short time later Kerensa cried out in nightmare and Oliver held her and rocked her like an infant. She seemed to sense him there and quieted, twisting her fingers in his shirt to keep him close. He smoothed her damp hair away from her pale face that accentuated its glossy redness, giving her an ethereal quality that frightened him. Tears glistened on his cheeks, and for once there was no Pengarron pride to forbid their display.

Doctor Charles Crebo arrived at the Manor house in the late afternoon. He was shown into the master bedroom by a weeping Ruth. He found a dirty fat old woman staring into space sitting at the side of an enormous heavily draped four-poster bed, and his apparently sleeping patient held too tightly by her black-haired husband whose head was buried in the pillow beside her.

'Sir Oliver… Dr Charles Crebo at your service, sir,' the surgeon-physician said briskly. 'The Reverend Ivey of Perranbarvah said you might have need of me.'

Oliver looked up, his voice pained and husky. 'My wife, doctor.' By now he was prepared to clutch at anything to save Kerensa's life. 'Can you help, please.'

'I'll do what I can,' promised Charles Crebo.

'All we can do now is to wait,' the doctor announced a short time later.

'Is there nothing you can give my wife?' asked Oliver. 'Are you sure?'

'Your servant says she managed to give her a few drops of strong camomile tea, Sir Oliver. In your wife's case that was probably the best thing to do. Hopefully it will have cleared her stomach and gone some way to purifying her system, and she's taken spoonfuls of cooled boiled water to ward off dehydration. There is nothing I can give her to make any difference to her condition.'

Kerensa moved her head from side to side and murmured, 'Dunstan… Dunstan…'

Charles Crebo looked at Oliver.

'Our old dog,' he explained. 'It was killed a few weeks ago.'

'I see. And your wife, presumably, was very fond of the dog?'

'Yes, she was… she's gone through some terrible experiences this year. Dr Crebo, last night my wife told me she thought she was with child. You've examined her, what is your opinion?'

'Well,' the doctor said, rubbing his chin and putting his thumbs in his faded waistcoat pockets, 'there were no visible signs of pregnancy that I could see. Without asking her one or two questions I really couldn't say at the moment. Of course, it could be early days yet.'

Kerensa stirred restlessly and murmured her husband's name.

'It's all right, my love,' he said, taking her hand and gently kissing it.

'What happens now?' he asked Charles Crebo.

The other man sighed. 'Your wife will reach crisis point before the night is over, Sir Oliver.'

'And what do you believe her chances to be, Dr Crebo?'

'I only hope she has a strong constitution and fighting spirit, or I'm afraid a lot more against than for. I'm sorry. She appears generally fit and strong and you say she's come through earlier ordeals. Cling to that. I'll call back later tonight.'

Oliver ordered Beatrice and the King sisters to stay out of the room unless he rang for them. He cradled Kerensa in his arms again. If he was going to lose her, he wanted to hold her close for every precious second. He thought back over the eight short months he had known her, recalling every moment, every word, every smile he could.

Gloom settled over the house like a heavy black cloud and did not go unnoticed when Dr Crebo returned at eight in the evening in the company of the Reverend Ivey whom he had met on the road. He shook his head sadly on declaring Kerensa's heartbeat and breathing had become weaker, and released his patient into the parson's hands. Declining to stay to join in the prayers, he retired downstairs to wait for the Reverend Ivey to join him in a glass of port.

As the doctor made his way to the parlour, Jack was sitting up in the hayloft of the stables, tears of grief and helplessness streaming down his thin young face as he stroked Kerensa's sleeping puppy. Elsewhere, Jake Angove and Barney Taylor sat together smoking their pipes in ominous silence. Ruth and Esther sniffed back tears as they went about their work, unable to sit still in the dreadful wait, while Beatrice sat on one side of Polly's bed, holding her hand, and on the other side Nathan O'Flynn did the same.

–

'Can I come in?'

Oliver was surprised to see it was Alice who had popped her head round the door.

'Of course,' he said. 'Close the door.'

She quietly crossed the room, sitting herself on the bed beside him. Gently she stroked Kerensa's deathly white cheek. Kerensa did not stir. She had not moved at all for a long time.

'The whole estate knows about her.'

Oliver looked at her swollen body.

'She was so happy last night,' he told her. 'Kerensa believed she was pregnant. If she is and if she… dies, I'll lose them both, Alice.'

He looked so wretched, quite unlike the self-assured, proud man she was used to seeing. Reaching out, she took his hand for a moment.

'You comforted me once when I needed someone badly. I wish there was something I could do now to help you, Oliver.'

He put his hand on her shoulder. 'I know. Just stay for a while and pray for her.'

Alice kept a short vigil with her ex-mistress, bending over to kiss Kerensa's cheek before making to leave.

'So pale and so hot,' she said, looking at the other girl and willing her to move if only a fraction, just to prove there was a small part of her fighting to live. 'Can I get you anything before I go?' she asked Oliver.

'No, but thank you for coming, Alice. It has meant a lot to me,' he replied, holding out his hand to her.

'Oliver,' she said, 'I don't want you to be upset by what I'm going to say, but – I didn't come alone. Clem's downstairs. He would like to see Kerensa.' She watched closely for his reaction.

He was thinking, his face holding no clue to his feelings. It was not long before he spoke.

'All right, Alice. Tell him he can come up.'

Clem was dressed in his Sunday best clothes, his fair hair brushed tidily back from his face. Oliver was struck by his youth and vulnerability, and an unexpected feeling of guilt replaced some of the dislike he had long harboured for the young man.

Clem said, 'Thank you for letting me see her.'

'You love her too,' Oliver replied simply.

He had laid Kerensa down and was standing beside the bed for Clem's visit. Clem moved forward, his heart turning at the sight of the girl lying on the lace-edged pillows. He had not seen her like this before, deathly pale except for a feverish spot on each cheek, looking as though she already belonged to another world. She did not move, not even an eyelash.

'It was bad enough when I lost her once,' Clem said very quietly, 'but at least I could see her from time to time. It helped. Hating you helped. But if she dies, if she's gone for good... I...' The words stuck in his throat and Oliver touched his arm.

'Will you take a glass of brandy with me, Trenchard? I think we both need one.'

Clem nodded, keeping his eyes on Kerensa as Oliver poured the brandy and handed him a large glassful.

'Kerensa always frowns at me having liquor in the bedroom. She never says anything, just has a way of looking at you to let you know how she feels and take the pleasure out of it at the same time.'

'Yes I know what you mean. She looked at me like that once or twice, and Old Tom all the time.'

'Of course, being bloody-minded, I do it all the more.'

It would not have been believed the day before: Sir Oliver Pengarron and Clem Trenchard, rivals in love, united now in grief and worry, conversing amiably and drinking brandy together.

Kerensa opened her eyes. Everything was hazy but as her vision cleared she blinked hard at seeing Clem's fair figure standing beside Oliver's taller dark one. The glasses they held caught the candle-light, hurting her eyes, and she closed them again. Finding the scene amusing, she smiled. The two men had seen her eyelids close and together they called her name. She did not hear them, having sunk deeply back into a dark floating warmth.

The Reverend Ivey opened the door, but on seeing the two men together quietly closed it again without either of them noticing. He walked slowly back down the stairs, gratified that they could put the past ill-feeling behind them at such an anxious time.

Clem put his glass down and held out his hand. Oliver accepted it.

'Kerensa's your wife,' Clem said, 'so I'll go now and leave you alone together. I don't know if I will ever forgive you for taking her from me, but if love has any power, then ours for her will be enough to bring Kerensa safely through this.'

When he reached the door, Oliver said, 'Trenchard, you and Alice may stay for the night if you would like to… stay until we know either way.'

Doctor Crebo made a last examination at ten o'clock. He could find no change in Kerensa's condition and affirmed his intention of returning soon after dawn of the following day. Alice slept fitfully on a sofa in the parlour, Clem getting up from his chair every so often to rearrange the blanket Beatrice brought in for her. He didn't sleep at all. The Reverend Ivey dozed in the armchair opposite him, dreading a shake on the shoulder that would summon him for final prayers in the master bedroom upstairs.

Chilled air, sharpened with a hint of frost, chased away the darkness, leaving a sky of moody grey. Oliver woke with a start, furious with himself for dropping off to sleep and frightened Kerensa might have slipped away from him without his knowledge. Of the numerous candles in the room only two had not burnt out and the curtained windows were keeping the room quite dark but he could see her grey-green eyes were wide open, not moving, not even blinking. He stared at her, his entire body cold and rigid with fear.

'Don't hold me so tightly, Oliver. I can hardly breathe,' she said in a voice which was barely audible.

'What did you say?' he said, quite stunned.

'Please… don't hold me so tightly.'

A cry of relief broke from the depths of his being. Half-laughing, half-crying, he smothered her with kisses until Kerensa weakly tried to push him away. She felt immediate relief as Oliver slackened his hold on her and knew the sickly sweet smell in the stuffy room came from her own sweating body. She badly wanted to be washed and put into a clean nightgown, and to be held lightly again by the strong arms that held her now, to have the same face close to hers, as it was when she had woken and her sight had cleared.

'Are you all right, my precious love? Are you feeling better? Can I get you anything? Oh, thank God! Thank God! Say something, anything.'

'Can I sit up, please?' she asked, her voice soft and weak.

Beatrice, woken up on her chair outside the door by his cries, shuffled into the room with a broad smile on her ugly face. 'Leave 'er be, boy,' she rasped, asserting her old authority over him and taking on the air that, as usual, women knew what was best where the sick were concerned, and men only got in the way. 'Yourn doin' the little maid no good like that.' She pushed Oliver aside and efficiently banged the pillows back into shape, sitting Kerensa up against them.

'Can we come in?' The Reverend Ivey was peeping round the door, the others from downstairs lined up behind him. 'We won't stay long, the doctor has just arrived too.'

'Yes, yes,' Oliver said joyfully, brushing back his hair, tidying his shirt and beckoning with bold hands. 'Come in, all of you.'

'Only for a while,' Beatrice rasped, now she was in charge of Kerensa.

Kerensa looked at each smiling face, returning a weak smile to them all. The smile changed to surprise when she saw Clem and Alice.

'I thought I was dreaming when I saw you with Oliver last night,' she said to Clem.

He smiled wanly at her. 'I will always be grateful to Sir Oliver for letting me visit you. It's so good to see you beginning to look well again.'

He placed his arm protectively on Alice's shoulders. He knew it must have been hard for her to have his love for Kerensa declared so publicly, and was grateful for and proud of his wife's forbearance.

'Thank the Lord for your recovery, Kerensa, we were so frightened we were going to lose you,' breathed Alice, quite forgetting all formalities. 'We'll be going now and will spread the good news.'

'I didn't realise you thought I was so ill,' said Kerensa.

'Well, you were, and you still have a long way to go before you'll be up and around again.'

Kerensa stretched out a hand to her friend. It dropped weakly almost at once as proof of Alice's words. 'I see what you mean.' She smiled. 'Thank you for coming, but don't go until you've had breakfast then Jack can take you home in the trap.'

'It's very kind of you but we'll be going all the same. We came over last evening in the cart and Clem has got to get back for the milking. Besides, the family will be anxious to know how you are.'

'All right, go if you must, but promise me you'll visit me soon.'

'I promise.'

To words of sincere thanks from Oliver, the Trenchards left, followed a short time later by the Reverend Ivey who hurried away to put Mrs Tregonning's worried mind at rest. The King sisters left the room to prepare the breakfast and to see to Polly while Beatrice helped Kerensa to freshen up and change her nightgown for the doctor's examination.

'So I arrive to good news, then?' remarked Charles Crebo brightly, tossing his cape on a chair on his way to the bed.

'Yes,' Oliver said, sitting down on the bed, suddenly overcome by exhaustion. He squeezed Kerensa's hand and kissed her cheek. 'You feel just nicely warm now, my love.'

'Out of my way, Sir Oliver,' said Dr Crebo sternly. 'In fact, out of the bedroom altogether while I examine her ladyship. Do something to make yourself more presentable. I'm sure you don't want to look at him like that for long, do you, my lady?' he said to Kerensa with a twinkle in his eye.

'I don't mind,' she said sleepily, the effect of her many visitors now telling on her.

'I'll be back soon,' he reassured Kerensa, aware for the first time of his need to shave and attend to the other things contributing to his unkempt appearance. He gave Kerensa one more kiss.

'You'll take breakfast with me later I trust, Doctor Crebo?'

'Most kind of you, Sir Oliver,' Charles Crebo accepted. 'Now, my lady, let's have these curtains opened and a window or two, eh? We'll have you up and about in no time, won't we, Beatrice? I must say, I did not expect to find that you had pulled through this morning. You must be quite a fighter.' He glanced at the door Oliver had passed through. 'Got something really important to live for...'

Fastening the studs on the sleeves of a clean shirt Oliver looked out of the window of his dressing room to where Jack could be seen playing with Bob, Kerensa's puppy. He shook his head sadly. When Kerensa was strong enough he had the hard task of telling her that Rudd Richards' wife and family were all dead. Naming her puppy was probably the last joyful thing Rudd's children had done.

Chapter 25

A few days later, as Kerensa sat cushioned and cosseted in front of a well built-up fire in her sitting room, Polly appeared to ask her if she would see a visitor.

'Yes!' Kerensa answered eagerly. 'Anyone. I'm going quietly mad, the way you all keep me just sitting about wrapped up like an old woman, Polly.' And she flicked at the blanket wrapped around her lap.

'You know his lordship won't let you do very much until he's sure you've completed your convalescence, as per doctor's orders.' Polly folded her arms and looked at Kerensa in a no-nonsense fashion. 'And neither will I.'

Kerensa made a face at Polly, but not unkindly. 'Well, tell me who my visitor is? It's not the good Doctor Crebo, Reverend Ivey, Alice, Lady Rachael or Mrs Tregonning. I can tell by your face it's someone who doesn't usually call on me.'

'You're right,' Polly replied, looking as if she wanted to say a lot more and was sorry she couldn't. 'It's a Miss Rosina Pearce.'

'Rosina! This is a welcome surprise. Show her in at once, Polly.'

'Don't get up, Kerensa,' Rosina implored her, as she shyly entered the room, 'I don't want to tire you.'

'Sit down,' Kerensa invited, as Polly departed to fetch the inevitable tea tray, 'and make yourself comfortable, Rosina. We're both recovering at the moment. How are you? It's good to see you again.'

Rosina was wearing good quality clothes and Kerensa, knowing she was staying at the house of Josephine Courtis, assumed the sharp-faced widow had provided them for her.

'I'm very well, thank you, and I'm glad to see you're getting over your ordeal. I'm sorry about Rudd Richard's family, they were good people.'

'Yes, it was a terrible tragedy,' Kerensa said, moved close to tears as she was every time the Richards were mentioned or she thought of them.

'I'm sorry. I didn't come to upset you, Kerensa.' Rosina said humbly.

'Oh, I'm all right, Rosina, don't you get worried about me getting weepy, that's not your fault. I'm delighted to see you, and now that… well, you can come as often as you like can't you?'

'I don't know,' Rosina answered in a small voice, 'after you've heard what I've come to tell you, you might not want me calling on you again.'

Kerensa looked at her sharply and made to protest but Polly came in, poured the tea and left again, before she could ask Rosina what she meant. 'It can't be that bad, surely, Rosina? What could you possibly do to upset anyone that much, let alone me?'

Rosina looked at the tea in her cup, then up at Kerensa. 'What if I say I'm going to marry Peter Blake?'

'You're what!' Kerensa didn't try to hide her shock.

Rosina put down her cup and saucer. 'You probably know what happened at Colly's hands up on Lancavel Downs? That Peter was there and I've been recovering at the home of his half-sister, Mistress Courtis?'

Kerensa stared and nodded.

'For quite a while before Colly hurt me that last time, I had been meeting Peter secretly on the moors. I know what he did to you, Kerensa, it was despicable, and if you can't forgive him, well, that's understandable. But Peter was good to me, he never looked to hurt me or behave in any forward way at all. This is probably hard for you to understand, Kerensa, but we fell in love on those innocent meetings on the moors and now we're getting married. I wanted to come and tell you myself. You've been a good friend to me and I believe I owe you that.'

Kerensa had gone a little pale. She gulped at her tea to give her time to think what to say. She didn't want to hurt Rosina but the memories of Blake's attack on her, and through that the loss of Dunstan, still filled her with pain. She could think of Peter Blake only with animosity.

'When… when will this marriage take place?' Kerensa said finally.

Rosina stood up. She knew, as she had expected, that Kerensa had received her news unfavourably.

'I know it's very quick, just three weeks since Peter took me away from Lancavel Downs, but we see no reason to wait. We don't want any fuss so we're getting married on special licence tomorrow. Only Peter's half-sister and his housekeeper, and Matthias Renfree who's befriended us, will be there. I'm sorry my news has distressed you, it wasn't my intention. I'll leave now. I hope you'll soon be completely recovered. Good bye, Kerensa.'

'Rosina!' Kerensa pushed off the blanket and rushed to the other girl. 'Please don't leave like this. I can't agree with what you're doing… but I don't want you to leave with any bad feelings between us.'

Rosina turned and smiled in her own serene way. 'Thank you, Kerensa. I know you'll find it hard to believe but Peter is sorry for what he did to you. I hope one day you will be able to forgive him, for your own sake as much as mine and his. I won't come again, I know it wouldn't be acceptable to you. You won't be able to look at me without thinking of Peter and I would find it difficult not being able to talk about him. Perhaps one day in the future things will be different.'

'Perhaps,' Kerensa said, but not seeing how or when that would be. 'It's been a difficult year for us both, Rosina. And even Alice has trouble facing me at times because she feels guilty about marrying Clem. But that's not fair because it was me who broke Clem's heart and it's no concern of mine what he does now. I do wish you happiness, Rosina. I hope it will turn out all right for you.'

They exchanged a brief hug and Rosina walked away to begin her new life. Kerensa sat down and wrapped the blanket around her tightly, and pondered sadly over the fact that yet another person in her life could now have very little to do with her.

A few days later Alice met Rosina at Marazion marketplace. Alice had been enjoying herself buying from the stalls. The previous night Clem had taken part in a smuggling run with Matthew King and Samuel Drannock, bringing in goods under canvas into Perranbarvah, and had given her the few shillings he had earned. She knew at once what she wanted to spend the money on, clothes for her baby, and had been set on buying them herself. She had nagged Florrie Trenchard, who had tried to insist she ought to stay at home with her feet up, until her mother-in-law had agreed on her going to market with Morley if she promised to be quick around the stalls and back to the farm cart.

Alice greeted Rosina with an affectionate hug and looked her up and down. 'Well, you're looking better than I've ever seen you, I'm glad to say,' she said, cutting through the noise of the hawkers, the animal grunts and squawks, and two middle-aged women with the look of tradesmen's wives who were arguing close by over their right to purchase a length of fine quality white lawn. Alice took pleasure in Rosina's happy shining face and her elegant but simple new clothes and shoes.

'Married life agrees with me,' Rosina returned, sweeping herself and Alice out of the way of a small boy desperately chasing a runaway piglet. 'I expect you heard...?'

'Yes, Kerensa told me,' Alice replied, not able to decide on a suitable expression for her face with her loyalty divided between her two friends, although she had been just as horrified as Kerensa at first.

'I take it you don't approve either?'

'Well, I don't know, Rosina,' Alice said truthfully. 'I understand Kerensa's feelings... it's rather a difficult situation. I suppose, when you look at it, all three of us have married men this year we wouldn't have dreamt of. I have to admit you look radiant, Rosina, and if anyone deserves some happiness it's you.'

'Thank you, Alice,' Rosina beamed. 'How are you keeping these days?'

'Well, not without my little discomforts,' she said, smoothing a hand down over her bulge. 'Anyway, I'm here to buy some clothes for this little one. Would you like to help me choose?'

'I'd love to,' Rosina replied, catching some of her excitement.

Alice was able to bypass the cheaper stalls and went straight to one known for its high quality because there was another sum of money burning a hole in her purse, one of the guineas Sir Oliver Pengarron had given to her, and she knew Clem would take little interest in what she bought or ask the cost. Alice was proud to be able to spend freely in front of Rosina, who was now a rich man's wife, and proud that her baby would begin its life in clothes of superior quality and appearance to those a working-class baby usually wore. With Rosina's encouragement she bought three beautifully smocked gowns, skeins of yellow and blue wool, to knit warm clothes for the baby's first winter, and a bolt of woollen material to make soft warm blankets.

Alice was glowing as Rosina walked along beside her, carrying her parcels, but kept stopping to raise each foot alternately and relieve it of her weight.

Rosina looked down at Alice's dusty hemline. 'You need a good rest off those poor feet of yours. Come back with me to our rooms over the shoemaker's and have some tea.'

'Well, I don't know about that,' she said doubtfully. 'Are you sure your husband won't mind?'

'No, no. Peter will be delighted. Please come,' Rosina implored, smiling radiantly. 'I haven't had a visitor of my own there yet. You will be the first… please, Alice?'

'Oh, go on then, just for a little while,' she capitulated, but for Rosina's sake rather than for herself.

Linking her other arm through Alice's, Rosina led the way through the heaving throng of people intent only on their own business, then helped Alice to climb the stairs over Angarrack's shop.

'You will have to keep off your feet more, Alice, if you can,' Rosina counselled, turning her key in the lock and ushering her guest into a large comfortable sitting room. 'Give me your shawl and choose the chair you will be most comfortable in.'

A girl of twelve appeared in the room and curtseyed to them both. 'Shall I make fresh tea for 'ee, Mistress Blake?' she asked shyly, ending with a giggle.

'Yes, please, Kate.' Rosina smiled at the young girl to put her at her ease. 'You know Mrs Trenchard, don't you?'

Alice greeted Kate, the daughter of the late miner Richard Astley, who quickly made off to the kitchen.

'It was good of you to take on little Kate, Rosina,' she remarked as she allowed her feet to be put up on an upholstered stool. 'You're as bad as Clem's mother, gran and little sister,' she added lightly, 'they're always on about me taking things easier.'

'Well, if a woman can't be pampered at a time like this, when can she?' Rosina said, piling cushions behind Alice's back. 'There,' she said when satisfied. 'You were saying something about Kate? Oh, yes. Peter's housekeeper is very good but inclined to outbursts of hysterics. He wanted me to have someone calmer about the place when he had to go out, to fetch and carry for me while I was getting better. Kate will be glad it's you who's here today, she's terrified of Peter's sister.'

'Are you completely recovered now, Rosina?' Alice asked, in the way one can only to a friend.

'Yes,' the other girl answered at once, her voice dropping with each succeeding word, 'it's only a short time since Colly nearly killed me and I've forgiven him for that. I'd feel a lot better if I knew where he is and if he's well.'

'Someone will find him soon, I'm sure.'

But Rosina was under no such illusions. 'To be honest with you, Alice, I think Colly must be dead.'

She nodded. She could think of nothing to say about Colly Pearce that his sister would like to hear. 'I thought at one time you and Matthias Renfree might marry,' she said instead.

'I think a lot of people shared your belief. He was on the verge of asking me once, but lost his nerve.'

'Really? Would you have accepted him?'

'No.'

'Why not? If you don't mind me asking.'

386

'I wasn't in love with him, and Matthias Renfree seems to be married to his calling.'

'You love your husband though, don't you?' Alice smiled, won over by Rosina's contentment with her new life. 'That much is obvious to me.'

'Yes, in spite of the dreadful things he'd done in the past, I love Peter very much.' Rosina smiled back, pleased the fact was so apparent.

'Bless you, Rosina. You always see the best in people, I could never be like that.'

'You're as good as the next person, Alice. And it's probably best we're all different. Excuse me while I go and fetch the tea tray. Kate can't manage to carry it by herself yet.'

Alone in the room, Alice looked around. It wasn't as richly furnished as any of the rooms of Pengarron Manor, but it was another rich man's dwelling she would never have dreamt of being invited into to take tea with the wife. If she had been there before she would have noticed the rapid changes Blake had had made for his new bride. Now, new curtains, coverings and cushions, carpets, pictures and ornaments with a distinctly feminine touch, chosen by Josephine Courtis, had replaced the previously typically austere bachelor appearance.

'You've obviously seen Kerensa since I called on her if she told you about me and Peter. How was she, Alice?' asked Rosina when they were sipping their tea.

'Getting stronger every day, thank the Lord, almost back to normal. That fever nearly did for her, left her so weak. I don't think I've ever been so frightened in all my life as I was throughout that night. She was terribly upset when she heard about the Richards.'

'I hear Rudd Richards has packed up and left the farm, poor man.'

'Yes. According to what Clem told me, the cause of the fever was an underground spring running beneath the outdoor closet. It tainted the drinking supply. Rudd wasn't affected much because of his liking for buttermilk and ale. Strange, isn't it? For all their filthy ways, the cause of their deaths was something that couldn't have been foreseen.'

'What becomes of a man who loses everything?' Rosina said with a faraway look in her eyes. Then, her delicate features brightening again, she asked, 'When are you expecting your baby to be born, Alice?'

'About three months from now, according to Gran Donald,' she answered, patting her spreading middle. 'Beatrice, though, reckons it'll come early.'

'Peter and I are hoping for a large family, four or five at least.'

Alice raised her skirt to display her swollen ankles. 'You may change your mind if you end up like this,' she said with feeling, then added on a lighter note, 'Still, be all worth it when she's born.'

'She?' Rosina smiled. 'Are you so sure it's going to be a little girl?'

'It had better be,' Alice said, half-seriously. 'I've always wanted to have my own daughter.'

'I'll pray for an easy delivery for you,' Rosina promised. 'I'm coming to the next Bible class at Jeb Bray's. It will be good to see everyone again, 'specially the children.'

'Oh? Any chance of your husband coming along as well? Do you think he'd get a favourable welcome if he did?'

'Peter says if he finds he would be accepted, he may go along sometime and sit and listen. Matthias Renfree calls on us occasionally, and they argue for hours over the Gospel and the need to have faith. Peter's a bit naughty, getting the preacher all fired up like he does, but Matthias has a wonderful sense of humour. I don't know if Peter'll ever change from his unbelief, but as Preacher Renfree says, at least he thinks and hasn't shut his mind completely.'

'Well, it will be good to see you back where you belong again, Rosina. No one's sat in your little corner since you were last there, you know.'

A key turning in the outside lock caused Rosina to look up expectantly. Peter Blake didn't even notice Alice's presence as he crossed the room and tenderly kissed his wife.

'We have a guest, Peter,' she said, blushing prettily.

'Oh,' said Blake, looking round the room until his eyes rested on Alice.

'This is Mrs Clem Trenchard, Peter. Her husband farms with his father on Trecath-en Farm. Alice, my husband, Peter.'

Rosina spoke with pride and Alice saw that the unwholesome look she had always found distasteful on Peter Blake's handsome face had now gone.

'I'm pleased to make your acquaintance, Mrs Trenchard,' he said amicably, briefly shaking her hand. 'Your name is Alice... let me see, you were once a bal-maiden with Rosina at the Wheal Ember, am I right?'

'Yes, Mr Blake, you are,' she answered, taken aback. She felt rather self-conscious sitting in her working clothes, her dusty shoes up on his furniture, the relaxed position accentuating her approaching mother-hood. She had not expected him to know anything about her or to refer to Rosina's past life.

Blake sat down beside his wife, and without embarrassment he and Rosina held hands.

'Rosina has told me about everyone who comes from Lancavel Downs, Mrs Trenchard,' he explained. 'You were a friend of hers. I'm grateful to anyone who was kind to her.'

'It was Rosina who was kind to me, and to everyone else,' Alice said.

'Have you two ladies been chatting over old times?'

'Yes,' Rosina answered. 'Do you want tea and biscuits, Peter?'

'Yes, please, my dearest,' he said, raising a hand to kiss it. 'Pour the tea in your cup to save Kate bringing another.'

Alice watched with growing amazement as Rosina poured tea, passed the cup to her husband, following it with a plate of biscuits – all without the two of them taking their eyes off each other. She began to feel forgotten.

'Well,' she said, struggling to her feet, 'I really must be going. Clem's father will be waiting by the animal pens for me by now and I don't want him to start worrying.'

Peter and Rosina Blake rose together. 'We'll see you safely down over the stairs, Alice,' Rosina said.

-

Her ankles were so swollen by the evening that Alice was ordered off early to bed. Clem came into the lean-to to change his shirt before having his supper. It was the first Alice had seen of him since dawn that morning.

'Had a busy day, Clem?' she said cheerfully.

'Mmm… been building hedges on our boundaries,' he answered.

Clem was in one of his quiet thoughtful moods and Alice knew he didn't want to talk. After supper he would go off somewhere with Charity, and not return until he came to bed in the small hours of the following morning.

'Mother said your ankles are swollen again,' he said, pulling off his shirt, then sitting on the bed as he unfolded the clean one.

Stretching across the bed Alice put her face on his bare back and wound her arms around his waist. Clem stiffened at once.

'Don't do that.'

'Why not?'

His reply was not unexpected. Alice had heard it before. 'It's not proper, for one thing.'

Her heart always sank a little when Clem was cool towards her, as he often was. She knew if it was Kerensa he was married to, he would be as loving a husband as Peter Blake appeared to be. Clem wasn't unkind to her and was gently considerate when making love, but those occasions were becoming less frequent, he using her pregnancy as a convenient excuse, she felt. There had been a new feeling of closeness between them when she had backed him against the advice of his father, mother and grandmother in going over to the Manor on hearing just how ill Kerensa was. But it had not lasted long and she had fought back her disappointment. Instead she clung to the hope things would improve when their child was born, but up to now he had shown a total lack of interest in that too.

Alice straightened up and picked up her knitting. 'I got your Sunday boots mended for you in town today,' she said, trying to keep her hurt feelings under control.

'Thanks.'

'Oh, look, Clem!' she exclaimed.

He turned round, his shirt halfway over his head. 'What's up?'

'Look at this,' she pointed to her stomach, 'the baby's moving. I've been hoping you'd get a chance to see it.'

Clem peered past her pointing fingers and gave a small shiver. 'Ugh, looks like a rat moving about in a sack of potatoes.'

'Clem! That's your son or daughter you're talking about in there.' Alice took his hand and tried to guide it towards her body but he snatched it away. 'Touch my stomach, Clem. It won't hurt you. It feels funny.'

'I'd rather not,' he said with distaste.

Alice cast her knitting down at the end of the bed and said with a sob in her voice, 'You don't seem very interested in our baby, Clem.' She turned her face away. There would be no point in showing him the things she had bought for the child.

He moved closer, placing a hand either side of her on the bed. He knew he had upset her and was sorry. 'It's not that, Alice. I feel a bit afraid of it, that's all.'

'Of the baby?' She turned back.

'Yes. Honestly,' Clem stressed. 'I was afraid of Rosie when she was born. I didn't even touch her until she could walk. Ask Mother or Gran.'

'Oh, Clem.' She stroked his fine hair. His eyes were so blue when he was concerned over something. Alice kissed his cheek and he did the same to her and allowed her to do up the front of his shirt.

Now she had him feeling contrite, she tried again at keeping his interest for a reasonable length of time. 'You'll never guess who I had tea with in Marazion today, Clem.'

'Tea? Let me see,' he teased, pulling one of her curls. 'Well, it had to be someone well-heeled… Mayor Oke, Cap'n Solomon, and Mother Clarry?'

'No, no,' she laughed. 'Rosina and Peter Blake.'

Clem jumped up as though the bed was red hot. 'What!' He was furious, so furious that Alice felt nervous with him for the first time. 'I don't believe this!' he shouted, banging his fist on the wall.

'What's the matter?' she said feebly. 'Why are you so angry, Clem?'

'Have you forgotten what that bastard did to Kerensa? What he tried to do to her?' His voice was getting louder.

'No, of course not.' Alice spoke rapidly in the hope he would calm down, becoming afraid of what her in-laws would think about Clem shouting at her. 'I met Rosina in the market actually, she was by herself at the time, and I was tired so she invited me to their rooms for some tea. I can't see that I did wrong by accepting, Clem.'

'Oh, don't you?' he went on at the same speech level. 'Peter Blake would have raped Kerensa without fear or regret if Jack and I hadn't stopped him. Not to mention unmercifully kicking an old defenceless dog near to death. The only thing I can say in favour of that swine Kerensa is married to is, he beat the hell out of Blake. It's a pity he didn't do the job properly and finish the bastard off.'

'But Peter Blake's a changed man now, Clem. You wouldn't believe he was the same since he married Rosina.'

'I don't give a damn about that! I've never understood how that girl could marry him,' Clem hurled at her, 'particularly with Matthias Renfree taking an interest in her.'

'He was only going to marry her out of pity because, like all you men, he didn't have the guts to stand up to her brother!' Alice retorted, defending her actions.

'But not many people marry for love, do they, Alice?' Clem said spitefully, his body shaking as he leaned forward and pointed a finger at her. 'You weren't in the Manor that day. You didn't see that poor animal. You didn't see how distressed Kerensa was, her face badly bruised from the punch he gave her. I'll never forgive that bastard Blake as long as I live!'

Alice had never seen him like this before. Huddled up in the corner of the bed she was frightened, angry and humiliated. 'I might not have been at the Manor that day,' she shouted back, sobbing, 'but you shouldn't have been there either. I don't believe for a minute you went over to see Nathan O'Flynn. It was her, wasn't it? Kerensa. Always Kerensa!'

'Shut up!'

'Why won't you admit it, Clem Trenchard, that she's married to someone else?' Alice screamed hysterically. 'She could have married you but she didn't, and I'm your wife, not her. You got me pregnant, you all but forced me the first time. It's time you faced up to reality and forgot her. I know you're still hanging about just to catch a glimpse of her—'

His face had grown red and ugly. 'Shut your filthy mouth, you bitch!' he snarled. 'You're not fit even to mention that girl's name!'

It made Alice gulp in shock. She would never have believed before that Clem could behave in such a cruel irrational way. To say the vicious things that spilled out of his mouth was worse than any obscenity. His whole manner was menacing. It terrified her that all the time, underneath his quiet moody exterior, such hatred and passion had lain, only waiting for something like her visit to the Blakes' home to provide the excuse for him to explode.

And yet she could not stop herself. 'The trouble with you, Clem, is you're really angry with yourself. You could have stopped her from marrying Oliver Pengarron if you'd really tried to, but you just stepped aside and let it happen. That's what is really eating away inside you, isn't it? Isn't it?'

The words were out before she knew it. 'I'm sorry, Clem,' she cried, trying desperately to grab hold of him, but he roughly fought her off. 'I'm sorry!'

The look in his eyes silenced her and she put a hand over her open mouth. She had spoken too close to the truth.

Very slowly and quietly, he said, 'I hate you.' He turned sharply and stormed out of the room, making the door rock violently on its hinges.

Alice stayed still, huddled in a corner of the narrow bed, until Gran Donald came into her. She was staring into space and shivering with the shock of the brutal row. The old woman pulled her shawl round her shoulders.

'Get yourself under the covers, m'dear,' she said kindly, sweeping back the sheet and patchwork coverlet. 'I'll get you a blanket from the linen chest, you're quite frozen.'

Alice obeyed mechanically. She lay down and let Gran Donald place the covers over her and tuck them in at the sides of the bed. How could this have happened? How could a day she had enjoyed so much come to such a terrible end? She blamed herself for her stupidity in telling Clem where she had gone. She should have realised he would be angry with her for going to Peter Blake's rooms.

If only she had not said all those things to him. Not hit on the truth of his innermost dark brooding feelings and tapped the wound, ripped it open. To allow the poison to burst to the surface, to be expelled with such a dangerous awesome force, and engulf them both.

It hurt so much, it cut painfully and deeply inside her, to know he loved Kerensa so overwhelmingly – to the point that even talking of a man who had once harmed her could scour his soul and turn all of his deep-rooted bitterness on his own wife.

Damn you, Kerensa Pengarron! You've got a husband who has grown to love you, and you don't even realise it! You live up in that big house and hold Clem, who should belong to me, by invisible strings. Let him go, why don't you let him go? Alice's distress was so great she could not hear Gran Donald speaking to her.

'Would you like me to get you a hot drink, Alice? It'll warm 'ee up.'

She clumsily pulled herself into a sitting position. 'Where's Clem gone?' she said hazily, her lower lip trembling as she spoke.

'He went out, maid. I believe he's found a litter of kittens for 'ee. Gone to check on 'em, I 'spect. You'll be able to pick one out for yourself soon.'

'He won't come back.' Alice began to cry, her whole body shaking.

Gran Donald put her arms round the girl and rocked her ample body. 'Now don't you take on so, m'dear. There's no need to upset yourself like this. All married folk do have a quarrel sometime or other.'

'Not like this, Gran,' Alice sobbed wretchedly. 'I never really had Clem. Now I never will.'

Chapter 26

After the long hot summer the weather deteriorated with frightening speed and intensity. Angry black clouds marred the sky, as black as night, the long-awaited rain refilling the empty river beds and streams to overflowing, and deluging cart tracks, lanes and the pot-holed roads until they were impassable. Winds roared like a pride of hungry lions seeking to devour all in their path. The rich stayed warm and comfortable in front of constantly replenished fires while the poor shivered and froze in damp and draughty cottages and mean hovels.

In the inhospitable early hours of one morning at the close of October, the three-masted sailing vessel, *Amy Christabel* was driven by hurricane winds like a helpless lump of driftwood on to the treacherous black granite at the foot of Pengarron Point. The tempest took only twenty-three minutes to wrench the ship asunder from bow to stern and claim a watery death for all its passengers, crew and livestock. Bodies, wreckage and cargo were strewn outwards to be swept east along the coastline to the sheer inaccessible cliffs below Painted Bessie's kiddley, and in the opposite direction to Trelynne Cove and beyond.

Anxious to avoid fighting and bloodshed on his property in an unstoppable, crazed, scramble to salvage the wreckage, Oliver gave permission for the inhabitants of the parish of Perranbarvah to comb the beaches, rocks, inlets and coves of Pengarron land, from dawn to dusk for a week. He gave a stern warning that any man, woman or child caught in the act of stealing flotsam from another, or of using violence to that end, would be brought before the magistrates and on his recommendation severely dealt with. People knew Sir Oliver would not make such a threat lightly. He was held in awe by those who knew him, or of him, and fear of his temper and personal retribution was enough to ensure that most kept themselves in line.

While the elements of nature had been unmerciful to the seafarers of the *Amy Christabel*, they favoured the beachcombers and plunderers. Washed ashore with each succeeding tide was timber, strips of canvas sail, bales of silk, trunks of clothing, containers of coffee, tea and spices, and ship's articles; lanterns, lengths of rope, carpenter's tools and water barrels, and the carcasses of fowls and animals. The bodies of mariners and wealthy passengers that floated inshore were swiftly robbed of all they had with them at point of death; jewellery, false teeth, wigs and shoes that had not floated off, and every item of clothing.

Oliver, Nathan and Jack made regular patrols of the clifftop and beaches, keeping a wary eye open for serious outbreaks of trouble. But even with the infiltration of outsiders from the parish in the scramble for the sacrifice thrown up from the sea, nothing more than minor skirmishes and the odd outburst of violent quarrelling disturbed the peace of the coastline when the winds dropped away.

The rain too eased off by the third day after the wrecking. Strong and healthy again, Kerensa had Jack saddle Kernick, and, warmly dressed to ward off the cold, joined Oliver on his ride along the coastline. By the time they had made their way down into Trelynne Cove the exercise after her enforced recuperation had left her feeling wonderfully light-hearted, her whole body invigorated, her mind clear and alert. The bracing cold air had touched a rosy glow to her cheeks, the scenic coastal beauty an added sparkle to the eyes.

For Kerensa it was the first time in the cove since her discovering her grandfather's body and it was a shock to see only an empty space where the cottage she had been born and brought up in had stood. The storm had removed all traces of the small garden she had carefully tended. She paced out its boundaries by memory as Oliver gazed up and down the length of the shingle beach.

'There were hundreds of people scavenging here only yesterday,' he called to her. 'Of the greedier variety, I suspect. Today, I can see only about thirty or forty.'

'Where do you think they have all gone?' Kerensa said, coming over to his side and looking down on the people dotted along the shoreline with handcarts, barrows and mules to take home their rewards.

'They must have heard wind of a rumour of better pickings elsewhere,' he said, 'probably think there's naught left but firewood to be washed ashore here now.'

'You can't tell anything for sure,' Kerensa said knowledgeably, 'Grandfather used to find many interesting things which he sold, years after any particular wreck.'

'Well, they have only one week on my property,' Oliver said drily, 'so they're obviously having a good look everywhere they can.'

They walked down the path that had once led from the cottage door and on to the crunch of the shingle. Kerensa bent down to pick up a handful of the smooth cold pebbles and realised with a small pang how much she had missed her old life.

'Looks like you have a visitor, my dear,' Oliver told her.

She straightened up to see a small girl with fair hair tearing across the shingle towards them and was delighted to see who it was.

'Rosie! It's wonderful to see you again.' The girl stopped in front of her, panting to get her breath back. 'Have you found anything interesting on the beach?'

Not sure of the correct term to be used now when addressing Kerensa, Rosie did not use any name or title. 'I got this,' she said, holding out her hand to show the oval shaped locket she was clutching. 'Lovely, isn't it?'

'It's very lovely,' Kerensa agreed.

'May I see it?' Oliver said, stretching out his hand.

Rosie closed her hand into a fist over the locket and glared up at the man who had caused her beloved elder brother so much heartbreak. Oliver put his hands on his hips and met her glare full on, and her expression changed to remind him of Clem in one of his sulky moods.

'I will not keep your locket for long, Miss Trenchard,' he said, amusement playing around his dark eyes. 'I may be able to tell you something of its value, that is all.'

Like all females encountering Sir Oliver Pengarron for the first time Rosie did not know what to make of him, especially with him calling her Miss Trenchard; no one had ever done that before. Her head came no higher than a point in the middle of his waist and shoulder and he seemed to tower over her like a giant. But the face that came closer to hers when he bent forward wore the handsomest of smiles and somehow he did not appear quite the demon she thought of him in her moments of fancy.

After a moment's pained thought she curtsied low, holding the corners of her skirt, to the baronet, but it was to Kerensa she handed her precious locket. Kerensa passed it to Oliver who moved away a short distance and held it up high to study it in a better light.

'You're not here by yourself, are you, Rosie?' Kerensa said, taking the little girl's cold hand.

'No, I come over with Father, Gran, and Clem and Alice. Did you know Alice is going to have a baby?'

'Yes, I did know. It will be nice for the whole family.' Kerensa was surprised to hear Alice was here in Trelynne Cove, with her pregnancy so well advanced, and because she had not been over to the Manor for several weeks.

'If it's a little maid,' Rosie said excitedly, 'Alice said she hopes it's like me, with lots of straight yellow hair, she hates her curls.'

'Well, the baby might have a few curls,' Kerensa smiled, craning her neck to see if she could locate Alice. 'And I think Alice's curls are beautiful.'

'So does everyone, but her. She's nice, is Alice. Got a cuddly sort of laugh and she made me a lovely dress for my birthday. First new one I've ever had. I really wanted Clem to marry you, but seeing as he couldn't cus you went off and had to marry Sir Oliver back there, I'm glad he chose Alice instead.' Rosie chatted away happily with the frankness of her youth, quite unaware of Kerensa's amazed look at her. 'She loves Clem, I heard her say so. Pity he don't love her.'

Kerensa threw a glance at her husband but he was absorbed with Rosie's locket. 'Why do you say that, Rosie? That Clem doesn't love Alice?' she probed gently.

'They fall out a lot these days. Ask Gran down there. Clem shouted at Alice proper awful once. It was horrible. I put my hands over my ears. He never used to shout, never used to be so blamed miserable.'

'Do you know why he shouted?'

'Dunno. He musta bin sorry for it though. He got her a kitten the next day, for Alice to try 'n' tame. She loves that kitten, spends nearly all her time in the lean-to with it now.' Rosie looked up suddenly. 'What does a–shamed mean?'

'Ashamed?' Kerensa's concern was rapidly increasing. 'It's how you should feel when you've done something bad and are sorry for it.'

'Then Clem musta done something bad,' the little girl said, drawing in her fair features tipped with a red button nose, ''cus Mother said to Gran, that he should be ashamed of himself.'

Kerensa felt it was time to steer the conversation away from Clem's and Alice's unhappy marriage. 'I can see your father and gran with Clem down on the shoreline, but where's Alice? Come to that, where's Charity?'

'Alice is sitting in the lee of they rocks over to Mother Clarry's, and Charity was up the other end just now with Bartholomew. He's chucking sticks for her.'

'Bartholomew Drannock?' asked Kerensa slowly.

'Yeh, that's him, horrid boy. He tried to kiss me just now, ugh.' Rosie suddenly pulled her hand away from Kerensa's and went over to Oliver. 'Can I have my locket back now? Please Sir,' she added hastily, remembering her manners.

Holding the locket over Rosie's open palm Oliver carefully let it drop into her cold–reddened hand.

'Is it val… val… is it a good one, Sir?' she asked hopefully.

'It's solid gold, little one,' Oliver was pleased to tell her, 'and may have belonged to a girl of your own age if the pictures inside are anything to be judged by. The small sparkling stone in the centre on the outside is a diamond.'

'A real one?' Rosie breathed.

'Indeed a real one. Keep it safe and it may serve you well in the future.'

'I must go tell Clem. It was him who found it for me,' said Rosie, racing off excitedly. 'Thank 'ee, Sir. Thank 'ee,' she called over her shoulder.

'The child has a lot more charm than her brother,' Oliver remarked. 'I wonder if he's searching for a trinket for Alice. I overheard the child say she was here.'

'You heard the rest too, then,' Kerensa said, with a sigh. 'Alice hasn't been to see me for a long time even though I sent Jack over with the trap, and when I enquired about it I was told she wasn't up to travelling. I can't think what she's doing here in her condition.'

'Poor Alice,' Oliver said with feeling. 'The girl deserves better than that moody Trenchard fellow. I find it difficult to understand what you saw in him that made you want to marry him.'

Kerensa knew a side to Clem that Oliver could never know. A young man, loving, tender and good-humoured, with plans, hopes and dreams… so he had been once. She said nothing, but watched as he turned to look in their direction after Rosie ran up and spoke to him. He did not wave. Turning back, he waded into the rushing grey sea.

Oliver had watched Kerensa for a reaction when he had made his detrimental remarks about Clem. Her face looked sad if anything, and he felt satisfied at Clem's rebuffal of her; if Trenchard kept up that behaviour, on the odd occasion their paths crossed, his own sulky disposition might just kill off any longing she still had for him.

'I'll scout around,' Oliver said, touching her shoulder. 'What will you do, my dear? Find Alice?'

'Yes,' Kerensa replied quietly, 'perhaps I will be able to cheer her.'

'I'll come and find you presently,' he said, striding away over the shingle to talk first to Morley Trenchard.

Kerensa moved in the opposite direction, holding up her skirts as she picked her way over the wet pebbles, calling hello to the people scavenging for anything that might add to their comfort for the winter. She threw back her head to enjoy the old familiar sounds: the rise and fall of frothy white foam over the coarse sand inches away from her feet, the light stinging wind in her ears, the shrieks of the outraged gulls disturbed in their isolation, and the tangy smell of salt and seaweed.

A dog came bounding past on its way to retrieve a stick that whistled past her ear, almost dislodging her hat.

'Charity!' she called out. 'Here, girl!'

The dog promptly forgot the stick at her command and came bounding back, excitedly jumping up, with wet paws all over her dress and cloak.

'So you do remember me, Charity?' Kerensa laughed, smoothing her hand over the young bitch's broad back. 'Is your paw better now?'

'Come on, Charity, get yerself here,' a young voice said crossly from behind her.

Kerensa turned to face Bartholomew Drannock. He stood feet astride, hands on hips, in much the same way as Oliver, and even for one so young he had a confident air about him as he looked her up and down. With his black hair and dark eyes it seemed incredible that the boy's resemblance to the Pengarrons had gone unnoticed, and rumours not spread about the identity of his father despite Oliver's absence from Cornwall at the time of his conception and infancy.

'I'm sorry to see your manners have not improved, Bartholomew,' she said, drily.

'Can't see no use fer 'em,' the boy retorted. 'You look pretty,' he added, moving closer to her in a most deliberate manner.

Kerensa refused to be shocked by the young rascal and ignored his precocious remark. 'How's your mother, Bartholomew? And little Jack, baby Cordelia, and the rest of your family?'

'What d'ya want to know about they for?' he said, cocking his head to one side. 'You'll find me much more interesting.'

Picking up a piece of driftwood Kerensa threw it back along the beach for Charity. She watched the bitch race off and turned back to the boy. With a sweetly superior voice, she said, 'As you are incapable of holding a sensible conversation, young man, I'll bid you a good afternoon.' And she walked on to resume her search for Alice.

'You walk pretty too!' Bartholomew shouted after her before running after Charity.

Kerensa shook her head but couldn't help smiling to herself. The boy was unmistakably of Pengarron stock.

–

Sitting in the shelter of the cliff, Alice saw Kerensa approaching. She sighed heavily, and with a great effort got to her feet. Kerensa waved the instant she saw Alice and hurried to meet her friend.

'Hello,' she said brightly, 'I was surprised when Rosie told me you were here.'

'Hello, Kerensa.' Alice sounded cold and unfriendly.

'Would you rather be alone?' she said uncertainly. 'I can go and find Oliver.'

'No, it's all right. It's just that I shouldn't have insisted on coming here,' Alice said miserably. 'Clem's cross now because I complained of the cold and asked to be taken home.'

'Here, take my cloak,' Kerensa said sympathetically, reaching to untie the ribbons.

'No!' snapped Alice. 'No, I'm all right, really. There's no need to fuss. You mustn't get cold on account of me.'

'Alice,' Kerensa said, hurt, 'I only want to help.'

Alice was comparing herself unfavourably with Kerensa, consciously adding to her own miseries. While she had grown gaunt in the face, with dark shadows under her eyes, and bloated in the body, Kerensa's natural beauty had returned in full measure since her illness. Here was a girl, Alice thought bitterly, who would soon blossom into full womanhood and grow more beautiful with every passing year. And not only did she have a husband of her own who would give her every attention, Alice's husband too would doubtless desire her all the more.

She must have remained in tight-lipped silence for a long time for Kerensa was walking away. It brought Alice back to her senses.

'Wait!' she called out. 'Please, Kerensa, come back.'

Kerensa stopped and slowly returned.

'I'm sorry,' Alice said quickly before she could say a word. 'If you'll take my arm we could go for a little walk. That should warm me up a bit, and make me less grouchy.' She forced a smile as Kerensa took her arm.

They made their way carefully down to the sand where it was easier to walk and moved closer to Mother Clarry's rock where the beach was isolated. Alice looked as though she had no intention of speaking further.

'I know you and Clem are having problems,' Kerensa said cautiously. 'Can I help?'

'No, no one can,' Alice returned shortly.

Kerensa was helpless, not knowing what to say, but Alice was her friend and one she deeply cared for. She tried to get her to look forward to the future.

'I'm sure things will get better for you when the baby's born.'

'Perhaps. I can't wait to get it over with. I seem to feel ill all the time.'

'I'm sorry, Alice.' Kerensa searched her mind for something positive to say. It was difficult. Alice looked pale and wan, her movements over the sand slow and listless.

Alice stopped walking and looked vacantly over the grey, churning sea. The beach was nearly at an end and they could hear the water slapping heavily against the rocks under the witch's seat.

'Do you remember the old days, Kerensa, when you and Clem were planning to marry? He was so happy back then… a different person to the one he is now.' Alice's voice sounded dull and regretful.

'Of course I remember, but—'

'He's changed such a lot,' Alice said acidly. 'He hates me.'

'What? I'm sure he doesn't, Alice.' Kerensa was fearful now.

'He hates me!' cried her friend. 'We had a terrible row and he told me so. He's stuck with me and the baby and he hates me!'

'I'm so sorry.'

'Why didn't you marry Clem!' Alice said viciously, pulling herself away. 'Why didn't you tell Oliver Pengarron to go to Hell, then none of this would have happened!'

'I didn't want to, Alice,' Kerensa pleaded. 'I loved Clem. I did it to protect him and his family as much as for my grandfather's sake.'

Alice stayed silent for a few moments then said, 'Yes, of course you did. I'm sorry… it's just that I've been so unhappy.'

'Is that why you haven't been to see me?'

'Yes. I thought I hated you, Kerensa. The Lord knows I wanted to.'
Then, lowering her voice, Alice said, 'But I can't… not you.'

Kerensa wanted to put her arm around her friend and hold her tight, but Alice's face stayed frozen, making such a gesture inadvisable for the moment. 'I'm sorry about you and Clem,' she said gently, 'but you have the baby to look forward to. Things might get better then. Don't give up hope, Alice.'

'Mayhap,' she said, rubbing at the heartburn under her breasts. 'And how about you, Kerensa? Have you been blessed yet, as they say?'

'No,' she replied, unsure how the question was to be taken. 'I thought I was, but it was the sickness. Beatrice came home from Marazion yesterday with the news that Rosina has just found out she's pregnant.'

'Is she? That was quick. She must have conceived on her wedding night. Your turn will come, Kerensa don't worry.' It was said with something of Alice's old friendliness and Kerensa breathed an inward sigh of relief.

'I hear you have a kitten, Alice,' she said, hoping it would add to the improvement in the other girl's humour.

'Oh, Scrap. Rosie tell you about that too, did she? How's your puppy? Strange our husbands have given us both a pet, but I'll warrant yours isn't a substitute for something else.' It seemed Alice's ill-humour was not to be lifted after all.

'What do you mean by that, Alice?'

'We're both married so there's no need to be coy,' she said bluntly. 'Does your husband want you at night?'

'Yes,' Kerensa replied at once, but dreading what was coming next.

'And has your feelings in mind as much as his own, I'm sure. Mine doesn't want me. Clem doesn't want me at all. Since the row he's taken to sleeping in the barn.' A sob rose in Alice's voice and she rubbed angrily at her eyes. 'Oh, Kerensa, I've been horrid to you and I'm sorry. But it's helped to take my anger and frustration out on you.'

'And I'm glad you did, Alice,' Kerensa said vehemently. 'It's what friends are for.'

Alice accepted a comforting hug and cried on Kerensa's shoulder, then smiled as she wiped away her tears. 'Let's go back and sit down, shall we?'

'I'll stay with you until Oliver's finished looking about, and with luck you'll soon be able to go home.' Kerensa took her arm again. She chatted to Alice as they walked, but her mind was on Clem.

She wanted to stalk across the beach and give him a stinging piece of her mind. How dare he treat Alice in this way? Where was his sense of decency, compassion, honour and responsibility? And where his backbone? He might have been upset, devastated even, when she married Oliver, but didn't he have any reserves of strength at all to call on? Had he no faith? She wanted to say all this and more but couldn't with Alice and Oliver in the cove. She would look for the earliest opportunity to do so.

Alice's foot slipped out of her shoe and she half-turned back towards the sea, holding on to Kerensa's arm as she retrieved it. She slid her foot back in then gripped the arm tightly.

'Are you all right, Alice?'

'What's there? There in the water?'

Kerensa could see nothing at first, but as the next wave rushed its way inshore it brought a little closer to land a chest that bobbed and lurched about like a drunken man.

'It's a chest or a trunk, Alice,' she said excitedly. 'You've found something! I'll get someone to pull it out for you.'

'No, look, we haven't got time.' Alice was excited too. 'It's going to be caught up on those rocks out there. If it bobs around the side of Mother Clarry's, it'll be lost forever.' Pulling her arm away, Alice hurried towards the rocks under the witch's seat.

'Where are you going?' Kerensa quickly sidestepped in front of her friend. 'What are you going to do?'

'If we get on those rocks there, we can pull in the chest together. It could be filled with beautiful clothes, Kerensa, I could make something fine for my baby to wear.'

'But those rocks are always slippery. It's far too dangerous, Alice.' Kerensa was walking backwards and could see her arguments were falling on deaf ears. Alice's face was set. 'Don't be silly, Alice, think of your baby. If you fall—ow!' Kerensa slipped and landed heavily on the sand.

Alice kept on going and began to run. By the time Kerensa regained her feet her friend was clambering over the first of the rocks where they edged the sea under the cliff.

'Alice!' she shouted, terrified. 'Come back! The water soon gets deep out there.'

As if to confirm her fears and warning, almost at once Alice slipped on seaweed and was brought down on her knees. She couldn't move forwards or backwards and panicked.

'Help me, Kerensa! Help me! I'm afraid to move!'

'Try to stay calm, Alice! I'll get help!'

It was the fastest Kerensa had ever run across the beach, shouting all the way.

'Clem! Oliver! Help! Help!'

They both heard her at the same time. Clem dropped a long beam of timber to splash back in the water. Oliver broke off his conversation with a wrinkled old fisherman. Although he was a good distance further away from Kerensa than Clem, his longer legs ensured they reached her at the same time. Clem caught her by the top of her arms but she shrugged him off.

'What is it?' Oliver demanded, flashing Clem a fierce look.

'It's Alice,' Kerensa cried fearfully, 'she's trapped on rocks under Mother Clarry's seat.' She looked wildly at both men. 'You must do something!'

They all ran off together, Kerensa panting to keep up. Oliver and Clem reached the rocks long before she did and when she ran up beside them they were both looking anxiously about.

The rocks were empty.

'Do you think she got back by herself?' Clem said doubtfully.

'We would have passed her,' said Oliver, shaking his head.

'There she is!' Kerensa screamed, pointing outwards across the sea. 'She's in the water, she must have fallen in.'

Kerensa was running again, throwing off her hat and cloak and kicking off her shoes. She didn't feel the coldness of the water as she ran into the rushing surf and fought like a wild animal as two strong arms swept her off her feet.

'Take my wife back on shore,' Oliver ordered, as he thrust her against Clem's chest, 'and make sure you keep her there.'

'What are you going to do?' Clem shouted above the roar of the surf while winding his arms around Kerensa to hold her against her struggles.

'I'm going in after Alice. I'm a strong swimmer and her only chance if she's pulled around those outer rocks. Go with Trenchard and wait on the shore,' he told Kerensa sternly, then waded into deep water and plunged into the icy sea.

Holding Kerensa up off her feet Clem carried her back to the shoreline. She turned to watch Oliver disappear and reappear in the undulation of the waves as he gained very slowly on the bobbing piece of cloth that was Alice's dress; all that could be seen of her. Clem stood close, his hands on Kerensa's shoulders.

'What will happen to them, Clem?' she said fearfully.

They were joined by others on the beach. Gran Donald picked up Kerensa's cloak. Clem took it from her and wrapped it round the shivering girl, resting his hands back on her shoulders.

All eyes were on the sea except for Morley Trenchard's. He was looking at his son. If the two people there drowned, then Clem and Kerensa would be free...

Alice closed her eyes, letting the waves take her where they would. She no longer felt the wetness and bitter cold, and the turmoil in her mind of the past few weeks had mercifully ceased. She was floating in a world of tranquil warm greyness and had not the slightest desire ever to be awakened from it. Something was touching her, drawing her away on a mystical journey of shapes and colours. She had no knowledge of the frantic struggle going on for her life and another's.

Alice was unconscious when Oliver reached her. If she had panicked and fought against him he would have been forced to leave her or let her drown them both. As it was it was easy enough to put his arm over her chest, his hand under her chin, and begin the swim back to the shore. But Alice had floated on her back too near the cliff's edge, and undercurrents swirling round the submerged rocks sucked them in close like the leaf and twig boats he and Arthur Beswetherick made as boys to be sent cascading over the waterfall of the river Withy. They were dragged under the water, Oliver needing all his strength to pull their heads above the surface to gasp for air before trying to move on to safety again. With his free hand he clutched at the rocks, propelling them along a short length at a time. Their arms, legs and heads were cut and bruised as they were flung like flotsam against the jagged granite. Many times they were dragged under, Alice so limp that as Oliver fought to keep his hold on her, he wasn't sure if she was still alive.

Clem and Morley and one other man were now gingerly making their way over the rocks from where Alice had fallen. Oliver did not realise he was so close inshore and did not hear their shouts of encouragement. When hands gripped Alice and tried to pull her out of the water he thought her clothes had caught on a rock and was dragging her away from him. He clung on to her until someone prised his numb fingers from her bodice and he realised at last that others were helping in her rescue.

Now he had only himself to think about. But the tremendous effort and prolonged immersion in freezing cold water had taken its toll on his great strength. He managed to gain a precarious hold on the edge of a rock but could not find the power to pull himself out. He tried his other hand to no avail and found no strength to hold on to the rock with both hands at the same time. Desperately he tried to get a foothold on a ledge of rock but none could be found. The strength to lift either arm failed him and his head sank below the water.

He thought his lungs would burst for air when a hand painfully grasped the hair at the nape of his neck and yanked his head up far enough to clear the surface. The hand that held the power of his life or death, the eyes that bored hatred into his, belonged to Clem Trenchard.

'I'll help you, Clem.'

Oliver could just make out the young voice above the rushing in his ears. Clem's expression did not change.

'Keep back out of the way, Bartholomew,' he snarled, 'I'll manage better on my own. Give me your hand, Pengarron,' he said to Oliver in the same tone.

Coughing and gasping in the icy air, Oliver could only raise the tips of his fingers out of the water in one last desperate attempt to help save his own life. Clem saw them, and grasping the hand cruelly tight he slipped and slid on the wet rocks as he hauled the other's exhausted body halfway out of the water, falling across his back in the effort. He pulled Oliver to a sitting position and both men panted heavily, staring at one another, as Bartholomew Drannock got between them and dragged Oliver's long weakened legs out of the sea.

The boy watched the two men curiously. He was too young to discern the look of animosity and regret on Clem's face, or Sir Oliver's expression of resentment mixed with gratitude and perplexity.

Looking at Oliver he said, 'Phew, I thought you was a dead 'un then, sir.'

Oliver could not speak but nodded to the boy and lay back on the rocks to breathe slowly in through his nose and out through his mouth in an effort to recover.

Bartholomew was told to go back over the rocks by two men who had come to help. He did so grudgingly. Clem rose and followed on the boy's heels. With his arms round the shoulders of the new helpers, Oliver half-walked and was half-dragged back to the safety of the shore.

Clem was met by his father. 'How's Alice?' he asked, without emotion.

'She's still alive… just,' Morley answered, his face stern.

Clem walked on.

Morley watched him then hurried to meet Oliver, whose boots he had tucked under his arm.

'You all right, sir?'

'Yes… just about,' Oliver said, his voice hoarse from the salt water.

'I'm grateful to 'ee for what you did for Alice, sir.'

409

'Think nothing of it, Morley. How is she?'

Leaving the unconscious body of Alice wrapped in her cloak in the care of Gran Donald, Kerensa ran to meet Oliver. She stopped in front of Clem without speaking but only for a moment, before running on again. Oliver pulled himself away from the men helping him, thanked them, and walked towards Kerensa on shaky limbs. She ran into his wet arms.

'Thank God you're all right,' she cried. 'I was so frightened.'

He kissed the top of her head. 'So was I,' he admitted.

Taking his arm she put it round her shoulders and they walked to the people huddled over Alice. Clem was kneeling beside her and holding her hand but it did not escape Oliver's notice that he was looking at Kerensa and following her every movement and gesture. He wished Clem had seen Kerensa running into his arms and the open display of affection that had passed between them. He wondered what Clem's reaction would have been to that?

What a young fool you are, Trenchard, he thought wryly. But Oliver still felt threatened by the youth, who lived in close proximity on the estate; first loves were special and Kerensa might only have ignored the young man a few moments ago because she was peeved with him for doing the same to her earlier, and angered by his apparently cruel treatment of Alice, her closest friend.

'We must get the maid up on the cart and home as soon as possible.' Gran Donald said, appealing to Morley, then looking pointedly at Clem.

'I've been thinking,' Kerensa interjected. 'It will be much quicker to take Alice to the Manor and Beatrice can tell if there's any harm done to the baby.'

'Well, if it's agreeable to you and Sir Oliver, it's important to get they wet clothes off her as quickly as can be done afore she catches a chill or something worse.' Morley said gravely. 'But it's up to Clem to make the final decision, Alice is his wife.'

'Alice is always welcome in my home,' Oliver said, glaring at Clem and emphasising his next sentence. 'We'll give her the very best of care.'

'It's fine by me,' Clem said, as though he had no real interest in the matter, his eyes still on Kerensa.

Morley pushed his son aside. Gathering Alice up in his arms he bore her off to the farm cart and plough horse tethered to a shrub up on the clifftop. Gran Donald, Rosie and Kerensa moved off close behind. Bartholomew, having received a reward of a guinea piece from Oliver, lost interest in the drama and wandered off with the rest of the beachcombers to scavenge the shore while daylight lasted.

Left alone with Clem, Oliver fell in step beside him as he followed the others.

'Tell me, Trenchard, whom do I thank for saving my life? You or the Drannock boy?'

Clem did not pay Oliver the courtesy of looking at him as he replied in a husky sarcastic voice, 'Did you think I would've let you drown?'

'I have no idea,' Oliver said dourly. 'Would you?'

'Shall we say…' Clem trained his eyes on Kerensa's back '…at the least I was sorely tempted.'

–

A week later Alice decided it was time for her to go home. She had woken up nearly three hours later after her ordeal in the sea to find herself in a big cosy bed in a room at Pengarron Manor.

Beatrice declared there was no harm caused to the baby and the only effect from her icy minutes in the water was a sniffly cold that lasted for forty-eight hours.

Clem was banned by mutual agreement of his father and Oliver from visiting Alice for the length of her stay. Morley was relieved at the prospect of a temporary parting for the young couple, hoping there would be an improvement in their shaky marriage on Alice's return to the farm. Oliver knew if Clem called at the Manor, it would be not Alice he was hoping to see.

She was sitting up in bed when Polly knocked and brought in her breakfast.

'I've got a feast for you this morning, Mrs Trenchard,' Polly said cheerfully. 'Her ladyship wants you well set up against the cold for your journey home. Word's been sent for your husband to collect you this afternoon.'

'I feel so much better since my stay here, the rest has done me the world of good. I can't thank her ladyship enough for all she's done for me,' Alice said, surveying the delicacies on the breakfast tray. 'She's fussed over me all week. Nothing's been too much trouble for her.'

'You gave her quite a fright falling off the rocks like that, and now it's up to you to take good care of yourself,' Polly counselled. 'It will mean a lot to her ladyship to see you with a happy and healthy baby.'

'Don't worry, Polly,' Alice said, as she began her breakfast, 'I won't let her down. I'll never do such a stupid thing again. What's the weather like today?'

Polly peered out of the window at the grey misty sky. 'Should clear up and be crisp and dry most of the day,' she said, giving a small wave to someone below.

'That Nat you're waving to?' asked Alice.

'Yes, he's been busy of late and I haven't seen much of him.'

'When are you getting married, Polly? If you don't mind me asking.'

'A week before Christmas, Mrs Trenchard. The same day as the big fisherman known as the Barvah Giant.'

'That'll be Matthew King and Lowenna Angove, Jake's niece,' Alice informed the Manor's housekeeper.

'Oh, is that who they are? Nathan goes with him on all his wrestling matches, you know, not that I approve of that sort of thing. It was Nathan's and this Matthew King's idea to have our weddings on the same day.'

Turning back from the window Polly saw that Alice was toying with her food. 'Oh, come on, Mrs Trenchard, eat up. You need to build up all the strength you can.'

There was an odd look on Alice's face. She said. 'Polly, would you take this tray away and tell her ladyship I would like to see her as soon as possible?'

'Are you all right, Mrs Trenchard?' Polly frowned, coming to stand at the foot of the bed.

'I'm perfectly well. Just get her for me, please.'

Kerensa's light step was heard almost at once running down the first-floor corridor. She rushed into the room.

'Alice, is something wrong?'

'Close the door, Kerensa, and come over here.' Alice spoke in a whisper. 'I don't want anyone to overhear.'

Kerensa did as she was asked. 'What is it?' she whispered too, alarm on her small face. 'The baby?'

'No,' said Alice, squirming about in the bed. 'I didn't want to tell Polly this. I couldn't help it, it just happened, but I've... wet the bed. I don't know how, I only used the chamber pot a few minutes before she brought my breakfast in. I'm awful sorry, Kerensa.'

Relief was sketched all over Kerensa's face and she laughed at Alice's embarrassment.

'Shush,' Alice hissed, 'I don't want anyone else to know about it. Help me get the linen out of the bed, will you? I'll scrub the mattress and it can air out before the bed's used again.'

'No need for you to do anything, Alice. I'll get you a clean night-shift and you can finish your breakfast in my sitting room. I've got a good blaze going down there, you'll be nice and warm.'

'There's a nightshift: on that chair there,' Alice said, pointing across the room to the pile of clean laundry beside a growing number of gifts of baby clothes that the females of the Manor had been industriously employed in making during her week's stay.

Picking up the garment Kerensa laid it on the bed, pulling back the covers to help Alice out and on to her feet. She gasped loudly. 'Alice, there's blood in the bed!'

Looking down at the red-stained wetness spreading out across the bottom sheet, Alice instinctively clutched her bulging stomach. 'Oh, dear Lord!' she cried out. 'My baby!'

Tossing back the covers Kerensa said more calmly than she felt, 'Stay there, Alice, I'll get Beatrice at once. Don't worry now, she'll know what's happened and what to do.'

'I hope you're right, Kerensa. Don't be long, will you?'

Alone, she prayed silently. If she lost the baby now there would be little chance left of her hopes of building something worthwhile out of her marriage to Clem. Please Lord, please. Let my baby be all right. I promise I'll be a better wife to Clem. I won't sulk any more. I won't keep pestering him with questions or try to make him feel guilty when he goes off to be alone. Please Lord, please... I won't even mind that he'll always love Kerensa.

Beatrice flapped into the bedroom seemingly moments later, breathless from the pace at which Kerensa had pushed her up the stairs. Folding back the bedcovers, Kerensa stood wringing her hands as they waited for the old woman's deliberations.

'Yourn lucky to find me 'ere, maid,' she rasped, wiping her nose on the back of her hand. 'Jus' off to Pain'ed Bessie's I wus. Now lemme see what's up with 'ee.' She peered shortsightedly at the wet bedsheet and Alice's nightshift for only a second. 'Thought as much,' she said, giving the anxious mother-to-be her lopsided grin.

'What's wrong with me?' asked Alice meekly.

'Nothin'. Tes nothin' but yer show, maid.'

'What does that mean?' Kerensa said, gripping Alice's shaking hand in both of hers.

'It means, m'dear, 'er babe's comin'. Tole 'ee it would be an early 'n' didn't I?'

Chapter 27

'My baby can't be coming!' Alice shrieked. 'I've had no pain, just a bit of wind.'

Beatrice snorted and prodded all over Alice's extended abdomen, looked into her eyes, and pulled open her mouth to examine her tongue. The girl gagged on the old woman's vile body odours and waved a hand in front of her nose.

'S'on the way, right 'nough. Not every woman gets a lot of pain. We're all different. Course, could get a mite painful fer 'ee later on at the end, or even not till tes all over. Some do git the pains after the birth.'

'What do we do now, Beatrice?' asked Kerensa.

'Change they bedclothes,' she said, beginning to shuffle out of the room.

The two girls exchanged worried glances.

'Surely that's not all?' Kerensa called sharply. 'Come back in here.'

'What shall I do?' Alice was praying Beatrice really did know all about childbirth.

'Git up 'n' walk around,' the old woman said at the door. 'It'll 'elp 'ee fer later on. Better 'n' jus' lyin' there.'

'How long do you think it'll be before the baby's born?' Alice asked nervously.

''ours yet, I d'reckon. There's nothin' fer 'ee to worry 'bout. Enjoy yer las' bit of rest, tes sleepless nights a'ead fer 'ee, maid.'

'Don't you dare leave the house,' Kerensa ordered Beatrice.

'Should we send for Clem?' Alice wanted to know.

'What fer? 'E's done 'is part innit, an' a man's no blamed use at a birthin'.'

Clem arrived for Alice soon after lunch. The labour was not yet far advanced and Beatrice ordered him to be packed off home until late at night, and as Alice was dozing comfortably in the warm bedroom, she was not to be disturbed. He was not asked to leave the Manor immediately, however, but to step into Kerensa's sitting room.

The neat and tidy room was empty, but looking around his surroundings he nodded, satisfied. It bore her mark and fragrance. Scrubbed shining clean in his Sunday best clothes, his hair tied back with a new strip of silk, he smiled to dazzle as Kerensa entered the room and quietly closed the door. Joining him at his station by the window, she kept her face serious.

'Hello, Clem, it was good of you to stay to see me.'

'You make it sound as though I've answered a summons. Your husband wouldn't approve of me being here so he's obviously out somewhere, kicking up his heels no doubt.'

Clem glanced out of the window. It was not particularly cold outside, but Kerensa's attitude was.

'Your garden is—'

Kerensa interrupted him. 'I didn't ask you here to talk about the garden, Clem.'

'If you're cross with me for not visiting Alice all week, I wasn't allowed to, remember?'

'Were you pleased about that, Clem?'

'Pleased?' He looked genuinely perplexed.

Kerensa's resolve to chastise him over his treatment of Alice wavered. She found herself in a role that didn't come easily to her and felt a measure of the responsibility for the change in Clem's character must lay on her own shoulders. But the memory of Alice's distress and feeling of hopelessness in the cove the week before made her continue.

'At not having to see Alice,' she said coolly, lifting her chin.

Clem knew what that last subtle movement meant. He moved closer to look directly down into her eyes. 'I don't know what you're getting at, Kerensa, but I suppose it hasn't been a bad thing for us to have a breathing space from each other.'

'Alice was very upset before she fell off those rocks. It has crossed my mind more than once that she might have jumped, rather than fallen.'

'And why should she do that?' he asked, his voice dropping to match her own tone.

'Perhaps because of you. Because of the way things have been between you. Alice is a girl who needs love, Clem. She needs to have her affection returned, to feel wanted and needed. She can't cope with your moods, with the way you cut yourself off from her. I asked you once not to hurt Alice—'

'Don't you play Lady of the Manor with me,' he angrily cut in. 'I'm not one of Pengarron's servants.'

'Clem, I only want to help you both, you and Alice,' Kerensa pleaded for his understanding.

'Help!' he snapped, then lowering his voice and looking at her full red mouth rather than her eyes, said, 'You're forgetting who you are, Kerensa Trelynne… and you've certainly forgotten who I am.'

Striding to the door, he threw it wide open. 'Tell my dear wife I'll be back to see her later tonight,' he said acidly. 'Tell her also to make the most of her stay – it will be her last.'

'Clem,' Kerensa rushed over to him, 'you are being unfair.'

'Am I?' He raised his eyes ceilingwards. 'I didn't want my child born under this roof, that is certain.'

When he had gone she shut the door of her sitting room and sat down, closing her eyes. How could Clem be so inconsiderate, so difficult? She pictured Alice lying in the big bed upstairs, about to become a mother, with all her hopes for the future. She had not spoken of Clem all week, but Kerensa knew she had been planning how to mend the broken bridges of her marriage. Kerensa put her face into her hands. What had she just done? She had broken one of her own golden rules and meddled between a man and his wife. What now?

Alice's contractions became painful, twenty minutes apart, as darkness fell. The sense of excitement that had been growing steadily in the Manor as the day progressed, reached a point that clashed with Beatrice's level of tolerance. She insisted Ruth and Esther go to their Bible meeting.

'What use is a coupla ole maids, anyway?' she grumbled to Kerensa. 'They went never find themselves in childbed. Went never know a man, come to that,' she snorted maliciously, digging the girl in the ribs with a cruel elbow.

The contractions were down to ten minutes apart when the King sisters returned. Beatrice wouldn't allow them into the bedroom so they retired to the kitchen to await the call for hot water.

Alice was nervous and begged Kerensa not to leave her alone with the old crone. She was convinced Beatrice was about to do something unthinkable to her body and her baby, and feverishly wished that she was back in the lean-to at Trecath-en, with Florrie Trenchard and Gran Donald in attendance. Kerensa asked Polly to search for books in the library with pictures in and bring them up to the bedroom to help pass the time. Polly could only find two.

One was the book of pictures Oliver had painted as a child; the other, illustrated verses of Heaven and Hell from the Bible.

Alice looked at the pages, Kerensa sitting on the bed beside her, with only a flickering interest for a short period of time before pushing them away and lying back on the pillows. She concentrated on her breathing according to Beatrice's instructions, unaware that Kerensa, holding her hand and murmuring encouraging phrases, was more nervous than she was herself.

Another hour slipped by, and as Alice felt the need to push her child into the world, Polly put her head round the door to inform them Clem had returned and was asking for news.

'Tell un to 'old on a bit longer,' Beatrice rasped across the room, 'us went be long now, the Good Lord willin'. Then git yerself back 'ere, us may 'ave need of 'ee.'

'Offer Mr Trenchard food and drink in the parlour, Polly,' Kerensa said, before the housekeeper shut the door.

Alice cried out as pain gripped her heaving body. Beatrice tied two strips of cloth to the bedhead, and forcing the girl's hands away from their tightening grip on Kerensa's, guided them to clutch the cloth.

''ang on to they, maid, or 'ee'll crush the missus,' she told the girl. 'You come 'ere,' she ordered Kerensa next. 'You the faintin' sort?'

'No, I don't think so,' she replied.

'Good, roll up they sleeves an' les git to work.'

With the bedcovers removed and old draw-sheets under her exposed lower half, Alice pushed down hard at the beginning of the next contraction.

Beatrice slapped her bare buttocks. 'Push from 'ere, maid, not yer throat, or we'll be 'ere all the blessed night.'

Dabbing a wet cloth to wipe perspiration from Alice's face and body, Kerensa urged her to push as Beatrice instructed. Minutes ticked by as Alice screwed up her face, grunting in the effort to bring to an end the most strenuous task of her young life. Polly had returned, and after attending the fire to keep the room warm, made up the cradle brought down from the nursery in readiness for its newest occupant.

'How... much... longer?' Alice gasped.

'Yourn almost there,' Beatrice told her.

''ere, missus,' she said to Kerensa, 'kneel yerself up on the bed and take the maid's arm. Git yerself on the other side,' she shouted to Polly, who was standing away at a discreet distance. ''old 'er up in a nigh sittin' position,' Beatrice ordered them. She then took Alice's hands and placed them under her knees. 'I can see the 'ead, maid. Pull on yer legs, push like Hell on yer next pain, and altogether we'll 'ave un out.'

Alice pushed, grunted and groaned for twenty minutes. Kerensa and Polly had to work hard, with their arms linked together behind her back and under her armpits, to hold her upright and stop her throwing herself off the bed.

'Is... it... nearly over?' Alice whimpered, her head falling back on Kerensa's shoulder.

'The next push, if it's a good un.'

Beatrice was right. Three and a half minutes later, Clem Trenchard's first child lustily bawled its way out of its mother's body, and into

Beatrice's waiting capable hands. Alice had thrown back her head with the last tremendous effort and together Kerensa and Polly lowered her back on the pillows.

Rapidly cleaning round the baby's nose and mouth, Beatrice wrapped the bawling infant in a piece of linen, held it up to Alice, and triumphantly croaked, ''ere 'ee are, Mother, 'old out yer arms. No need to smack its little arse.'

Alice blinked hard as Kerensa wiped perspiration away from her tired face.

'Look, Alice,' she said, her voice choked with emotion. 'You've got a little boy.'

Alice took her son into her arms and cuddled him against her breast. She touched the fine wet hair on the top of his tiny round head. 'Oh, Kerensa, did you ever see such fair hair on a baby?' she breathed in awe.

'He's just like his father,' said Polly, her face full of wonder, the same as the others.

Gently, very gently, Kerensa stroked a fingertip over the baby's cheek. 'He is like Clem,' she whispered.

'Gis on with 'ee all,' Beatrice scoffed. 'Tes too soon for the babe to look like anything but a babe yet. He's a mite small, but a thriver, I d'reckon.'

Kerensa got slowly and very carefully off the bed, not taking her eyes away from Alice's son for a moment. She walked to the door.

'An' where do 'ee think yourn off to?' Beatrice demanded of her.

'To tell Clem he has a son.'

'You git yerself back, me 'an'some. We got more work to do 'ere yet.'

—

It was three-quarters of a hour before Kerensa joined Clem in the parlour. He was lounging back in an armchair by the fireplace, his long legs stretched out with one foot on the fender of the hearth. He was staring into the flames, his elbow on the chair's plump arm, the backs of his fingers held to his mouth. He didn't know she was there, and all

420

the anger and frustration she'd felt at his behaviour melted like snow held up to a flame. His coat lay at the side of the chair, his shirt was pulled open at the neck and she could sense how things would have been if she could walk in on him relaxing like this every night after a hard day's work. He looked young and vulnerable and handsome in the flickering firelight that painted his hair a deeper gold.

Kerensa wanted to hold him tight, the desire so intense she caught her breath. Seeing her there Clem stood up, and reading the expression on her face, held out his hands to her. Without hesitation she put her hands into his, confused for an instant at the reason for them being there together.

Then she was smiling radiantly. 'I've got wonderful news for you, Clem.'

'Well?' he said softly, moving closer until he could almost touch her body with his.

'You have a son,' she said, the excitement inside her bubbling over. 'In fact, you have two sons!'

'What? Two! Are you sure?'

'Of course I'm sure. I've just witnessed their births,' she laughed. 'The second baby was no surprise to Beatrice, but quite a shock to the rest of us. He's only half the size of your first born and can't be any more than three pounds in weight. You must go up and see Alice, she's so proud.'

'She's all right, isn't she?'

'Yes, she's fine. Come upstairs and see her.'

'In a minute. I want to say something to you first.' His hands were warm as he pressed them tighter around hers. 'I'm sorry about this afternoon, Kerensa. I behaved like a rat towards you.'

'Forget that now, Clem. And, anyway, it's me who should be sorry. I had no right to say those things to you.'

'You were right,' he said. 'Right in what you said and right to say it.' With his eyes fixed firmly on hers he raised her hands to his lips, kissing them both tenderly. 'I could never hurt you, believe that.'

Before Kerensa could respond to this a flurry of movement, ending at her skirts, made them both look down.

'Bob,' Kerensa laughed, 'how did you get in here?'

'I let him in,' Oliver said coldly from the doorway. 'Take your hands away from my wife, Trenchard.'

'It's all right, Oliver,' Kerensa said, as Clem released her hands and she scooped Bob up into her arms. 'I've just come down to tell Clem that Alice has delivered twin sons.'

'How nice for him,' Oliver retorted, crossing the room and standing pointedly between them. 'Then I suggest he goes upstairs and sees how his wife is.'

Clem met the anger in Oliver's dark eyes with a direct gaze. Inside he was jubilant. He had taken back a little of the girl the other man had stolen from him.

'If you'll excuse me, my lord,' he said, pride and defiance in his voice, 'I'll go up and see my son. That is… both my sons.' Sweeping his coat up from the floor, he hung it in careless fashion over his shoulder and with a more than friendly smile to Kerensa, jauntily left the parlour.

Holding back his outrage at the youth's behaviour Oliver faced his wife. Her eyes shone as she told him all about the newly born Trenchard twins, totally unaware of his growing irritation with her.

How naive you still are, he thought, his poor wife upstairs only just delivered in childbed, and Clem Trenchard here holding your hands, standing far too close to you… almost making love to you… but you did not notice it at all.

'Beatrice was marvellous,' Kerensa was saying. 'She didn't give the second little baby a smack to make it cry when he was born, says she doesn't believe in it. She just gently blew on his little belly and he cried at once. The first one was born crying lustily. Oh, Oliver, you should see them, the babies are—'

He rudely snatched Bob away. 'If you don't mind, this little fellow deserves some attention, or have you forgotten all about him because of the Trenchard brats? I'm taking Bob for a long walk, a very long walk.'

'—so tiny,' Kerensa finished stupidly as her husband stormed out of the room.

'Is it all right to come in?' Oliver whispered. The Manor was quiet for the night and every sound would echo throughout its length and breadth in the stillness.

'Yes, of course you can,' Alice whispered back from the bed.

He closed the door behind him and crept over to her, glancing around the room by the light of the candle he was holding before putting it down.

'Where are your babies?' he asked, speaking now in his normal voice.

'Beatrice and Polly have taken them into the next room so I can rest better until their next feed.'

Sitting on the bed he studied her face by candlelight, then picked up her hand. 'How are you feeling, Alice?'

'I'm feeling very well, thank you, Oliver. I don't know how I would have managed without Kerensa staying with me all the time through it. Beatrice said it was all over very quickly for a first labour.' Alice's voice was weak and her face looked strained but she had taken on a new maturity and Oliver could feel her elation.

'Having twins must have been a shock too, but then twins run in your family, don't they?'

'Well, I must admit I was frightened at first when the pains started again, but once Beatrice told me what was happening I was all right. I'll never forget the look on Kerensa's face, bless her. Sometimes she looks so very young.'

'I know what you mean, Alice,' he said vexedly.

Alice tapped him firmly on the arm. 'Have you said anything to upset her, Oliver? She seemed so different when she came back in here after Clem had left for home. You're not upset because she hasn't become pregnant herself, are you?'

'No, of course not.' He smiled at her. 'I wouldn't be that unfair, Alice. I won't be able to stay long and I've come to talk about you, not Kerensa. What does your husband think of his sons?' he asked. 'And you? You wanted a daughter and received not one son, but two. Are you very disappointed?'

'Clem didn't say much, but I think he's quietly pleased. As for me, I was disappointed for a minute or so… but never mind, they're both seemingly healthy. Perhaps I'll have a daughter one day, and you your son, Oliver.'

'I'd drink to that, if I'd brought one with me,' he said lightheartedly.

'And your future with Clem, what do you think that will hold?' Oliver had serious doubts for Alice's future happiness as unwelcome thoughts of her husband holding Kerensa's hands as a lover would, filtered into his mind.

'Oh, I'll make it work somehow. Don't worry about me. You just look after Kerensa, she's very dear to me.' Alice kissed his cheek.

'You're a good friend to have, Oliver Pengarron. I owe you my life, I'll never forget that.'

He retrieved his candlestick and moved to the door. 'Goodnight, Alice. God bless you.'

'Goodnight, Oliver, and God bless you too.' Oliver made his way to Kerensa. He would go to her now and make it up to her for being short with her… but he wished he knew how she felt about the young man she had once been betrothed to.

Chapter 28

Dozing in front of a small cosy fire in her sitting room, with Bob curled up contentedly on her lap, a sudden spattering of rain on the window panes woke Kerensa from a pleasant dream. Stroking the puppy who was getting too big to be on her lap, something for which Oliver would have reprimanded her if he was at home, she glanced at the clock on the mantelpiece. It was almost eleven o'clock and she was the only one in the house not in bed. She remained still, listening to the frenzied dance of rain on the glass, until the long case clock in the hall competed with the one over the fireplace to chime in the twenty-third hour.

She settled Bob for the night and looked in on Alice, who, like her sons, was sound asleep. The twins, to be baptised Philip and David, although very small, had given no cause for any concern in the two days since their birth, and Alice was to take them home to the lean-to on Trecath-en Farm on the morrow.

Clem had turned up the evening after their births to be met by Oliver who made it plain in no uncertain terms he was not welcome and his presence in the Manor house was only tolerated for Alice's sake. He'd come again that evening but stayed only long enough to inform Alice he would arrive with his mother the next morning to take his family home. As soon as Clem had gone Oliver left for Sir Martin's for a night at the card table, and after that planned to pay a brief call on his distant cousins at Zennor before going on to look over property at Penzance.

Kerensa was thinking of Clem as she walked through the door of the master bedroom from her dressing room, tying the satin ribbons at the neck of her nightgown. As she closed the door terror raced through

425

her when a hand was placed firmly over her mouth. She turned round to face her assailant and a quiet voice told her not to be afraid. The hand was taken away.

'Dear Lord, Clem,' she whispered shakily, 'what on earth are you doing here?'

'When I was leaving I noticed Jack saddling Conomor and as soon as he rode off, I slipped back into the house and hid.' He had a brightness in his eyes and voice. 'When I heard the King sisters and Daniel's cousin going to bed, I came in here to wait for you.'

'But why, Clem? I... I don't understand,' she said, endeavouring to regain her composure. 'You must leave at once. Oliver will be back at any moment.'

'No, he won't. I listened in on a conversation between Jack and Nathan. I know exactly where he's gone and how long he will be away... all night.'

Moving quickly away to the other side of the room she turned back to face him squarely. 'Why have you done this, Clem?'

'To see you, Kerensa,' he replied, knowing she could read his secret thoughts, 'why else?'

She dared to ask the next question. 'But why exactly?'

He came over to her, the nearness of him shouting a warning to her. She felt him drawing her to him in more than spirit, compelling her to look at him, the desire on his face plain in the glow from the bright restless firelight. His lips hardly moved as he spoke the words.

'There's only one reason why I'm here, Kerensa—to make love to you.'

'No...' she breathed.

He cut off her escape before she completed a single step away from him, drawing her body to his and raising her face to look into his summer-blue eyes.

'Let me go, Clem,' she implored him, beating her fists on his back and shoulders, kicking her bare feet against his legs. 'Let go of me!'

'No, Kerensa, I won't, not this time. You were meant to be mine from the beginning and I'm not leaving this room until I have not just a part of you, but all of you... every last part of you.'

426

He crushed his mouth down on hers, kissing her until her arms fell to her sides and she felt he would drain her very soul.

'Clem, for pity's sake,' she gasped, when at last he brought the kiss to an end, 'think of Alice.'

'Forget Alice, forget everyone, now is not the time for me to search my conscience.'

She was aware of the intensity of her desire and arousal and forced herself not to look into the eyes that would melt the harshest heart. He was running his lips down her neck, behind her ears, back to her temples; demanding a response; heightening her awareness of his masculine scent, the leanness of his body; coaxing her to yield, tempting her sensuality to rise and break to the surface...

'You must stop this,' she murmured.

'I'll stop this moment if you tell me you don't want me,' Clem challenged her, his breath hot on her flushed face. 'Tell me you don't want me, tell me you don't love me, and I'll disappear into the night and out of your life forever.'

She did not move or struggle. She did not say a word. He only had to look down into her eyes to know he had won. Victory flooded him, body, mind and soul. There was no longer need for words. At last he could take what he wanted more than life itself. Soft, smooth arms slid up his chest and around his neck, tender fingers undid the strip of silk catching his hair and let it float to the floor. Warm, moist red lips returned the delicious pain of his next possessive kiss.

Slowly, he lowered them on to the luxurious thick carpet under their feet, opening her mouth wider with his, caressing her body through the silkiness of her gown. He touched the places forbidden to him before, then pulled apart those satin ribbons at her throat, sliding the smooth material down to present himself with her fragrant soft bare flesh. He kissed and tasted this tribute to him, so soft and silky and perfectly shaped and formed.

'I love you, Kerensa,' Clem whispered tenderly. 'I love you so much it hurts, it's eating away inside of me.'

She stroked his silky hair and traced a line down his face with a gentle fingertip.

'You do love me, Kerensa… say it… tell me…'

She smiled dreamily. 'I love you, Clem.'

Easing his shirt from his breeches she ran her hands over the bare skin of his back and neck, opening her lips to his again and again. Keeping his lips on hers, he lifted her nightgown.

At that instant something inside her froze. Clem's kisses were as tender and as passionate as the moment required, his touch as silky smooth, exciting, demanding. His body was eager for hers as it sought to claim her. But he was not Oliver.

Oh my God! her mind screamed. What am I doing… Oliver!

With all the strength she could summon, she pushed Clem violently aside. Caught offguard he fell heavily towards the fire, his hand hitting a log, sending sparks flying.

'I… I can't, Clem. I'm sorry,' she cried, horrified with herself. Rolling away she sat up, straightening her gown and shaking it down to her feet.

Kerensa thought he might be angry, or beg her to return to him, or come after her and try to rouse her again with more kisses. But Clem sat on the carpet with his head down in defeat. Like her he was trembling violently, but she couldn't make out if he was laughing or crying.

She did not know what to do. 'Clem?'

'You love me, yes,' he said wearily. 'But you love him more, don't you?'

'Yes,' Kerensa replied quietly. 'I… I'm sorry. I didn't realise that I did love him – how much – until just now.'

Clem patted the carpet beside him and sighed. 'Sit down, Kerensa, I won't touch you again, I promise.'

There had not been a moment before tonight when Kerensa felt she couldn't trust Clem and quickly she decided she risked nothing by trusting him now. She returned to the carpet, sitting down close and facing him. Faces flushed by their amorous behaviour and its abrupt end, they talked.

'I thought if I could make love to you just once, Kerensa, it would be enough to take away this terrible longing I have for you. I thought

428

I could then face all the long lonely years I have ahead, knowing you will never be mine.' He sighed heavily. 'But I was wrong. If you hadn't stopped me it would have sparked off an even greater desire inside me for you… and I would have wanted you more and more.'

'You were thinking this way on the night the twins were born, weren't you?' she said. 'Oliver noticed it but I didn't… he must think me very young and foolish at times.'

Clem gave a short ironic laugh. 'It's part of the reason why he loves you.'

Kerensa's eyes widened in surprise. 'Loves me? Oliver?'

Clem looked away and stared into the flames of the fire. 'Has he never told you?'

'No.' She was incredulous. 'He has said nothing of the kind. Clem, why do you say he does?'

'Because,' he said with a feeling of desolation, 'he told me so.'

'You, Clem! Of all people, he told you? But why? I don't understand.'

Clem sighed again. 'Do you think I could have some of that fine brandy he keeps in this room?' he said, shrugging his shoulders as if he was trying to shake off some horror. 'I'm not finding this easy and my throat's so dry I feel as though I'm choking.' He rubbed at his throat to reinforce his words then got up and moved away from the burning heat of the fire while tucking his shirt into his breeches.

Kerensa brought him a glass with very little brandy in it. 'I'm sorry it can't be more, but Oliver would notice,' she said, looking anxiously at Clem and feeling torn apart by his look of abject misery. She hated herself at that moment. Why did she have to keep hurting him?

'This will do,' he said, drinking it straight down and handing her back the glass. He took a deep breath and let the fiery liquid burn, then soothe, the churning of his gut.

'I've got an idea how you're feeling, Clem. I wanted you too,' she murmured, looking down at her hands tightly clasped in her lap. 'Part of me still does… and part of me always will.'

'It means a lot to me to hear you say that, Kerensa, but it's better we try and forget what nearly happened. I'll tell you how I know your husband loves you and then I'll go.' He gulped and cleared his throat. 'The night you nearly died of the fever, Alice asked him... Sir Oliver... if I could see you. I was really surprised when she came downstairs and told me he had agreed. When I entered this bedroom, I thanked him. The look on his face alone was enough to tell me how he felt about you. Then he said, "You love her too." Do you understand, Kerensa? "You love her too." In that one short sentence he told me he loved you.'

Clem got slowly to his feet and stood in front of her. She raised her face to his. 'There you are, my little sweet, you've made even the high and mighty Lord of the Manor fall in love with you.'

'I had no idea,' Kerensa said. 'I've never known how he's felt one minute to the next. His moods can swing so very quickly... he's so different to anyone else I know.'

'Perhaps that is why you love him,' Clem said, pain burning in his eyes. Touching her hair with the lightest of caresses, he turned to go.

'Clem, wait.' Kerensa jumped up and took his arm. 'When I married Oliver I felt so bad about what it did to you, but now... now I've realised that I love him... I feel as though I've betrayed you again.'

'There's no need for you to feel like that,' he returned. 'You've betrayed no one, but I nearly betrayed my love for you by putting you in an impossible situation just now. I nearly betrayed Alice too.'

'What will you do now?'

'Try to be a good father to my sons, a better husband to Alice... I've treated her so badly, I have a lot to make up to her. It's ironic,' and Clem laughed in the manner of his last word, 'I resented Alice because I believed that by having her as my wife she had taken me further away from you, yet all the time you were falling in love with your husband and moving away from me yourself. You asked me once not to hurt her and I'll do my best to give her some of the happiness she deserves. And you, Kerensa? What will you do?'

'Go on as before. Don't concern yourself about me, Clem.'

'He's a proud man, your husband. I suspect he's not sure of your feelings for him, or whether or not you still love me. It won't be him who declares his love first.'

Kerensa nodded. She knew Clem was right.

From somewhere he summoned a smile. 'If you ever need me...' he murmured, then quickly he was gone and she was alone.

Huddled on the carpet before the fire, Kerensa reflected on the bitter-sweet events of the last few months. So she loved Oliver, did she? Well that was no surprise to her really. After all, she had been drawn to him since that very first day he had come to Trelynne Cove... and she had been drawn to this huge old house the very first time she had come here.

Dear sad Clem... What was it Rachael had said to her about him? 'You don't sound as though you have an all consuming passion for him'... But she still felt love for him, even now. Kerensa knew that would never change.

And Alice, who had been her friend, her maid, and then Clem's wife? Thank God you will always be my friend, Alice, she thought, embarrassed by thoughts of what she had almost done with Clem.

Now Alice had Philip and David, but not the daughter she had hoped for. Was there to be a hopeful future for them, would Clem be able to change and treat Alice with the kindness and affection she deserved? 'I hope so, with all my heart,' Kerensa whispered.

Why did Clem being here tonight and their nearly making love remind her of the mysterious Hezekiah? He had smiled his angel smile, then told her: 'You are innocent of this world. Take care someone like me does not destroy you. There will always be someone who may try. Not necessarily an enemy, perhaps someone who loves you...' Clem... if she had made love with him, how would she now be able to face Oliver, knowing she loved him? Kerensa shuddered at that thought. It frightened her a little.

She stared into the deep red and gold flames. How like they were to the human emotions... slowly kindled or raging... twisted, contorted... burning themselves out... to be relit again?

What now that I know I love you, Oliver? she thought with intense longing. It's warm and cosy here in our bedroom tonight. I wish with all my heart you were with me.

Chapter 29

Having ridden early to Marazion, Kerensa left Kernick with Ned Angove for an inspection of the pony's shoes. The town was already busy for the Thursday market. There were traders putting up stalls, farmers herding livestock into pens, farmers' wives with large baskets of butter, cheese, eggs, cream and preserves to sell. Travelling herbalists and apothecaries, dried flower sellers and knife sharpeners, and pedlars offering a multitude of cheap and gaudy wares.

She had a guinea in her purse in case she saw anything that took her fancy on the numerous, bunched together stalls as she left the blacksmith's shop to join the early shoppers and bargain hunters. There was nothing that Kerensa particularly wanted to do, or see, or buy. She wandered slowly in and out of the groups of people and rickety tables of colourful wares, keeping a sharp eye open for pickpockets and early drunkards. She thanked a filthy looking farmhand who threw a pile of fresh straw over a recently made heap of pig droppings so she wouldn't have to defile her riding boots as she passed him by.

She was pleased it was too early for the talents of the showmen, acrobats, freak shows and card tricksters to be put on display. As always, she was repulsed at the moth-eaten appearance of a wretched muzzled brown bear, who never seemed to perform for its master despite the all too frequent lashes it would receive. Kerensa was wondering if the owner would accept her guinea for the bear, and if there was a hut big enough to house the poor animal in at the back of the Manor, when the man in question looked up in front of her. She opened her mouth to speak but the bear trainer looked fiercer than his animal so she turned and beat a hasty retreat.

Leaving the marketplace she walked the length of the town's long dusty street to make her way down to the beach facing the castle on the Mount. She would have liked to take off her boots to feel the cold rough sand under her bare feet, but her position as wife of the Lord of the Manor forbade any such frivolous action. Gazing across the quarter mile of deep sea, the tide being fully in, she watched the rocking sails of the merchant ships moored up at the Mount's splendid new pier. Her thoughts travelled to far distant exotic ports and countries, trying to picture what it might be like in Brittany, the Channel Islands, the Caribbean, the West Indies, or Portsmouth, Plymouth; Penzance even. She'd never been on a sailing ship, the farthest distance she had ever been away from home was here, Marazion.

A pitiful wailing broke rudely through her contemplations. An infant who could just about walk, and dressed only in a filthy tattered rag to its knees, was heading in her direction, crying at the highest pitch of its young voice. Looking quickly about Kerensa could see no one who might be responsible for the infant and she ran over to meet it. The child stopped dead when it saw her and she crouched down in front of it.

'Hello, what's the matter, my handsome?' she said very gently, not wanting to frighten the child. 'Are you lost?'

Kerensa was shocked by the child's appearance. Unable to tell if it was a boy or a girl she reckoned it to be about fifteen months old, with skin so dirty that lice were crawling over its body and through its hair. Bruises and scratches could be easily detected through the dirt, and the smell of dried urine and excreta that assaulted her nose was foul in the extreme.

'You poor little thing. Who on God's earth has left you like this?'

The infant held out its tiny arms to the source of comfort it had suddenly found and Kerensa picked it up. Holding its small light body in close she wiped away its tears and some of the dirt as it stared at her with huge eyes that seemed permanently startled.

'It's all right, little one,' she said soothingly, 'You poor little soul, you'll be all right with me.'

''ere! What the 'ell do 'ee think yer doin' with that brat!' An unkempt sailor was bearing down upon them with an angry scowl on his face.

Kerensa was angry too. She held protectively on to the child and hurled an accusing question at the sailor. 'Are you responsible for this child and the dreadful state it's in?'

'What if I am? Tes no bisness of yourn. Git yer 'ands off 'im.'

'So it's a little boy, is it?' she snapped back. 'No one can tell in this filthy rag he's got on. Where's his mother?'

'Dead, an' a good job too.'

The sailor made a step forward and the little boy began its pitiful wail again in obvious fear of the overbearing man. Kerensa stood her ground, glaring back into the evil face that bore a deep scar across one eye that slanted from forehead to cheek-bone. The sailor scratched his bald head and Kerensa was amazed at the long wiry hair on the back of his hand. He was a grotesquely hairy individual except for his bald head, his face and throat adorned with a thick matted beard, more of the same bursting from the top of his shirt. A pot belly spilled over his breeches and the breezes off the sea wafted his beastly smell of stale alcohol and sweat and vomit over her. He smelled like the shroud of a long dead corpse.

Kerensa felt sick and more than a little afraid of this repulsive man, but her anger and indignation were much stronger. 'Are you the child's father?' she said, raising an authoritative voice above the infant's wailing.

'Ais, what's that to thee?'

'Why is he in such a filthy state and quite obviously beaten? No one has the right to treat a child like this.'

Putting his hairy hands on his hips the sailor swayed his lower body from side to side and leered at her. 'My, aren't we a grand lady with our fine clothes, askin' questions an' tellin' a man 'ow 'e can treat 'is rightful child. Course, the brat mebbe mine, mebbe not. Some other's bastard is more like it. Who are 'ee anyway? 'ee looks like a piece o' quality but yer voice tells a diff'rent story. Someone's fancy mistress, eh?'

The infant stopped crying and turning his frightened eyes from the sailor he rested his head on Kerensa's shoulder. He smelled dreadful but she held back her disgust as the man snickered at his son's filth soiling the sleeves on her riding habit and cloak.

Clearing her throat she said haughtily, 'My name is Kerensa Pengarron. I am the wife of Sir Oliver Pengarron. You may have heard of him.'

The sailor chuckled and muttered something vile under his breath. 'Well, well, well. A real lady, 'pon my soul. Ais, my pretty, I d'know that Pengar'n bastard. Accused me once of wreckin' and plunderin' a ship that run aground nearly in this very spot four years ago... taken to beddin' little small maids, 'as 'e? Got an eye fer young'uns these days, eh? What'd 'e marry thee fer? Yer not gentry, though I d'reckon 'e went find none as pretty as thee 'mong that God-fer-sakin' lot.' Spitting at Kerensa's feet he jeered as she jumped back.

'What are you going to do with your son?' she said, keeping her eyes fixed on the sailor lest he rapidly advance on her. 'Who looks after him when you're away at sea?'

''arlots. That's who's bin mindin' 'im since that bitch 'is mother died. She wus an 'arlot too, curse 'er rotten soul. Died of the pox more 'n' likely. Well, they went 'ave 'im no more since I come ashore so I'm going to sell the brat in the market. Now give 'im 'ere!'

He thrust out a brutal hand and snatched the little boy's thin arm and tried to yank him from Kerensa's tight hold. The child screamed and clutched at her hair and clothes.

'You can't sell your own child!' she shouted wildly, pulling back as hard as she could.

'I can do what I damn well like with 'im!'

'Wait! Please! Wait a moment.'

The sailor smirked lewdly at her frantic face. 'Well, pretty lady, yer goin' to give me somethin' worth waitin' fer?'

'How much do you want for him? For the child? I'll buy him from you.'

'Now yer talkin' my language,' he said, taking his hand off the boy's arm. ''ow much yer off'rin'?'

'A guinea,' Kerensa said, hoping it would be enough to satisfy the sailor's greed. 'I have a guinea in my purse.'

'A guinea!' he laughed out. 'Now a rich young lady like yerself can do better than that. I'll git a shillin' or two in the market fer 'im so I'm not takin' no bloody measly guinea from the gentry.'

'But I have no more with me today,' Kerensa pleaded. 'Surely a guinea is better than a shilling, and you have no use for the child. I'll give him a good home and see he is brought up properly for you.'

'I don't give a damn 'ow the brat's brung up. Got any jewellery on 'ee, 'ave 'ee?'

The only jewellery of value Kerensa could call her own was the exquisite pearl necklace Oliver had presented her with for her birthday. She would have handed it over to the sailor without compunction, risking Oliver's wrath; but market day in Marazion was neither the time nor place to wear such a valuable thing and so she hadn't put it on.

'No,' she replied, her stomach knotting, 'I would not wear jewellery here for fear of it being stolen.'

'Very wise of yer, pretty lady, but that's no good to me, is it?' 'Ow good in bed are 'ee? 'Alf 'our in some quiet little place might 'elp me change me mind 'bout the guinea.'

Fighting down the nausea rising in her throat Kerensa looked again at the ships moored up at the Cornish Mount. If only Hezekiah Solomon was there she could ask him to lend her some money, but there was no sign of *Free Spirit* or its white haired captain. The sailor had followed her eyes and winked when she looked back at him.

'Lookin' fer a lover mebbe?' He touched his body in a crude gesture making Kerensa wince.

'Please take the guinea,' she begged him. 'The purse too if you like… and my hat and my cloak.'

'They went be no use to me, can't be bothered to go round sellin' 'em,' retorted the sailor. 'Now give that brat to me or I'll 'ave the law on 'ee.'

'No!' Kerensa cried angrily. 'I'm quite sure you wouldn't go one step near a magistrate. But I will. And I wonder what he'll have to say about the wilful ill-treatment of this poor child.'

436

'You'll what! A man can do what 'e likes to 'is rightful son in any way 'e God-damned chooses!' The sailor was furious. He gripped the infant by his arm and the back of his neck, causing him to scream in pain and terror.

Kerensa fought to hold on to him, screaming, 'No! No! I won't let you take him!'

Some rough looking acquaintances of the sailor were gathering round as he and the grim-faced girl struggled and fought over the little boy. They laughed and clapped and uttered vile innuendoes as the tussle continued, cheering wildly as the sailor won the battle by brute force as he hurled Kerensa back on the sand, having wrenched the child out of her despairing hands. Thrusting the child under his arm he stalked off, laughing loudly and heartily with his cronies.

But Kerensa was not beaten yet. Quickly scrambling to her feet she raced after the sailor and grabbed his free arm, clinging on, like a limpet to a shoreline rock, as he tried to shake her off while keeping up his long bow-legged strides. He twisted his hand round to stroke her face and she recoiled from his rough touch.

'Changed yer mind, me 'an'some,' 'bout 'aving a little lie-down with me, 'ave 'ee?' he laughed crudely, his cronies joining in.

'I have a pony at the blacksmith's,' she got out breathlessly. 'Its saddle is made of the finest quality leather. You could sell it for at least ten or fifteen guineas, maybe a lot more.'

The sailor stopped short. With a nod he thrust the screaming infant back to her. 'You 'ave a deal, pretty lady, lead me to it an' the brat's yourn,' he said, rubbing his dirty hands together.

'Only the two of us and the child,' Kerensa said, warily eyeing the other rough-looking men.

'Looks like she fancies 'ee after all, shipmate,' one said, nudging the sailor with an elbow and winking a bloated eye.

'You dock-rats 'eard what she said. Clear off, you scum!' the sailor growled. 'An' show some respect. Me an' this lady 'ere is doin' bisness.'

Walking as fast as she could towards Ned Angove's shop, Kerensa tried to keep a few steps in front of the sailor. She cooed to the little boy who gradually became quiet, putting his thumb into his mouth and staring up at her with large frightened eyes. Stallholders, shoppers and passersby stared curiously at the small group as they reached the marketplace, but Kerensa ignored them.

As they approached the blacksmith's shop Ned dropped his hammer with a clatter on the stone floor and hurried to find out the meaning of this strange situation. His wide brow furrowed as Kerensa explained all that had happened and the clear plan she had conceived of what she wanted to do next. Ned wasn't sure whether he should try to talk her out of her plans or not. But he could see she was firmly set on having her own way, so he called his daughter, Lowenna, to fetch a clerk from Nancarrow and Holborn, Notaries and Commissioners of oaths. Before Lowenna left, Kerensa scribbled and signed a note for her to take to Mistress Gluyas' shop, asking the dressmaker to send back with Lowenna some infant's clothes suitable for the little boy to wear.

Close to the blacksmith's was Araminta Bray's grocer's shop, its windows well stocked with goods from Oliver's freetrading activities. Quite unable to bear being in the presence of the sailor for a moment longer, Kerensa took the child into the shop, leaving Ned Angove to pick up his hammer and keep a watchful eye on the boy's father.

Leaving her other customers at once, Araminta Bray, a widow with a vacuous face and sharply receding chin, ushered Kerensa into a back room. She asked Oliver no questions about the goods he provided to sell in her shop, and none to Kerensa about her reasons for having a filthy ragged infant in her possession.

Peering over the top of her circular-framed spectacles, Araminta listened without comment as Kerensa outlined a brief account of her encounter with the child and his father and the reason for the errand Lowenna Angove had been sent on. As she listened she put an old tin bowl of hot water, a cake of harsh-smelling soap, and clean towels on a wooden table in the corner of the room for the child to be washed. Then leaving Kerensa to return to the shop, she promised to look out for Lowenna's return and to send her in with the clerk and the clothes.

Sitting the little boy on the table, Kerensa laid her cloak aside and began to wash him with gentle hands. Carefully she tugged off the close-fitting filthy rag and threw it on the fire. She could have cried at the condition of his body. His stomach was distended from constant hunger, his skin thinly stretched over protruding bones and covered with weeping sores. If Kerensa could hate anyone, it was the people responsible for this sort of cruelty.

Lowenna joined her with the information that the clerk would be along shortly with pen, ink and paper as requested. She brought with her a baby's linen gown, a square of cloth for a napkin, a thick knitted shawl and a small blanket. She helped Kerensa to finish washing the boy, gently rubbing off more filth from his tiny body while Kerensa held him on her lap. Although he looked uncomfortable at all the unaccustomed and unwelcome attention he was receiving, he sat still without complaint, looking from one girl to the other with wonderfully sad brown eyes.

'Don't make much fuss, do he, m'lady?' Lowenna said, frowning as she rubbed at his sore skin.

'Probably has received too many beatings even to try now,' Kerensa said, with an exasperated sigh.

'I made some enquiries about the little boy on the way back from getting the clothes, m'lady,' Lowenna said excitedly. 'These, by the way, were made up for Mayor Oke's grandson but Mistress Gluyas said she'll arrange for some more to be done for him.' It was like an adventure to the girl, all this intrigue over the little boy and making an expedition to Mistress Gluyas' shop, a place she had always dreamed of going into but never believing she would.

'Never mind about Mayor Oke's grandson, Lowenna, what did you find out about the little boy here?' Kerensa asked eagerly.

'Well, m'lady, seems he was born to one of they women from the brothel on the outskirts of the west side of the town. Tis reckoned just about anyone could be his father, poor little beggar. Seems his mother was married to that sailor in Father's shop, but she went into the brothel, what with him being out to sea most of the time.'

'I see,' Kerensa said, wrapping the boy in a towel and patting him dry. 'That will do for now, I think, it will take days to get all this dirt completely off and he's beginning to shiver again. Will you help me get the gown on him, please?'

Lowenna carefully lowered the gown over the boy's head and helped Kerensa pull his arms through the sleeves. 'I thought this would be better for his sore skin than a little shirt and leggings,' Lowenna said. 'It was so exciting choosing the things Mistress Gluyas' assistants showed me.'

'You were right in your choice and I'm grateful to you, Lowenna. I'll give you another note and you go back there again and choose something for yourself.' Kerensa smiled. 'I've seen a lot of undernourished children, Lowenna, but never one as badly treated as this before. I wonder how old he is.'

'About two years, according to one woman I spoke to. Don't know how she knew, mind you, and thanks for what you said about the note, m'lady. You caused quite a stir walking through the market with him and that awful sailor. Everybody's talking about it.'

'I don't care what anyone says. And if this child's two years old he's far too small for his age, but then that's no surprise. I'll have to get plenty of good food inside of him.' Finding a clean patch on the boy's cheek, Kerensa kissed him there and he nestled close to her and put his thumb into his mouth.

'That clerk should be in the smithy by now, I'll go fetch him,' Lowenna said, making for the shop door. 'Mrs Bray said to warm up some milk for the young'un, I'll do it when I come back.' She hesitated before leaving, 'M'lady…'

'Yes, Lowenna?'

'Are… are you really going to buy that little boy from his father?'

'Yes,' came the wavering reply.

'But, if you don't mind me saying so, what if Sir Oliver doesn't like it?'

Kerensa held the little boy close and lifted her chin high. 'Well, he'll just *have* to like it.'

The boy noisily lapped up warm milk from a spoon while the clerk from Nancarrow and Holborn, a hooked-nose young man with an air of importance about him, sat at the table and wrote out a legal document. Kerensa gave clear information for the transfer of the child from his father to her as legal guardian. She emphasised the wording was to be precise, and his father would have no claim on him at any future date.

The sailor was sent for and brought in through a back door of the grocer's shop by Ned Angove, who stood like a sentry watching and listening for any signs of trouble. Kerensa signed the document hiring first had it read out for their joint approval, then the sailor did so with a scrawled X. Ned and the clerk witnessed it. The boy slept, comfortably folded in Kerensa's arms, as his father signed him away without a single look.

'You come with me now,' Ned Angove rumbled after Kerensa handed over the guinea. 'I'll give you the saddle and then you can clear off.'

'Wait… please,' Kerensa called out, as Ned lifted the latch of the door.

The sailor made no attempt to stop but the burly blacksmith blocked his way. Reluctantly the sailor turned round. 'What do 'ee want?' he scowled at Kerensa.

'What's his name, the boy's?' she said.

'Lemme see.' He scratched flakes of dirty dry skin off his bald head. 'Kane… Kane, I d'believe 'is mother called him.'

'And his other name?'

'That's no concern of yourn,' the sailor spat. 'From now on the little bastard can be called Pengar'n.'

Chapter 30

The driver of the carriage Kerensa hired helped her down on to the gravel driveway outside the Manor house. She thanked him, then shifted the sleeping child who had grown heavy in her arms.

'If you'll wait, I'll have some money sent out to you,' she said.

'No need for that, m'lady,' replied the friendly driver. 'Someone can settle up next time they're in town.'

The carriage was drawing away when Polly opened the huge main door to her. 'My lady!' she gasped, at the unexpected sight before her.

'Is Sir Oliver still here, Polly?' asked Kerensa, bringing Kane into the warmth of his new home.

'Yes, my lady,' Polly said, following closely at the girl's heels and peering over her shoulder at the child who was waking up. 'He was about to leave for Ker-an-Mor Farm but has just come back for something and gone into his study.'

'Good. Will you fetch me a tray of food and tea please, Polly? I'm ravenously hungry.'

'And in need of a clean dress,' the housekeeper remarked, wrinkling her nose.

'That can wait. I've put up with the smell this past hour and more so a bit longer won't hurt me.'

Polly excitedly dashed off to the kitchen and Kerensa walked into her husband's study.

'Oliver, I owe some money for a carriage I hired from Marazion, and Jack will have to ride over to Ned Angove's and collect Kernick.'

Not having heard such a blunt statement, delivered so directly and positively from her before, Oliver looked up from his desk. He gazed at her as she stood in the doorway, holding a small child who was looking up at her with its thumb in its mouth.

'There's no fire in here,' she went on disapprovingly. 'I'll take him through to my sitting room. Ruth should have lit one in there by now. This is Kane, by the way.'

'Kerensa…' Oliver began.

But she had already left the room. He followed her into her sitting room where she placed the child in an armchair and pulled off her hat and cloak.

'Kerensa,' Oliver started again, 'will you tell me what's been happening and what you're doing with that child?'

He didn't sound cross, only puzzled, but she was still in a protective mood. 'I'm not giving Kane up, whatever you say,' she told him fiercely, taking the boy into her arms again. 'I had to fight to get him.'

'What do you mean, you had to fight to get him?'

'Just exactly what I said. I'll leave here before I give him up.'

'You don't have to do that, my dear,' Oliver said, becoming alarmed. 'I wasn't about to make any such suggestion, but I would like to know what this is all about.'

Kerensa sat down with Kane cuddled against her. 'I bought him in Marazion, from a dreadful sailor,' she said. 'That is, I exchanged him for my saddle and a guinea, and I had a legal document drawn up to prove it, so no one can take him away from me.'

Oliver rubbed his chin. 'You amaze me, Kerensa.'

'Have you nothing else to say?' she asked, her resolution undiminished.

'All right,' said Oliver, never one to shy away from a challenge. 'Why did you acquire the child from this… dreadful sailor?'

'Because the little boy's been so cruelly ill-treated,' she replied, anger rising in her again. 'Just look at his poor little body.'

Pulling aside the blanket and shawl, she lifted the boy's gown. Oliver came and crouched at her feet, looking intently at the bruises, scratches and sores on the child's torso. He gingerly took one tiny hand.

'Hello, Kane. You are in a sorry state, aren't you?' he murmured very softly.

'These aren't the clothes he was wearing when I came across him crying miserably on the beach. He had nothing more than a filthy rag on then. I cleaned him up in the back of Araminta Bray's shop, and Lowenna Angove took a note for me to Mistress Gluyas' for these,' Kerensa said, holding out a piece of the child's gown, pleased at Oliver's interest. 'I couldn't bear to leave him. He was going to be sold for a shilling in the market, and goodness knows what would have happened to him then.'

'Mmm, he's crawling with lice too, poor little fellow, and smells nearly as bad as Beatrice.'

'Mrs Bray gave me some soap and hot water to clean him up but it hasn't made a lot of difference. You don't mind me bringing him home, do you, Oliver?' she asked earnestly.

'I don't know… I'll have to think about it. I haven't had time to get used to the idea yet.'

With his thumb stuck firmly in his mouth, Kane's brown eyes followed all of Oliver's movements as he allowed the big man to tickle his wet dribbly chin.

'He seems to like you,' Kerensa smiled. 'The poor little mite was terrified of the sailor. He frightened me too.'

'Did he hurt you?' Oliver asked quickly, his face darkening. 'Because if he did…'

'No, it was just a horrible experience,' Kerensa replied, putting a hand on Oliver's shoulder in case he was about to ride off to Marazion to thrash the life out of the sailor.

Oliver knew what her gesture had meant. He took her hand and kissed it, then bent forward and kissed her cheek. 'Well, my love, I am very proud of you. Not many men would have had the courage to stand up to such a bully, as you obviously must have done.'

'Of course, I owe money to Nancarrow and Holborn's too for having the document drawn up, Oliver,' she said weakly, a feeling of tiredness coming over her after the excitement.

'I'll settle that, don't you worry about it.'

'What about the saddle? I told the sailor he could sell it for about fifteen guineas.'

'Double the amount is more likely.'

'Do you mind very much, Oliver? I only had a guinea and he said it wasn't enough and I couldn't think of anything else to do.'

'A saddle isn't important, my love. A child's well-being is. You sit quietly and rest while I get Beatrice to take the boy up to the nursery and Polly to see to you. What you need now is a rest and a change of clothes,' Oliver said soothingly.

'No!' Kerensa said. 'Kane won't let anyone near him but me at the moment and I don't care about myself, I won't do anything until we've settled what's to happen to him right now.'

Oliver looked taken aback but he could see her determination – and he admired her for it. 'What would you like to do with him?' he asked quietly.

'I thought of nothing else all the way home. I want to bring him up as ours, Oliver. I found him when he needed me and as far as I'm concerned he'll always need me. I felt he belonged to me at the moment I held him in my arms.' Kerensa's eyes filled with tears as she spoke. 'I couldn't let him go now, Oliver. Please try to understand, I don't want him put to a kind family on the Estate or something like that. I want him to be ours, but if you can't accept that I'll go away and keep him all to myself.'

'Dear life, Kerensa,' Oliver said, moved by her tears and intensity and fearful at her threat, 'you don't have to go, I've already told you that. In fact, you can fill the house with every stray brat in the parish if only you'll stay and never leave.'

'Do you mean it?' she said, looking into his deep dark eyes. 'That you don't ever want me to leave here and Kane can stay?'

'Yes, I couldn't bear it if you left me now, my love,' he answered softly. 'And Kane can stay.'

'As ours?'

Oliver looked into the large startled brown eyes of the child. The little boy might be between him and Kerensa now in the physical sense but there was no reason for him ever to part them. 'As ours,' Oliver whispered.

'Oh, Oliver!' Throwing an arm around his neck, Kerensa kissed him. 'I know you'll grow to love him as I do already. You're wonderful, Oliver Pengarron, for all your proud and stern ways, do you know that? And do you know that I love you so very, very much?'

'What!' Oliver exclaimed, sweeping an arm around her closely and making Kane protest at being squashed between them. 'Do you mean it, Kerensa?'

'Yes, yes, yes. I love you, and have done for a long time.'

'I love you, Kerensa Pengarron. You're wonderful. I've also loved you for a long, long time.' He was serious for a moment but then they kissed and laughed, and kissed and hugged, trying to placate Kane at the same time. 'I'd kiss the boy too if he wasn't so dirty,' Oliver asserted, but doing it anyway.

A small group of women had gathered in the room but were ignored. Having told Ruth and Esther and Beatrice about Kerensa's arrival home with the infant, Polly had come with them to view the Manor's tiny guest.

'I do 'ope they baint goin' to keep that up fer long or that little small boy there will be starved to death,' muttered Beatrice, with her lopsided grin.

Ruth and Esther exchanged indulgent glances and Polly whispered to them, 'I was beginning to think they were never going to realise how they felt about each other.'

'Yer noticed too, did 'ee?' Beatrice said, wiping away a long drop from her nose. 'Wonder 'ow long it would 'ave took 'em without the young'un coming along.'

'Good Lord,' Oliver whispered, much later in their bedroom, 'he's got the same colour hair as you.'

'You would never have guessed it,' said Kerensa, as she looked fondly down on Kane's sleeping form in the cradle only recently vacated by the Trenchard twins. 'It took three good washes to get him this clean and there's still some ground-in dirt in places. Poor little soul, I put him in the kitchen sink and he screamed and screamed so I had to take him out after only a short time. He's got a thin scar running from the side of his neck right down his back, something he'll carry for the rest of his life to remind him of his terrible beginning.'

'Do you know,' Oliver said thoughtfully, looking at Kane's head from all angles, 'he looks a cross between Arthur Beswetherick and Esau the fieldmouse.'

'Oh, he doesn't, he's beautiful. Of course I can't speak on Arthur Beswetherick,' Kerensa gave her husband a playful slap on the chest. 'What did he look like, Oliver?'

'Nothing like Martin or William. He was considered most handsome. He would have taken quite a fancy to you, my love,' Oliver said, with a saucy wink. 'I would have had to watch him very closely.' Looking back at Kane, he added, 'Arthur had the same shade of brown eyes. What's that strange smell? Reminds me of one of Beatrice's herbal ointments.'

'It is. He's got one ointment for the sores on his little body and another one to get rid of the lice.'

As they peered over the cradle Kane turned over on his side, put his thumb in his mouth, and slept on. 'Why isn't he in the nursery?' Oliver asked.

'It's too far away from our bedroom and I want to see to Kane myself. He only really seems happy with me at the moment so I asked Jack to bring the cradle in here.'

'He likes to suck his thumb, doesn't he? He'd better give up the habit if he doesn't want children like that Drannock boy teasing him when he gets older.'

'You mean Bartholomew?' Kerensa said, her face reddening at the thought of the secret she shared concerning the other, older boy. She wished she could tell Oliver what she knew. With the declaration of their love fresh in her mind she wanted to keep nothing from him, wanted nothing ever to act as a barrier between them. Perhaps one day soon the time would be right and she would tell him about his fisherman half-brother in Perranbarvah.

'Yes, that's him,' Oliver went on, taking her into his arms. 'Have a good look at him the next time you see him, my love. I believe there's Pengarron blood somewhere in that brat.'

'Why? Because he's rude and already showing more than a passing interest in girls of his own age and older?'

'No,' he said, feigning indignation. 'The day he helped pull me out of the sea I saw the look of a Pengarron in his face, I swear. Quite clear, it was. It wouldn't surprise me if one of my grandfathers was more than friendly with one of his grandmothers.'

Kerensa didn't know what to say to this and returned her attention to Kane as he stirred. 'It's a bit of a squeeze for him in here, I'll have to sort out a bed for him.' She stroked his straggly hair. 'I hope that sailor is not his real father. Any man would be better than him.'

'Well, at least he will have a better life with us than he would have had left in that wretch's hands. By the way, I got your saddle back from Ned Angove while I was in Marazion. Seems he got the sailor to agree to part with it just for one guinea. I returned Ned's guinea and gave him one for his daughter for coming to your aid. I don't think we'll ever see that sailor again.'

'Why?' Kerensa said, alarmed. 'Have you done something to him, Oliver?' She would never forget the retribution served out to Peter Blake after he had abused her.

'If I had come across him he would not have escaped a thorough thrashing, but Hezekiah is to see he will sail with him and never set foot on Cornish soil again. He'll spend the rest of his life languishing in some foreign backwater port. *Free Spirit* came in on the evening tide and Hezekiah had heard all about you and the sailor. Seems you were prepared to fight tooth and nail for the boy. I'm very proud of you, my precious love.' Kissing her warmly, Oliver pulled Kerensa to her feet. 'Come on, to bed now, and I hope the little fellow doesn't wake up for quite a while…'

'I love you with my whole being, Oliver Pengarron,' she said. 'And if I ever have to, I'll fight tooth and nail for you.'

—

'Do you think I need more holly over the mantelpiece, Beatrice?' Kerensa asked, critically viewing her handiwork at decorating her sitting room for Christmas Day.

'Naw, that'll do I d'believe, young missus. I'd best git these other bits cleared up afore the boy 'ere eats they berries.'

Kerensa looked affectionately at Kane who was lying on his stomach on the floor, happily playing tug-of-war over a wooden toy with Bob. With plenty of good food and goat's milk and an over-abundance of love and attention, the boy had undergone a remarkable change during the last few weeks. His protruding bones had gradually disappeared as his body filled out, and he quickly became sturdy on his feet while showing a notable strength at pulling apart his toys and any other item that found its way into his searching hands.

His weeping sores had healed and vanished, his red hair became straight and shiny, and although his milk teeth were either missing or rotten, Doctor Crebo, who had been called in to look him over, advised that with the correct diet and fresh air every day, his second teeth would be healthy and strong.

Kerensa was happy at last, and not the only one to dote freely on Kane. Beatrice often sat him on what little lap she had left, Jack would take his tiny hand and show him the Manor's horseflesh. Nathan held him to look up into the nests and cages of any injured animals in the hut, Jake laughed to himself and turned a blind eye when he liberally watered his plants rather than ask to be taken to the water closet, and Polly, Ruth and Esther indulged in his every whim. Oliver, who was probably the most indulgent of them all and had no belief in a child having to 'behave himself', delighted in giving him endless rides on Conomor around the stableyard.

Looking back at the mantelpiece Kerensa decided one more piece of holly would be required to complete the effect she desired and climbed up on the chair in front of her, reaching upwards.

'You be careful, m'dear,' Beatrice rasped, gathering up holly branches and sniffing noisily as her nose ran. 'I'll 'ave these outside an' the gard'ners can do what they like with 'em.'

'Why must I be careful?' Kerensa smiled. 'I'm not going to eat holly berries, Beatrice.'

'Careful of climbin' about, young missus, is what I d'mean.'

'The mantelpiece isn't that high.'

'Gis on with 'ee,' blurted Beatrice. 'I seen it in yer face days ago. Don't 'ee know yerself yet, cheeil?'

'Know what, Beatrice?' Kerensa asked, stepping down from the chair, 'What are you talking about?'

Clutching holly in one hand, Beatrice wiped the drip from her nose with the heel of the other. 'Think 'bout it,' she said, broadly grinning at the puzzled girl. 'When did Nature last pay 'ee a monthly call, eh? You haven't seen nothin' since the young'un's been 'ere, 'ave 'ee?'

It took a full ten seconds before it dawned on Kerensa what Beatrice was hinting at. Then… 'You mean?'

'Ais. Yer good 'n' proper with child at last.'

'Oh! I… that's wonderful! Oh, Beatrice!' Rushing across the room Kerensa hugged the old woman. 'Where's Oliver?' she said, jumping up and down with excitement. 'He's going over to Ker-an-Mor Farm this morning. Has he left yet? He said goodbye to us earlier.'

'Dunno, m'dear, let un go anyway, no need to run after un like every other female 'as all 'is life. Let un wait till later.'

A heavy step was heard heading towards the back of the house for the stableyard.

'That's him now,' said Kerensa.

'Let un wait, maid, like I tole 'ee. Went 'urt un.'

Kerensa paced up and down, rapidly thinking things over. She stopped and looked at Kane, then Bob, then Beatrice, rubbing her hands together before placing them over her flat stomach.

With a sudden rush she gathered up Kane in her arms. Beatrice chuckled as the girl dashed past her and her light steps could be heard running through the house.

'Oliver!' Kerensa shouted at the top of her voice, Kane bobbing up and down as she ran. 'Wait for me! Oliver…'

The Pengarron Sagas

Pengarron Land
Pengarron Pride
Pengarron's Children
Pengarron Dynasty
Pengarron Rivalry